Betty and Veronica®

Best Friends Forever

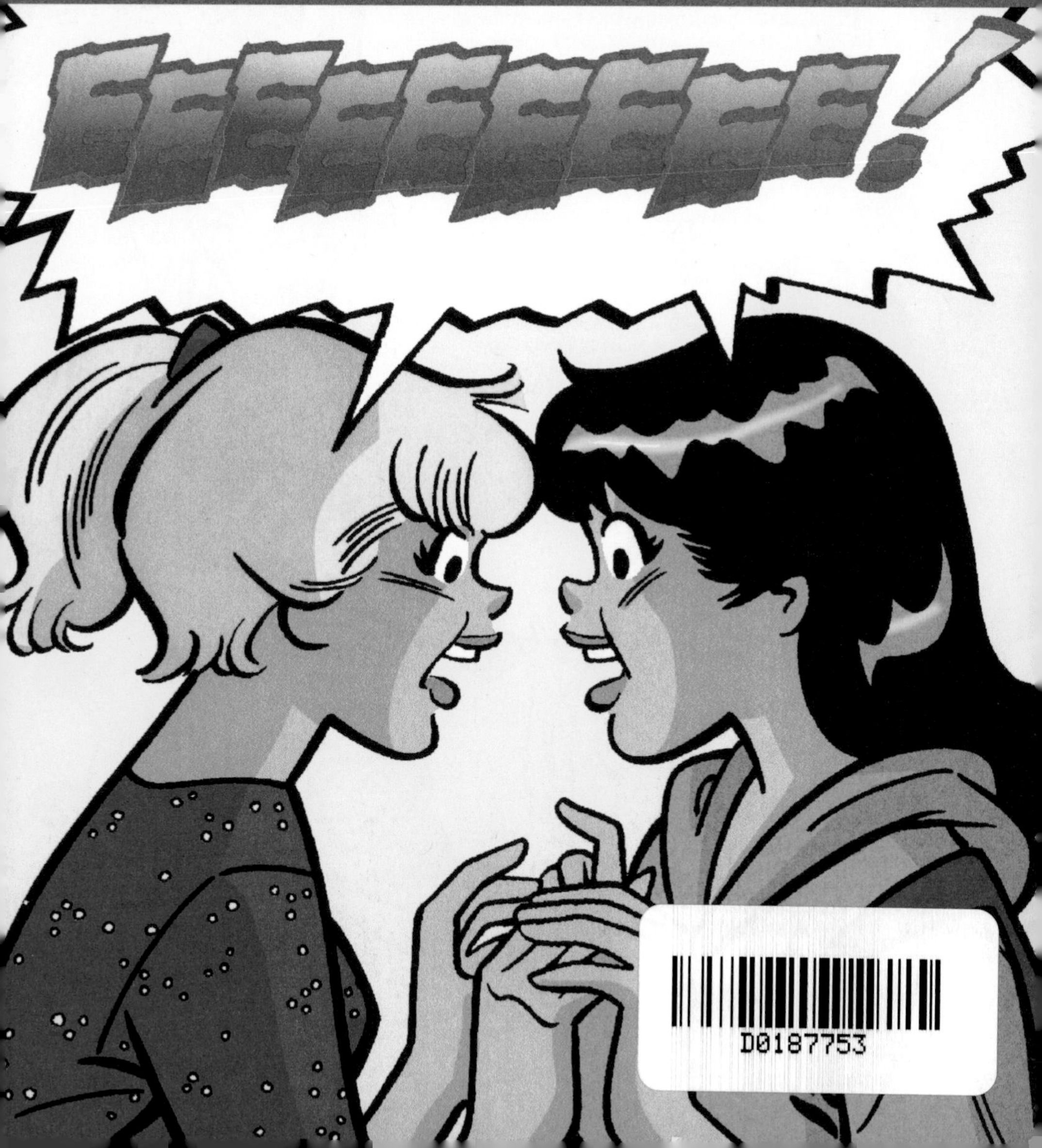
EEEEEEEEE!

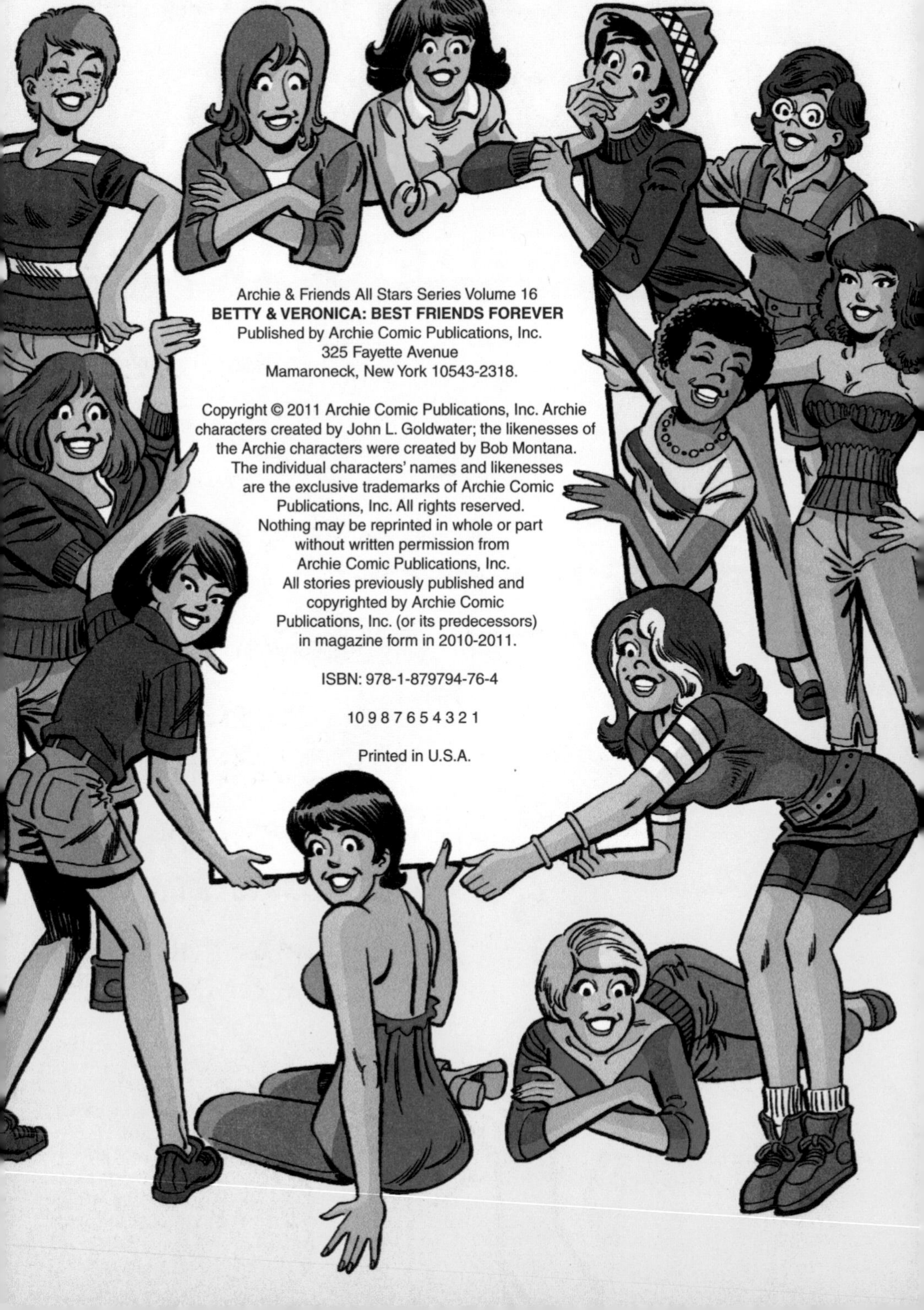

Archie & Friends All Stars Series Volume 16
BETTY & VERONICA: BEST FRIENDS FOREVER
Published by Archie Comic Publications, Inc.
325 Fayette Avenue
Mamaroneck, New York 10543-2318.

ISBN: 978-1-879794-76-4

10 9 8 7 6 5 4 3 2 1

Printed in U.S.A.

Betty and Veronica®

Best Friends Forever

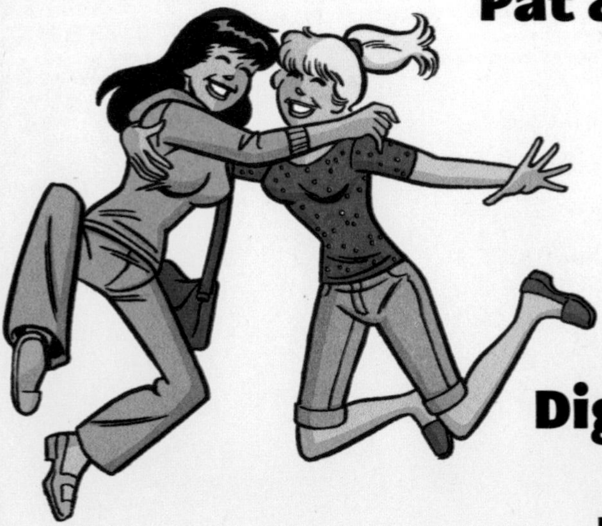

Written by:
Dan Parent

Pencils by:
Pat & Tim Kennedy

Inking by:
Mike DeCarlo

Lettering by:
Jack Morelli

Coloring by:
Digikore Studios

Cover Colors by:
Rosario "Tito" Peña

Co-CEO: Jon Goldwater
Co-CEO: Nancy Silberkleit
President: Mike Pellerito
Co-President/Editor-In-Chief: Victor Gorelick
Director of Circulation: Bill Horan
Executive Director of Publishing/Operations: Harold Buchholz
Executive Director of Publicity & Marketing: Alex Segura
Project Coordinator & Book Design: Joe Morciglio
Production Manager: Stephen Oswald
Production: Jon Gray, Kari Silbergleit, Pat Woodruff
Proofreader: Jamie Rotante

Chapter 1: The Battle Begins!

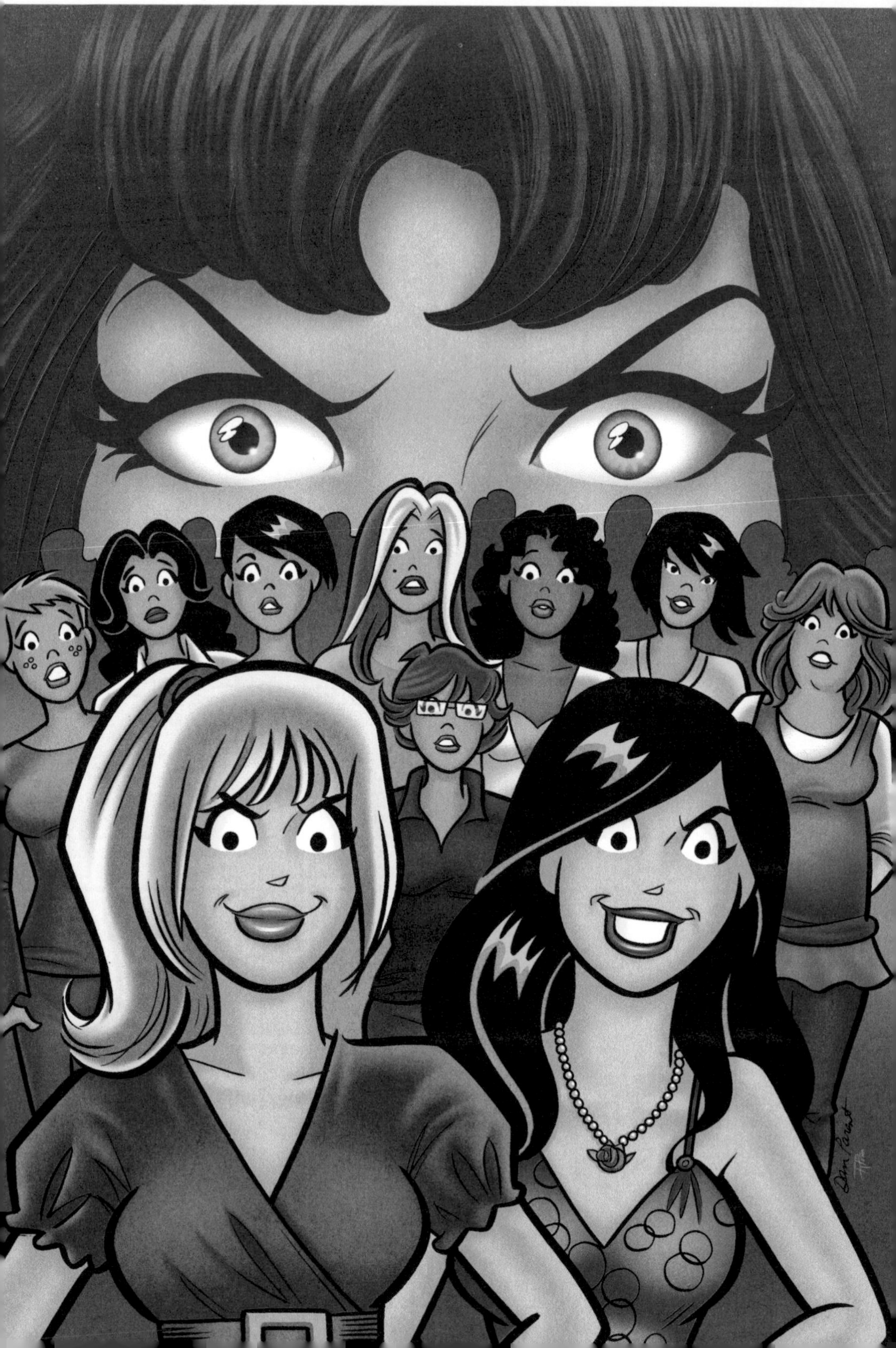

Betty in BATTLE OF THE BFFs!

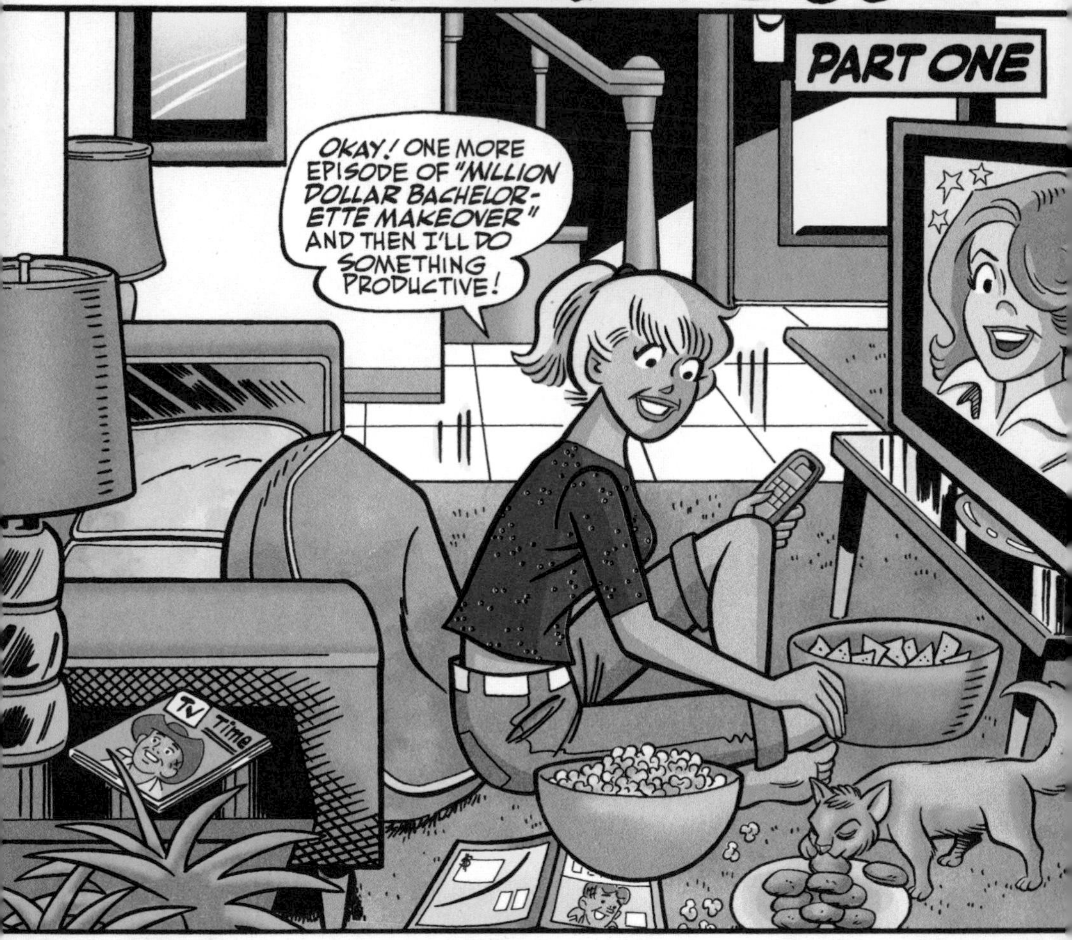
PART ONE
OKAY! ONE MORE EPISODE OF "MILLION DOLLAR BACHELOR-ETTE MAKEOVER" AND THEN I'LL DO SOMETHING PRODUCTIVE!
TV Time

SCRIPT: DAN PARENT PENCILS: PAT & TIM KENNEDY INKING: MIKE DECARLO LETTERING: JACK MORELLI COLORING: DIGIKORE STUDIOS MANAGING EDITOR: MIKE PELLERITO EDITOR/ EDITOR-IN-CHIEF: VICTOR GORELICK

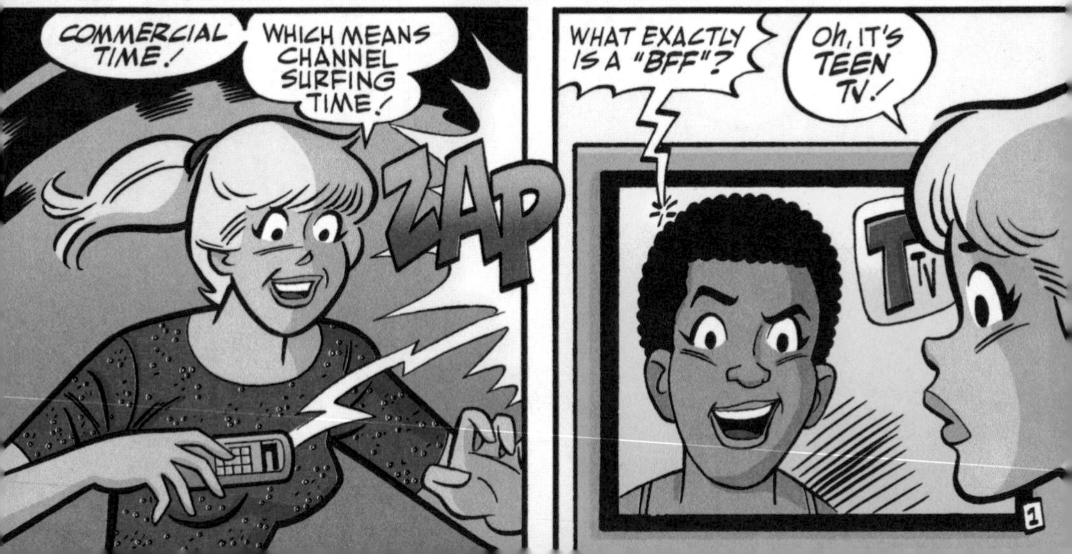
COMMERCIAL TIME!
WHICH MEANS CHANNEL SURFING TIME!
ZAP
WHAT EXACTLY IS A "BFF"?
Oh, IT'S TEEN TV!
T TV

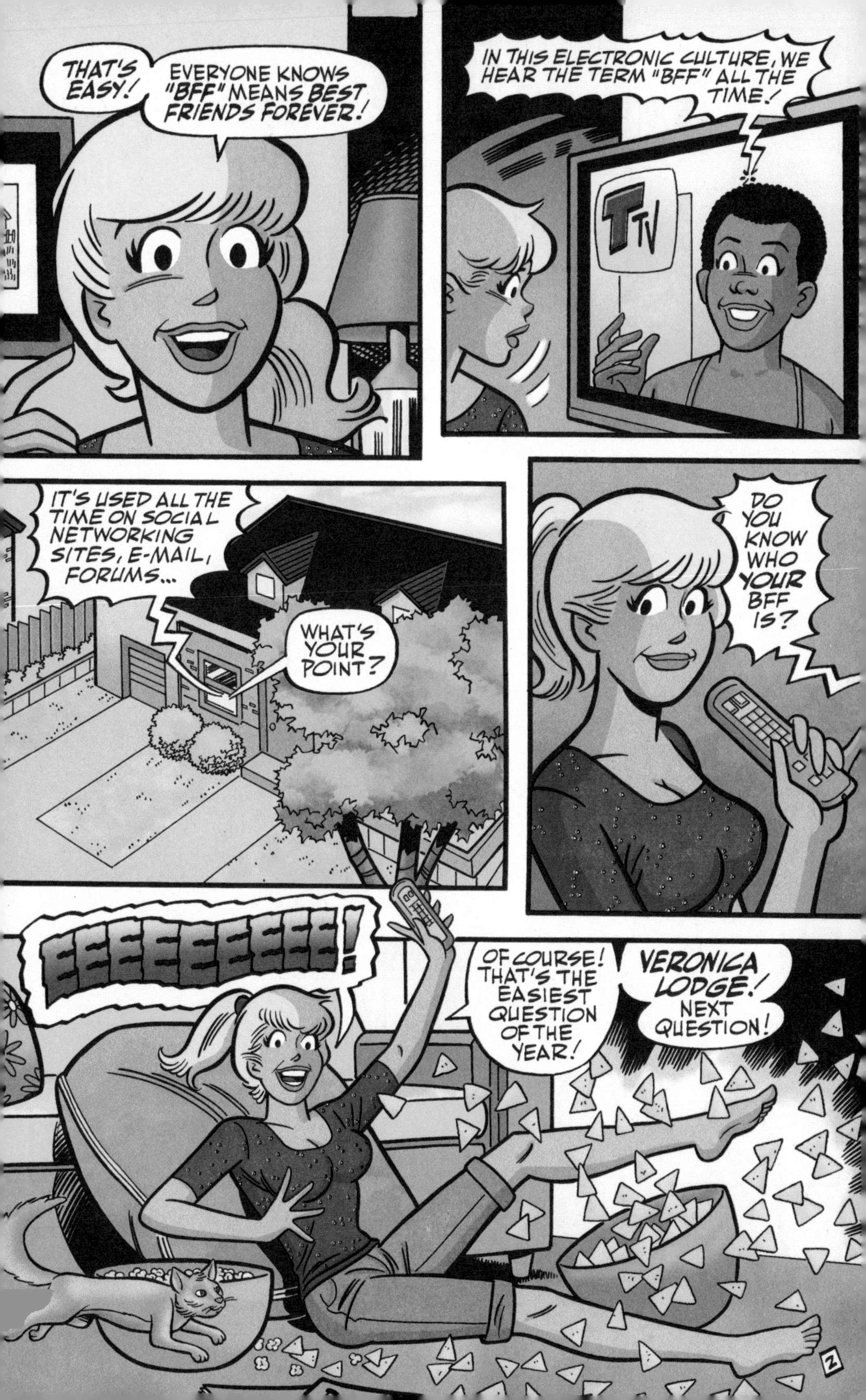
THAT'S EASY!
EVERYONE KNOWS "BFF" MEANS BEST FRIENDS FOREVER!
IN THIS ELECTRONIC CULTURE, WE HEAR THE TERM "BFF" ALL THE TIME!
TTV
IT'S USED ALL THE TIME ON SOCIAL NETWORKING SITES, E-MAIL, FORUMS...
WHAT'S YOUR POINT?
DO YOU KNOW WHO YOUR BFF IS?
EEEEEEEEE!
OF COURSE! THAT'S THE EASIEST QUESTION OF THE YEAR!
VERONICA LODGE! NEXT QUESTION!
2

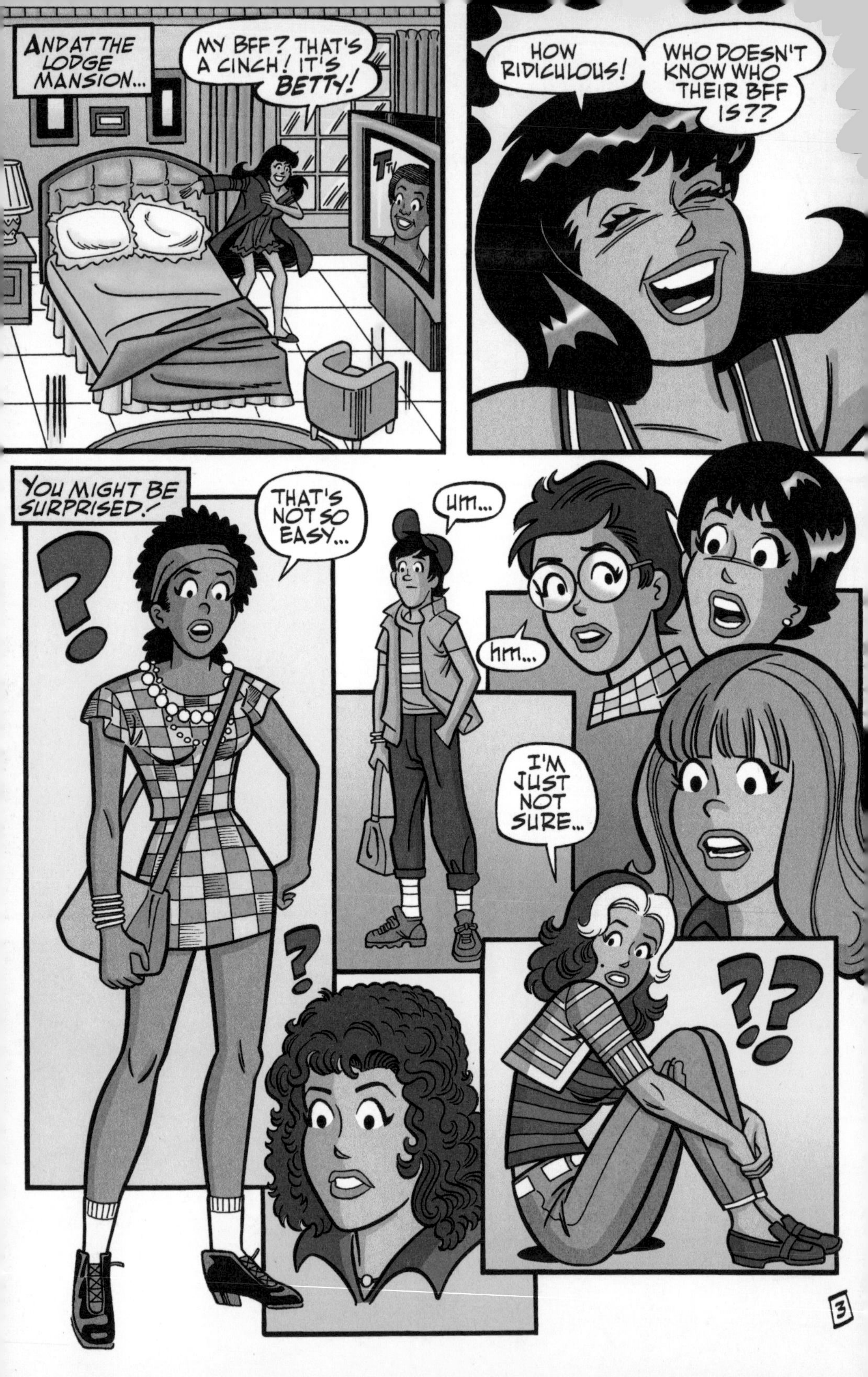
AND AT THE LODGE MANSION...
MY BFF? THAT'S A CINCH! IT'S BETTY!
HOW RIDICULOUS!
WHO DOESN'T KNOW WHO THEIR BFF IS??
YOU MIGHT BE SURPRISED!
THAT'S NOT SO EASY...
UM...
HM...
I'M JUST NOT SURE...
??

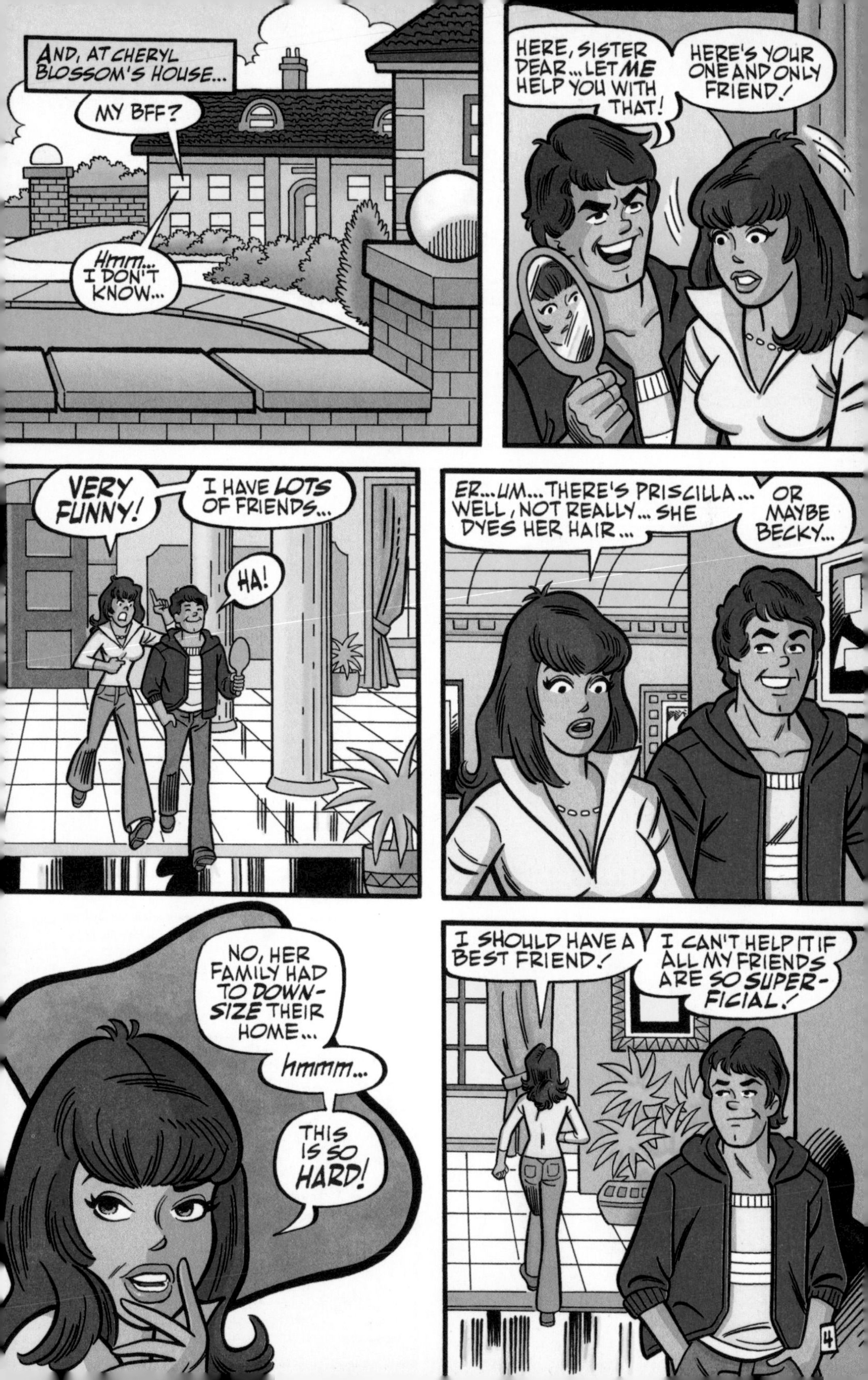
AND, AT CHERYL BLOSSOM'S HOUSE...
MY BFF?
Hmm... I DON'T KNOW...
HERE, SISTER DEAR... LET ME HELP YOU WITH THAT!
HERE'S YOUR ONE AND ONLY FRIEND!
VERY FUNNY!
I HAVE LOTS OF FRIENDS...
HA!
ER... UM... THERE'S PRISCILLA... WELL, NOT REALLY... SHE DYES HER HAIR...
OR MAYBE BECKY...
NO, HER FAMILY HAD TO DOWN-SIZE THEIR HOME...
hmmm...
THIS IS SO HARD!
I SHOULD HAVE A BEST FRIEND!
I CAN'T HELP IT IF ALL MY FRIENDS ARE SO SUPER-FICIAL!
4

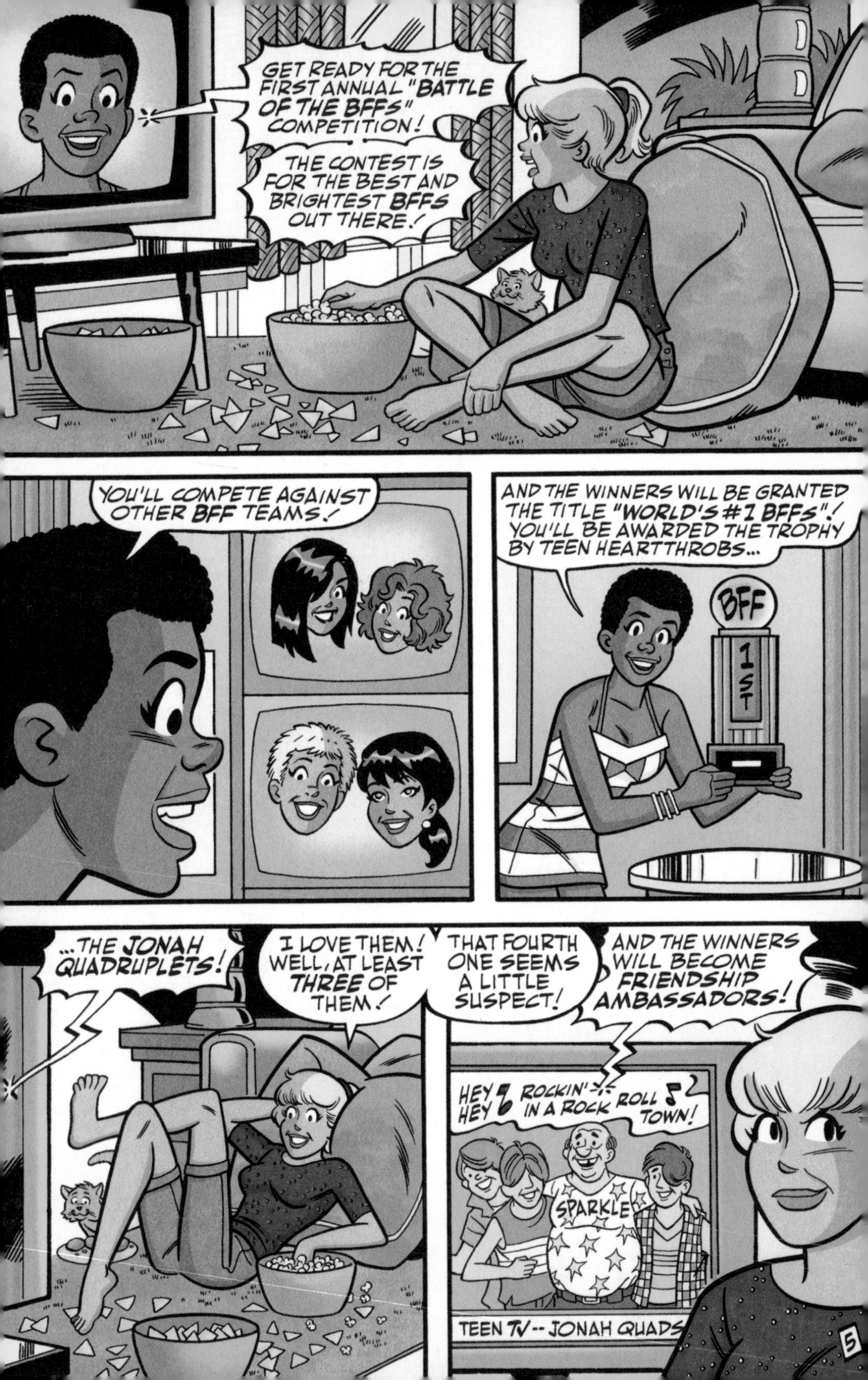
GET READY FOR THE FIRST ANNUAL "BATTLE OF THE BFFs" COMPETITION!
THE CONTEST IS FOR THE BEST AND BRIGHTEST BFFs OUT THERE!
YOU'LL COMPETE AGAINST OTHER BFF TEAMS!
AND THE WINNERS WILL BE GRANTED THE TITLE "WORLD'S #1 BFFs"! YOU'LL BE AWARDED THE TROPHY BY TEEN HEARTTHROBS...
BFF
1ST
...THE JONAH QUADRUPLETS!
I LOVE THEM! WELL, AT LEAST THREE OF THEM!
THAT FOURTH ONE SEEMS A LITTLE SUSPECT!
AND THE WINNERS WILL BECOME FRIENDSHIP AMBASSADORS!
HEY HEY ROCKIN' IN A ROCK ROLL TOWN!
SPARKLE
TEEN TV -- JONAH QUADS
5

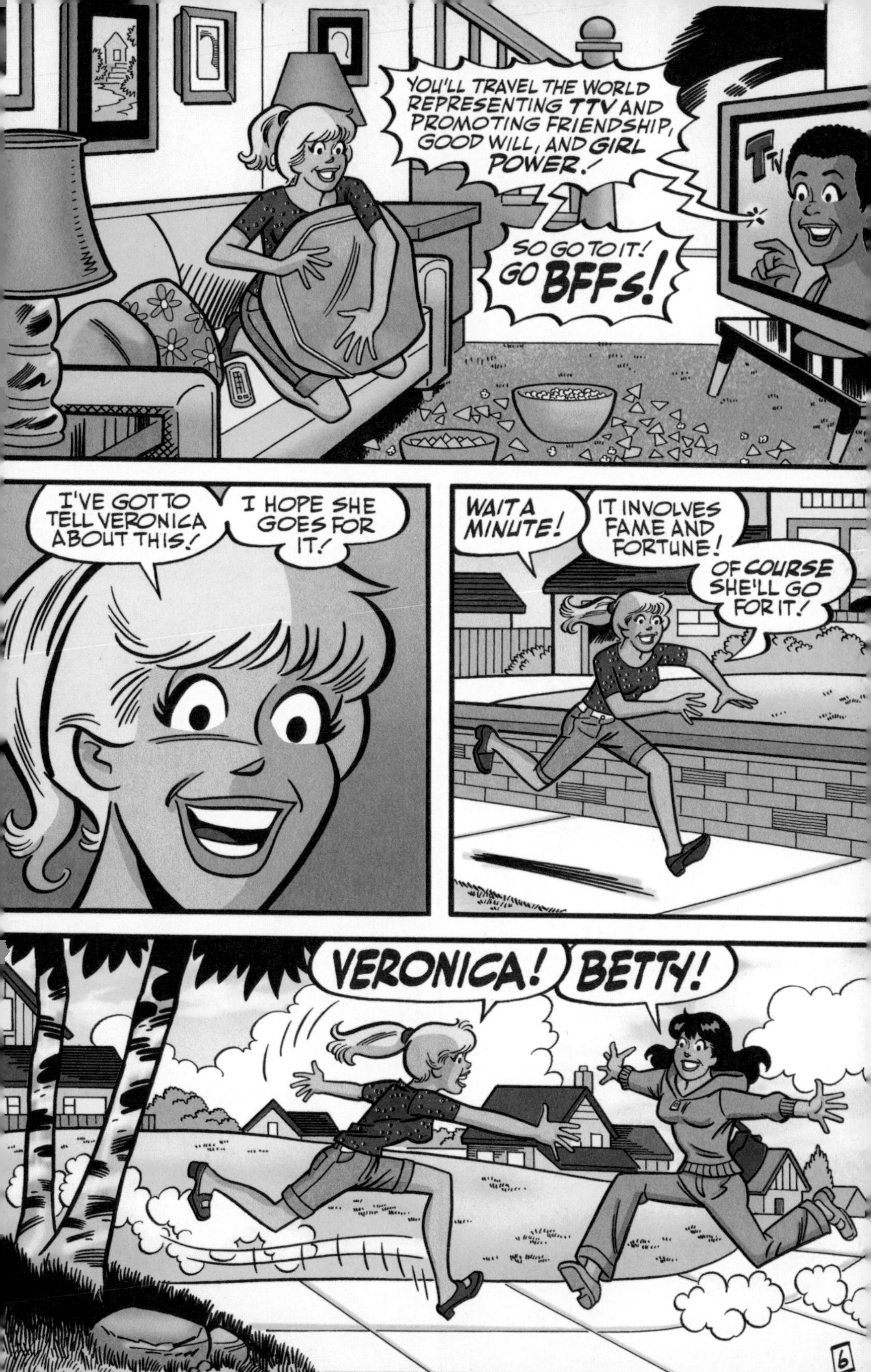
YOU'LL TRAVEL THE WORLD REPRESENTING TTV AND PROMOTING FRIENDSHIP, GOOD WILL, AND GIRL POWER!
TTV
SO GO TO IT! GO BFFs!
I'VE GOT TO TELL VERONICA ABOUT THIS!
I HOPE SHE GOES FOR IT!
WAIT A MINUTE!
IT INVOLVES FAME AND FORTUNE!
OF COURSE SHE'LL GO FOR IT!
VERONICA!
BETTY!

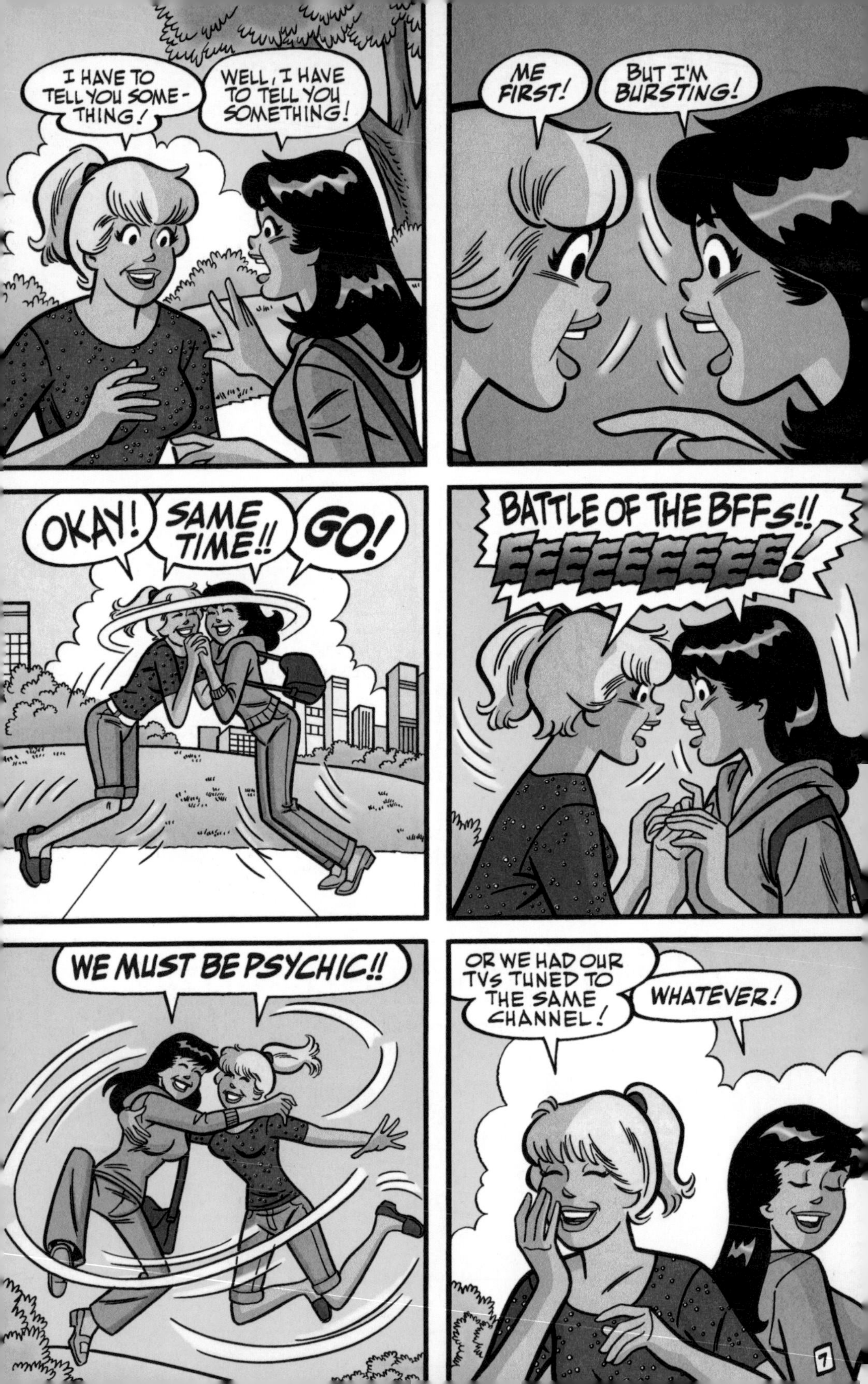
I HAVE TO TELL YOU SOME-THING!
WELL, I HAVE TO TELL YOU SOMETHING!
ME FIRST!
BUT I'M BURSTING!
OKAY!
SAME TIME!!
GO!
BATTLE OF THE BFFs!! EEEEEEEEE!
WE MUST BE PSYCHIC!!
OR WE HAD OUR TVs TUNED TO THE SAME CHANNEL!
WHATEVER!
7

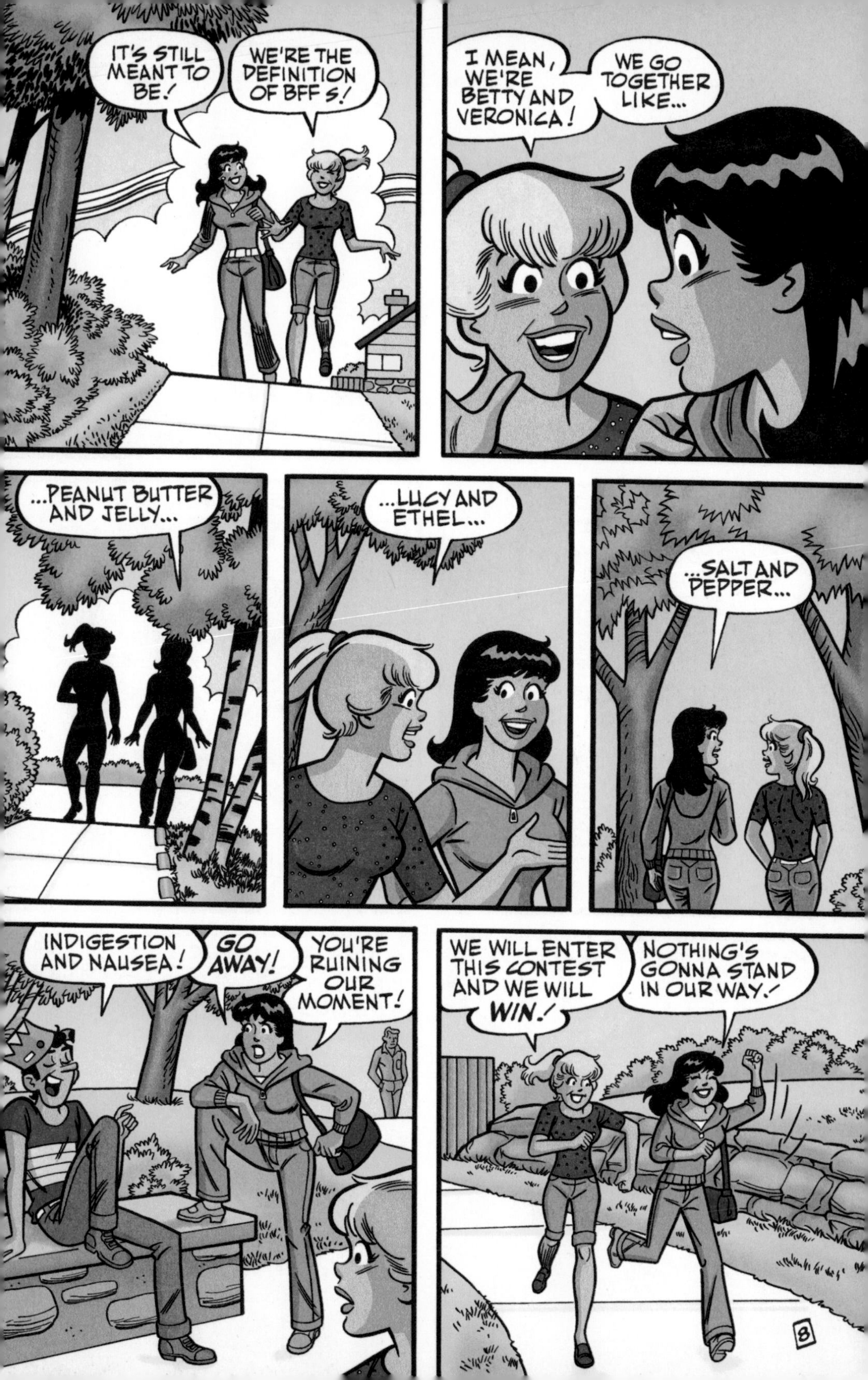
IT'S STILL MEANT TO BE!
WE'RE THE DEFINITION OF BFF S!
I MEAN, WE'RE BETTY AND VERONICA!
WE GO TOGETHER LIKE...
...PEANUT BUTTER AND JELLY...
...LUCY AND ETHEL...
...SALT AND PEPPER...
INDIGESTION AND NAUSEA!
GO AWAY!
YOU'RE RUINING OUR MOMENT!
WE WILL ENTER THIS CONTEST AND WE WILL WIN!
NOTHING'S GONNA STAND IN OUR WAY!
8

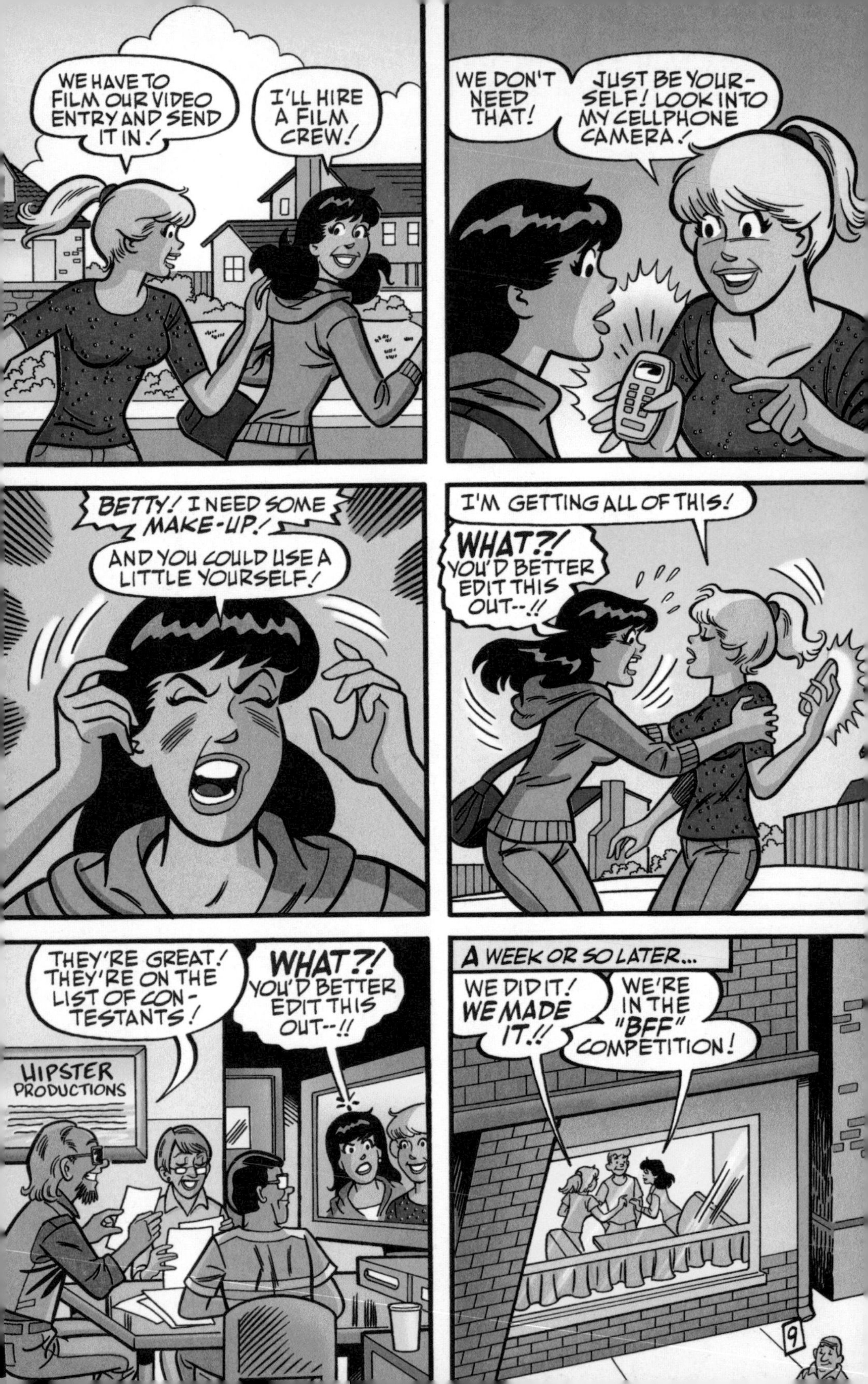

WE HAVE TO FILM OUR VIDEO ENTRY AND SEND IT IN!
I'LL HIRE A FILM CREW!
WE DON'T NEED THAT!
JUST BE YOURSELF! LOOK INTO MY CELLPHONE CAMERA!
BETTY! I NEED SOME MAKE-UP!
AND YOU COULD USE A LITTLE YOURSELF!
I'M GETTING ALL OF THIS!
WHAT?! YOU'D BETTER EDIT THIS OUT--!!
THEY'RE GREAT! THEY'RE ON THE LIST OF CONTESTANTS!
WHAT?! YOU'D BETTER EDIT THIS OUT--!!
HIPSTER PRODUCTIONS
A WEEK OR SO LATER...
WE DID IT! WE MADE IT!!
WE'RE IN THE "BFF" COMPETITION!

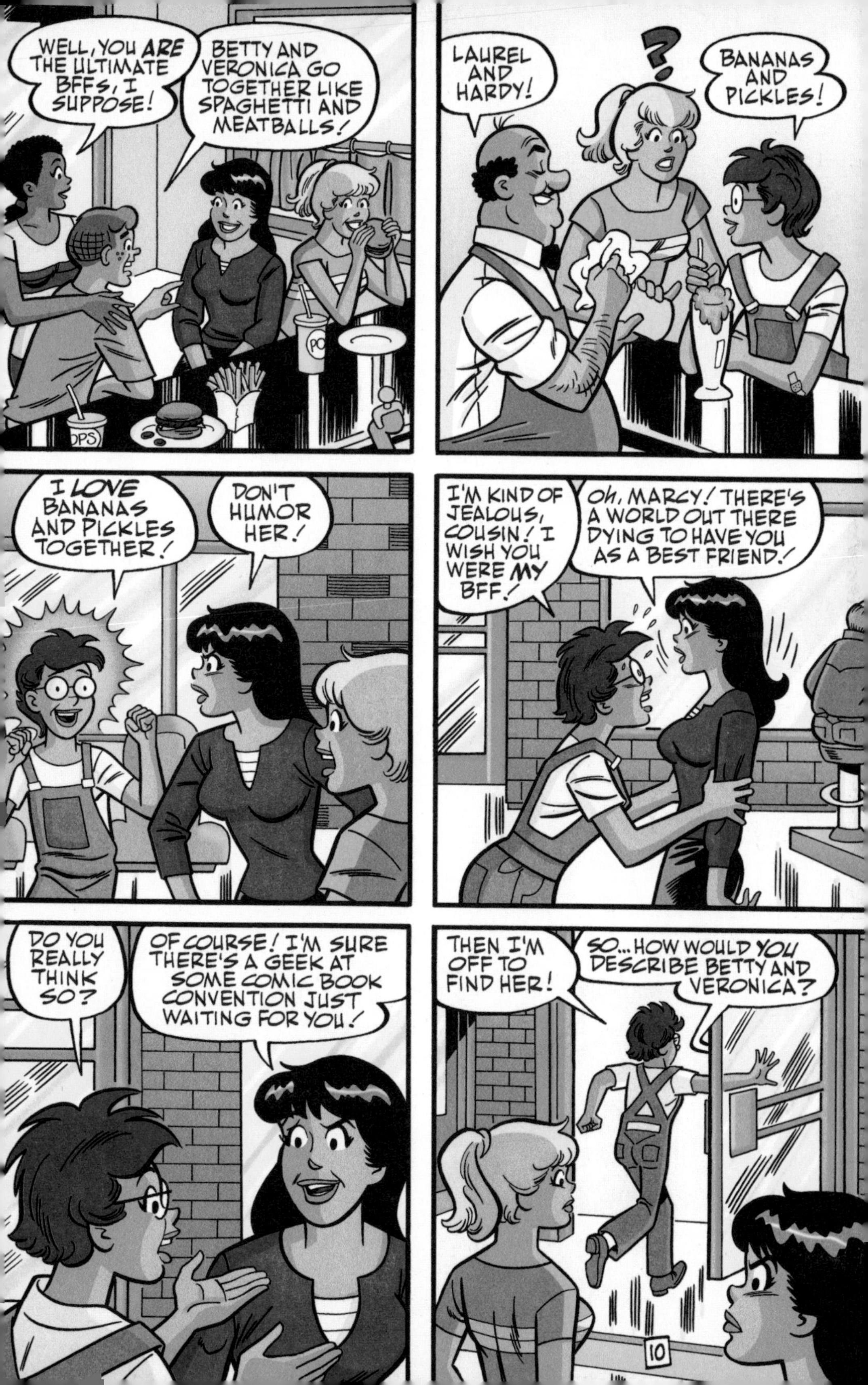
WELL, YOU ARE THE ULTIMATE BFFs, I SUPPOSE!
BETTY AND VERONICA GO TOGETHER LIKE SPAGHETTI AND MEATBALLS!
LAUREL AND HARDY!
?
BANANAS AND PICKLES!
I LOVE BANANAS AND PICKLES TOGETHER!
DON'T HUMOR HER!
I'M KIND OF JEALOUS, COUSIN! I WISH YOU WERE MY BFF!
OH, MARCY! THERE'S A WORLD OUT THERE DYING TO HAVE YOU AS A BEST FRIEND!
DO YOU REALLY THINK SO?
OF COURSE! I'M SURE THERE'S A GEEK AT SOME COMIC BOOK CONVENTION JUST WAITING FOR YOU!
THEN I'M OFF TO FIND HER!
SO...HOW WOULD YOU DESCRIBE BETTY AND VERONICA?

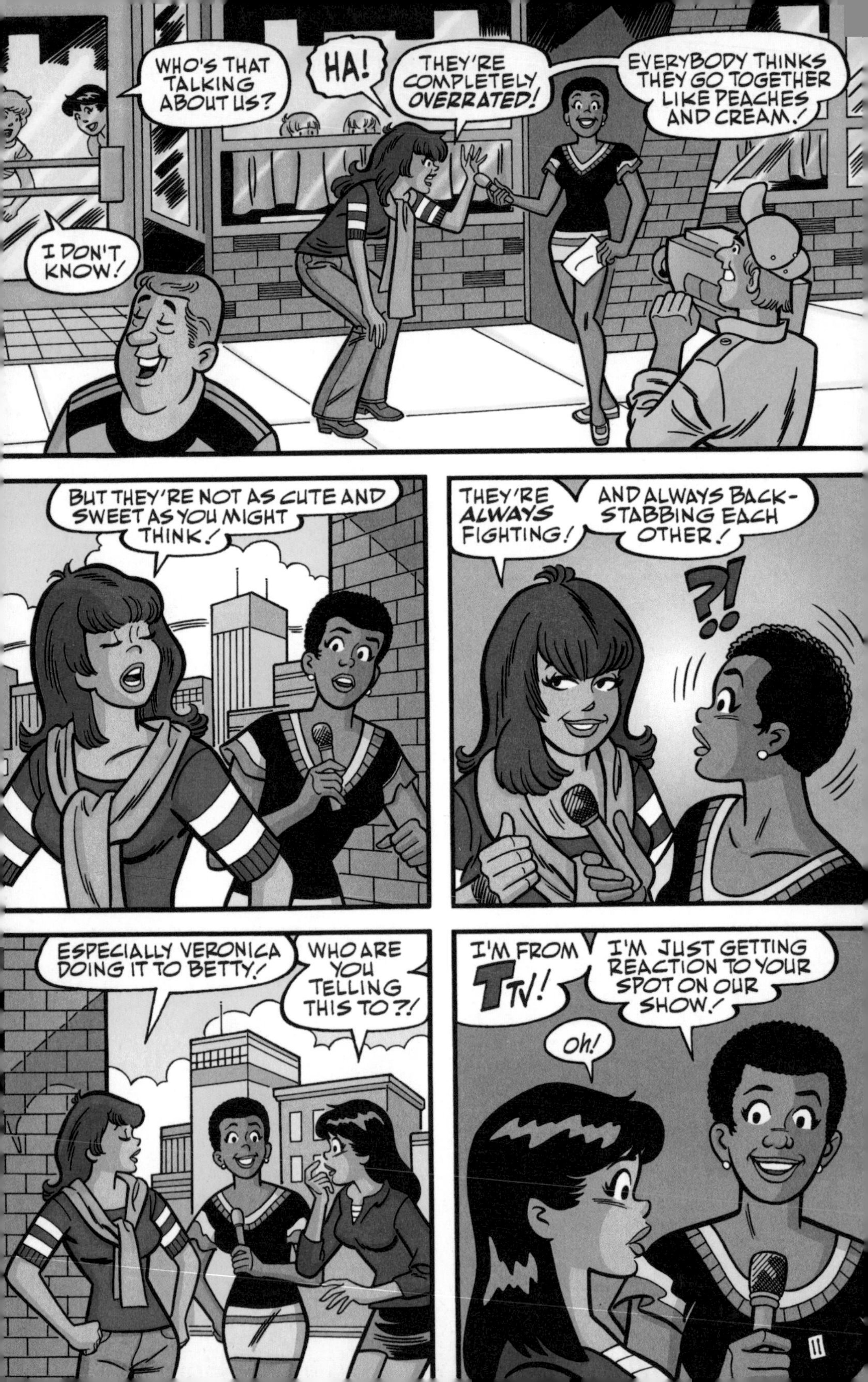
WHO'S THAT TALKING ABOUT US?
HA!
THEY'RE COMPLETELY OVERRATED!
EVERYBODY THINKS THEY GO TOGETHER LIKE PEACHES AND CREAM!
I DON'T KNOW!
BUT THEY'RE NOT AS CUTE AND SWEET AS YOU MIGHT THINK!
THEY'RE ALWAYS FIGHTING!
AND ALWAYS BACK-STABBING EACH OTHER!
?!
ESPECIALLY VERONICA DOING IT TO BETTY!
WHO ARE YOU TELLING THIS TO?!
I'M FROM TTV!
I'M JUST GETTING REACTION TO YOUR SPOT ON OUR SHOW!
Oh!
11

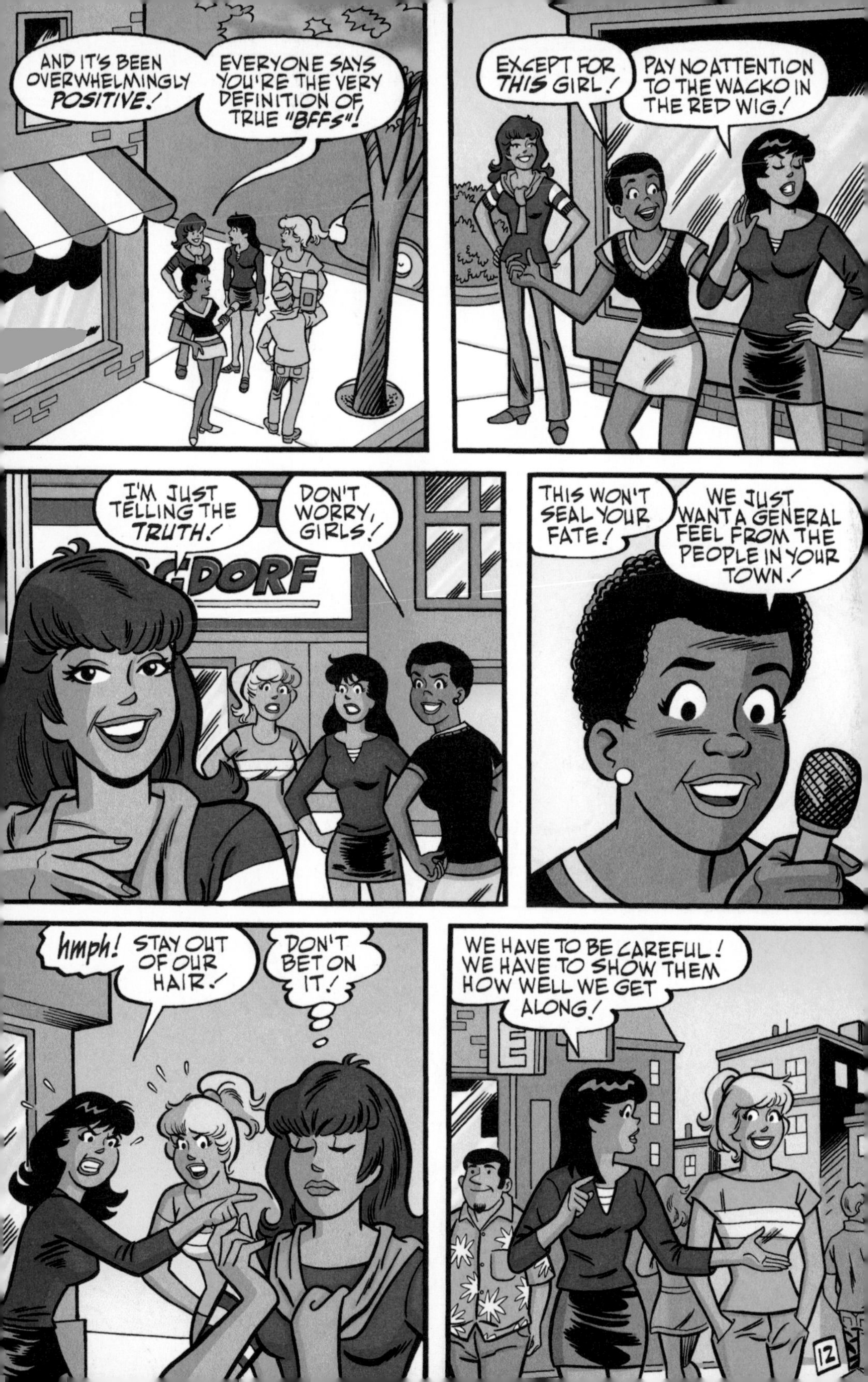

AND IT'S BEEN OVERWHELMINGLY POSITIVE!
EVERYONE SAYS YOU'RE THE VERY DEFINITION OF TRUE "BFFS"!
EXCEPT FOR THIS GIRL!
PAY NO ATTENTION TO THE WACKO IN THE RED WIG!
I'M JUST TELLING THE TRUTH!
DON'T WORRY, GIRLS!
GDORF
THIS WON'T SEAL YOUR FATE!
WE JUST WANT A GENERAL FEEL FROM THE PEOPLE IN YOUR TOWN!
hmph! STAY OUT OF OUR HAIR!
DON'T BET ON IT!
WE HAVE TO BE CAREFUL! WE HAVE TO SHOW THEM HOW WELL WE GET ALONG!

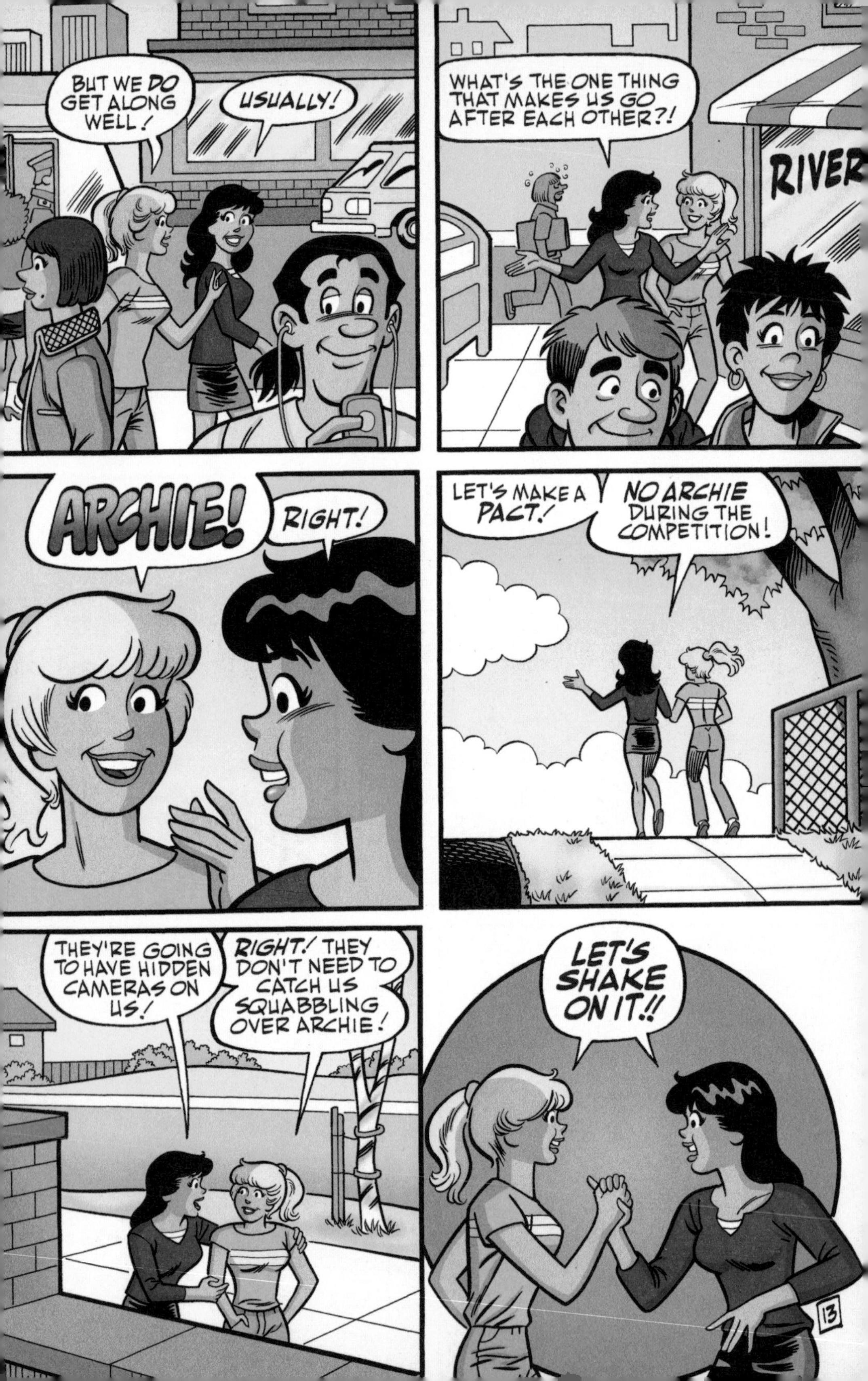

BUT WE DO GET ALONG WELL!
USUALLY!
WHAT'S THE ONE THING THAT MAKES US GO AFTER EACH OTHER?!
RIVER
ARCHIE!
RIGHT!
LET'S MAKE A PACT!
NO ARCHIE DURING THE COMPETITION!
THEY'RE GOING TO HAVE HIDDEN CAMERAS ON US!
RIGHT! THEY DON'T NEED TO CATCH US SQUABBLING OVER ARCHIE!
LET'S SHAKE ON IT!!
13

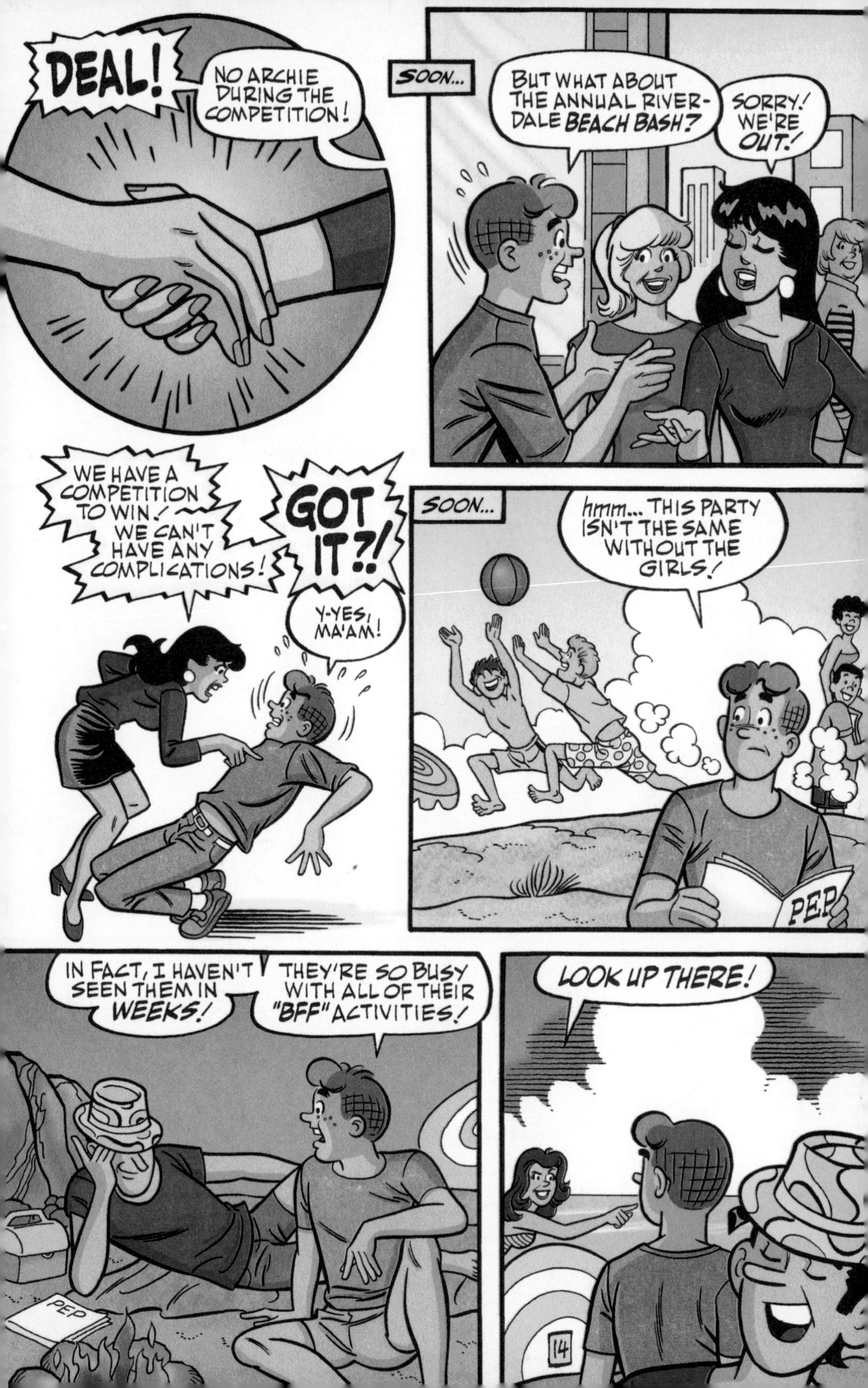
DEAL!
NO ARCHIE DURING THE COMPETITION!
SOON...
BUT WHAT ABOUT THE ANNUAL RIVER-DALE BEACH BASH?
SORRY! WE'RE OUT!
WE HAVE A COMPETITION TO WIN! WE CAN'T HAVE ANY COMPLICATIONS!
GOT IT?!
Y-YES, MA'AM!
SOON...
hmm... THIS PARTY ISN'T THE SAME WITHOUT THE GIRLS!
PEP
IN FACT, I HAVEN'T SEEN THEM IN WEEKS!
THEY'RE SO BUSY WITH ALL OF THEIR "BFF" ACTIVITIES!
PEP
LOOK UP THERE!
14

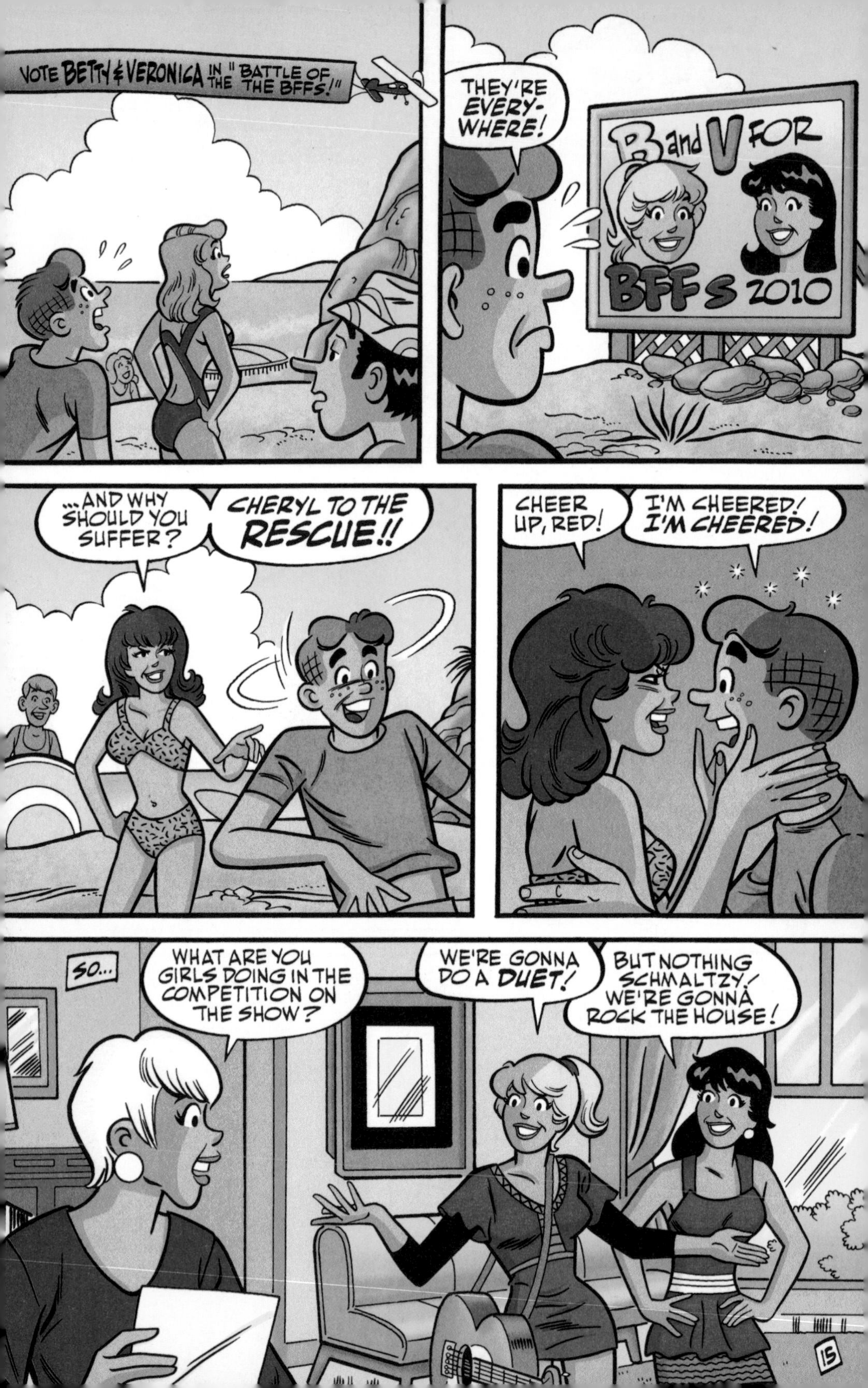
VOTE BETTY & VERONICA IN THE "BATTLE OF THE BFFS!"
THEY'RE EVERY-WHERE!
B and V FOR BFFs 2010
...AND WHY SHOULD YOU SUFFER?
CHERYL TO THE RESCUE!!
CHEER UP, RED!
I'M CHEERED! I'M CHEERED!
SO...
WHAT ARE YOU GIRLS DOING IN THE COMPETITION ON THE SHOW?
WE'RE GONNA DO A DUET!
BUT NOTHING SCHMALTZY! WE'RE GONNA ROCK THE HOUSE!
15

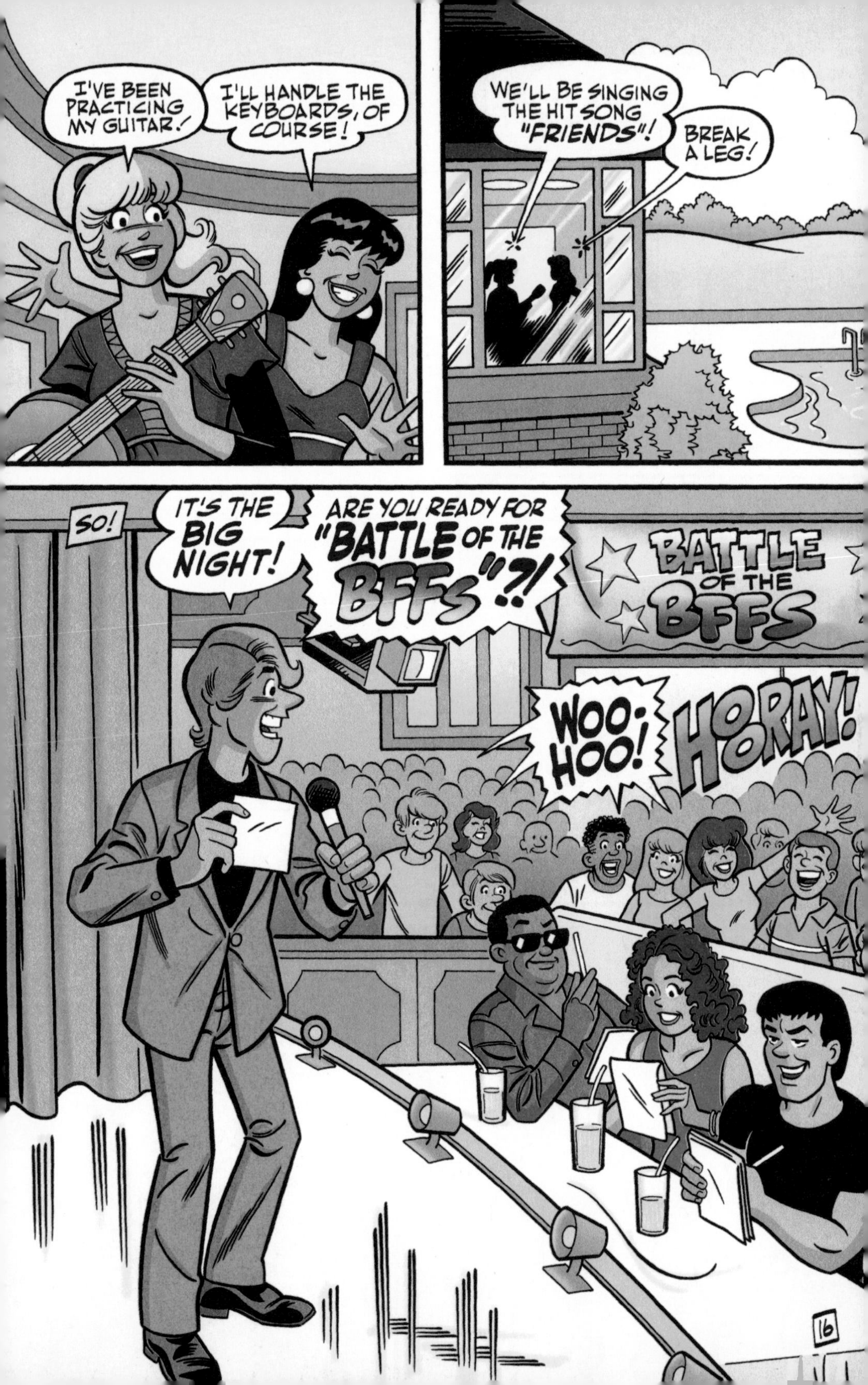

I'VE BEEN PRACTICING MY GUITAR!
I'LL HANDLE THE KEYBOARDS, OF COURSE!
WE'LL BE SINGING THE HIT SONG "FRIENDS"!
BREAK A LEG!
SO!
IT'S THE BIG NIGHT!
ARE YOU READY FOR "BATTLE OF THE BFFs"?!
BATTLE OF THE BFFS
WOO-HOO!
HOORAY!

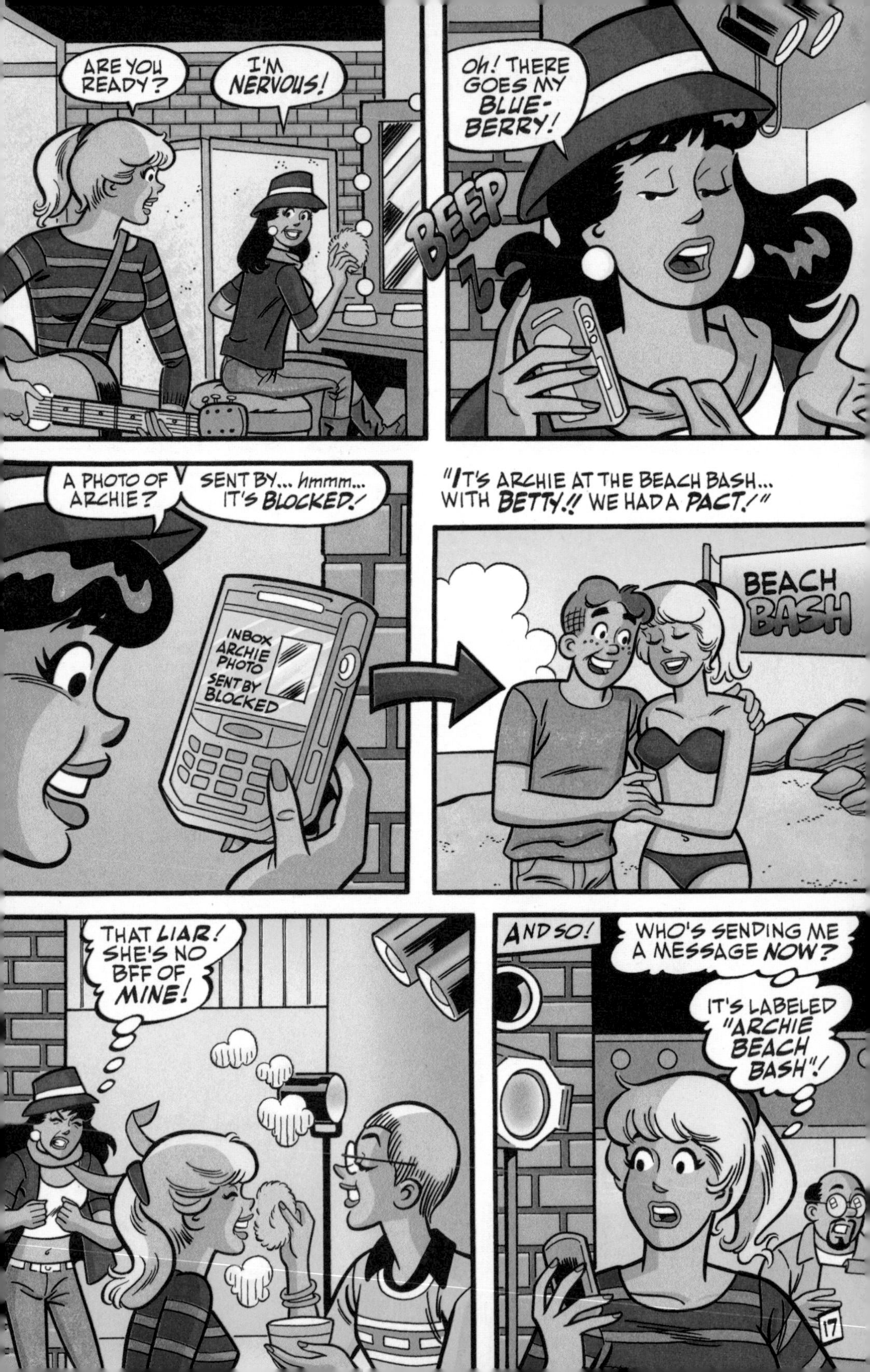
ARE YOU READY?
I'M NERVOUS!
Oh! THERE GOES MY BLUE-BERRY!
BEEP
A PHOTO OF ARCHIE?
SENT BY... hmmm... IT'S BLOCKED!
INBOX ARCHIE PHOTO SENT BY BLOCKED
"IT'S ARCHIE AT THE BEACH BASH... WITH BETTY!! WE HAD A PACT!"
BEACH BASH
THAT LIAR! SHE'S NO BFF OF MINE!
AND SO!
WHO'S SENDING ME A MESSAGE NOW?
IT'S LABELED "ARCHIE BEACH BASH"!
17

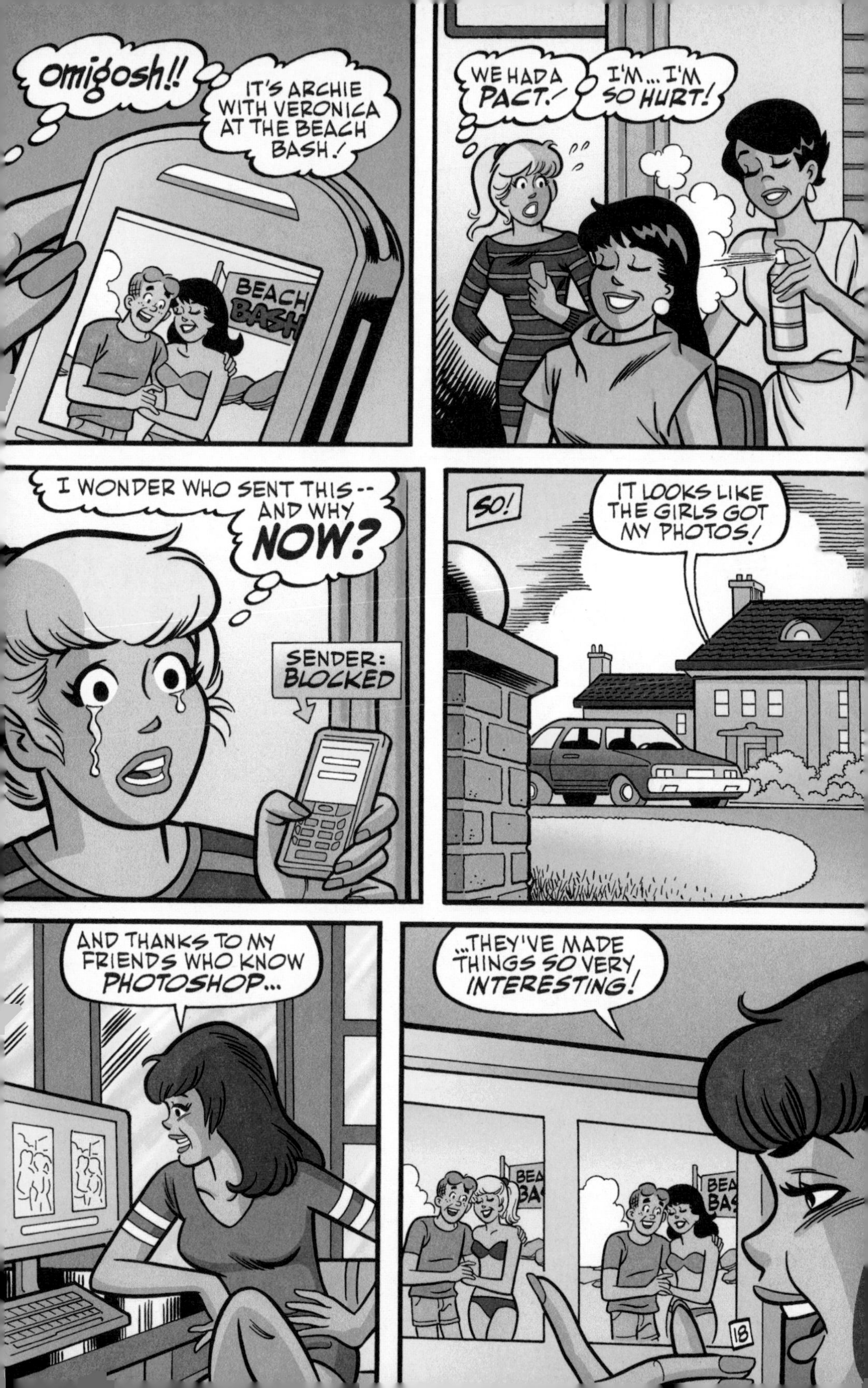

OMIGOSH!!
IT'S ARCHIE WITH VERONICA AT THE BEACH BASH!
BEACH BASH
WE HAD A PACT!
I'M... I'M SO HURT!
I WONDER WHO SENT THIS-- AND WHY NOW?
SENDER: BLOCKED
SO!
IT LOOKS LIKE THE GIRLS GOT MY PHOTOS!
AND THANKS TO MY FRIENDS WHO KNOW PHOTOSHOP...
...THEY'VE MADE THINGS SO VERY INTERESTING!

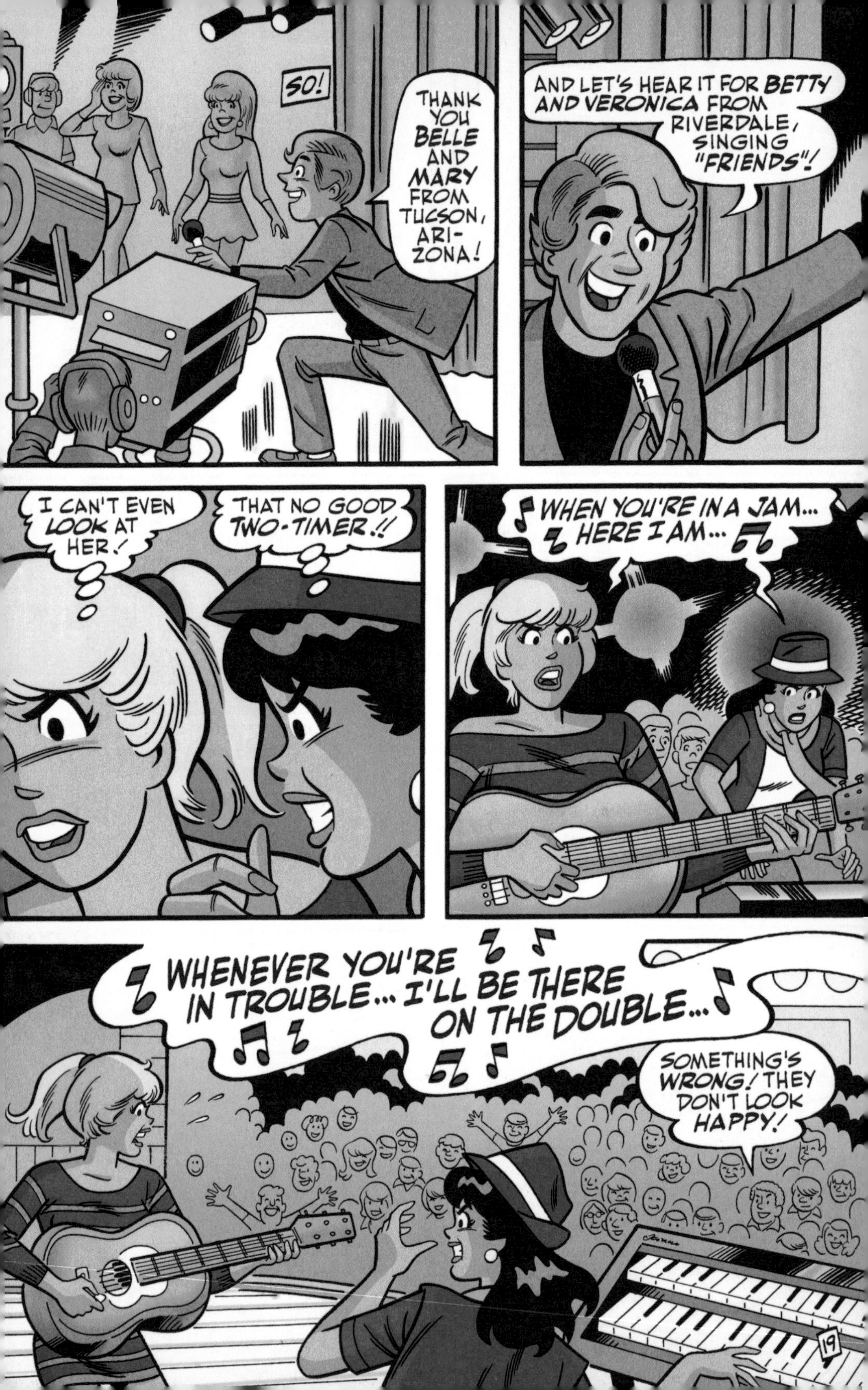
SO!
THANK YOU BELLE AND MARY FROM TUCSON, ARI-ZONA!
AND LET'S HEAR IT FOR BETTY AND VERONICA FROM RIVERDALE, SINGING "FRIENDS"!
I CAN'T EVEN LOOK AT HER!
THAT NO GOOD TWO-TIMER!!
WHEN YOU'RE IN A JAM... HERE I AM...
WHENEVER YOU'RE IN TROUBLE... I'LL BE THERE ON THE DOUBLE...
SOMETHING'S WRONG! THEY DON'T LOOK HAPPY!
19

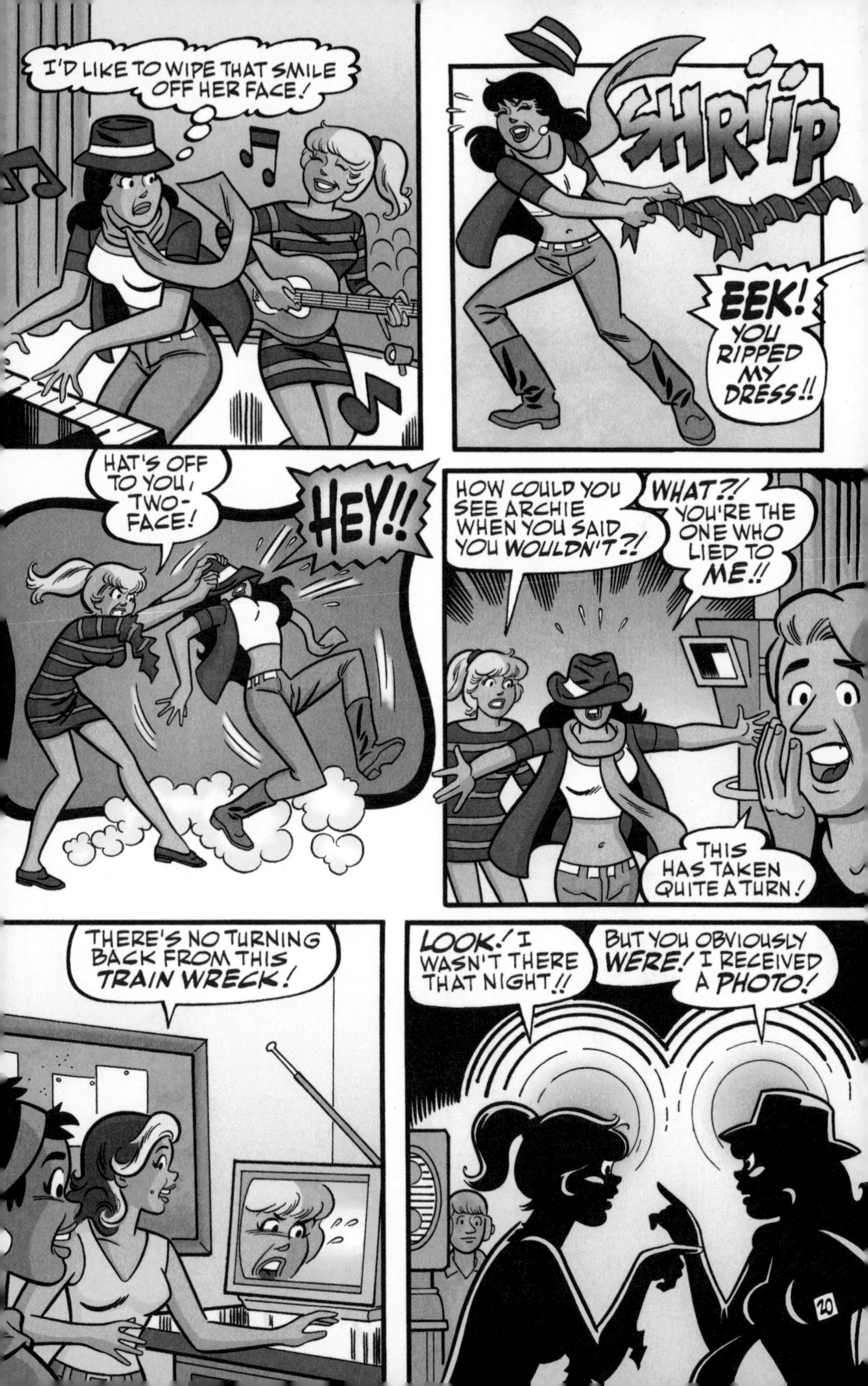
I'D LIKE TO WIPE THAT SMILE OFF HER FACE!
SHRIIP
EEK! YOU RIPPED MY DRESS!!
HAT'S OFF TO YOU, TWO-FACE!
HEY!!
HOW COULD YOU SEE ARCHIE WHEN YOU SAID YOU WOULDN'T?!
WHAT?! YOU'RE THE ONE WHO LIED TO ME!!
THIS HAS TAKEN QUITE A TURN!
THERE'S NO TURNING BACK FROM THIS TRAIN WRECK!
LOOK! I WASN'T THERE THAT NIGHT!!
BUT YOU OBVIOUSLY WERE! I RECEIVED A PHOTO!
20

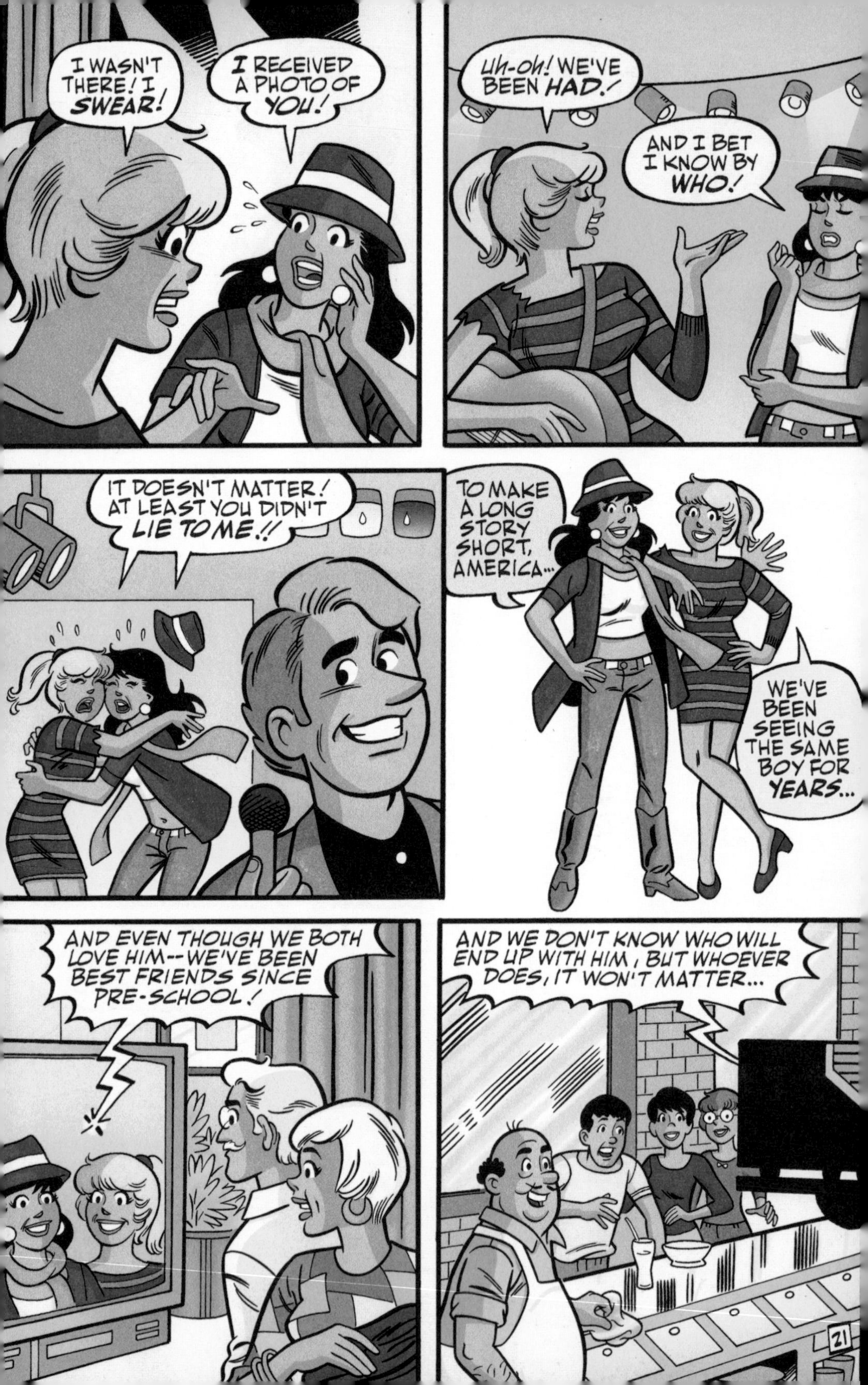
I WASN'T THERE! I SWEAR!
I RECEIVED A PHOTO OF YOU!
Uh-oh! WE'VE BEEN HAD!
AND I BET I KNOW BY WHO!
IT DOESN'T MATTER! AT LEAST YOU DIDN'T LIE TO ME!!
TO MAKE A LONG STORY SHORT, AMERICA...
WE'VE BEEN SEEING THE SAME BOY FOR YEARS...
AND EVEN THOUGH WE BOTH LOVE HIM--WE'VE BEEN BEST FRIENDS SINCE PRE-SCHOOL!
AND WE DON'T KNOW WHO WILL END UP WITH HIM, BUT WHOEVER DOES, IT WON'T MATTER...
21

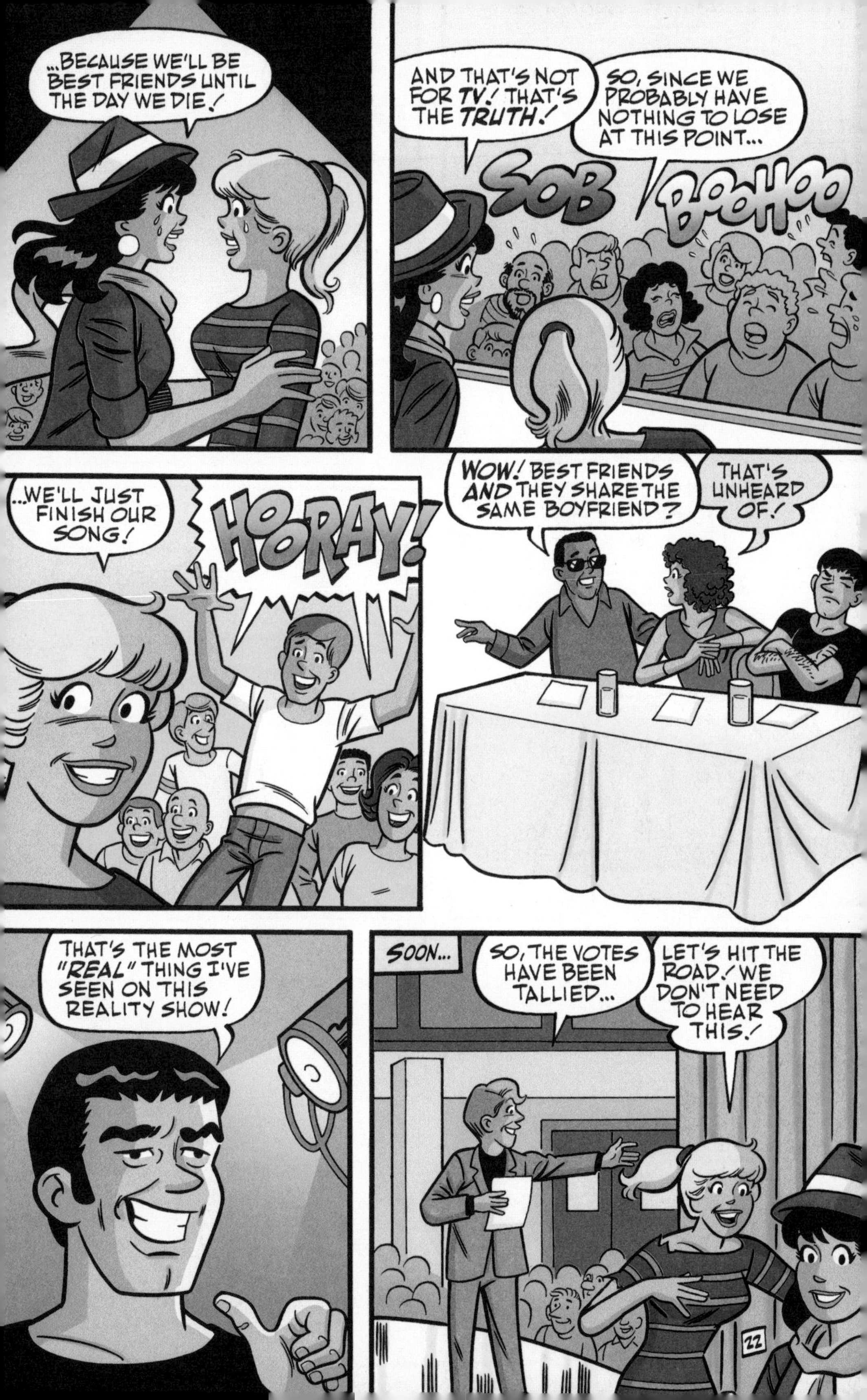
...BECAUSE WE'LL BE BEST FRIENDS UNTIL THE DAY WE DIE!
AND THAT'S NOT FOR TV! THAT'S THE TRUTH!
SO, SINCE WE PROBABLY HAVE NOTHING TO LOSE AT THIS POINT...
SOB
BOOHOO
...WE'LL JUST FINISH OUR SONG!
HOORAY!
WOW! BEST FRIENDS AND THEY SHARE THE SAME BOYFRIEND?
THAT'S UNHEARD OF!
THAT'S THE MOST "REAL" THING I'VE SEEN ON THIS REALITY SHOW!
SOON...
SO, THE VOTES HAVE BEEN TALLIED...
LET'S HIT THE ROAD! WE DON'T NEED TO HEAR THIS!
22

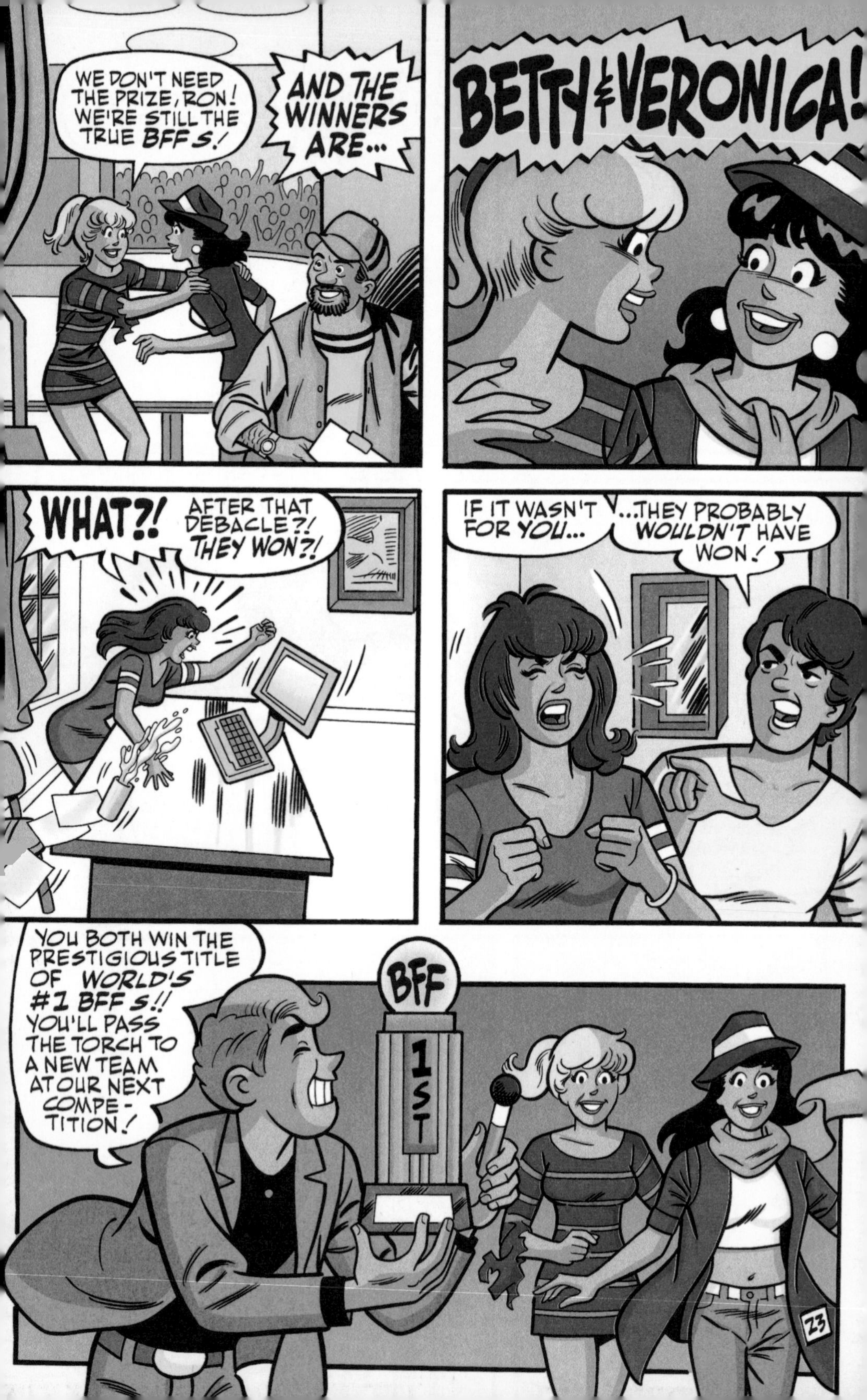
WE DON'T NEED THE PRIZE, RON! WE'RE STILL THE TRUE BFF S!
AND THE WINNERS ARE...
BETTY & VERONICA!
WHAT?!
AFTER THAT DEBACLE?! THEY WON?!
IF IT WASN'T FOR YOU...
...THEY PROBABLY WOULDN'T HAVE WON!
YOU BOTH WIN THE PRESTIGIOUS TITLE OF WORLD'S #1 BFF S!! YOU'LL PASS THE TORCH TO A NEW TEAM AT OUR NEXT COMPE-TITION!
BFF
1ST
23

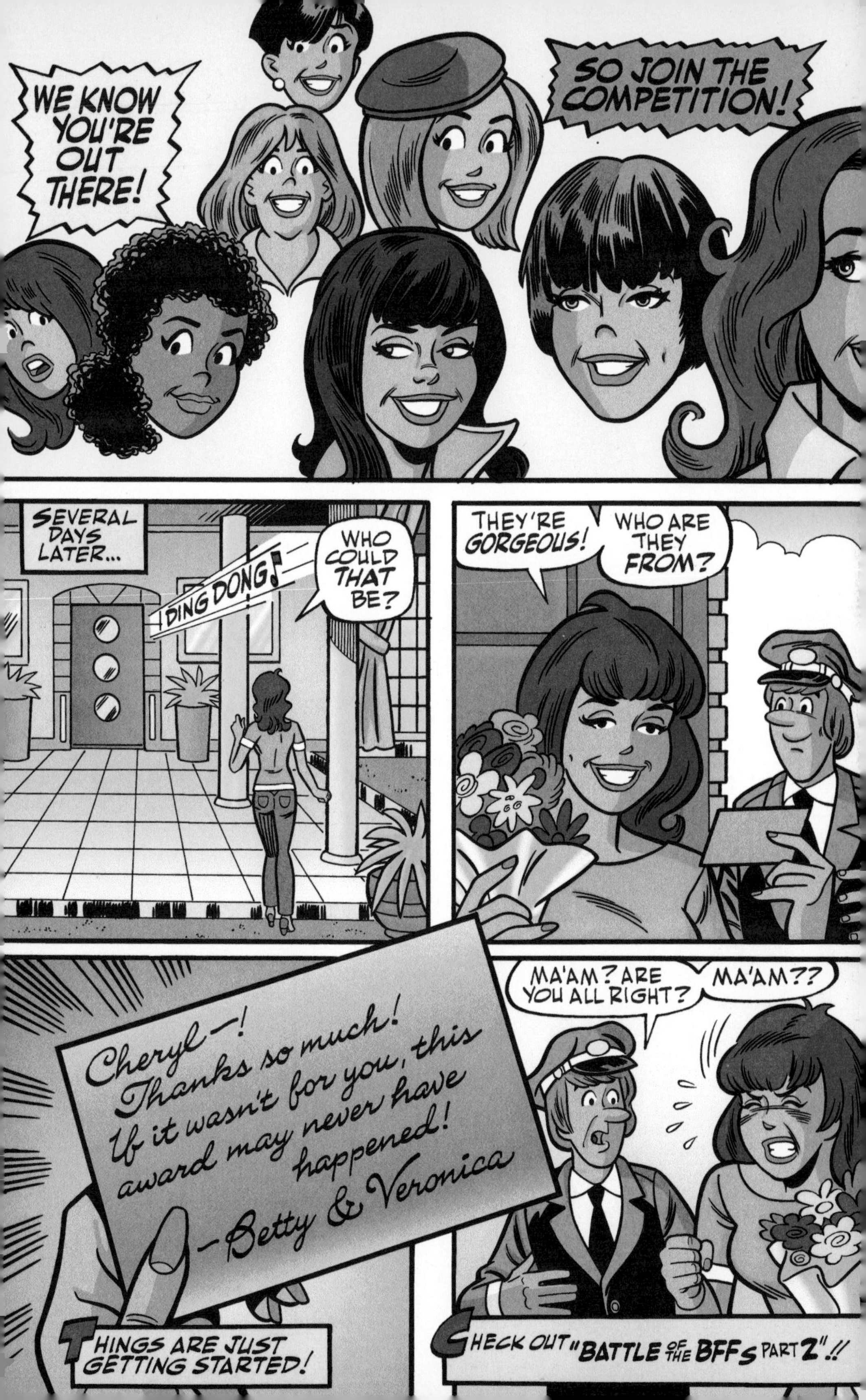

WE KNOW YOU'RE OUT THERE!
SO JOIN THE COMPETITION!
SEVERAL DAYS LATER...
DING DONG
WHO COULD THAT BE?
THEY'RE GORGEOUS!
WHO ARE THEY FROM?
Cheryl—! Thanks so much! If it wasn't for you, this award may never have happened! —Betty & Veronica
THINGS ARE JUST GETTING STARTED!
MA'AM? ARE YOU ALL RIGHT?
MA'AM??
CHECK OUT "BATTLE OF THE BFFs PART 2"!!

Chapter 2: Cheryl Strikes Back!

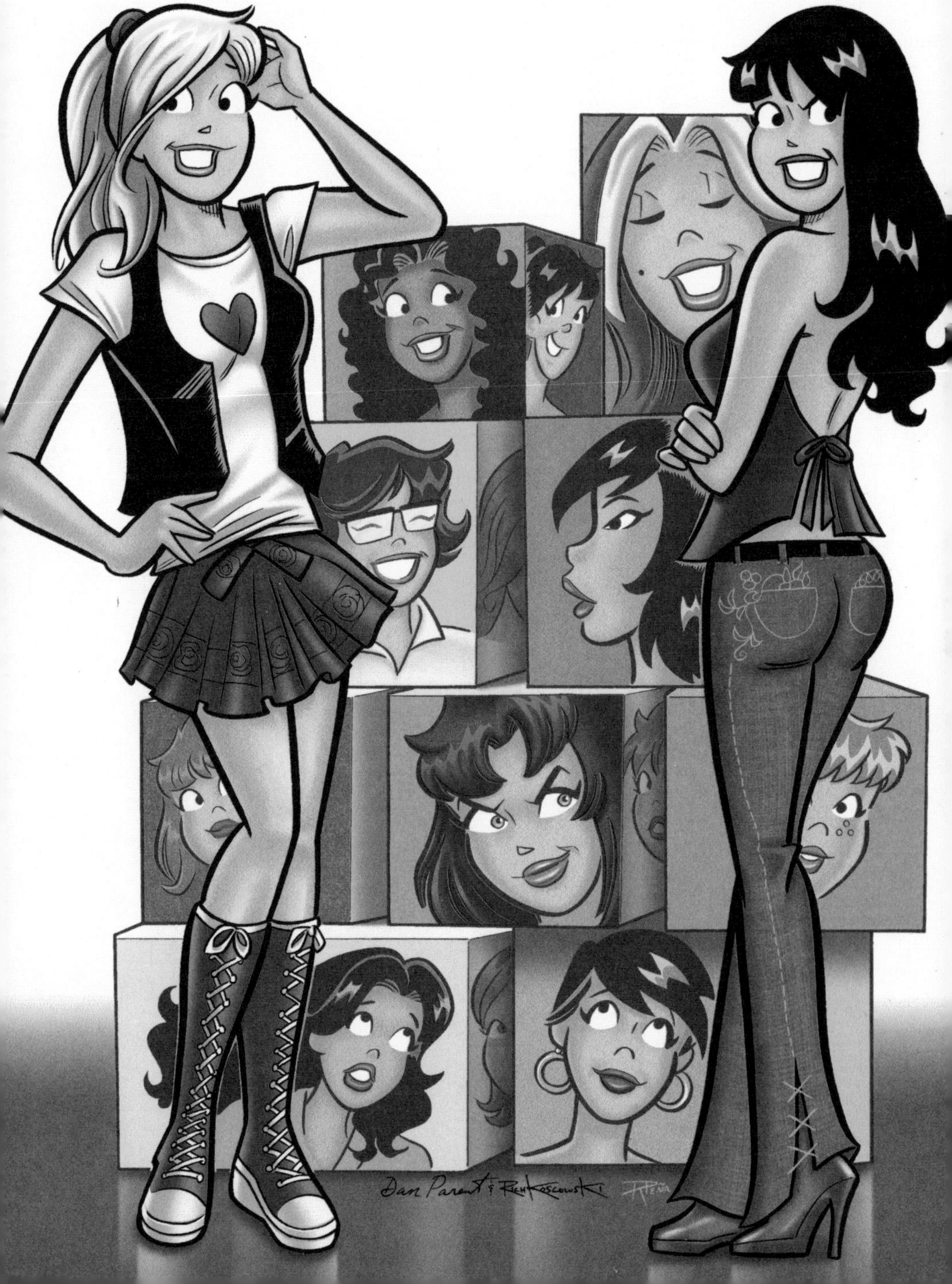

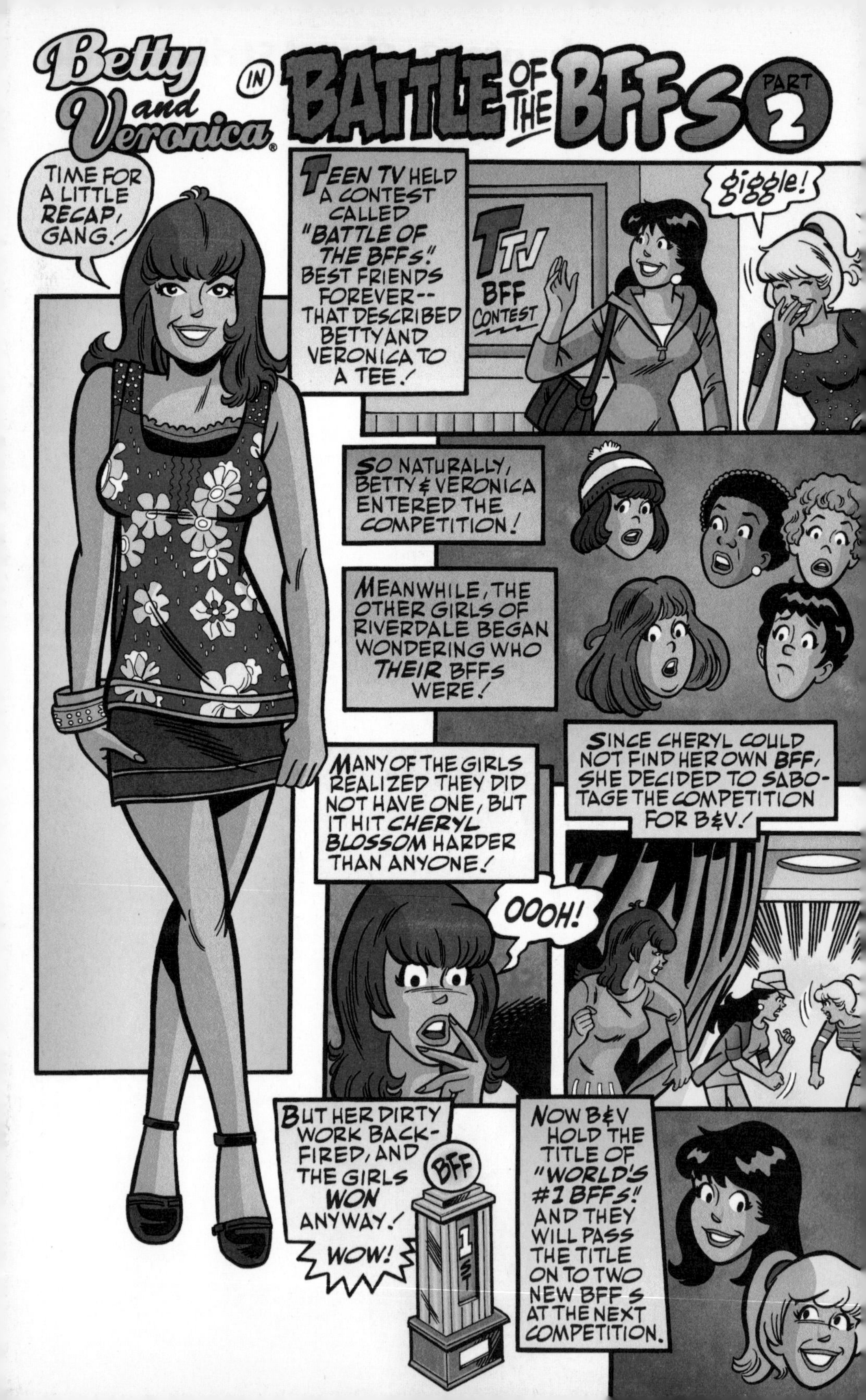

Betty and Veronica
IN
BATTLE OF THE BFFs PART 2
TIME FOR A LITTLE RECAP, GANG!
TEEN TV HELD A CONTEST CALLED "BATTLE OF THE BFFs!" BEST FRIENDS FOREVER-- THAT DESCRIBED BETTY AND VERONICA TO A TEE!
TTV BFF CONTEST
giggle!
SO NATURALLY, BETTY & VERONICA ENTERED THE COMPETITION!
MEANWHILE, THE OTHER GIRLS OF RIVERDALE BEGAN WONDERING WHO THEIR BFFs WERE!
MANY OF THE GIRLS REALIZED THEY DID NOT HAVE ONE, BUT IT HIT CHERYL BLOSSOM HARDER THAN ANYONE!
OOOH!
SINCE CHERYL COULD NOT FIND HER OWN BFF, SHE DECIDED TO SABOTAGE THE COMPETITION FOR B&V!
BUT HER DIRTY WORK BACKFIRED, AND THE GIRLS WON ANYWAY!
WOW!
BFF
1ST
NOW B&V HOLD THE TITLE OF "WORLD'S #1 BFFs!" AND THEY WILL PASS THE TITLE ON TO TWO NEW BFFs AT THE NEXT COMPETITION.

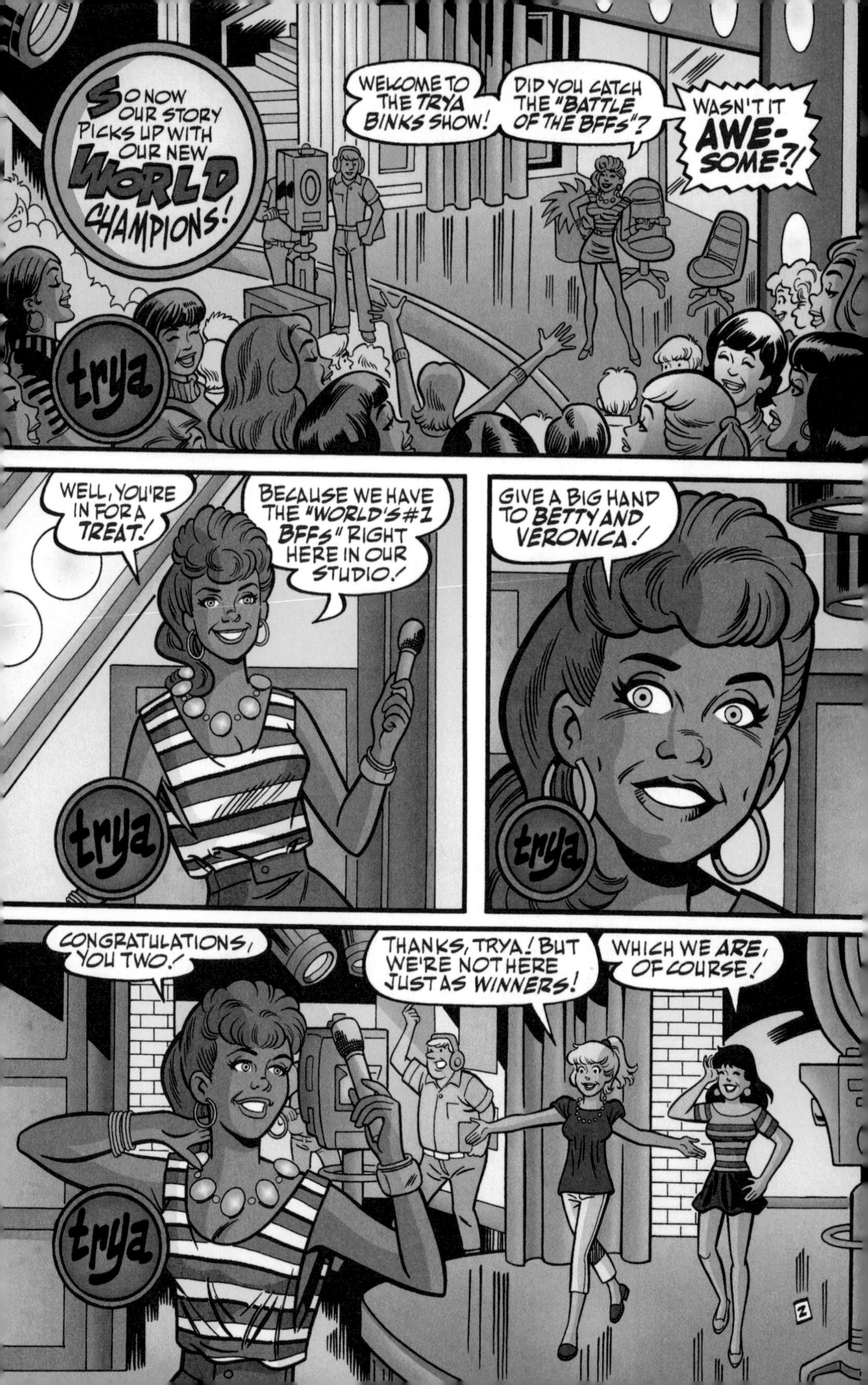
SO NOW OUR STORY PICKS UP WITH OUR NEW WORLD CHAMPIONS!
WELCOME TO THE TRYA BINKS SHOW!
DID YOU CATCH THE "BATTLE OF THE BFFS"?
WASN'T IT AWE-SOME?!
tryа
WELL, YOU'RE IN FOR A TREAT!
BECAUSE WE HAVE THE "WORLD'S #1 BFFS" RIGHT HERE IN OUR STUDIO!
tryа
GIVE A BIG HAND TO BETTY AND VERONICA!
tryа
CONGRATULATIONS, YOU TWO!
THANKS, TRYA! BUT WE'RE NOT HERE JUST AS WINNERS!
WHICH WE ARE, OF COURSE!
tryа
2

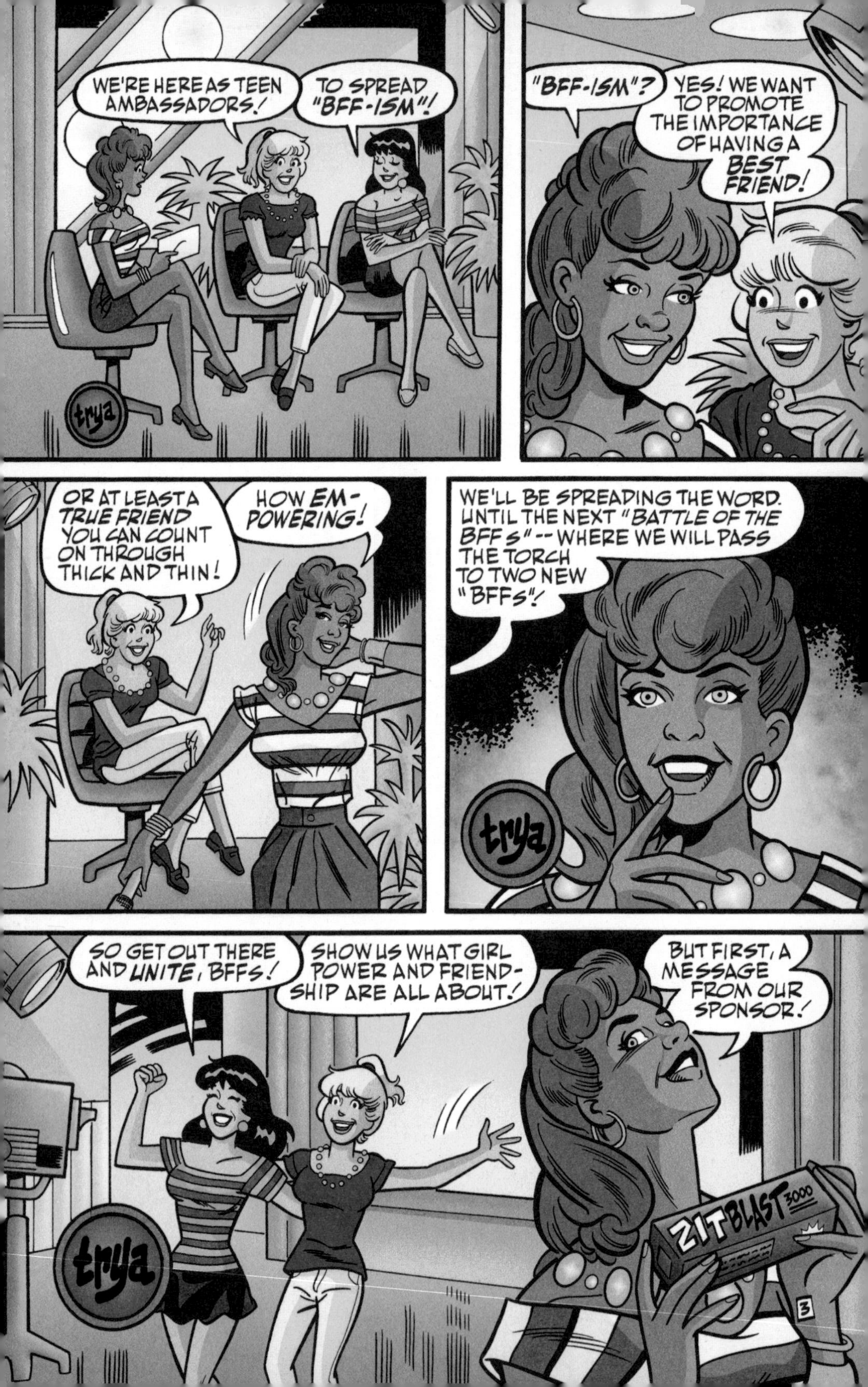
WE'RE HERE AS TEEN AMBASSADORS!
TO SPREAD "BFF-ISM"!
trya
"BFF-ISM"?
YES! WE WANT TO PROMOTE THE IMPORTANCE OF HAVING A BEST FRIEND!
OR AT LEAST A TRUE FRIEND YOU CAN COUNT ON THROUGH THICK AND THIN!
HOW EM-POWERING!
WE'LL BE SPREADING THE WORD. UNTIL THE NEXT "BATTLE OF THE BFFs" -- WHERE WE WILL PASS THE TORCH TO TWO NEW "BFFs"!
trya
SO GET OUT THERE AND UNITE, BFFs!
SHOW US WHAT GIRL POWER AND FRIENDSHIP ARE ALL ABOUT!
BUT FIRST, A MESSAGE FROM OUR SPONSOR!
trya
ZIT BLAST 3000
3

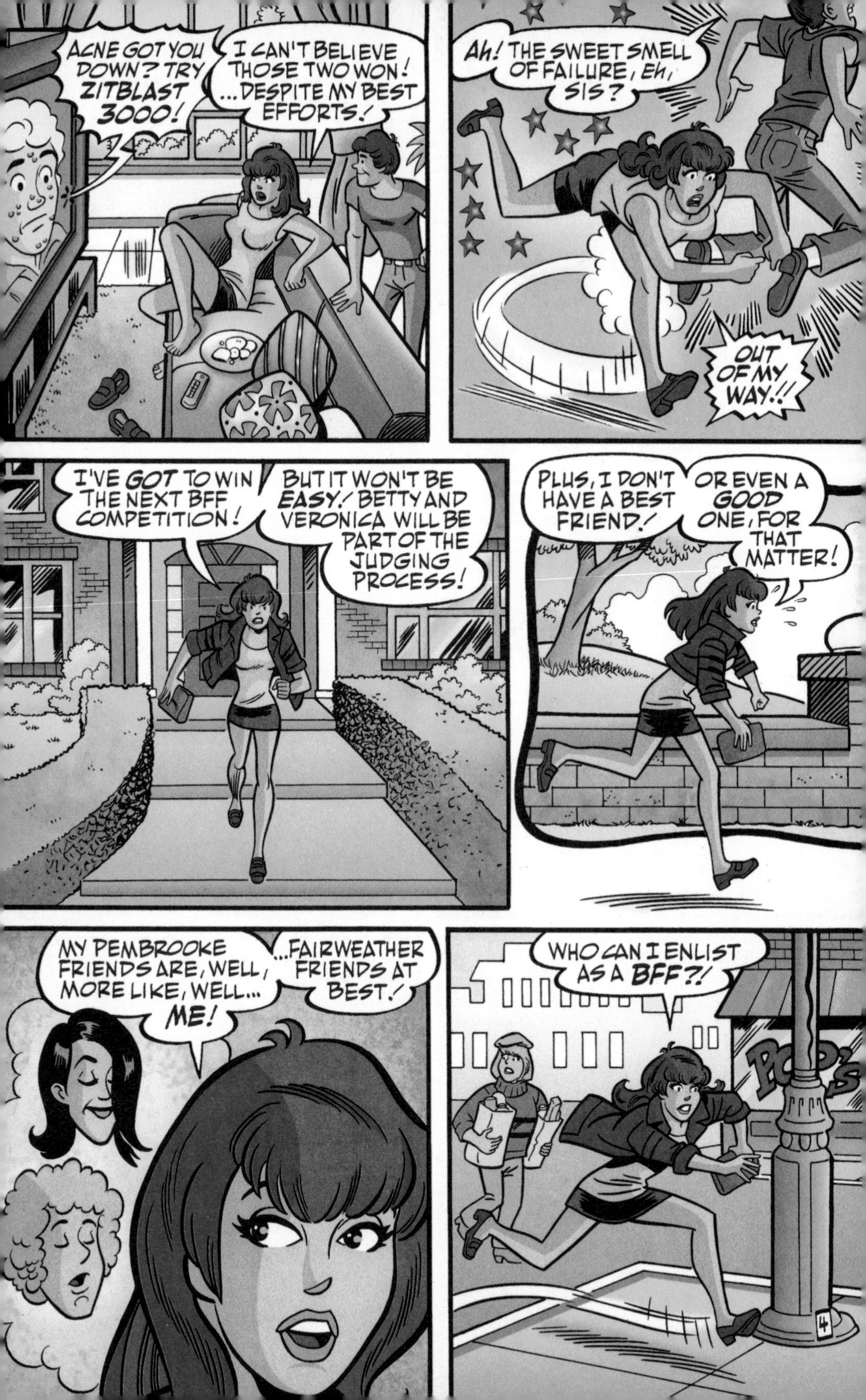
ACNE GOT YOU DOWN? TRY ZITBLAST 3000!
I CAN'T BELIEVE THOSE TWO WON! ...DESPITE MY BEST EFFORTS!
Ah! THE SWEET SMELL OF FAILURE, Eh, SIS?
OUT OF MY WAY!!
I'VE GOT TO WIN THE NEXT BFF COMPETITION!
BUT IT WON'T BE EASY! BETTY AND VERONICA WILL BE PART OF THE JUDGING PROCESS!
PLUS, I DON'T HAVE A BEST FRIEND!
OR EVEN A GOOD ONE, FOR THAT MATTER!
MY PEMBROOKE FRIENDS ARE, WELL, MORE LIKE, WELL... ME!
...FAIRWEATHER FRIENDS AT BEST!
WHO CAN I ENLIST AS A BFF?!
POP'S
4

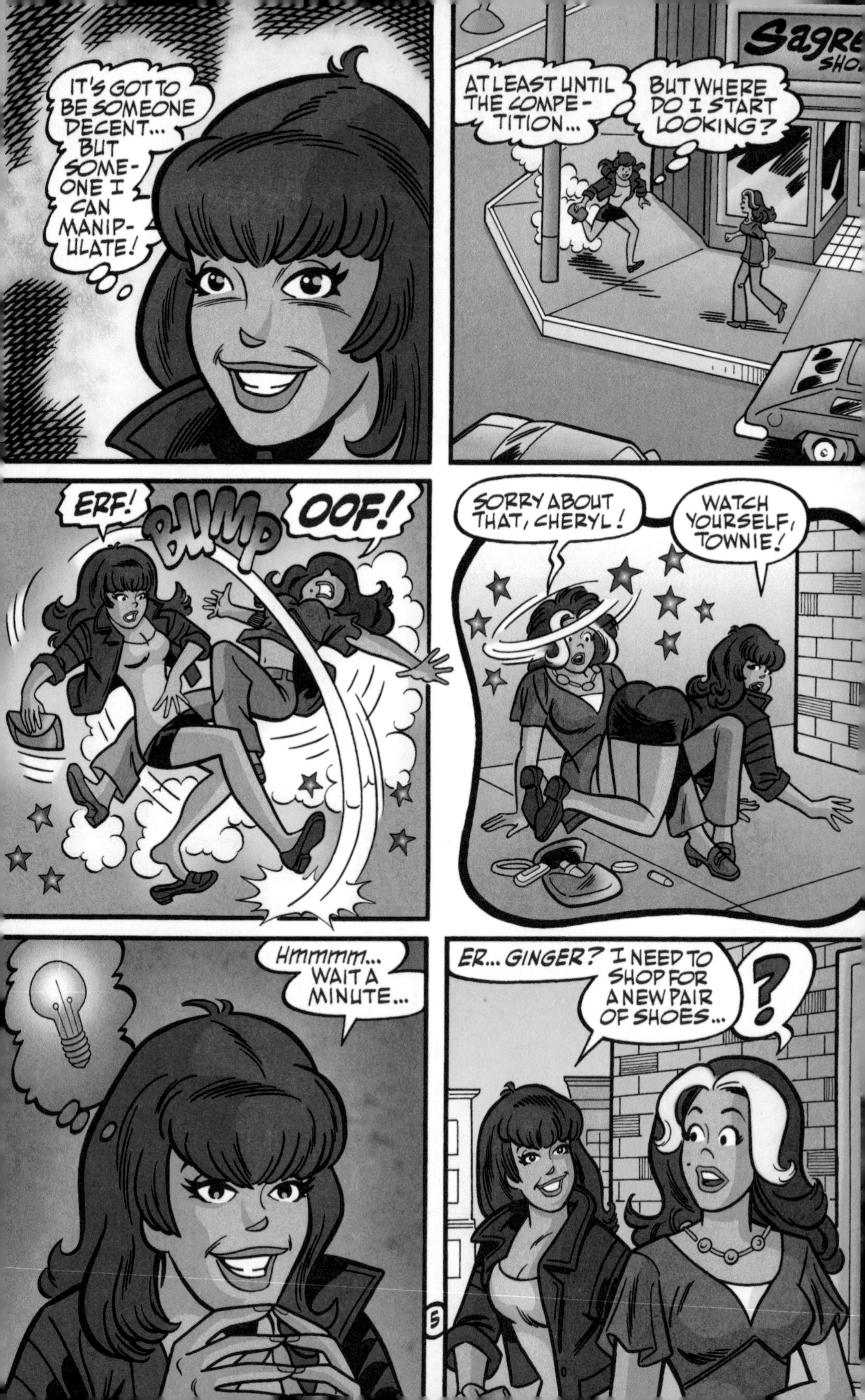

IT'S GOT TO BE SOMEONE DECENT... BUT SOMEONE I CAN MANIPULATE!
AT LEAST UNTIL THE COMPETITION...
BUT WHERE DO I START LOOKING?
ERF!
BUMP
OOF!
SORRY ABOUT THAT, CHERYL!
WATCH YOURSELF, TOWNIE!
Hmmmm... WAIT A MINUTE...
ER... GINGER? I NEED TO SHOP FOR A NEW PAIR OF SHOES...
?
5

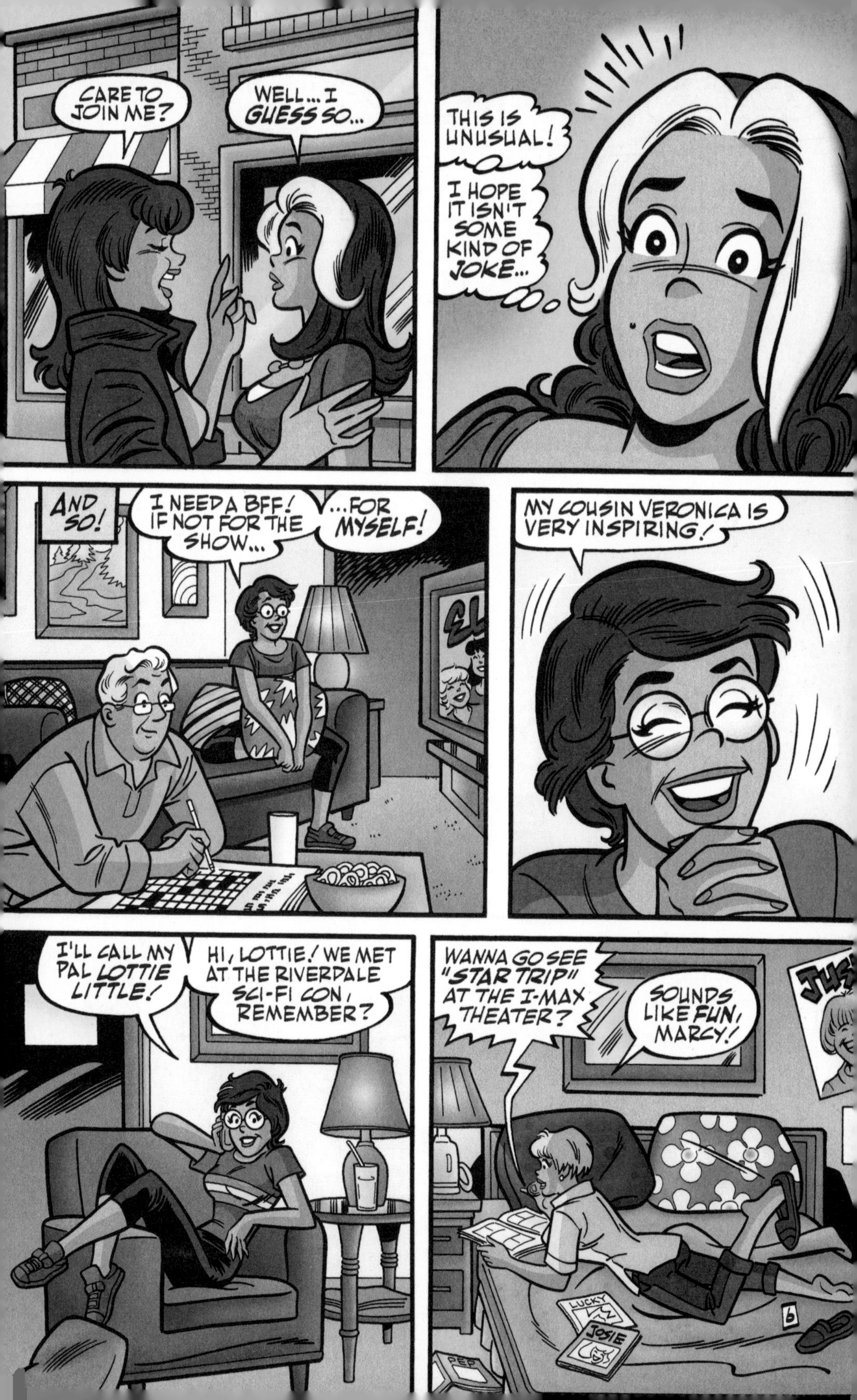
CARE TO JOIN ME?
WELL... I GUESS SO...
THIS IS UNUSUAL!
I HOPE IT ISN'T SOME KIND OF JOKE...
AND SO!
I NEED A BFF! IF NOT FOR THE SHOW...
...FOR MYSELF!
MY COUSIN VERONICA IS VERY INSPIRING!
I'LL CALL MY PAL LOTTIE LITTLE!
HI, LOTTIE! WE MET AT THE RIVERDALE SCI-FI CON, REMEMBER?
WANNA GO SEE "STAR TRIP" AT THE I-MAX THEATER?
SOUNDS LIKE FUN, MARCY!
LUCKY
JOSIE
PEP
6

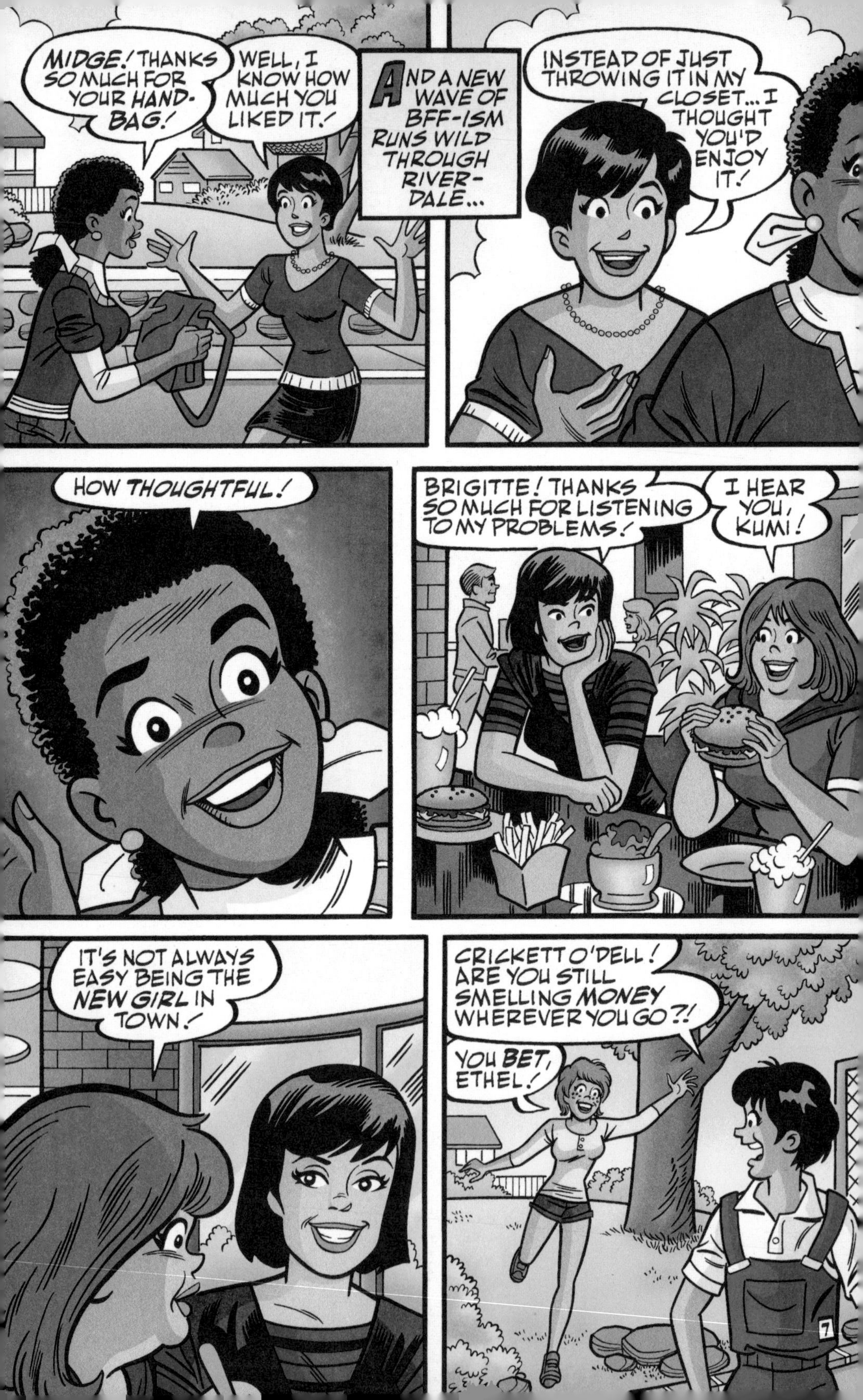
MIDGE! THANKS SO MUCH FOR YOUR HAND-BAG!
WELL, I KNOW HOW MUCH YOU LIKED IT!
AND A NEW WAVE OF BFF-ISM RUNS WILD THROUGH RIVER-DALE...
INSTEAD OF JUST THROWING IT IN MY CLOSET... I THOUGHT YOU'D ENJOY IT!
HOW THOUGHTFUL!
BRIGITTE! THANKS SO MUCH FOR LISTENING TO MY PROBLEMS!
I HEAR YOU, KUMI!
IT'S NOT ALWAYS EASY BEING THE NEW GIRL IN TOWN!
CRICKETT O'DELL! ARE YOU STILL SMELLING MONEY WHEREVER YOU GO?!
YOU BET, ETHEL!
7

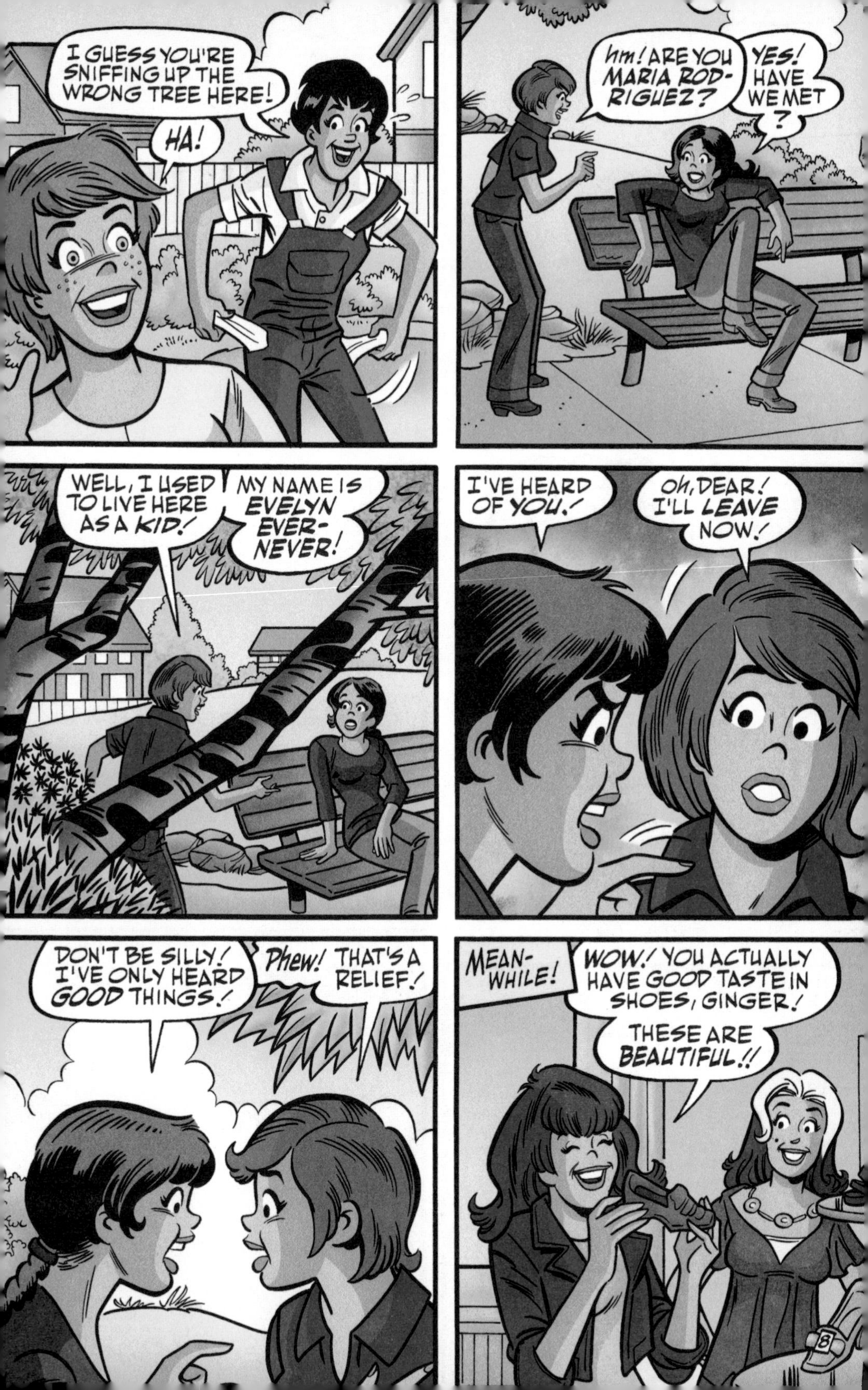
I GUESS YOU'RE SNIFFING UP THE WRONG TREE HERE!
HA!
hm! ARE YOU MARIA RODRIGUEZ?
YES! HAVE WE MET?
WELL, I USED TO LIVE HERE AS A KID!
MY NAME IS EVELYN EVER-NEVER!
I'VE HEARD OF YOU!
Oh, DEAR! I'LL LEAVE NOW!
DON'T BE SILLY! I'VE ONLY HEARD GOOD THINGS!
Phew! THAT'S A RELIEF!
MEANWHILE!
WOW! YOU ACTUALLY HAVE GOOD TASTE IN SHOES, GINGER!
THESE ARE BEAUTIFUL!!

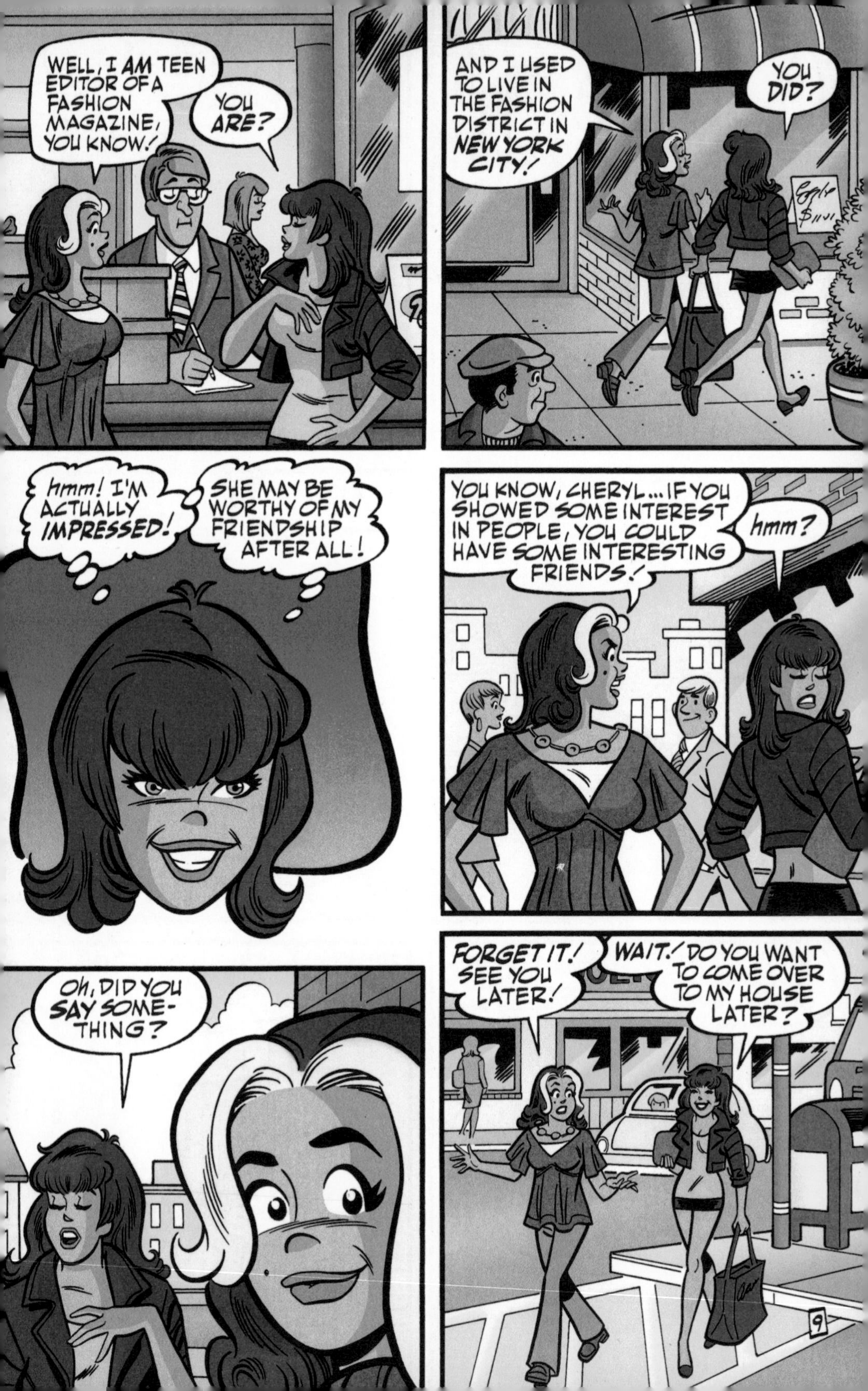
WELL, I AM TEEN EDITOR OF A FASHION MAGAZINE, YOU KNOW!
YOU ARE?
AND I USED TO LIVE IN THE FASHION DISTRICT IN NEW YORK CITY!
YOU DID?
hmm! I'M ACTUALLY IMPRESSED!
SHE MAY BE WORTHY OF MY FRIENDSHIP AFTER ALL!
YOU KNOW, CHERYL... IF YOU SHOWED SOME INTEREST IN PEOPLE, YOU COULD HAVE SOME INTERESTING FRIENDS!
hmm?
Oh, DID YOU SAY SOME-THING?
FORGET IT! SEE YOU LATER!
WAIT! DO YOU WANT TO COME OVER TO MY HOUSE LATER?
9

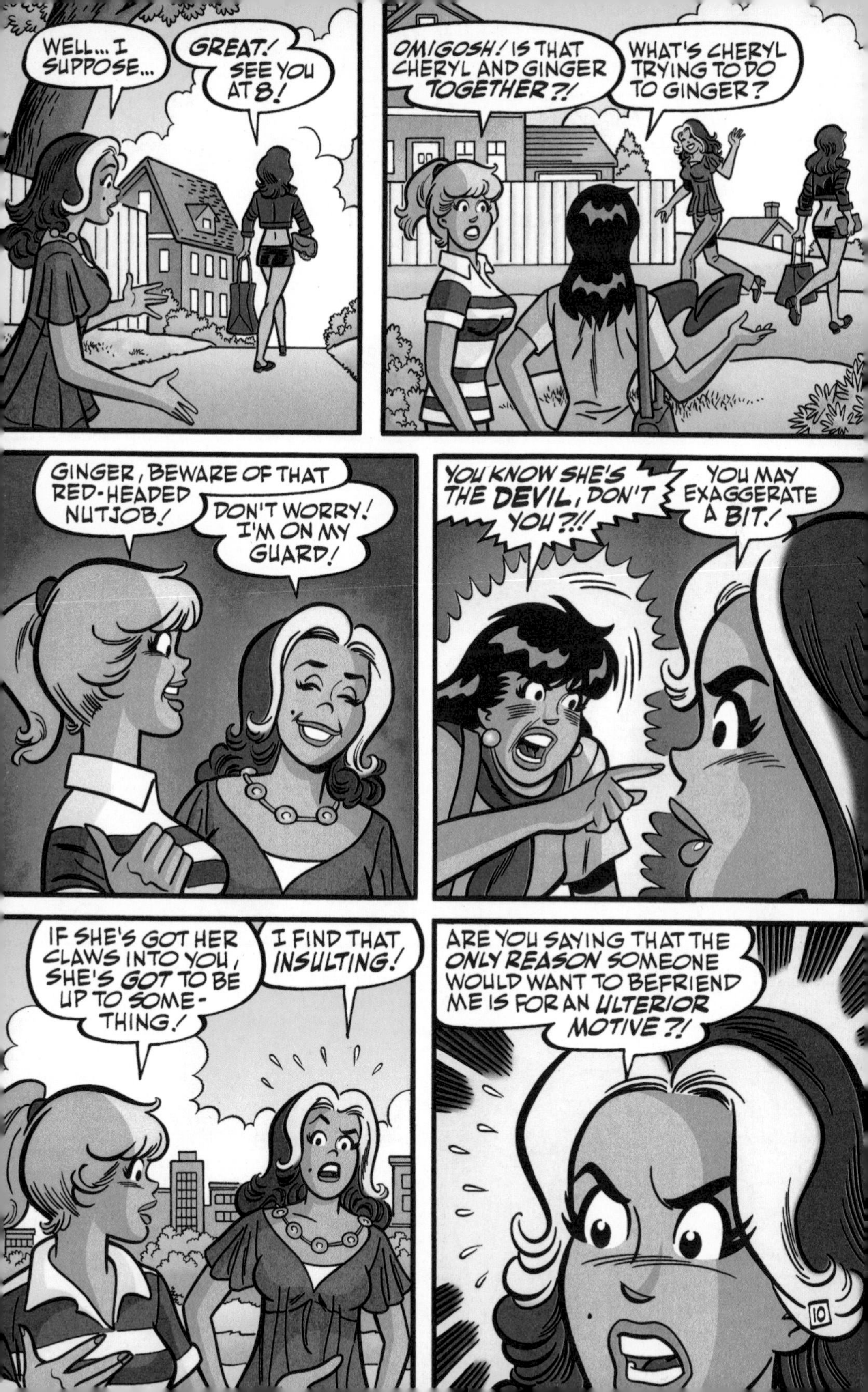
WELL... I SUPPOSE...
GREAT! SEE YOU AT 8!
OMIGOSH! IS THAT CHERYL AND GINGER TOGETHER?!
WHAT'S CHERYL TRYING TO DO TO GINGER?
GINGER, BEWARE OF THAT RED-HEADED NUTJOB!
DON'T WORRY! I'M ON MY GUARD!
YOU KNOW SHE'S THE DEVIL, DON'T YOU?!!
YOU MAY EXAGGERATE A BIT!
IF SHE'S GOT HER CLAWS INTO YOU, SHE'S GOT TO BE UP TO SOME-THING!
I FIND THAT INSULTING!
ARE YOU SAYING THAT THE ONLY REASON SOMEONE WOULD WANT TO BEFRIEND ME IS FOR AN ULTERIOR MOTIVE?!
10

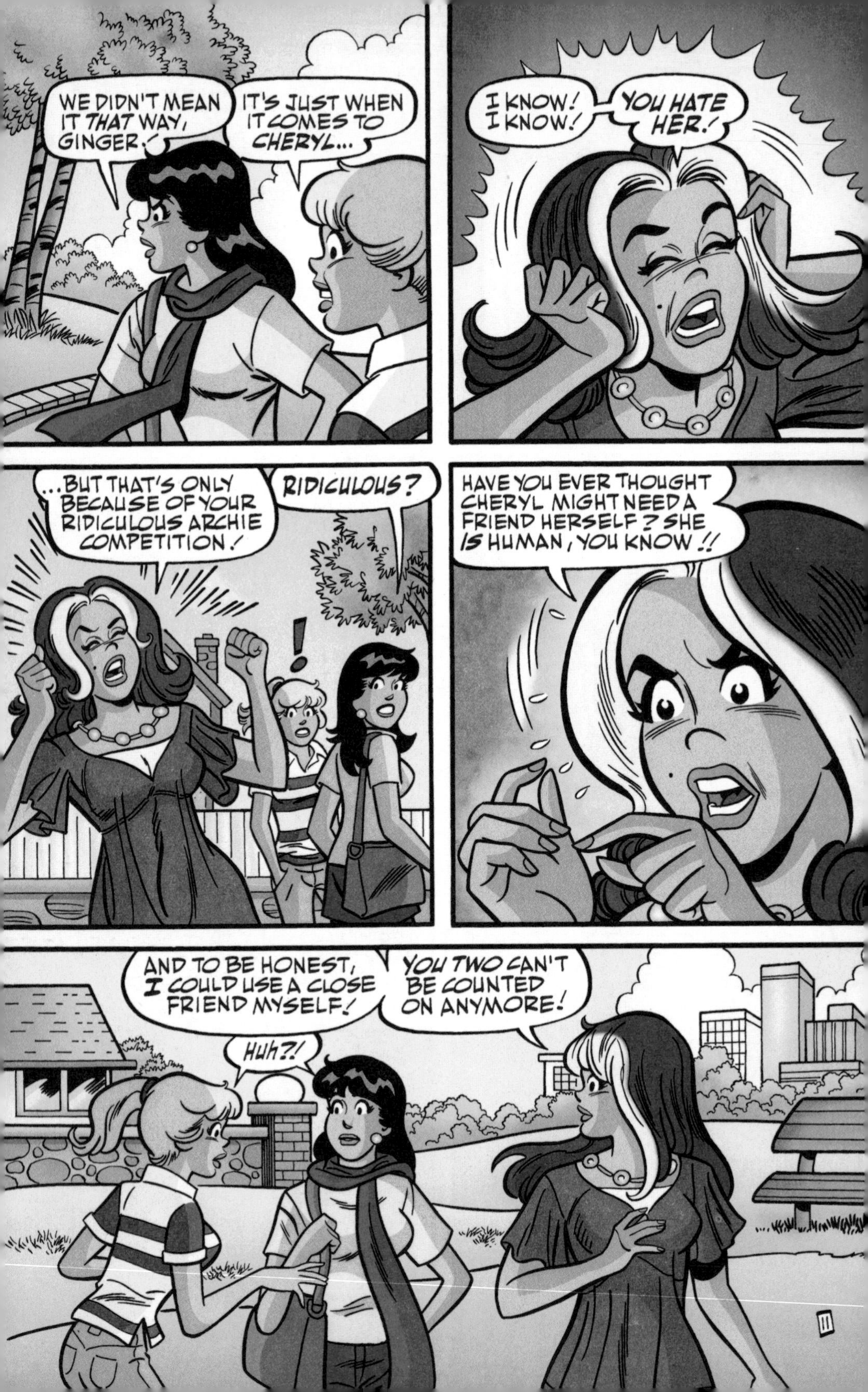
WE DIDN'T MEAN IT THAT WAY, GINGER!
IT'S JUST WHEN IT COMES TO CHERYL...
I KNOW! I KNOW!
YOU HATE HER!
...BUT THAT'S ONLY BECAUSE OF YOUR RIDICULOUS ARCHIE COMPETITION!
RIDICULOUS?
!
HAVE YOU EVER THOUGHT CHERYL MIGHT NEED A FRIEND HERSELF? SHE IS HUMAN, YOU KNOW!!
AND TO BE HONEST, I COULD USE A CLOSE FRIEND MYSELF!
YOU TWO CAN'T BE COUNTED ON ANYMORE!
HUH?!

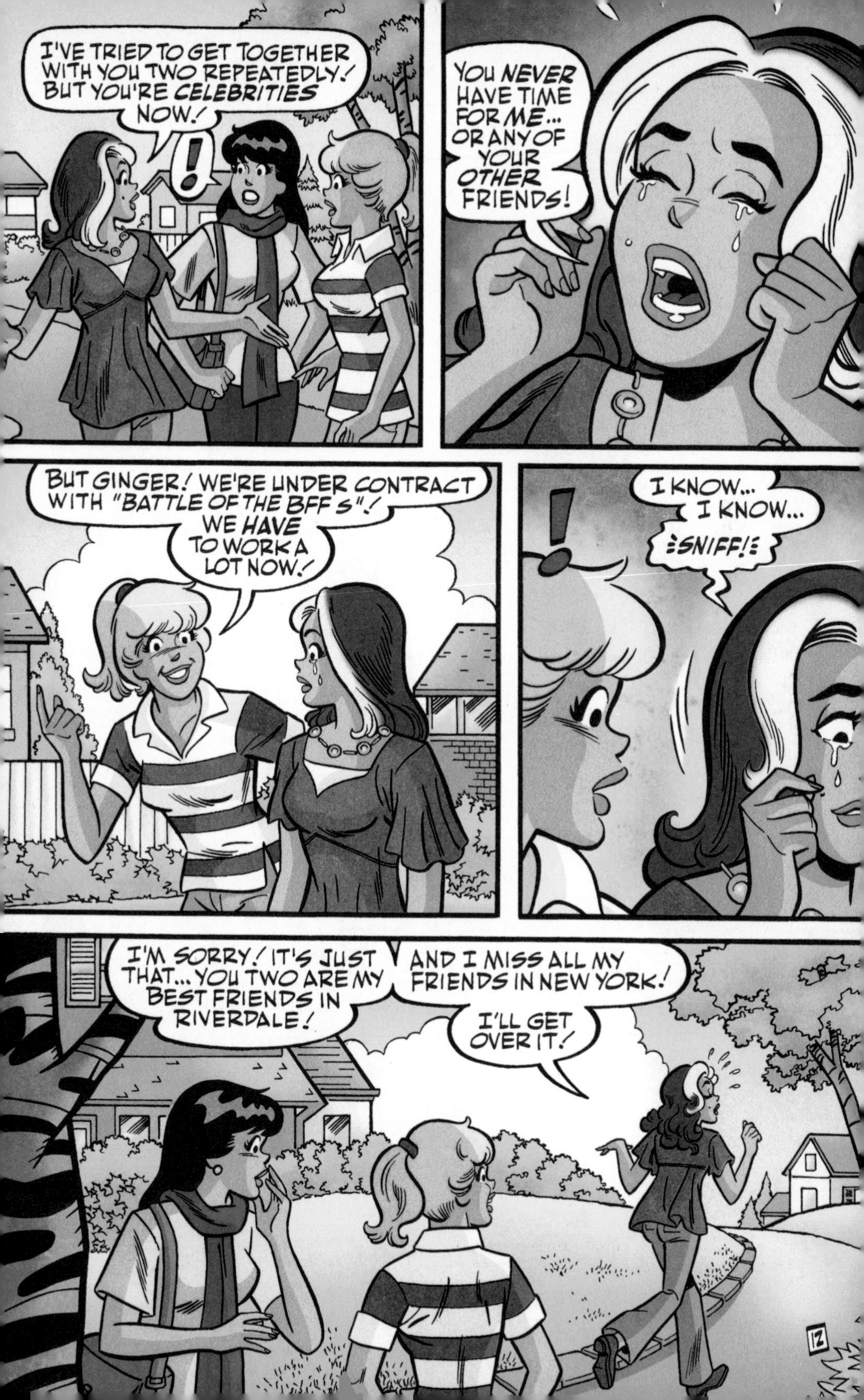
I'VE TRIED TO GET TOGETHER WITH YOU TWO REPEATEDLY! BUT YOU'RE CELEBRITIES NOW!
!
YOU NEVER HAVE TIME FOR ME... OR ANY OF YOUR OTHER FRIENDS!
BUT GINGER! WE'RE UNDER CONTRACT WITH "BATTLE OF THE BFF's"! WE HAVE TO WORK A LOT NOW!
!
I KNOW... I KNOW...
SNIFF!
I'M SORRY! IT'S JUST THAT... YOU TWO ARE MY BEST FRIENDS IN RIVERDALE!
AND I MISS ALL MY FRIENDS IN NEW YORK!
I'LL GET OVER IT!
12

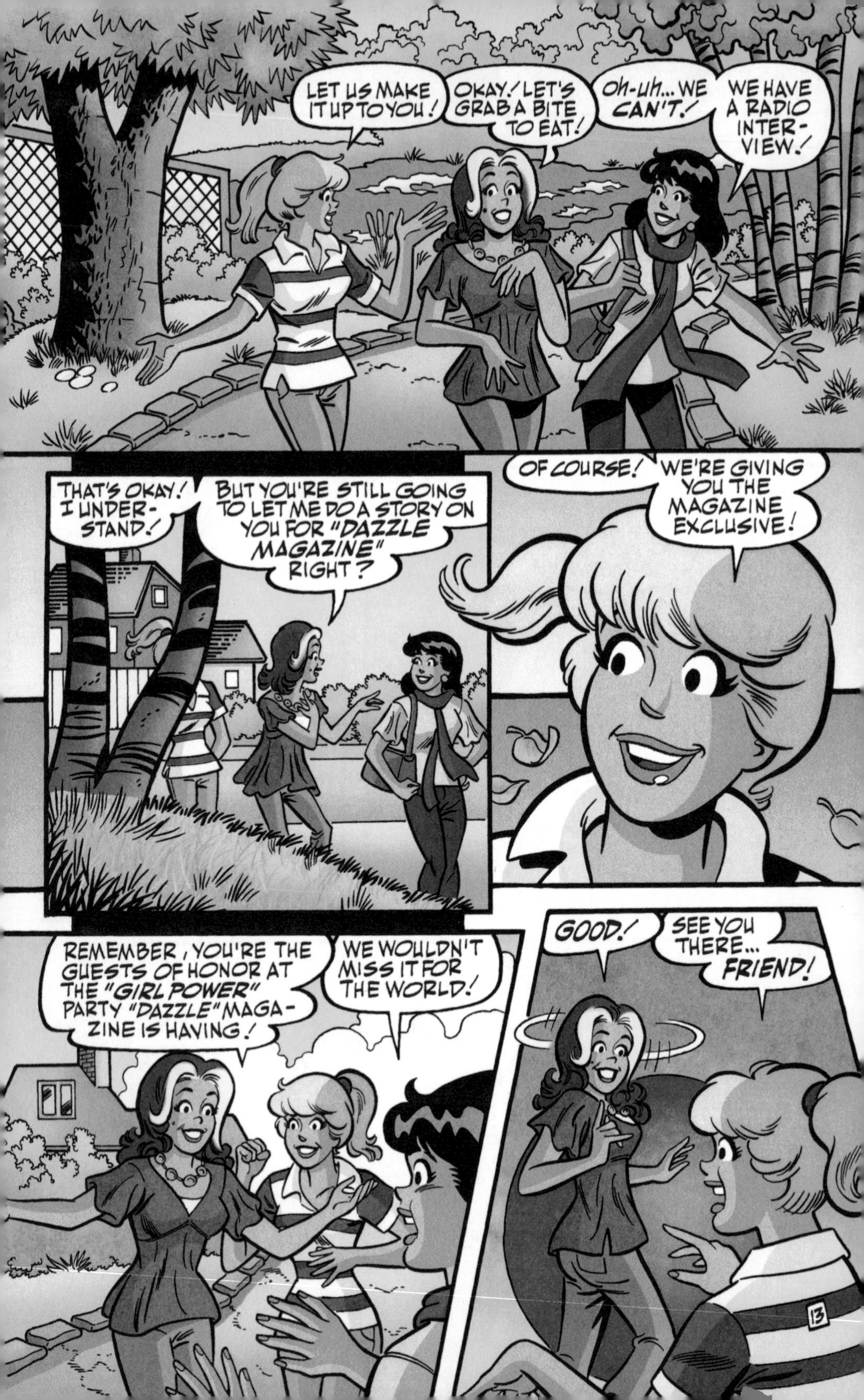
LET US MAKE IT UP TO YOU!
OKAY! LET'S GRAB A BITE TO EAT!
Oh-uh... WE CAN'T!
WE HAVE A RADIO INTER-VIEW!
THAT'S OKAY! I UNDER-STAND!
BUT YOU'RE STILL GOING TO LET ME DO A STORY ON YOU FOR "DAZZLE MAGAZINE" RIGHT?
OF COURSE!
WE'RE GIVING YOU THE MAGAZINE EXCLUSIVE!
REMEMBER, YOU'RE THE GUESTS OF HONOR AT THE "GIRL POWER" PARTY "DAZZLE" MAGA-ZINE IS HAVING!
WE WOULDN'T MISS IT FOR THE WORLD!
GOOD!
SEE YOU THERE... FRIEND!
13

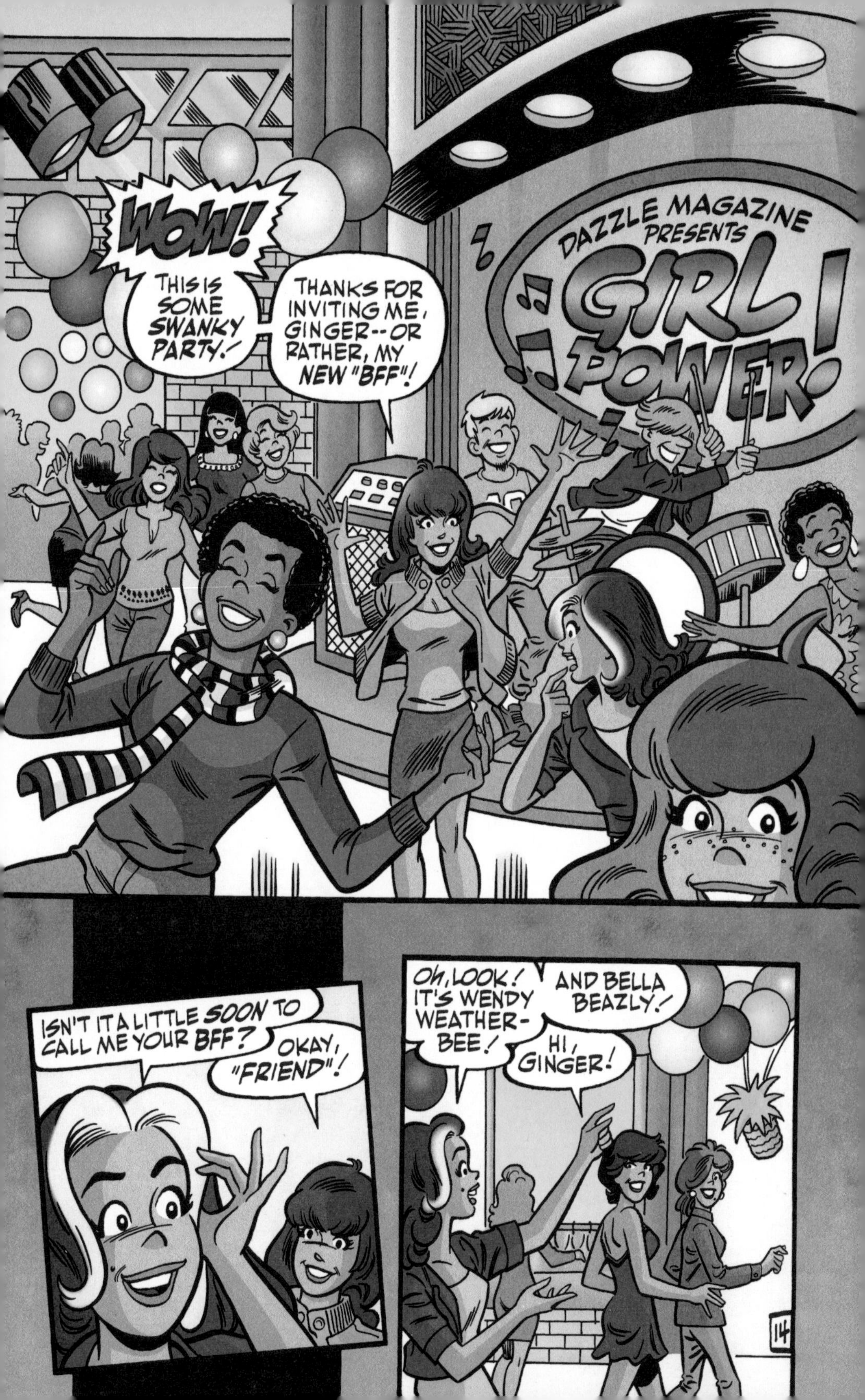
DAZZLE MAGAZINE PRESENTS
GIRL POWER!
WOW!
THIS IS SOME SWANKY PARTY!
THANKS FOR INVITING ME, GINGER--OR RATHER, MY NEW "BFF"!
ISN'T IT A LITTLE SOON TO CALL ME YOUR BFF?
OKAY, "FRIEND"!
OH, LOOK! IT'S WENDY WEATHER-BEE!
AND BELLA BEAZLY!
HI, GINGER!
14

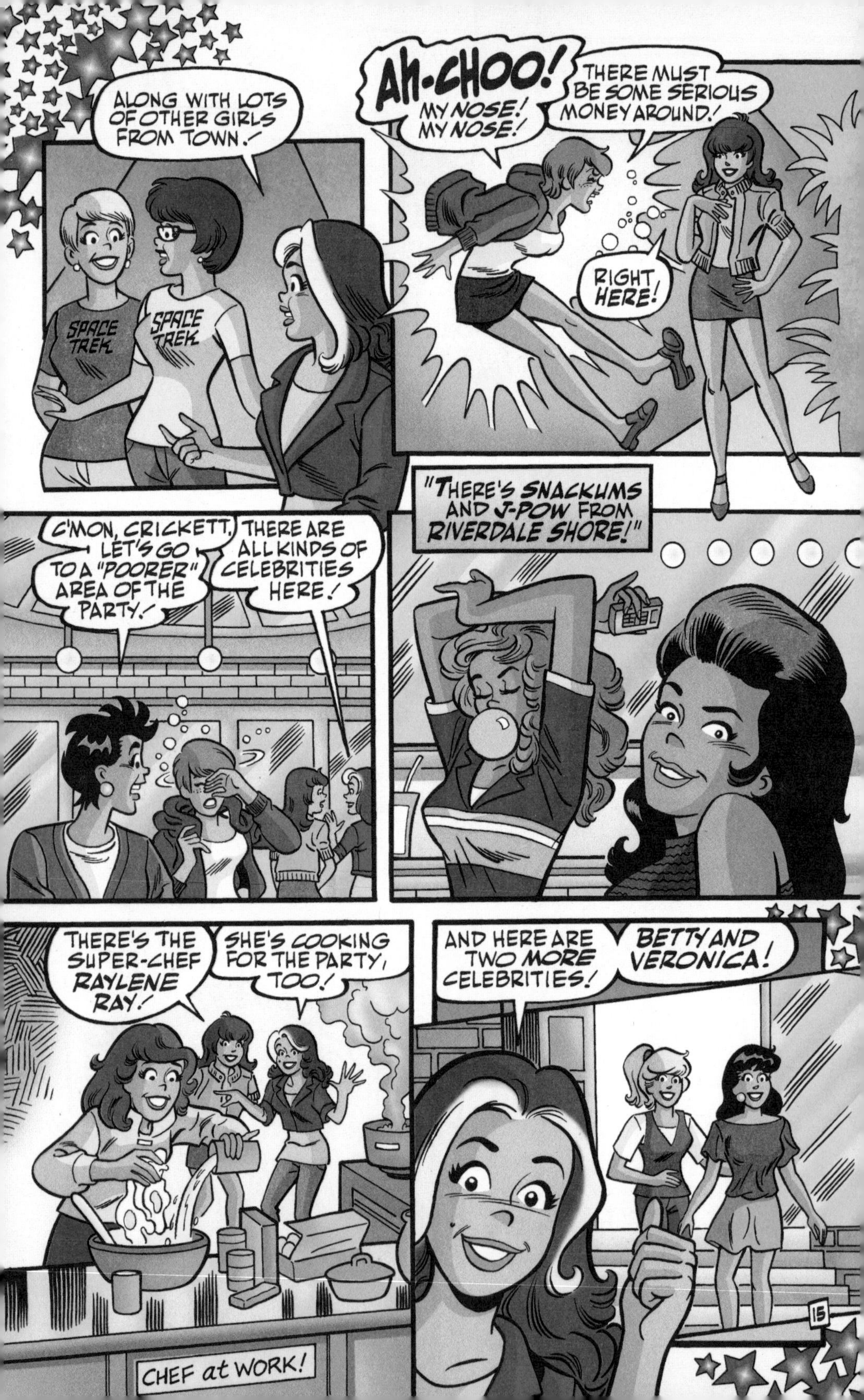

ALONG WITH LOTS OF OTHER GIRLS FROM TOWN!
SPACE TREK
SPACE TREK
AH-CHOO! MY NOSE! MY NOSE!
THERE MUST BE SOME SERIOUS MONEY AROUND!
RIGHT HERE!
C'MON, CRICKETT, LET'S GO TO A "POORER" AREA OF THE PARTY!
THERE ARE ALL KINDS OF CELEBRITIES HERE!
"THERE'S SNACKUMS AND J-POW FROM RIVERDALE SHORE!"
THERE'S THE SUPER-CHEF RAYLENE RAY!
SHE'S COOKING FOR THE PARTY, TOO!
CHEF at WORK!
AND HERE ARE TWO MORE CELEBRITIES!
BETTY AND VERONICA!
15

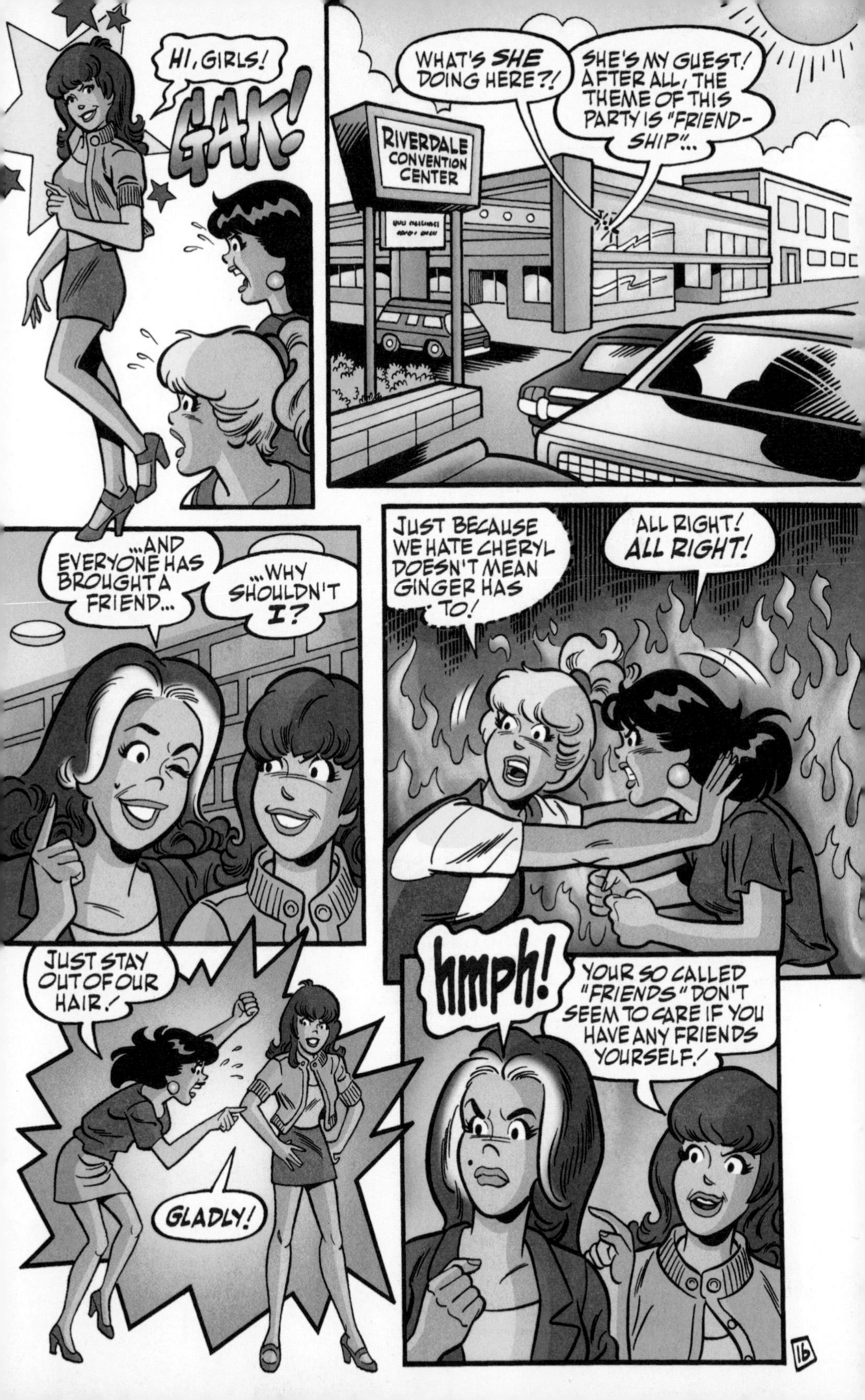
HI, GIRLS!
GAK!
WHAT'S SHE DOING HERE?!
SHE'S MY GUEST! AFTER ALL, THE THEME OF THIS PARTY IS "FRIEND-SHIP"!...
RIVERDALE CONVENTION CENTER
...AND EVERYONE HAS BROUGHT A FRIEND...
...WHY SHOULDN'T I?
JUST BECAUSE WE HATE CHERYL DOESN'T MEAN GINGER HAS TO!
ALL RIGHT! ALL RIGHT!
JUST STAY OUT OF OUR HAIR!
GLADLY!
hmph!
YOUR SO CALLED "FRIENDS" DON'T SEEM TO CARE IF YOU HAVE ANY FRIENDS YOURSELF!

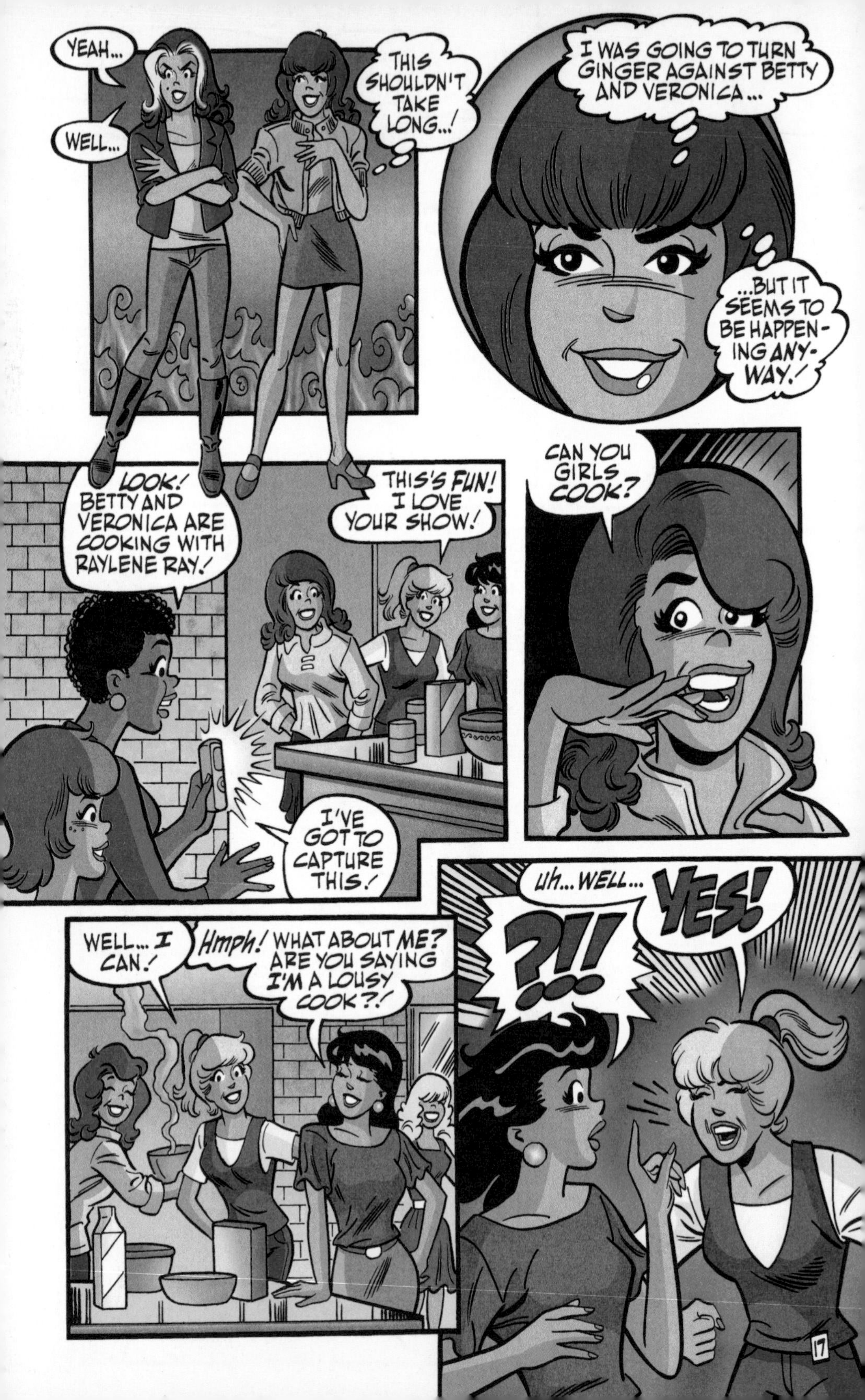
YEAH...
WELL...
THIS SHOULDN'T TAKE LONG...!
I WAS GOING TO TURN GINGER AGAINST BETTY AND VERONICA...
...BUT IT SEEMS TO BE HAPPENING ANYWAY.!
LOOK! BETTY AND VERONICA ARE COOKING WITH RAYLENE RAY.!
THIS'S FUN! I LOVE YOUR SHOW!
I'VE GOT TO CAPTURE THIS.!
CAN YOU GIRLS COOK?
WELL... I CAN.!
Hmph! WHAT ABOUT ME? ARE YOU SAYING I'M A LOUSY COOK?!
uh... WELL...
YES!
?!!...
17

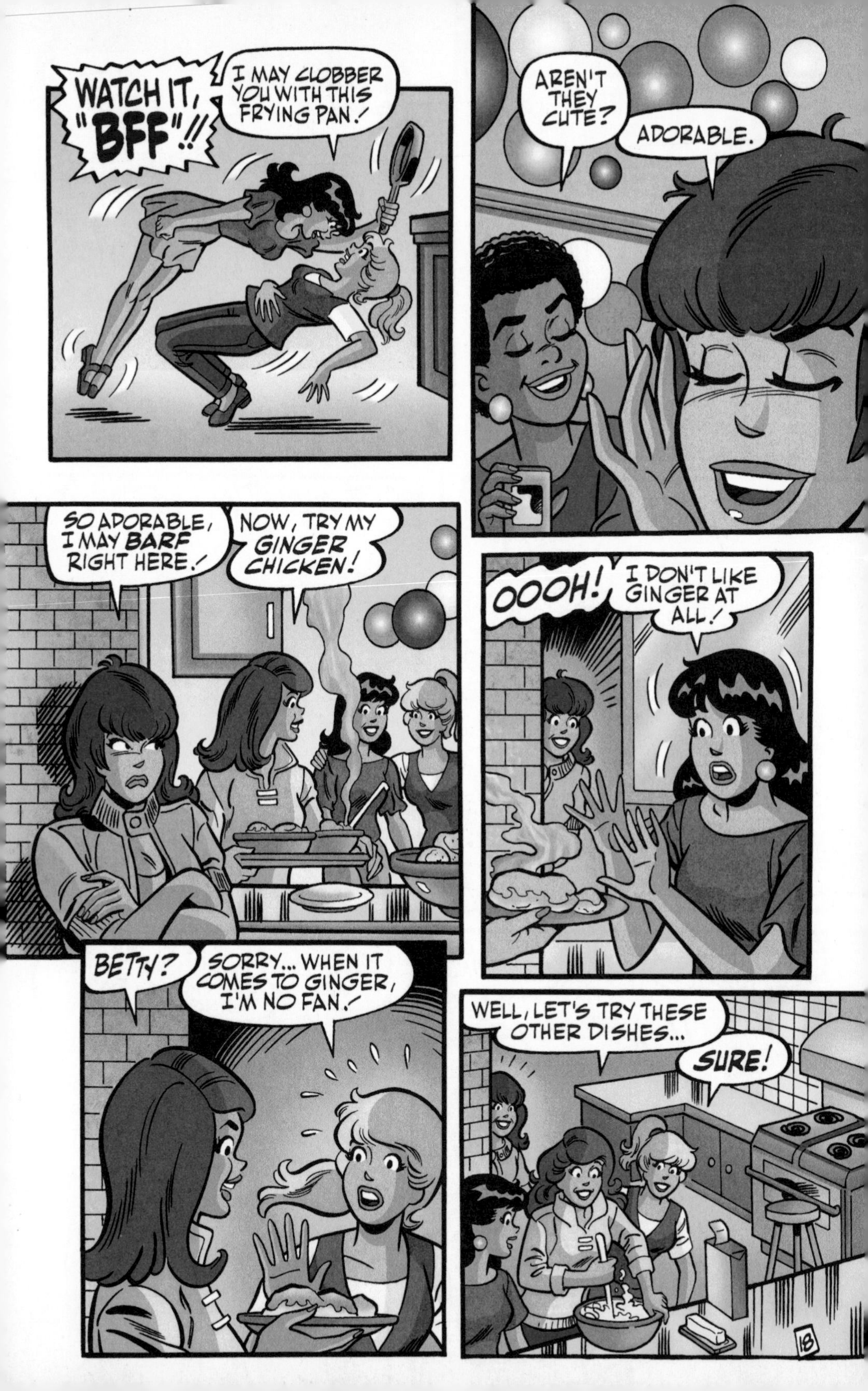
WATCH IT, "BFF"!!
I MAY CLOBBER YOU WITH THIS FRYING PAN!
AREN'T THEY CUTE?
ADORABLE.
SO ADORABLE, I MAY BARF RIGHT HERE!
NOW, TRY MY GINGER CHICKEN!
OOOH!
I DON'T LIKE GINGER AT ALL!
BETTY?
SORRY... WHEN IT COMES TO GINGER, I'M NO FAN!
WELL, LET'S TRY THESE OTHER DISHES...
SURE!
18

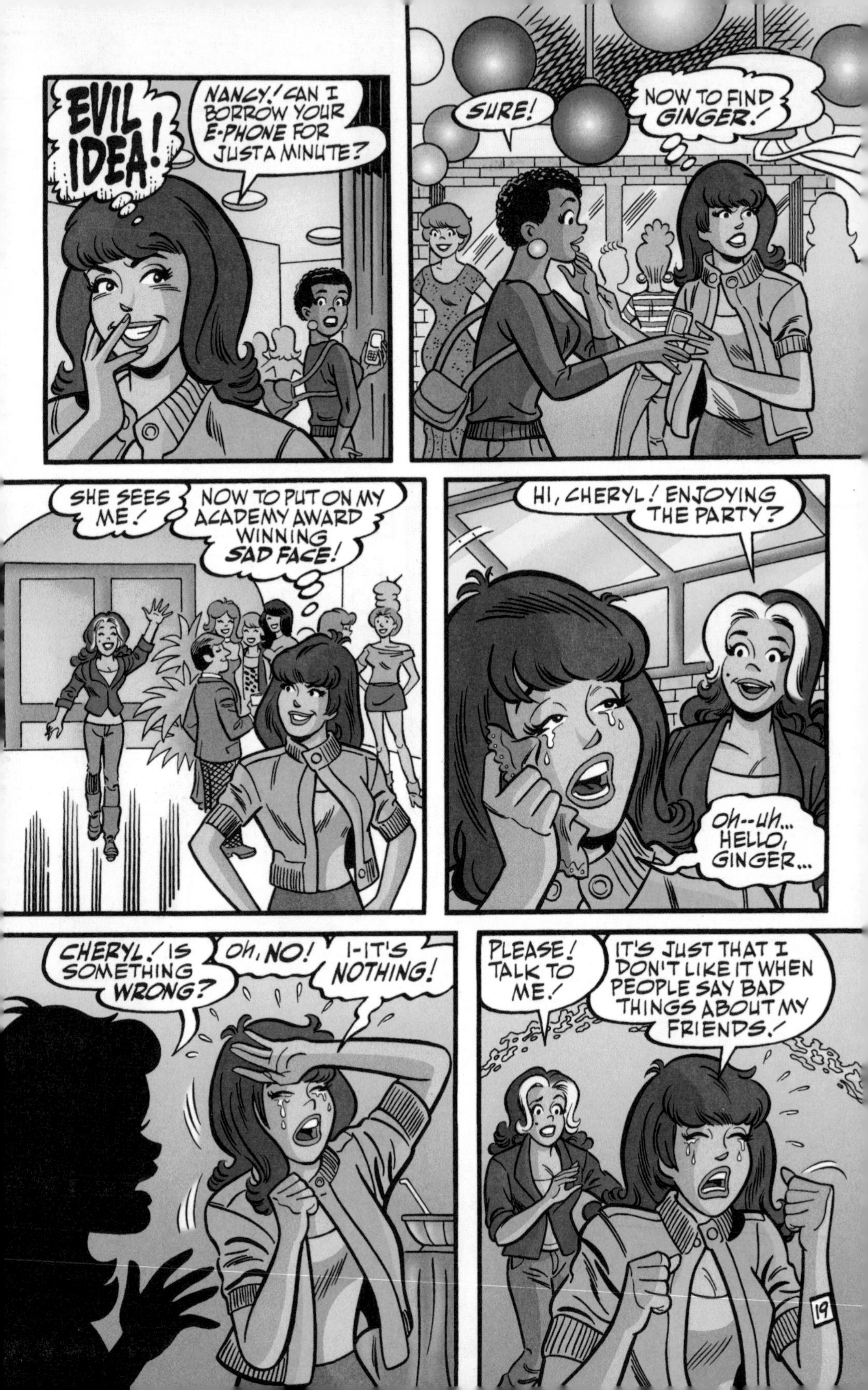
EVIL IDEA!
NANCY! CAN I BORROW YOUR E-PHONE FOR JUST A MINUTE?
SURE!
NOW TO FIND GINGER!
SHE SEES ME!
NOW TO PUT ON MY ACADEMY AWARD WINNING SAD FACE!
HI, CHERYL! ENJOYING THE PARTY?
Oh--uh... HELLO, GINGER...
CHERYL! IS SOMETHING WRONG?
Oh, NO!
I-IT'S NOTHING!
PLEASE! TALK TO ME!
IT'S JUST THAT I DON'T LIKE IT WHEN PEOPLE SAY BAD THINGS ABOUT MY FRIENDS!
19

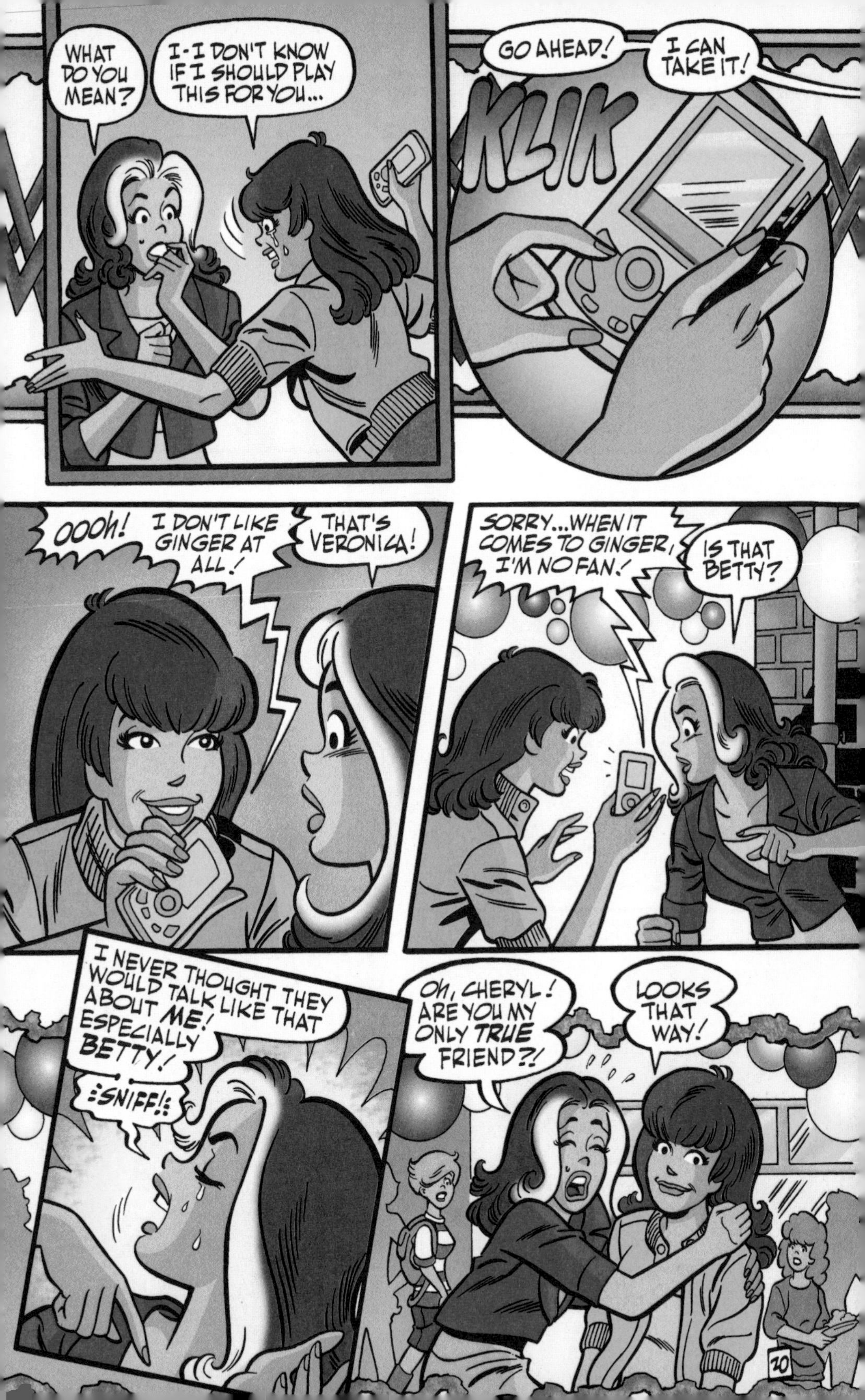
WHAT DO YOU MEAN?
I-I DON'T KNOW IF I SHOULD PLAY THIS FOR YOU...
GO AHEAD!
I CAN TAKE IT!
KLIK
OOOH!
I DON'T LIKE GINGER AT ALL!
THAT'S VERONICA!
SORRY...WHEN IT COMES TO GINGER, I'M NO FAN!
IS THAT BETTY?
I NEVER THOUGHT THEY WOULD TALK LIKE THAT ABOUT ME! ESPECIALLY BETTY!
SNIFF!
OH, CHERYL! ARE YOU MY ONLY TRUE FRIEND?!
LOOKS THAT WAY!
20

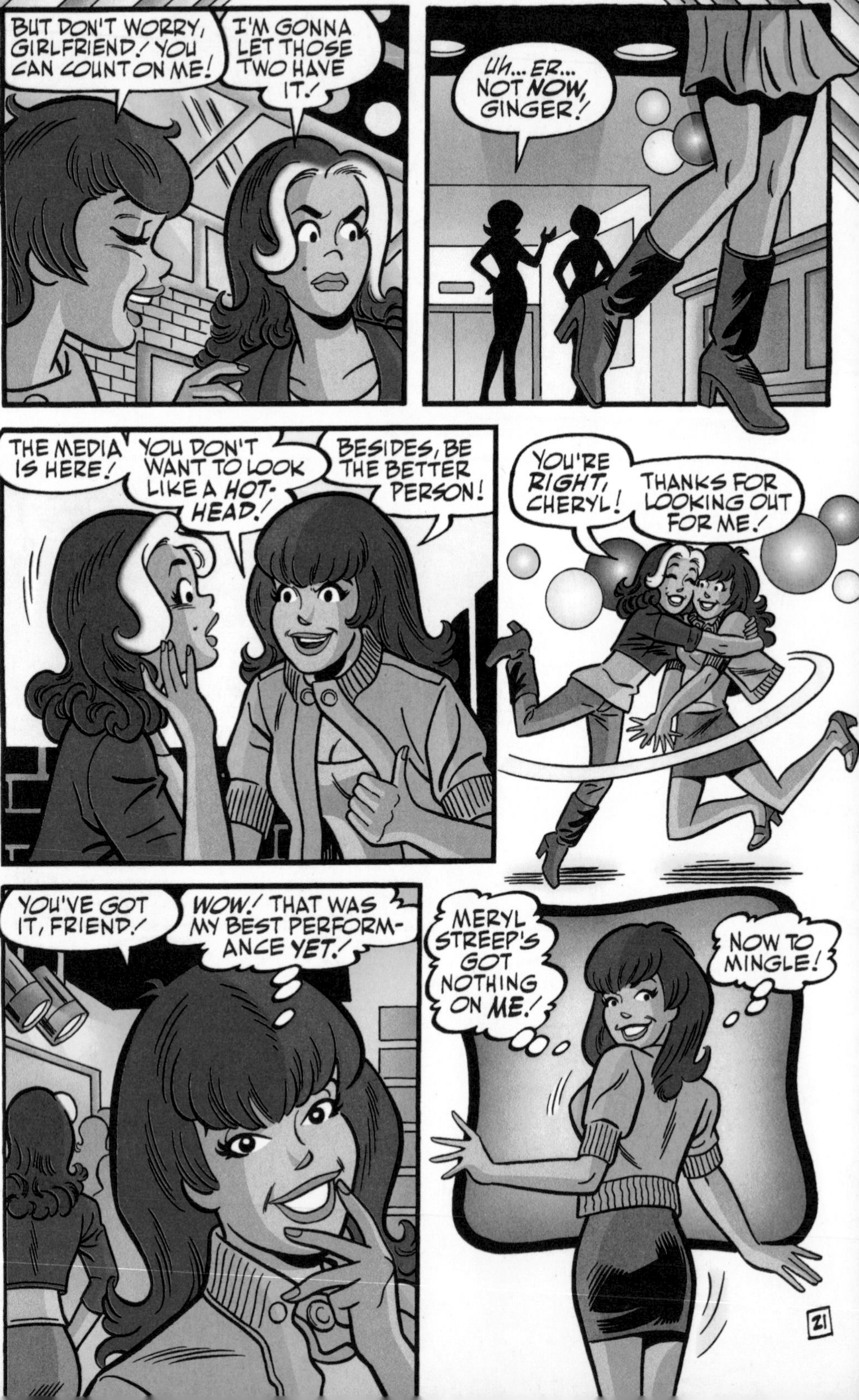
BUT DON'T WORRY, GIRLFRIEND! YOU CAN COUNT ON ME!
I'M GONNA LET THOSE TWO HAVE IT!
UH... ER... NOT NOW, GINGER!
THE MEDIA IS HERE!
YOU DON'T WANT TO LOOK LIKE A HOT-HEAD!
BESIDES, BE THE BETTER PERSON!
YOU'RE RIGHT, CHERYL!
THANKS FOR LOOKING OUT FOR ME!
YOU'VE GOT IT, FRIEND!
WOW! THAT WAS MY BEST PERFORM-ANCE YET!
MERYL STREEP'S GOT NOTHING ON ME!
NOW TO MINGLE!

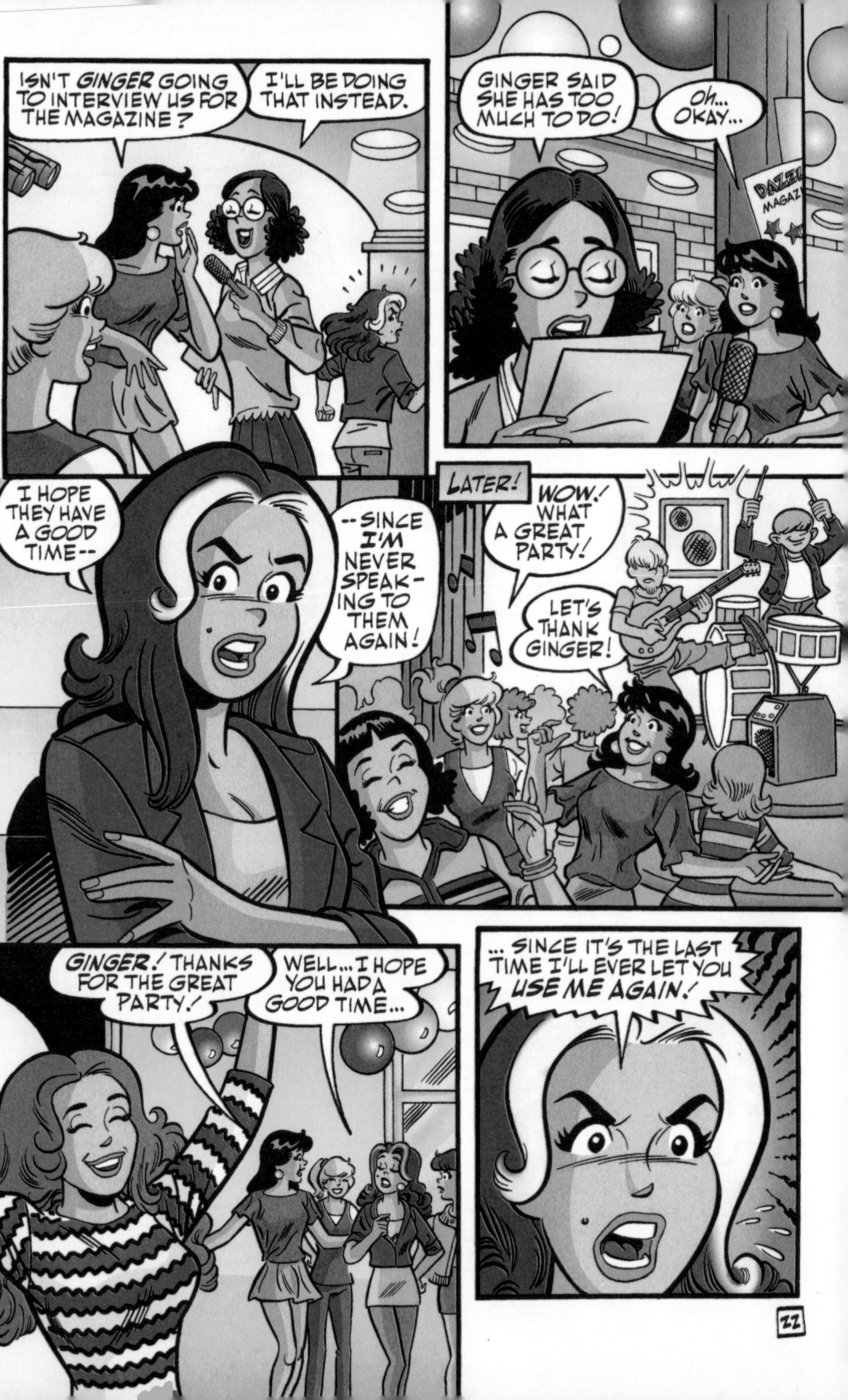
ISN'T GINGER GOING TO INTERVIEW US FOR THE MAGAZINE?
I'LL BE DOING THAT INSTEAD.
GINGER SAID SHE HAS TOO MUCH TO DO!
Oh... OKAY...
DAZZL MAGAZ
I HOPE THEY HAVE A GOOD TIME--
--SINCE I'M NEVER SPEAKING TO THEM AGAIN!
LATER!
WOW! WHAT A GREAT PARTY!
LET'S THANK GINGER!
GINGER! THANKS FOR THE GREAT PARTY!
WELL... I HOPE YOU HAD A GOOD TIME...
... SINCE IT'S THE LAST TIME I'LL EVER LET YOU USE ME AGAIN!

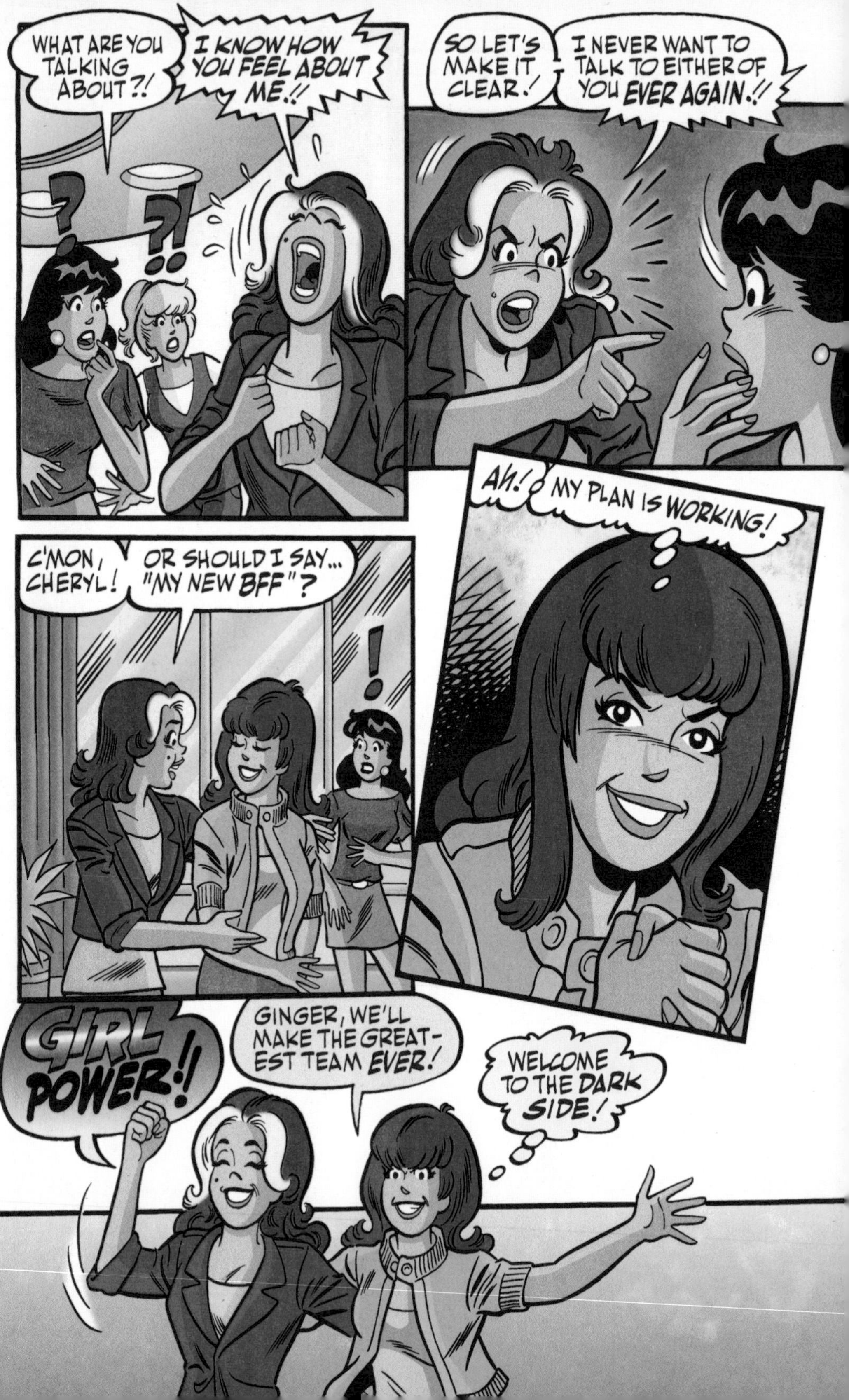
WHAT ARE YOU TALKING ABOUT?!
I KNOW HOW YOU FEEL ABOUT ME.!!
SO LET'S MAKE IT CLEAR.!
I NEVER WANT TO TALK TO EITHER OF YOU EVER AGAIN.!!
Ah!
MY PLAN IS WORKING!
C'MON, CHERYL!
OR SHOULD I SAY... "MY NEW BFF"?
GIRL POWER!!
GINGER, WE'LL MAKE THE GREATEST TEAM EVER!
WELCOME TO THE DARK SIDE!

Chapter 3: BFFs Unite!

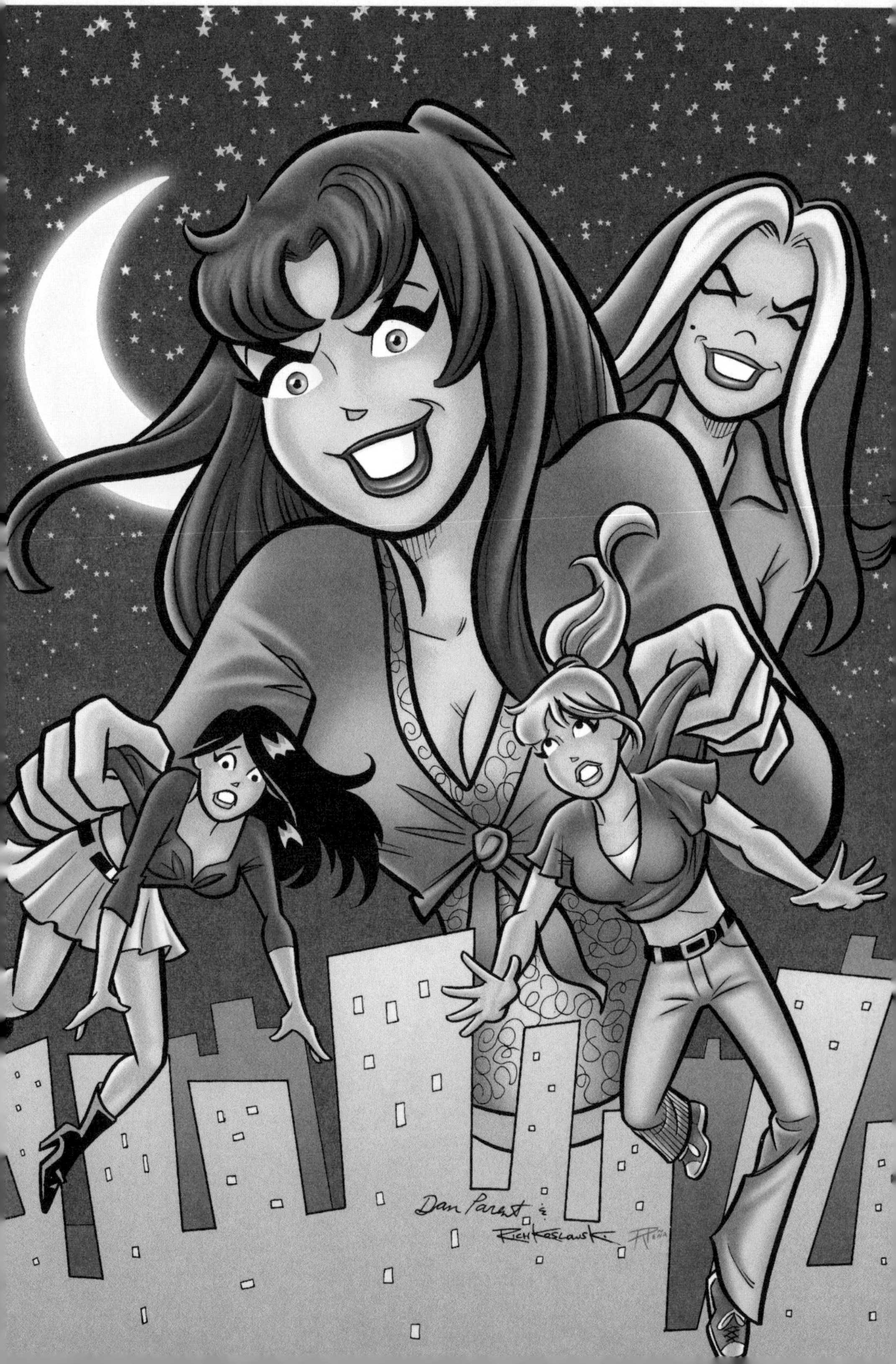
Dan Parent &
Rich Koslowski

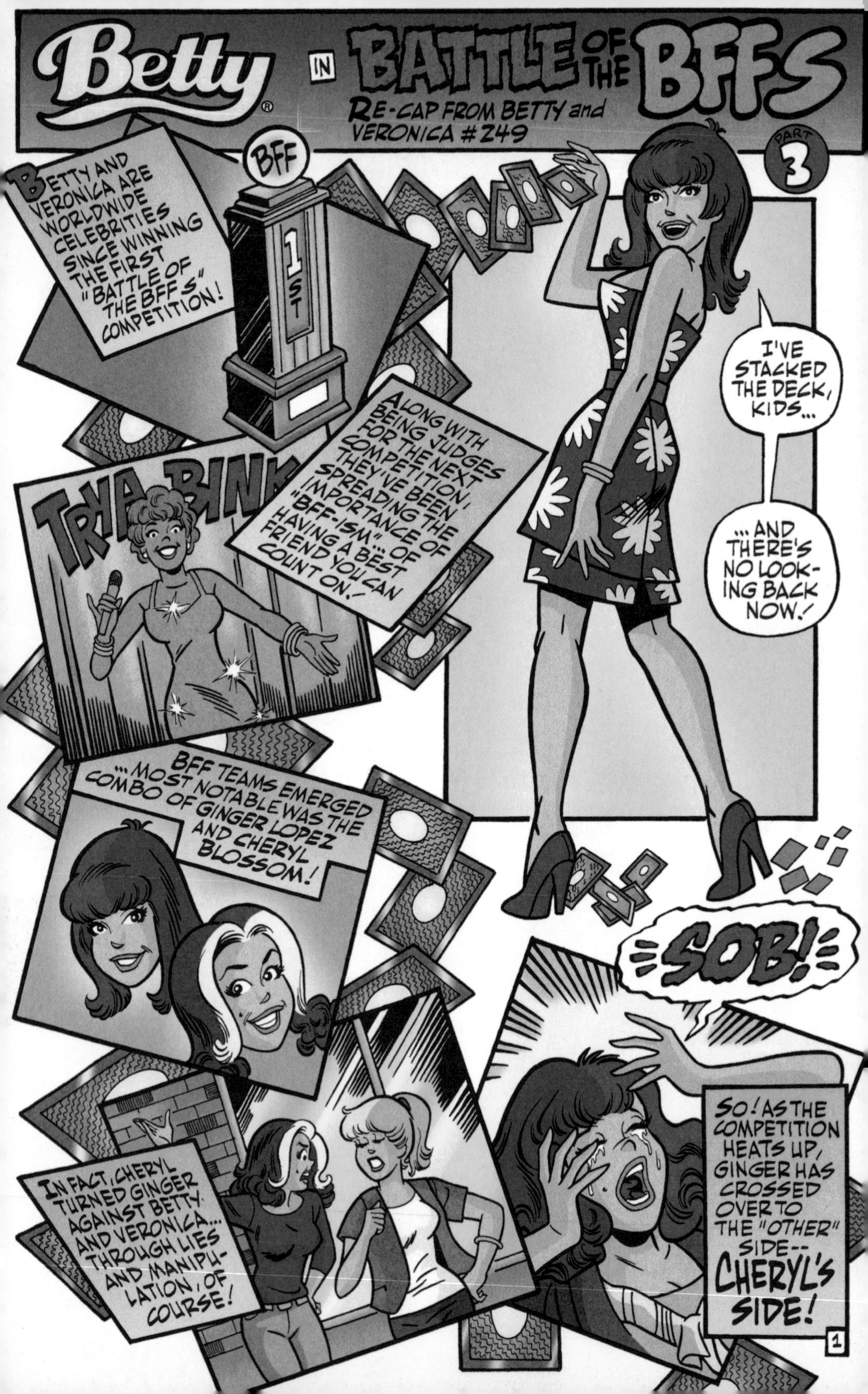
Betty® IN BATTLE OF THE BFFS
RE-CAP FROM BETTY and VERONICA #249
PART 3
BETTY AND VERONICA ARE WORLDWIDE CELEBRITIES SINCE WINNING THE FIRST "BATTLE OF THE BFF'S" COMPETITION!
BFF
1 ST
I'VE STACKED THE DECK, KIDS...
...AND THERE'S NO LOOKING BACK NOW!
ALONG WITH BEING JUDGES FOR THE NEXT COMPETITION, THEY'VE BEEN SPREADING THE IMPORTANCE OF "BFF-ISM"... OF HAVING A BEST FRIEND YOU CAN COUNT ON!
TRYA BINK
BFF TEAMS EMERGED ...MOST NOTABLE WAS THE COMBO OF GINGER LOPEZ AND CHERYL BLOSSOM!
SOB!
IN FACT, CHERYL TURNED GINGER AGAINST BETTY AND VERONICA... THROUGH LIES AND MANIPULATION, OF COURSE!
SO! AS THE COMPETITION HEATS UP, GINGER HAS CROSSED OVER TO THE "OTHER" SIDE-- CHERYL'S SIDE!
1

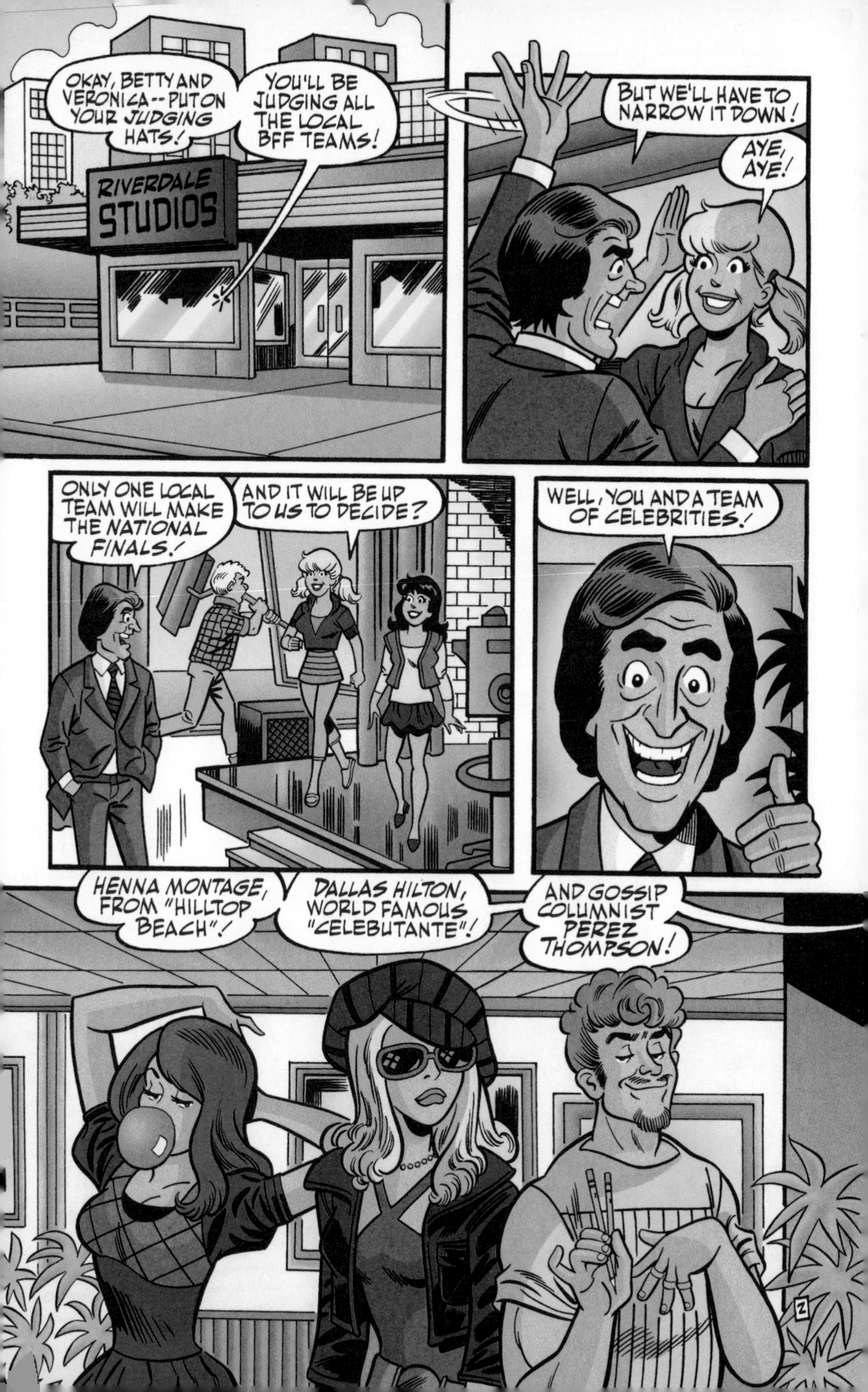
RIVERDALE STUDIOS
OKAY, BETTY AND VERONICA-- PUT ON YOUR JUDGING HATS!
YOU'LL BE JUDGING ALL THE LOCAL BFF TEAMS!
BUT WE'LL HAVE TO NARROW IT DOWN!
AYE, AYE!
ONLY ONE LOCAL TEAM WILL MAKE THE NATIONAL FINALS!
AND IT WILL BE UP TO US TO DECIDE?
WELL, YOU AND A TEAM OF CELEBRITIES!
HENNA MONTAGE, FROM "HILLTOP BEACH"!
DALLAS HILTON, WORLD FAMOUS "CELEBUTANTE"!
AND GOSSIP COLUMNIST PEREZ THOMPSON!
2

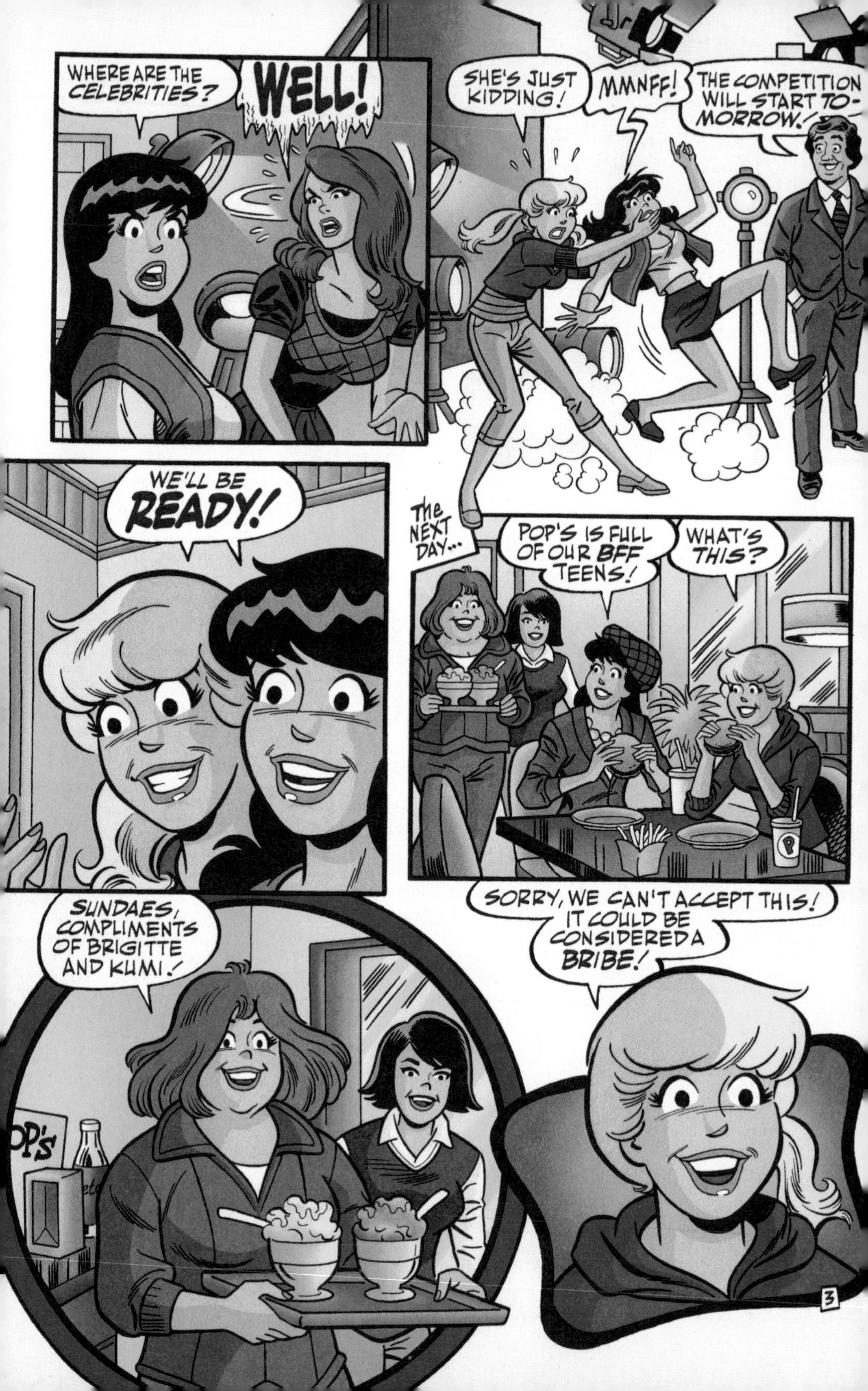

WHERE ARE THE CELEBRITIES?
WELL!
SHE'S JUST KIDDING!
MMNFF!
THE COMPETITION WILL START TO-MORROW!
WE'LL BE READY!
The NEXT DAY...
POP'S IS FULL OF OUR BFF TEENS!
WHAT'S THIS?
SUNDAES, COMPLIMENTS OF BRIGITTE AND KUMI!
SORRY, WE CAN'T ACCEPT THIS! IT COULD BE CONSIDERED A BRIBE!

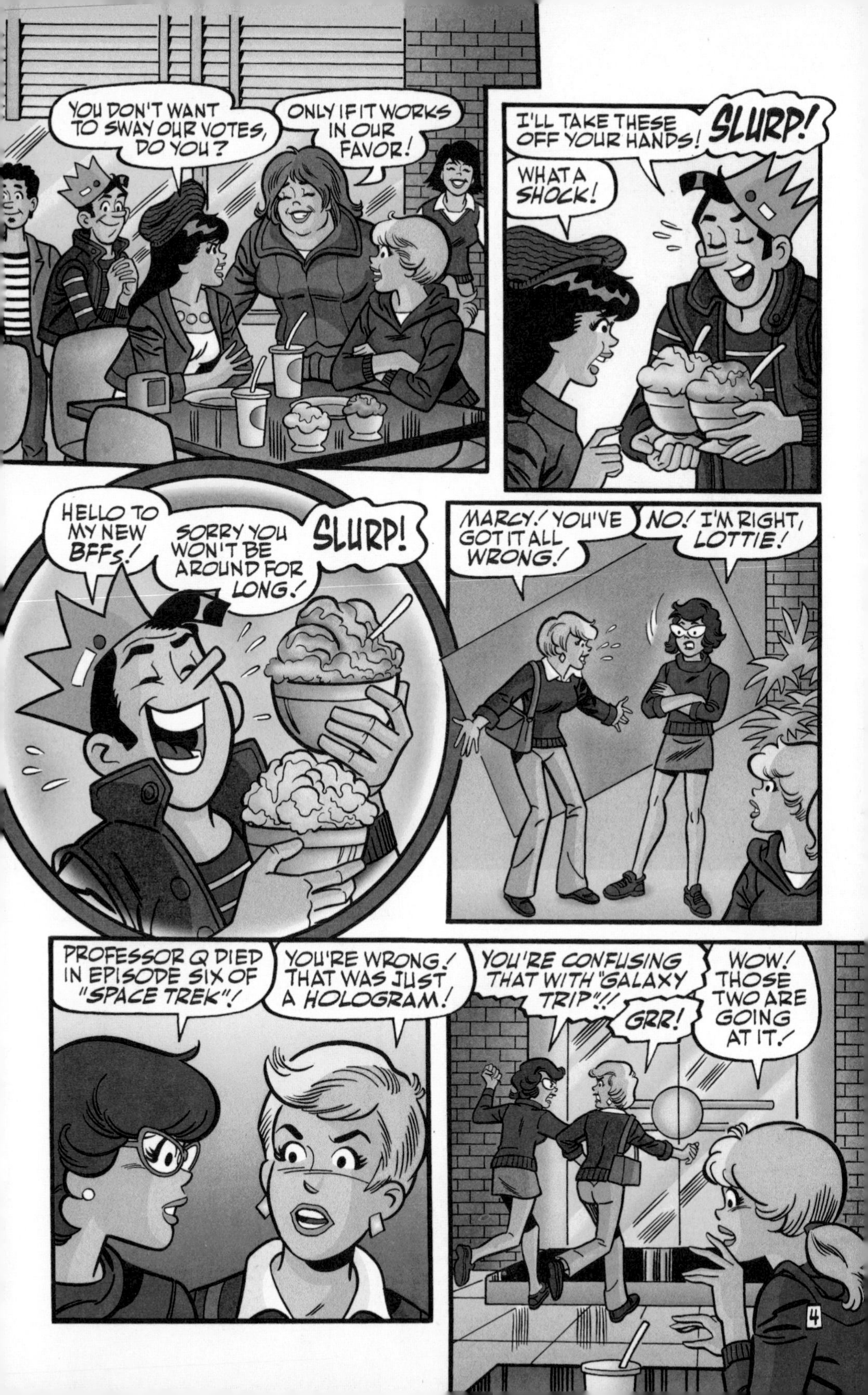
YOU DON'T WANT TO SWAY OUR VOTES, DO YOU?
ONLY IF IT WORKS IN OUR FAVOR!
I'LL TAKE THESE OFF YOUR HANDS!
SLURP!
WHAT A SHOCK!
HELLO TO MY NEW BFFs!
SORRY YOU WON'T BE AROUND FOR LONG!
SLURP!
MARCY! YOU'VE GOT IT ALL WRONG!
NO! I'M RIGHT, LOTTIE!
PROFESSOR Q DIED IN EPISODE SIX OF "SPACE TREK"!
YOU'RE WRONG! THAT WAS JUST A HOLOGRAM!
YOU'RE CONFUSING THAT WITH "GALAXY TRIP"!!
GRR!
WOW! THOSE TWO ARE GOING AT IT!
4

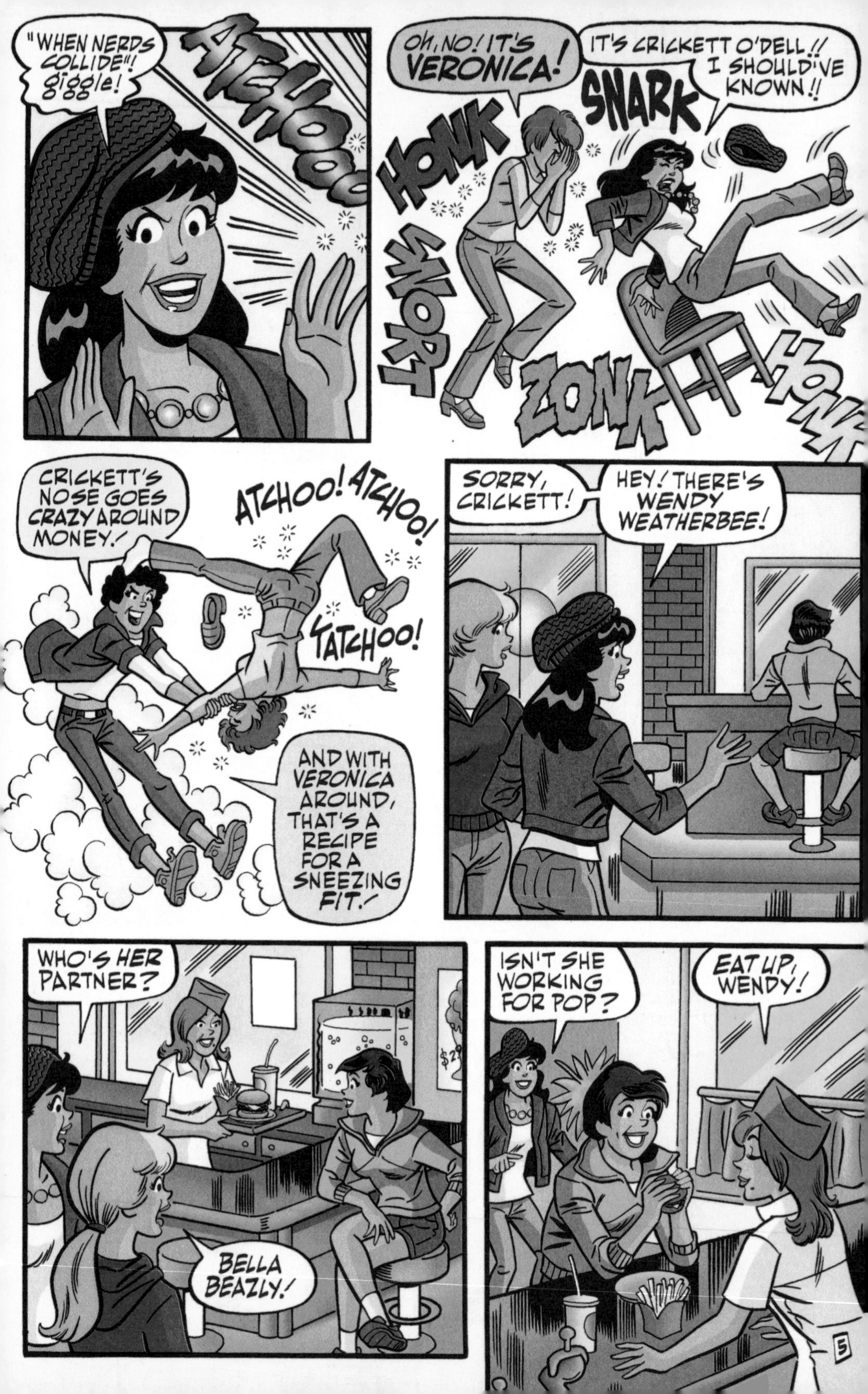

"WHEN NERDS COLLIDE"! giggle!
ATCHOOO
OH, NO! IT'S VERONICA!
IT'S CRICKETT O'DELL!! I SHOULD'VE KNOWN!!
HONK
SNARK
SNORT
ZONK
HONK
CRICKETT'S NOSE GOES CRAZY AROUND MONEY!
ATCHOO! ATCHOO!
ATCHOO!
AND WITH VERONICA AROUND, THAT'S A RECIPE FOR A SNEEZING FIT!
SORRY, CRICKETT!
HEY! THERE'S WENDY WEATHERBEE!
WHO'S HER PARTNER?
BELLA BEAZLY!
ISN'T SHE WORKING FOR POP?
EAT UP, WENDY!

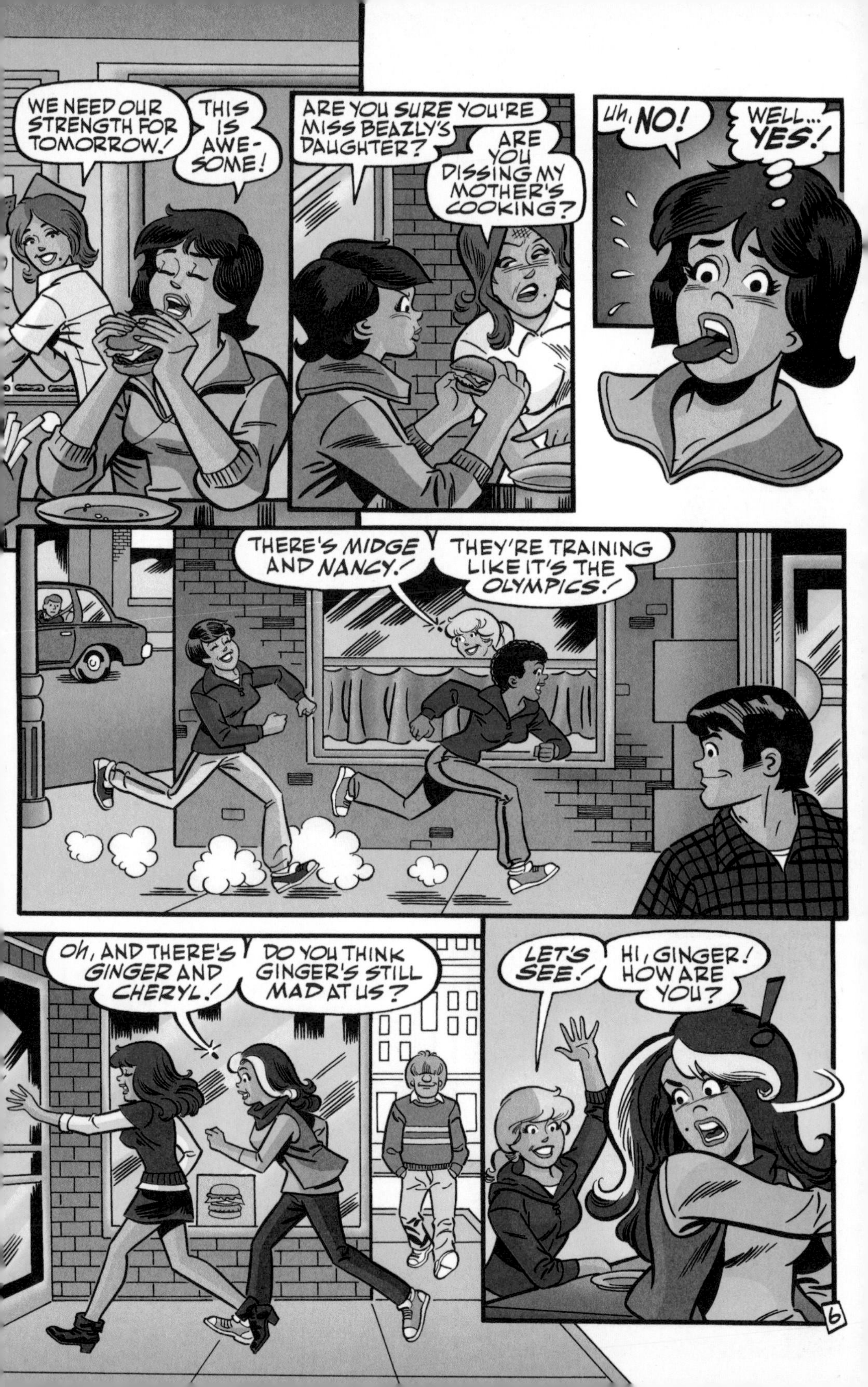

WE NEED OUR STRENGTH FOR TOMORROW!
THIS IS AWESOME!
ARE YOU SURE YOU'RE MISS BEAZLY'S DAUGHTER?
ARE YOU DISSING MY MOTHER'S COOKING?
Uh, NO!
WELL... YES!
THERE'S MIDGE AND NANCY!
THEY'RE TRAINING LIKE IT'S THE OLYMPICS!
Oh, AND THERE'S GINGER AND CHERYL!
DO YOU THINK GINGER'S STILL MAD AT US?
LET'S SEE!
HI, GINGER! HOW ARE YOU?
6

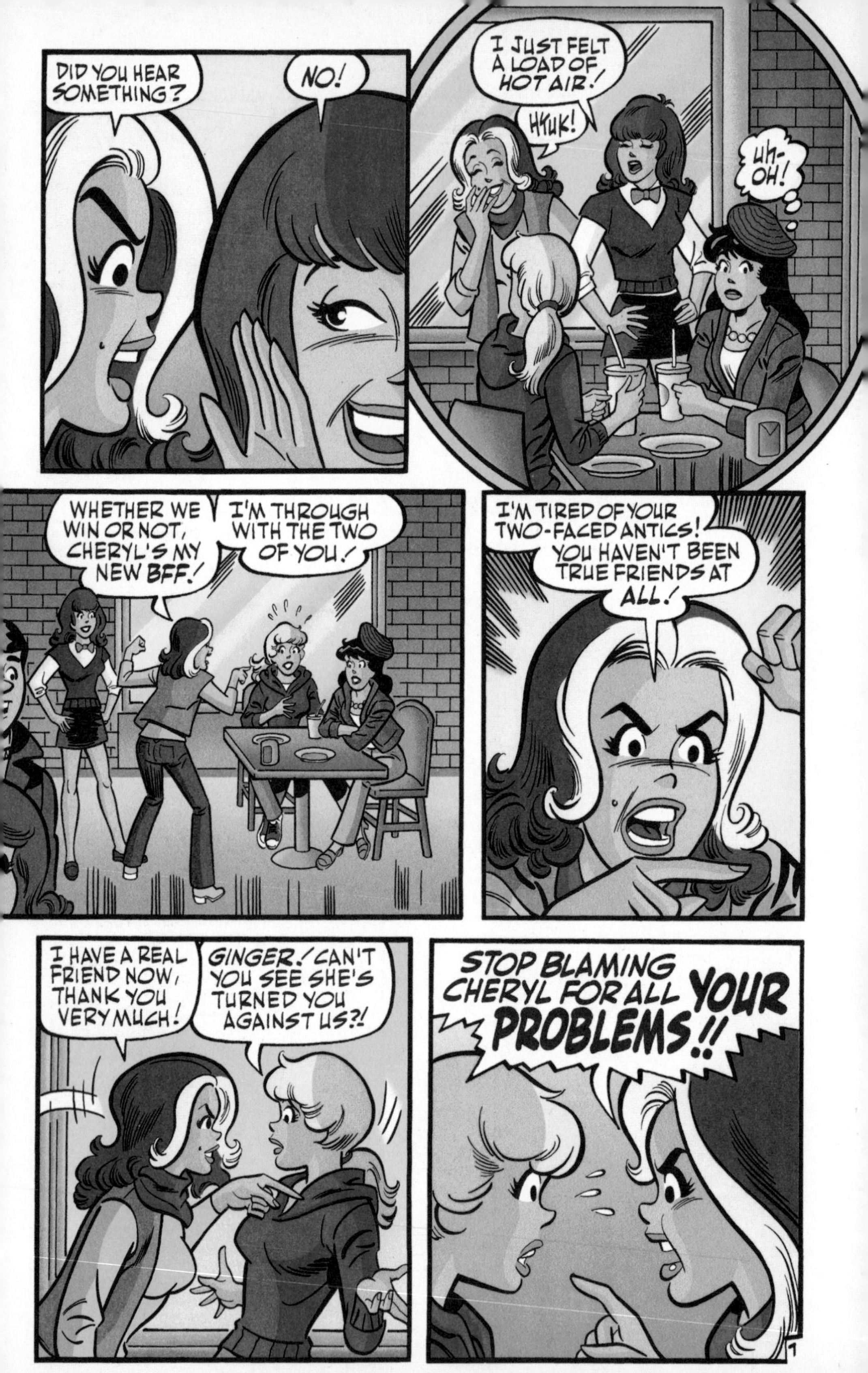
DID YOU HEAR SOMETHING?
NO!
I JUST FELT A LOAD OF HOT AIR!
HYUK!
UH-OH!
WHETHER WE WIN OR NOT, CHERYL'S MY NEW BFF!
I'M THROUGH WITH THE TWO OF YOU!
I'M TIRED OF YOUR TWO-FACED ANTICS! YOU HAVEN'T BEEN TRUE FRIENDS AT ALL!
I HAVE A REAL FRIEND NOW, THANK YOU VERY MUCH!
GINGER! CAN'T YOU SEE SHE'S TURNED YOU AGAINST US?!
STOP BLAMING CHERYL FOR ALL YOUR PROBLEMS!!

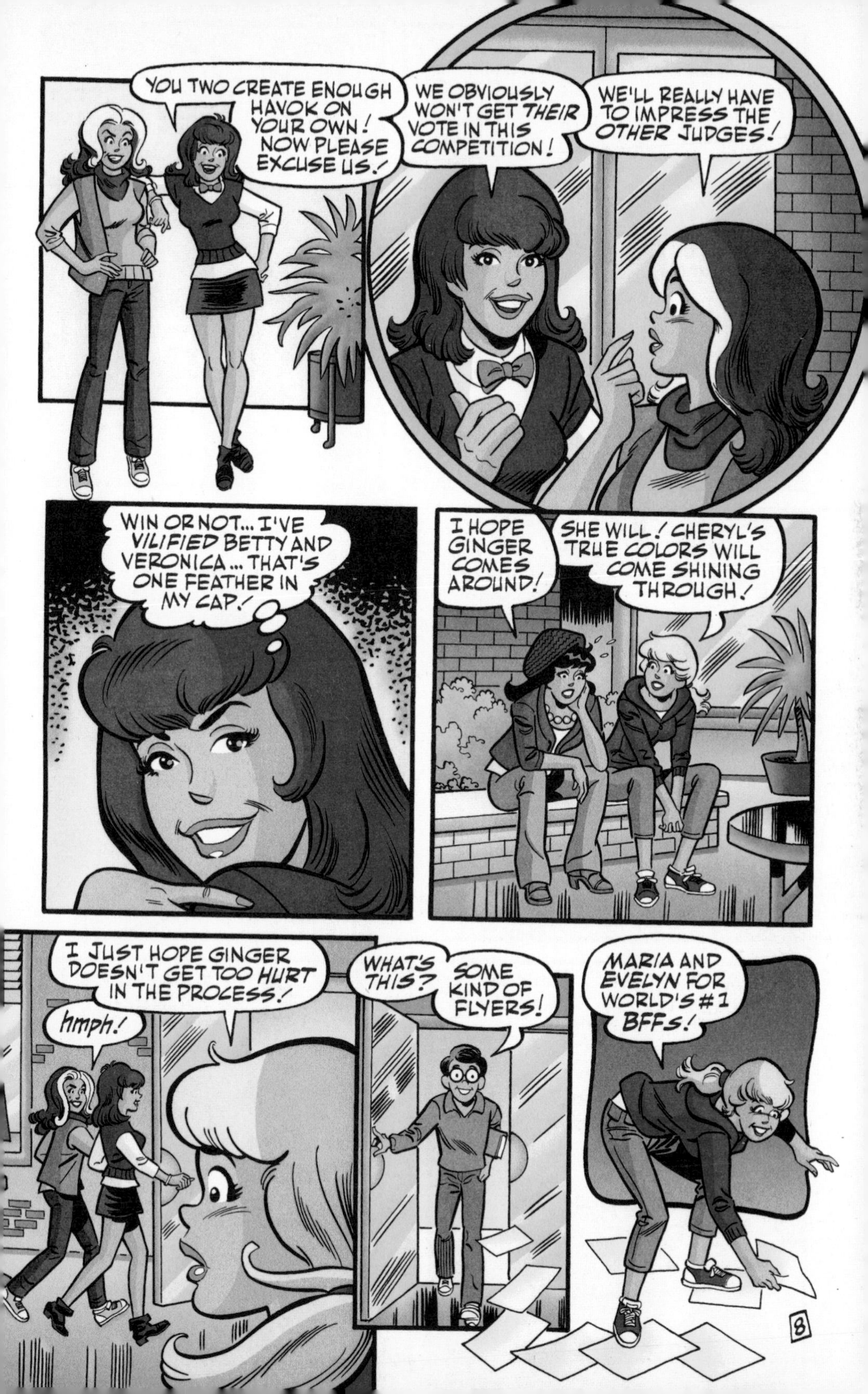
YOU TWO CREATE ENOUGH HAVOK ON YOUR OWN! NOW PLEASE EXCUSE US.!
WE OBVIOUSLY WON'T GET THEIR VOTE IN THIS COMPETITION!
WE'LL REALLY HAVE TO IMPRESS THE OTHER JUDGES!
WIN OR NOT... I'VE VILIFIED BETTY AND VERONICA... THAT'S ONE FEATHER IN MY CAP!
I HOPE GINGER COMES AROUND!
SHE WILL! CHERYL'S TRUE COLORS WILL COME SHINING THROUGH!
I JUST HOPE GINGER DOESN'T GET TOO HURT IN THE PROCESS!
hmph!
WHAT'S THIS?
SOME KIND OF FLYERS!
MARIA AND EVELYN FOR WORLD'S #1 BFFS!
8

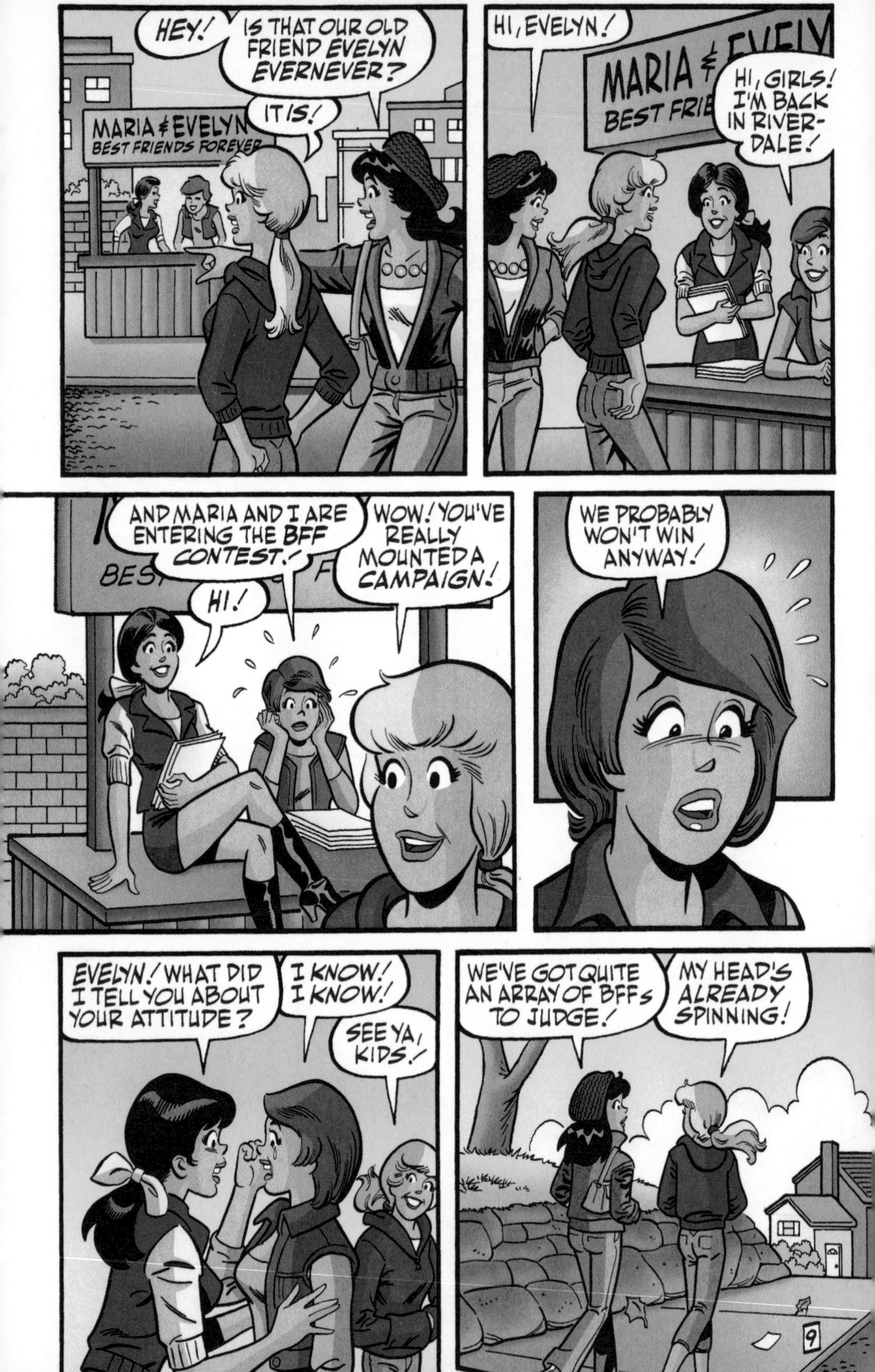
HEY!
IS THAT OUR OLD FRIEND EVELYN EVERNEVER?
IT IS!
MARIA & EVELYN BEST FRIENDS FOREVER
HI, EVELYN!
HI, GIRLS! I'M BACK IN RIVERDALE!
AND MARIA AND I ARE ENTERING THE BFF CONTEST!
HI!
WOW! YOU'VE REALLY MOUNTED A CAMPAIGN!
WE PROBABLY WON'T WIN ANYWAY!
EVELYN! WHAT DID I TELL YOU ABOUT YOUR ATTITUDE?
I KNOW! I KNOW!
SEE YA, KIDS!
WE'VE GOT QUITE AN ARRAY OF BFFs TO JUDGE!
MY HEAD'S ALREADY SPINNING!
9

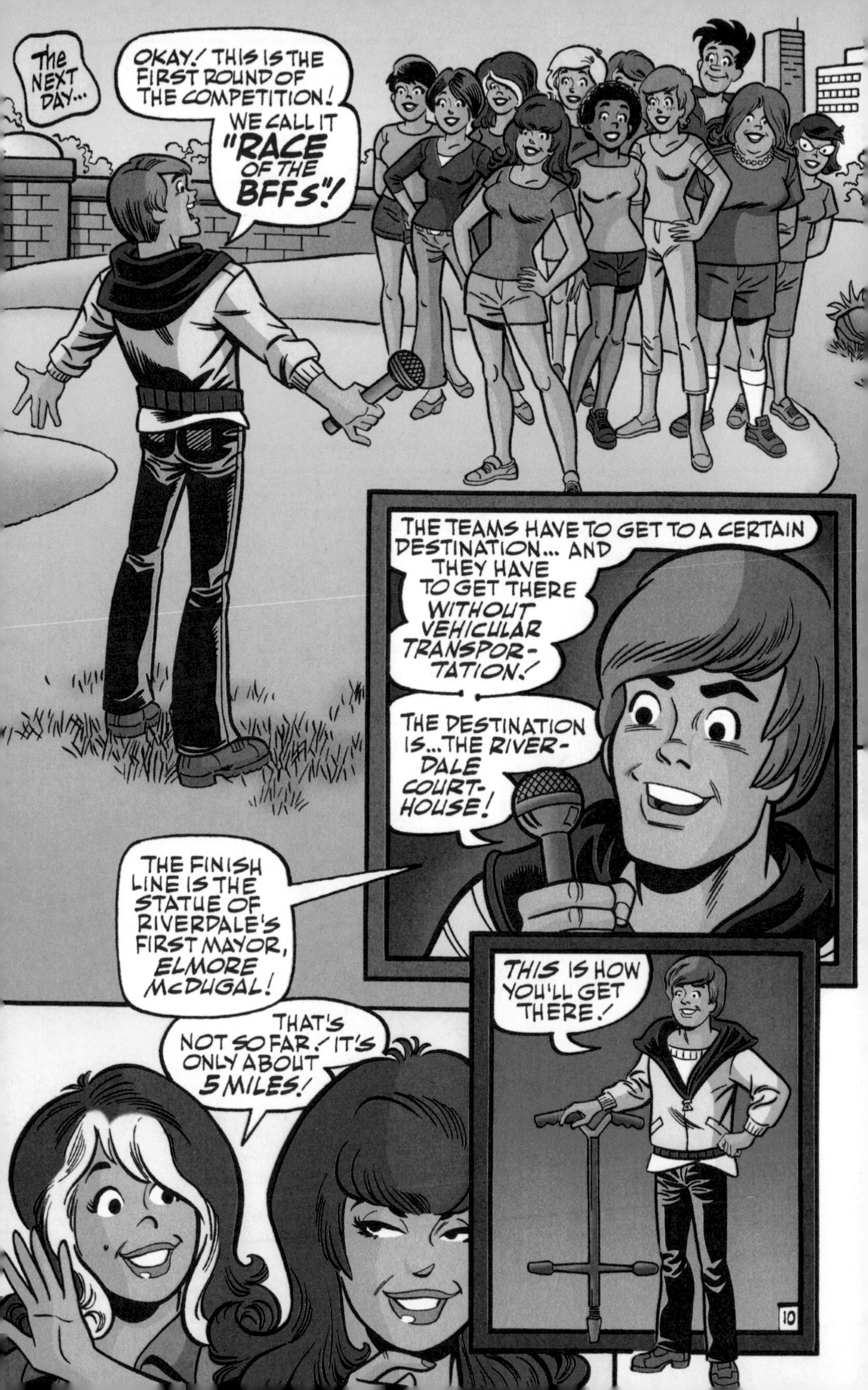
The NEXT DAY...
OKAY! THIS IS THE FIRST ROUND OF THE COMPETITION!
WE CALL IT "RACE OF THE BFFS"!
THE TEAMS HAVE TO GET TO A CERTAIN DESTINATION... AND THEY HAVE TO GET THERE WITHOUT VEHICULAR TRANSPOR-TATION!
THE DESTINATION IS...THE RIVER-DALE COURT-HOUSE!
THE FINISH LINE IS THE STATUE OF RIVERDALE'S FIRST MAYOR, ELMORE McDUGAL!
THAT'S NOT SO FAR! IT'S ONLY ABOUT 5 MILES!
THIS IS HOW YOU'LL GET THERE!
10

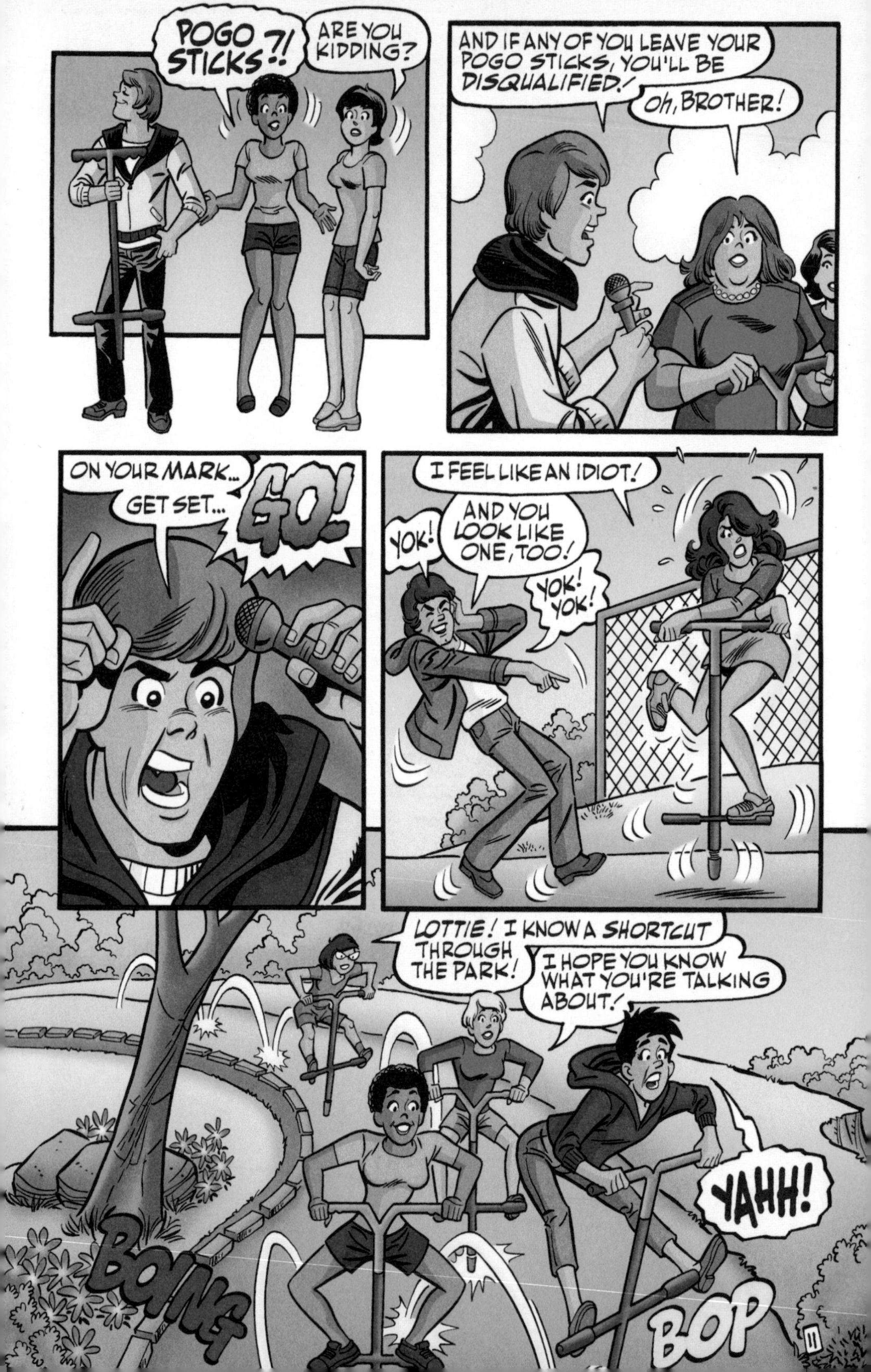
POGO STICKS?!
ARE YOU KIDDING?
AND IF ANY OF YOU LEAVE YOUR POGO STICKS, YOU'LL BE DISQUALIFIED!
Oh, BROTHER!
ON YOUR MARK...
GET SET...
GO!
I FEEL LIKE AN IDIOT!
YOK!
AND YOU LOOK LIKE ONE, TOO!
YOK! YOK!
LOTTIE! I KNOW A SHORTCUT THROUGH THE PARK!
I HOPE YOU KNOW WHAT YOU'RE TALKING ABOUT!
YAHH!
BOING
BOP

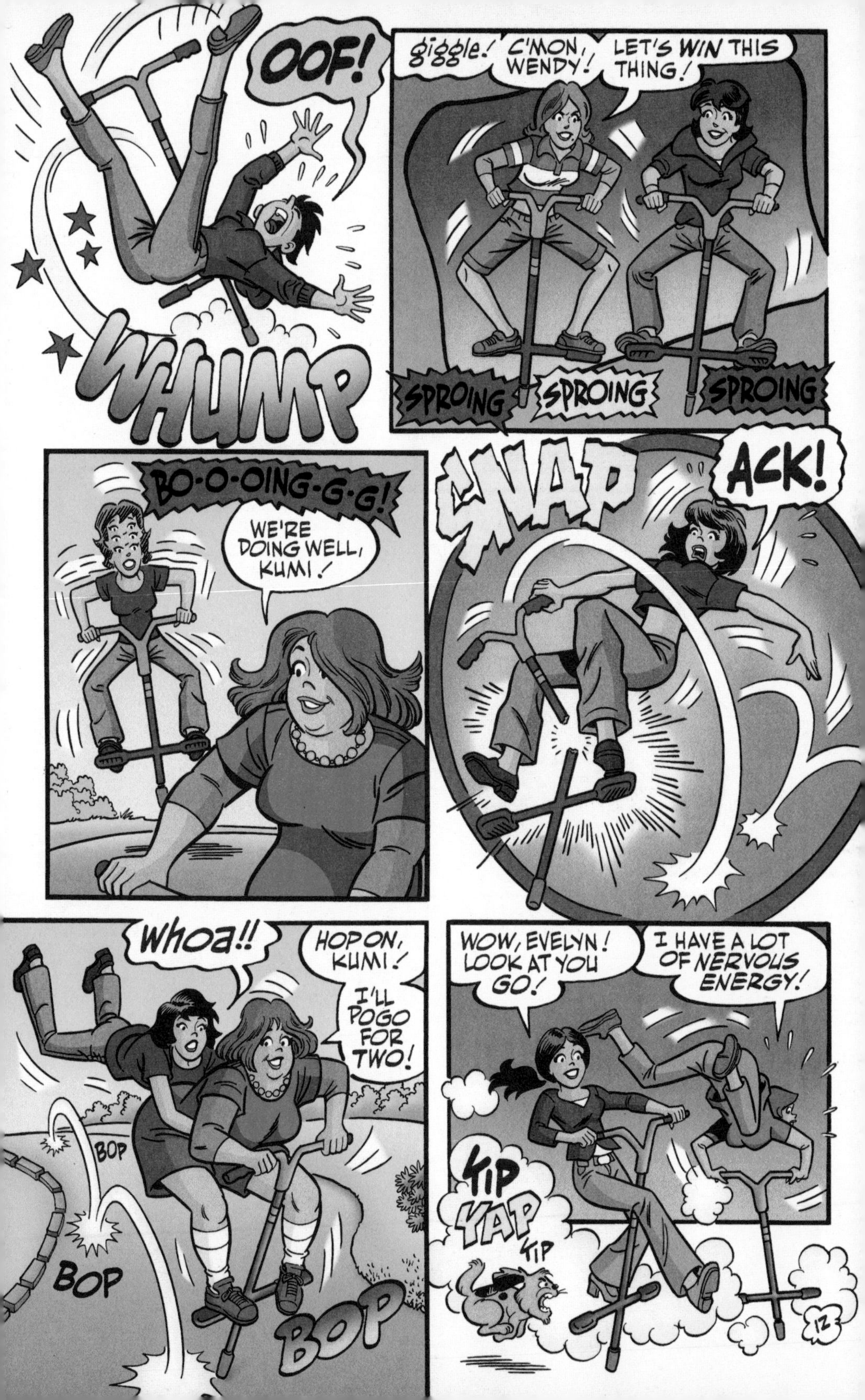
OOF!
WHUMP
giggle!
C'MON, WENDY!
LET'S WIN THIS THING!
SPROING
SPROING
SPROING
BO-O-OING-G-G!
WE'RE DOING WELL, KUMI!
SNAP
ACK!
Whoa!!
HOP ON, KUMI!
I'LL POGO FOR TWO!
BOP
BOP
BOP
WOW, EVELYN! LOOK AT YOU GO!
I HAVE A LOT OF NERVOUS ENERGY!
YIP
YAP
YIP
12

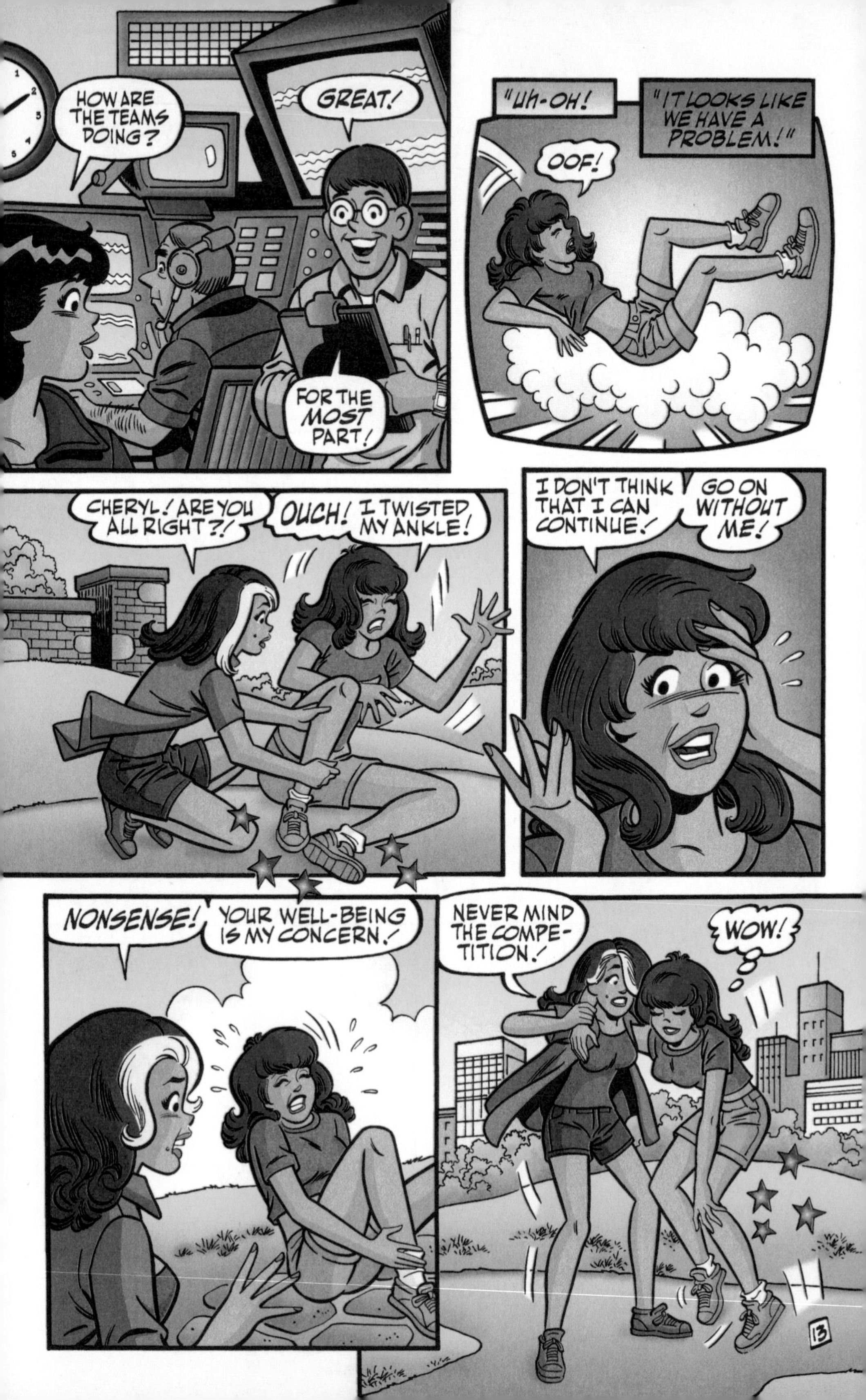

HOW ARE THE TEAMS DOING?
GREAT!
FOR THE MOST PART!
"UH-OH!
"IT LOOKS LIKE WE HAVE A PROBLEM!"
OOF!
CHERYL! ARE YOU ALL RIGHT?!
OUCH!
I TWISTED MY ANKLE!
I DON'T THINK THAT I CAN CONTINUE!
GO ON WITHOUT ME!
NONSENSE!
YOUR WELL-BEING IS MY CONCERN!
NEVER MIND THE COMPE-TITION!
WOW!
13

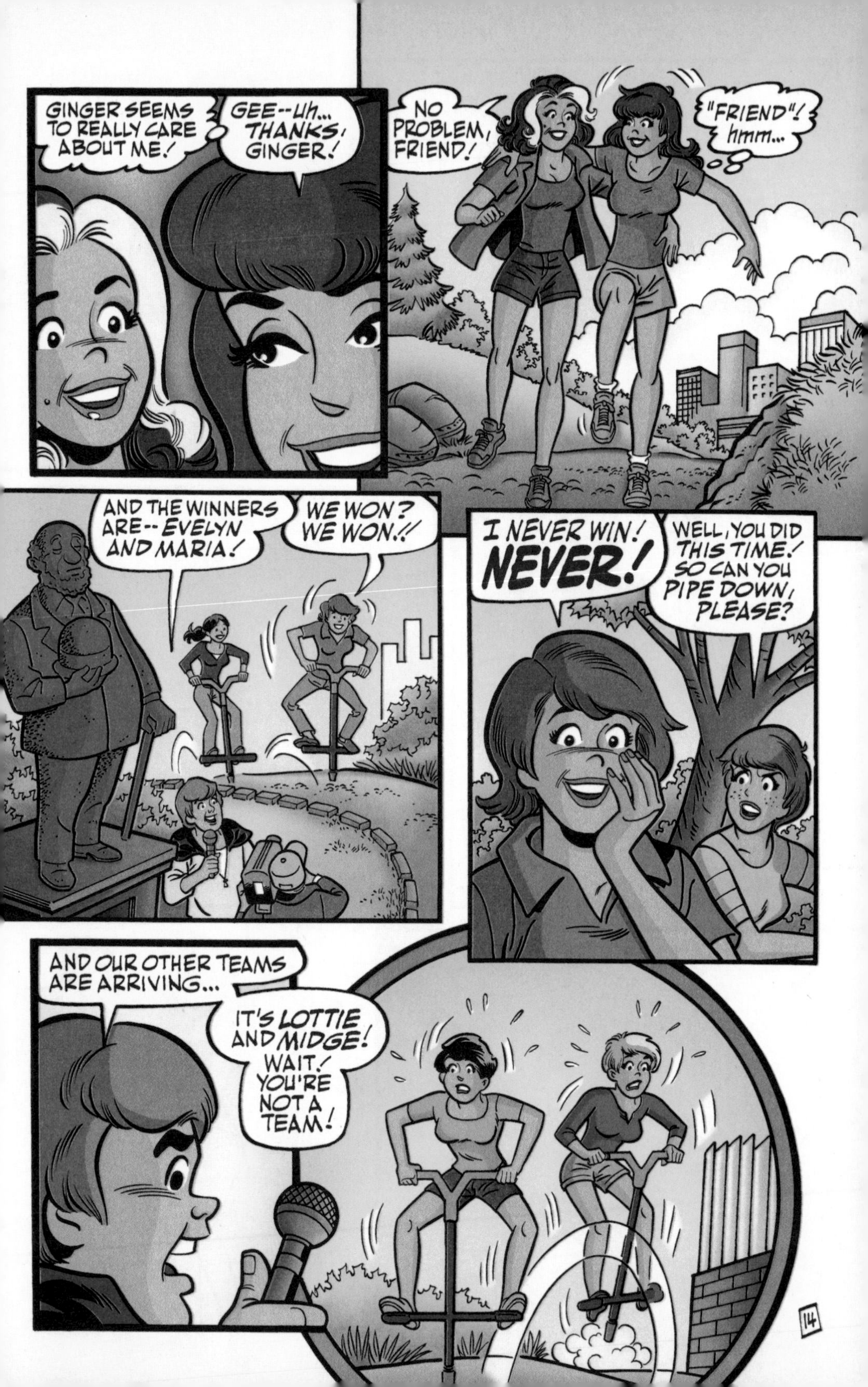
GINGER SEEMS TO REALLY CARE ABOUT ME!
GEE--uh... THANKS, GINGER!
NO PROBLEM, FRIEND!
"FRIEND"! hmm...
AND THE WINNERS ARE-- EVELYN AND MARIA!
WE WON? WE WON.!!
I NEVER WIN! NEVER!
WELL, YOU DID THIS TIME! SO CAN YOU PIPE DOWN, PLEASE?
AND OUR OTHER TEAMS ARE ARRIVING...
IT'S LOTTIE AND MIDGE! WAIT! YOU'RE NOT A TEAM!
14

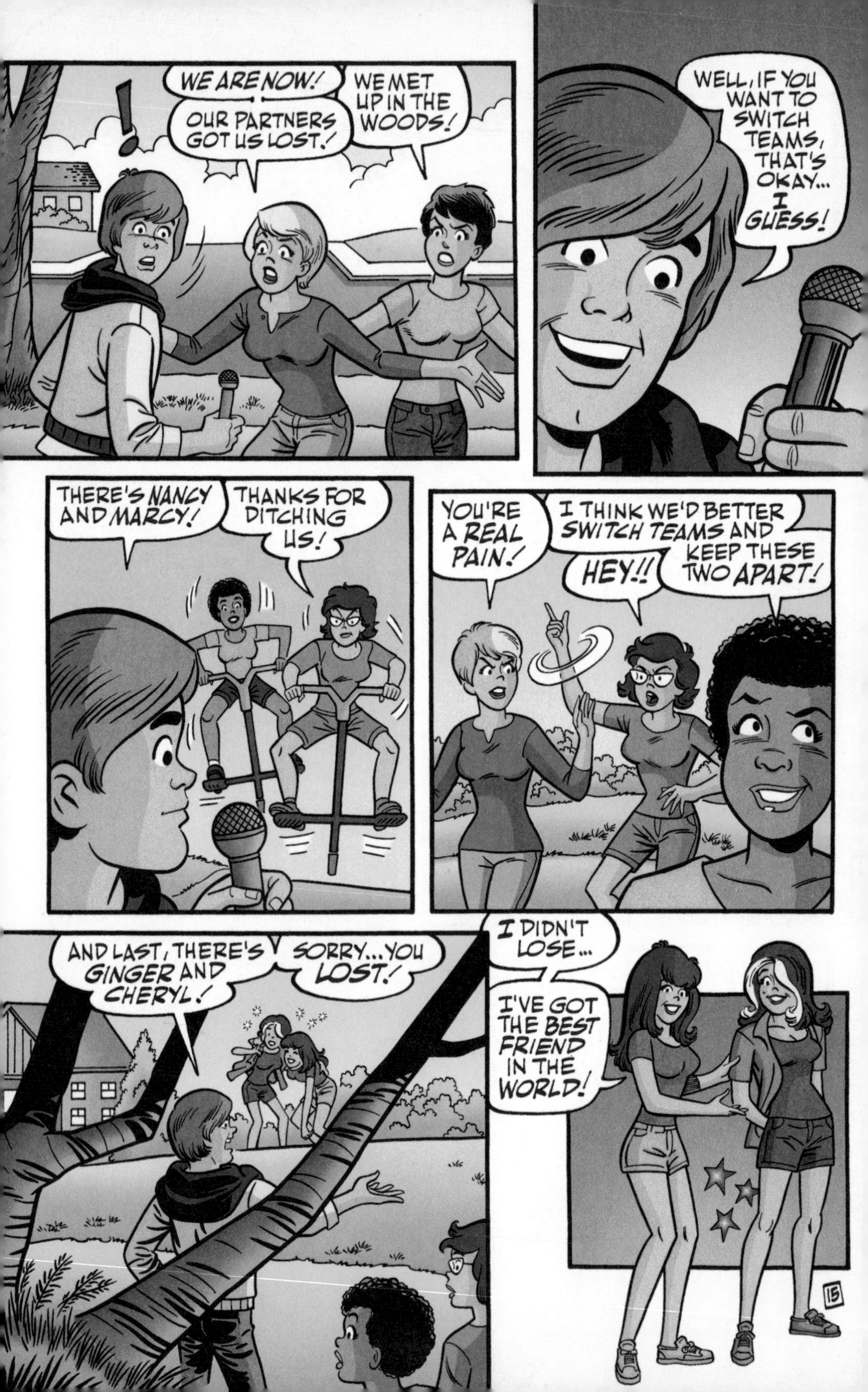
WE ARE NOW!
OUR PARTNERS GOT US LOST!
WE MET UP IN THE WOODS!
WELL, IF YOU WANT TO SWITCH TEAMS, THAT'S OKAY... I GUESS!
THERE'S NANCY AND MARCY!
THANKS FOR DITCHING US!
YOU'RE A REAL PAIN!
I THINK WE'D BETTER SWITCH TEAMS AND
HEY!!
KEEP THESE TWO APART!
AND LAST, THERE'S GINGER AND CHERYL!
SORRY... YOU LOST!
I DIDN'T LOSE...
I'VE GOT THE BEST FRIEND IN THE WORLD!
15

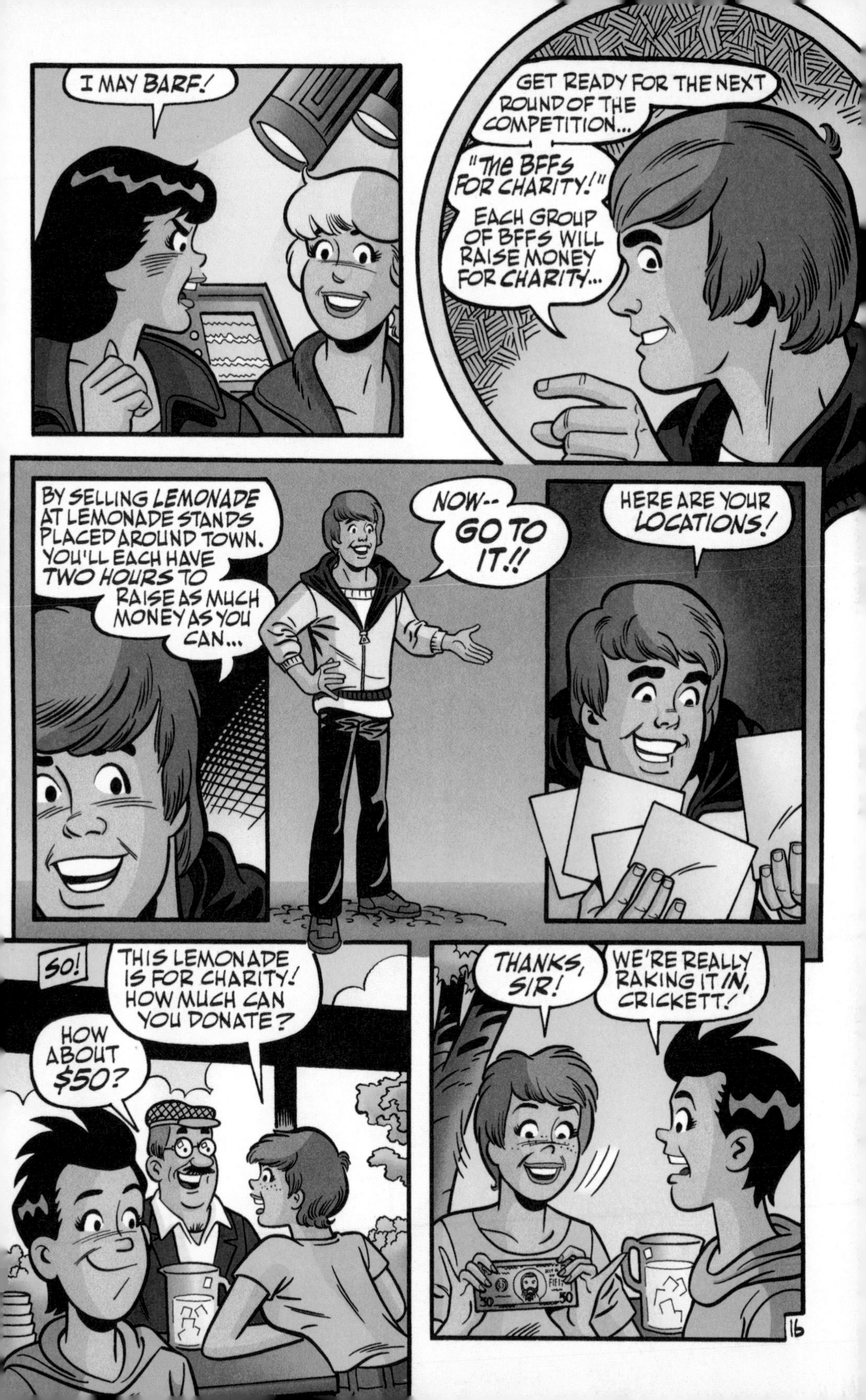
I MAY BARF!
GET READY FOR THE NEXT ROUND OF THE COMPETITION...
"THE BFFS FOR CHARITY!"
EACH GROUP OF BFFS WILL RAISE MONEY FOR CHARITY...
BY SELLING LEMONADE AT LEMONADE STANDS PLACED AROUND TOWN. YOU'LL EACH HAVE TWO HOURS TO RAISE AS MUCH MONEY AS YOU CAN...
NOW-- GO TO IT!!
HERE ARE YOUR LOCATIONS!
SO!
THIS LEMONADE IS FOR CHARITY! HOW MUCH CAN YOU DONATE?
HOW ABOUT $50?
THANKS, SIR!
WE'RE REALLY RAKING IT IN, CRICKETT!
16

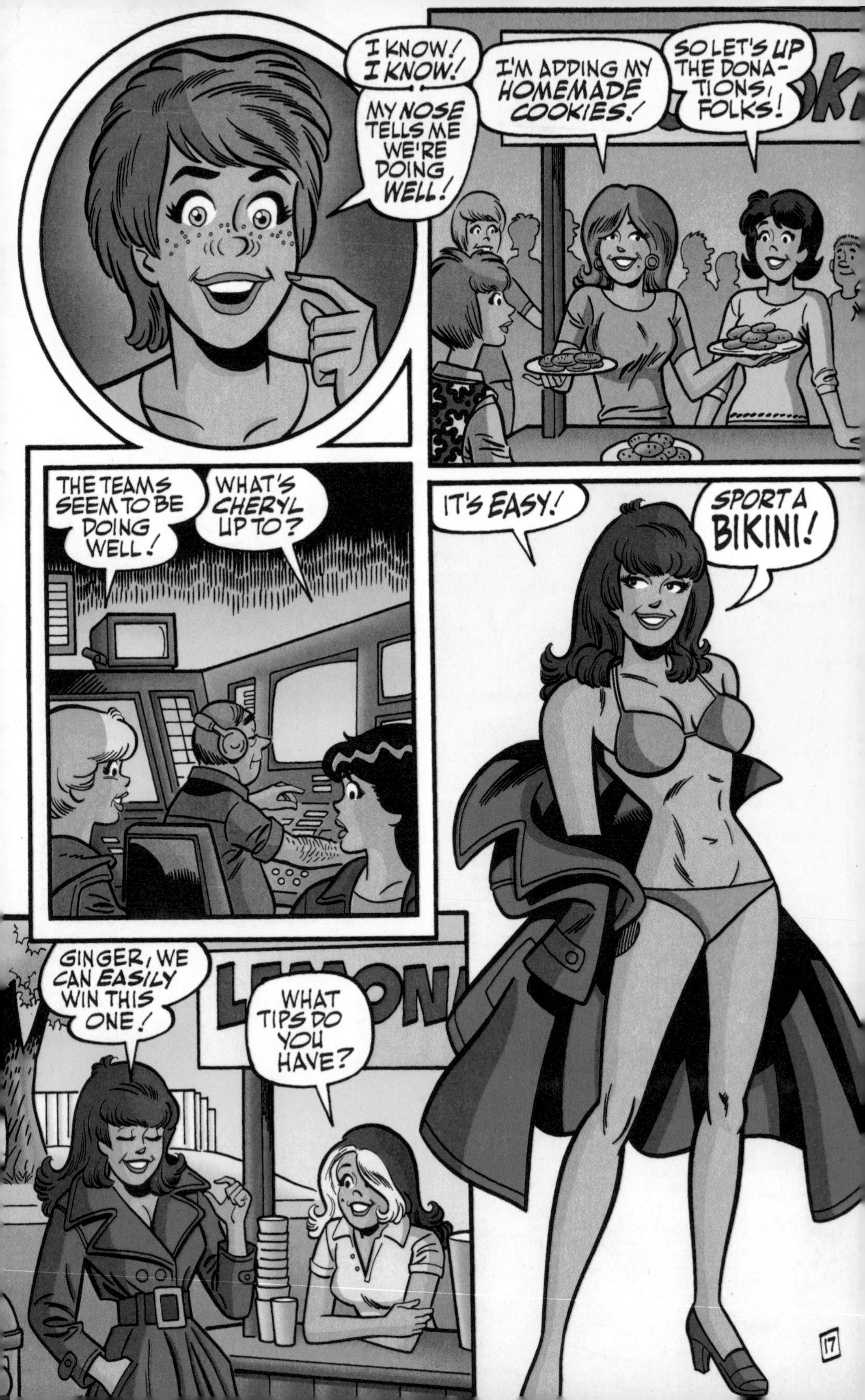

I KNOW! I KNOW!
MY NOSE TELLS ME WE'RE DOING WELL!
I'M ADDING MY HOMEMADE COOKIES!
SO LET'S UP THE DONA-TIONS, FOLKS!
THE TEAMS SEEM TO BE DOING WELL!
WHAT'S CHERYL UP TO?
GINGER, WE CAN EASILY WIN THIS ONE!
WHAT TIPS DO YOU HAVE?
IT'S EASY!
SPORT A BIKINI!
17

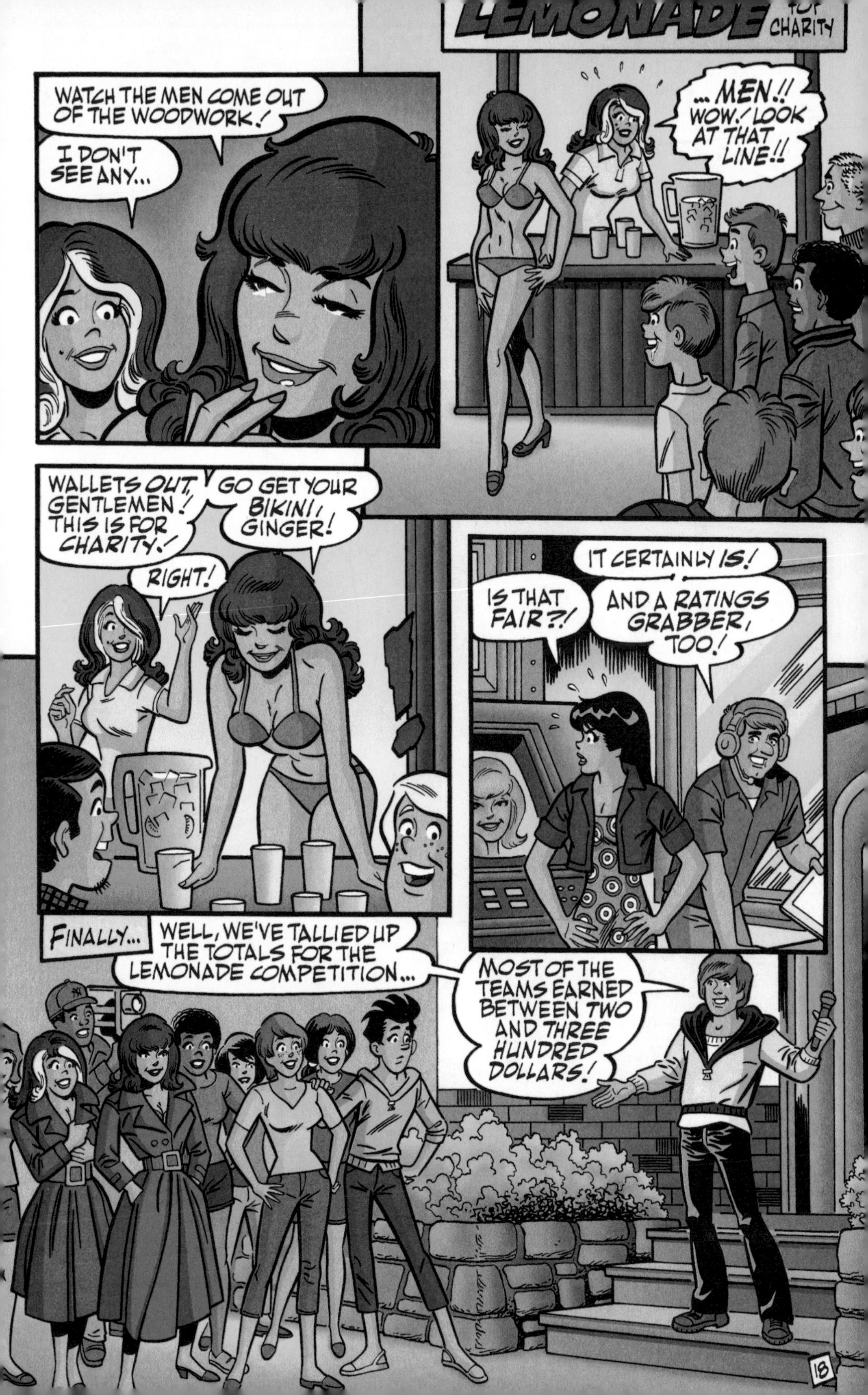
LEMONADE FOR CHARITY
WATCH THE MEN COME OUT OF THE WOODWORK!
I DON'T SEE ANY...
...MEN!! WOW! LOOK AT THAT LINE!!
WALLETS OUT, GENTLEMEN! THIS IS FOR CHARITY!
GO GET YOUR BIKINI, GINGER!
RIGHT!
IS THAT FAIR?!
IT CERTAINLY IS!
AND A RATINGS GRABBER, TOO!
FINALLY...
WELL, WE'VE TALLIED UP THE TOTALS FOR THE LEMONADE COMPETITION...
MOST OF THE TEAMS EARNED BETWEEN TWO AND THREE HUNDRED DOLLARS!
18

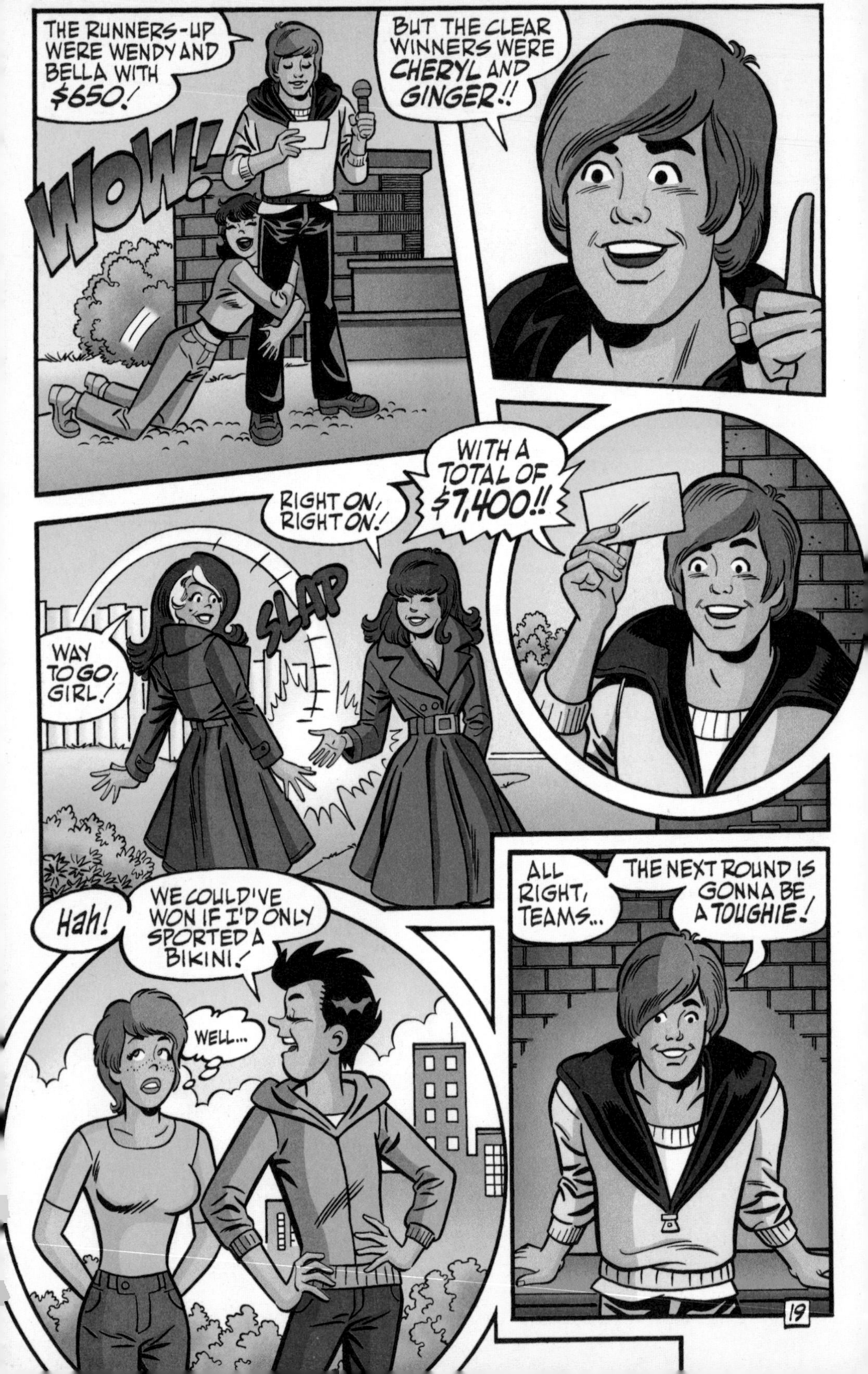
THE RUNNERS-UP WERE WENDY AND BELLA WITH $650!
WOW!!
BUT THE CLEAR WINNERS WERE CHERYL AND GINGER!!
RIGHT ON, RIGHT ON!
WITH A TOTAL OF $7,400!!
SLAP
WAY TO GO, GIRL!
Hah!
WE COULD'VE WON IF I'D ONLY SPORTED A BIKINI!
WELL...
ALL RIGHT, TEAMS...
THE NEXT ROUND IS GONNA BE A TOUGHIE!

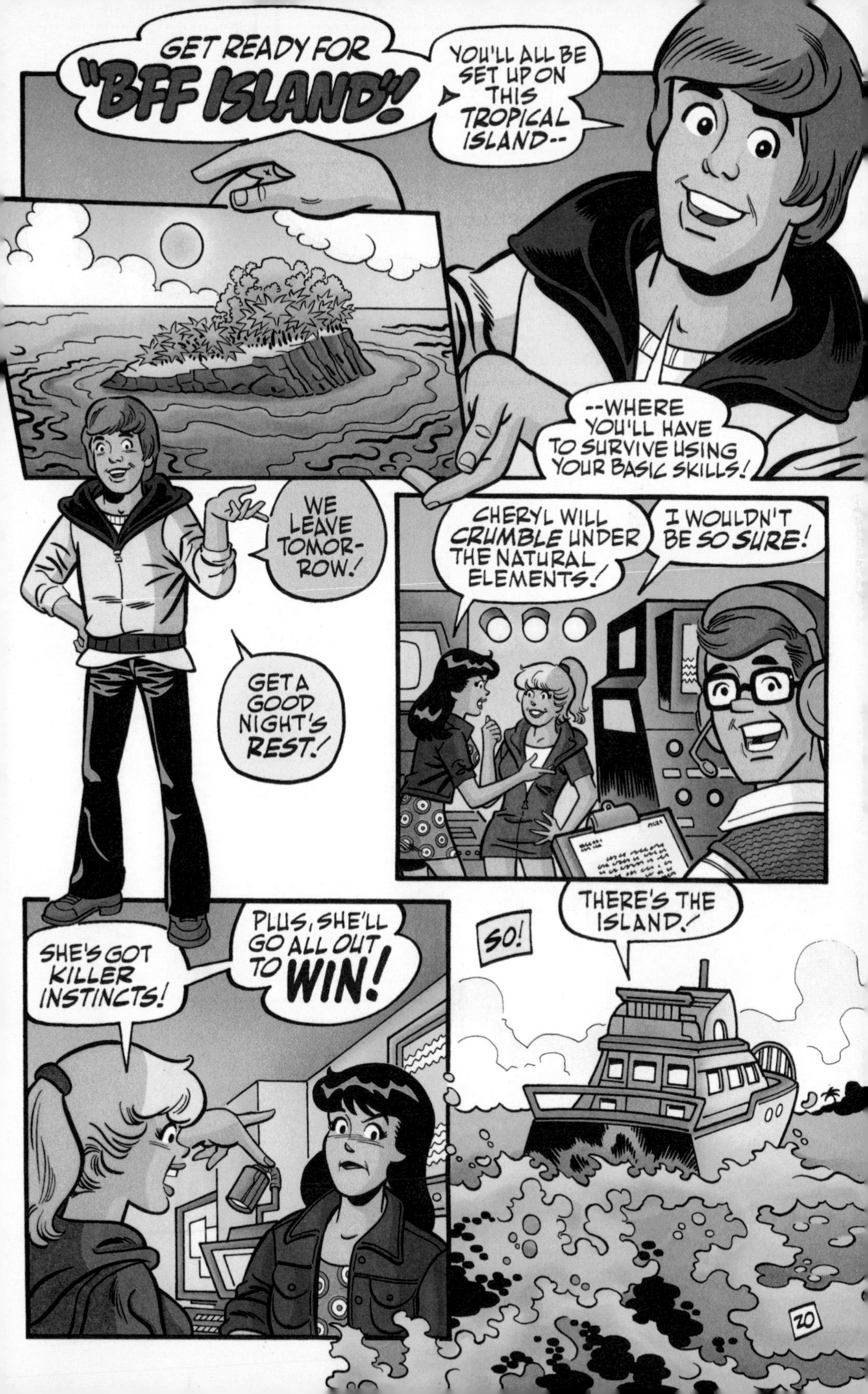
GET READY FOR "BFF ISLAND"!
YOU'LL ALL BE SET UP ON THIS TROPICAL ISLAND--
--WHERE YOU'LL HAVE TO SURVIVE USING YOUR BASIC SKILLS!
WE LEAVE TOMORROW!
GET A GOOD NIGHT'S REST!
CHERYL WILL CRUMBLE UNDER THE NATURAL ELEMENTS!
I WOULDN'T BE SO SURE!
SHE'S GOT KILLER INSTINCTS!
PLUS, SHE'LL GO ALL OUT TO WIN!
SO!
THERE'S THE ISLAND!
20

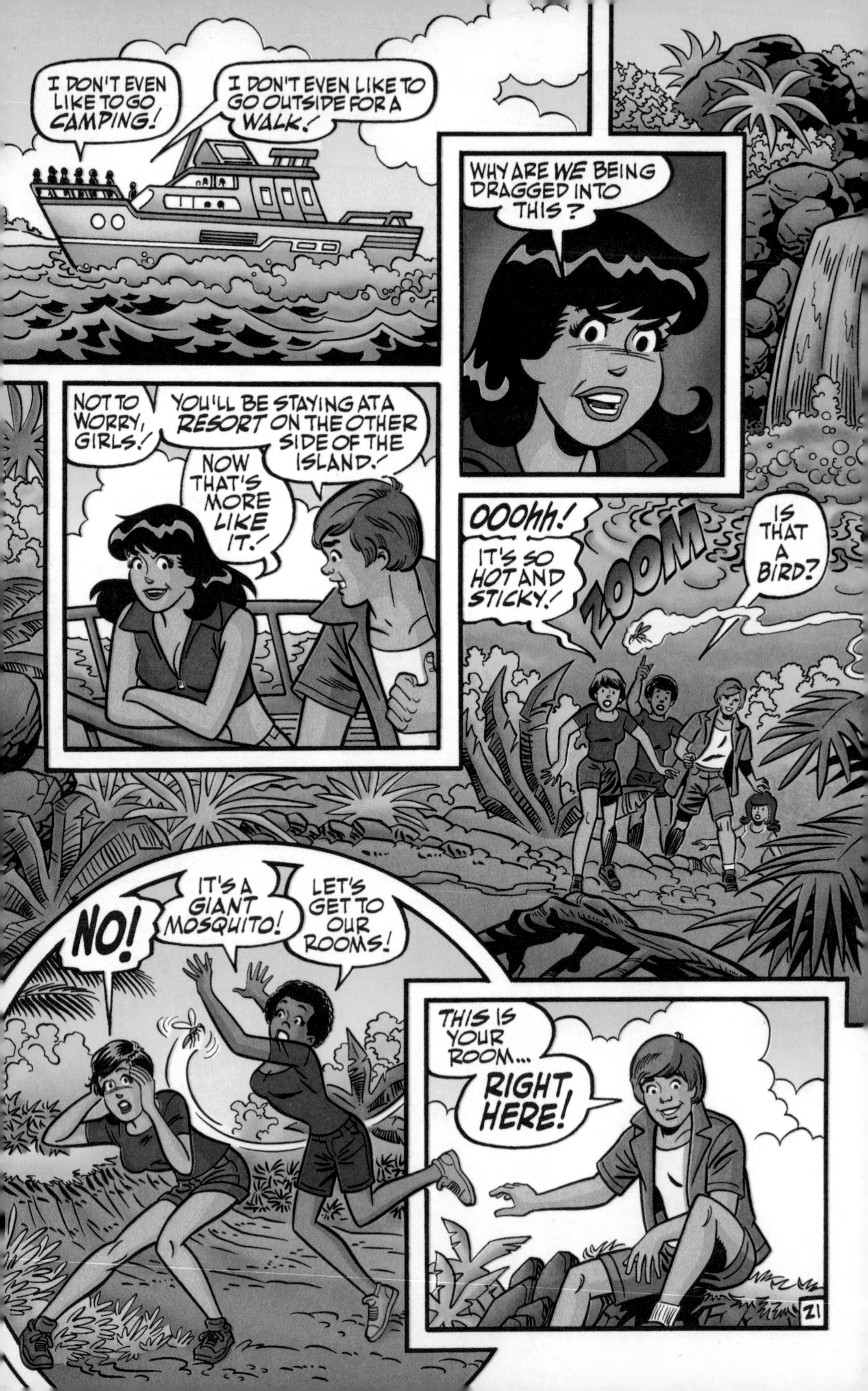
I DON'T EVEN LIKE TO GO CAMPING!
I DON'T EVEN LIKE TO GO OUTSIDE FOR A WALK!
WHY ARE WE BEING DRAGGED INTO THIS?
NOT TO WORRY, GIRLS!
YOU'LL BE STAYING AT A RESORT ON THE OTHER SIDE OF THE ISLAND!
NOW THAT'S MORE LIKE IT!
OOOhh!
IT'S SO HOT AND STICKY!
ZOOM
IS THAT A BIRD?
NO!
IT'S A GIANT MOSQUITO!
LET'S GET TO OUR ROOMS!
THIS IS YOUR ROOM...
RIGHT HERE!
21

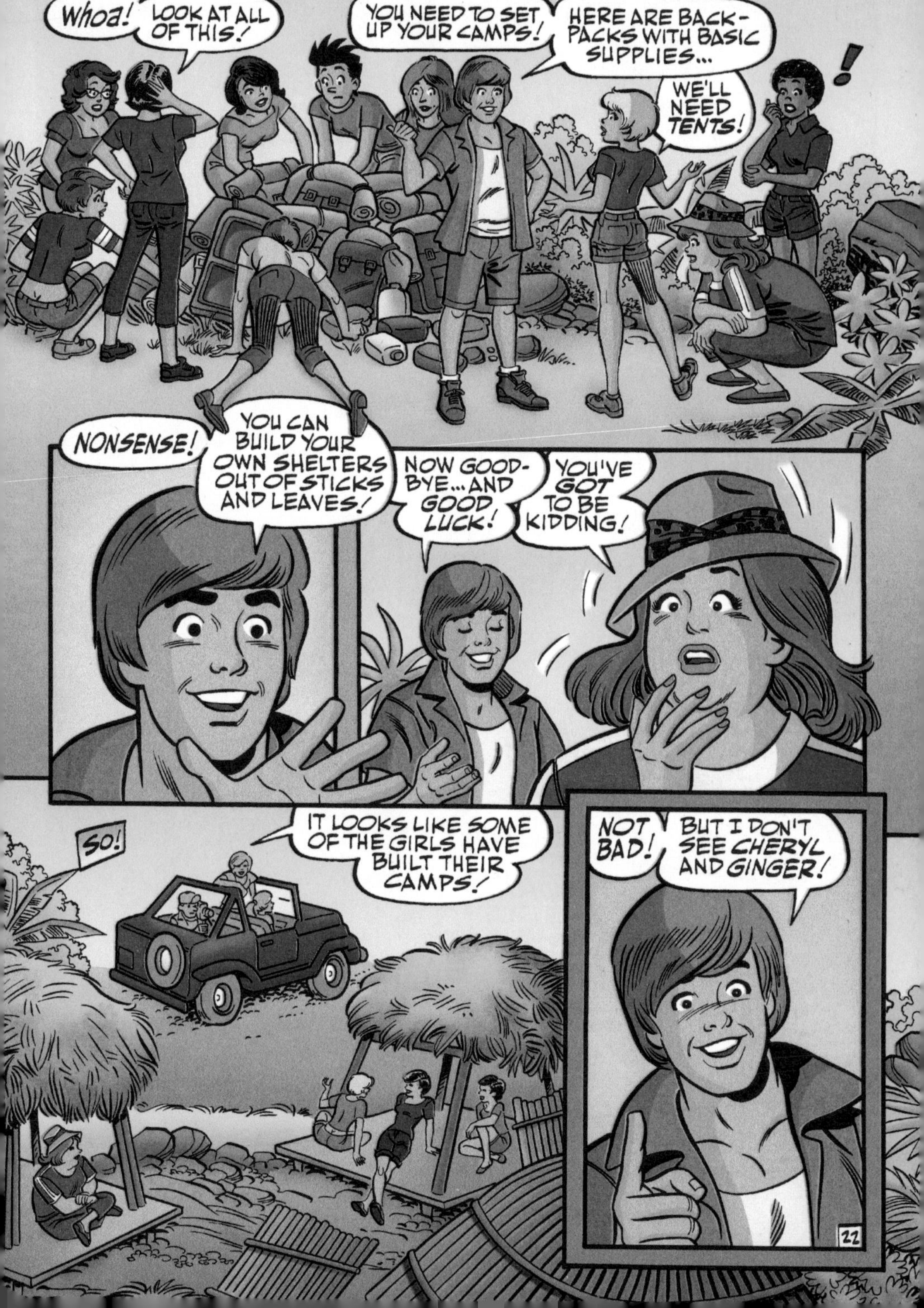
Whoa!
LOOK AT ALL OF THIS!
YOU NEED TO SET UP YOUR CAMPS!
HERE ARE BACK-PACKS WITH BASIC SUPPLIES...
WE'LL NEED TENTS!
!
NONSENSE!
YOU CAN BUILD YOUR OWN SHELTERS OUT OF STICKS AND LEAVES!
NOW GOOD-BYE... AND GOOD LUCK!
YOU'VE GOT TO BE KIDDING!
SO!
IT LOOKS LIKE SOME OF THE GIRLS HAVE BUILT THEIR CAMPS!
NOT BAD!
BUT I DON'T SEE CHERYL AND GINGER!
22

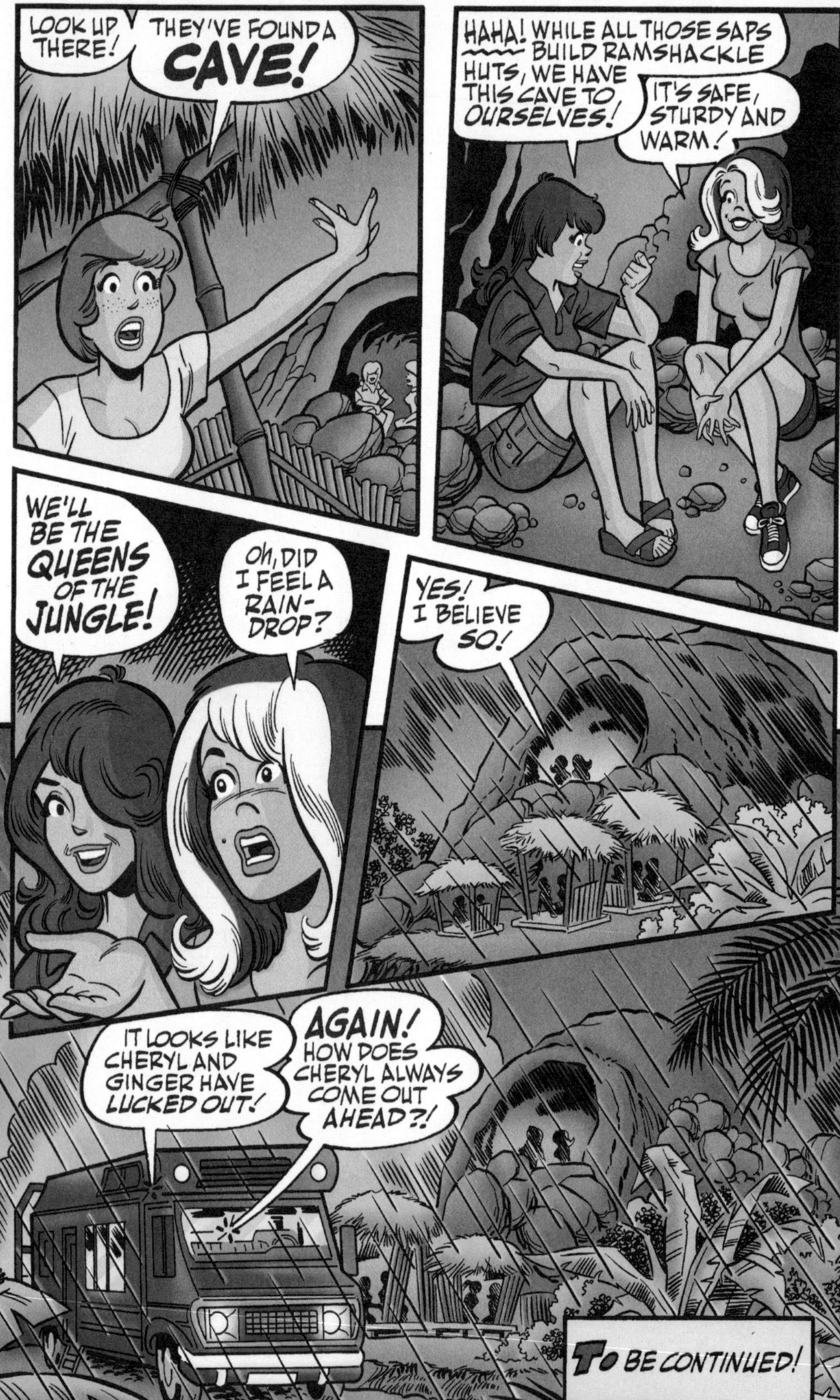
LOOK UP THERE!
THEY'VE FOUND A CAVE!
HAHA! WHILE ALL THOSE SAPS BUILD RAMSHACKLE HUTS, WE HAVE THIS CAVE TO OURSELVES!
IT'S SAFE, STURDY AND WARM!
WE'LL BE THE QUEENS OF THE JUNGLE!
OH, DID I FEEL A RAIN-DROP?
YES! I BELIEVE SO!
IT LOOKS LIKE CHERYL AND GINGER HAVE LUCKED OUT!
AGAIN! HOW DOES CHERYL ALWAYS COME OUT AHEAD?!
TO BE CONTINUED!

Chapter 4: All's Well That Ends Well!

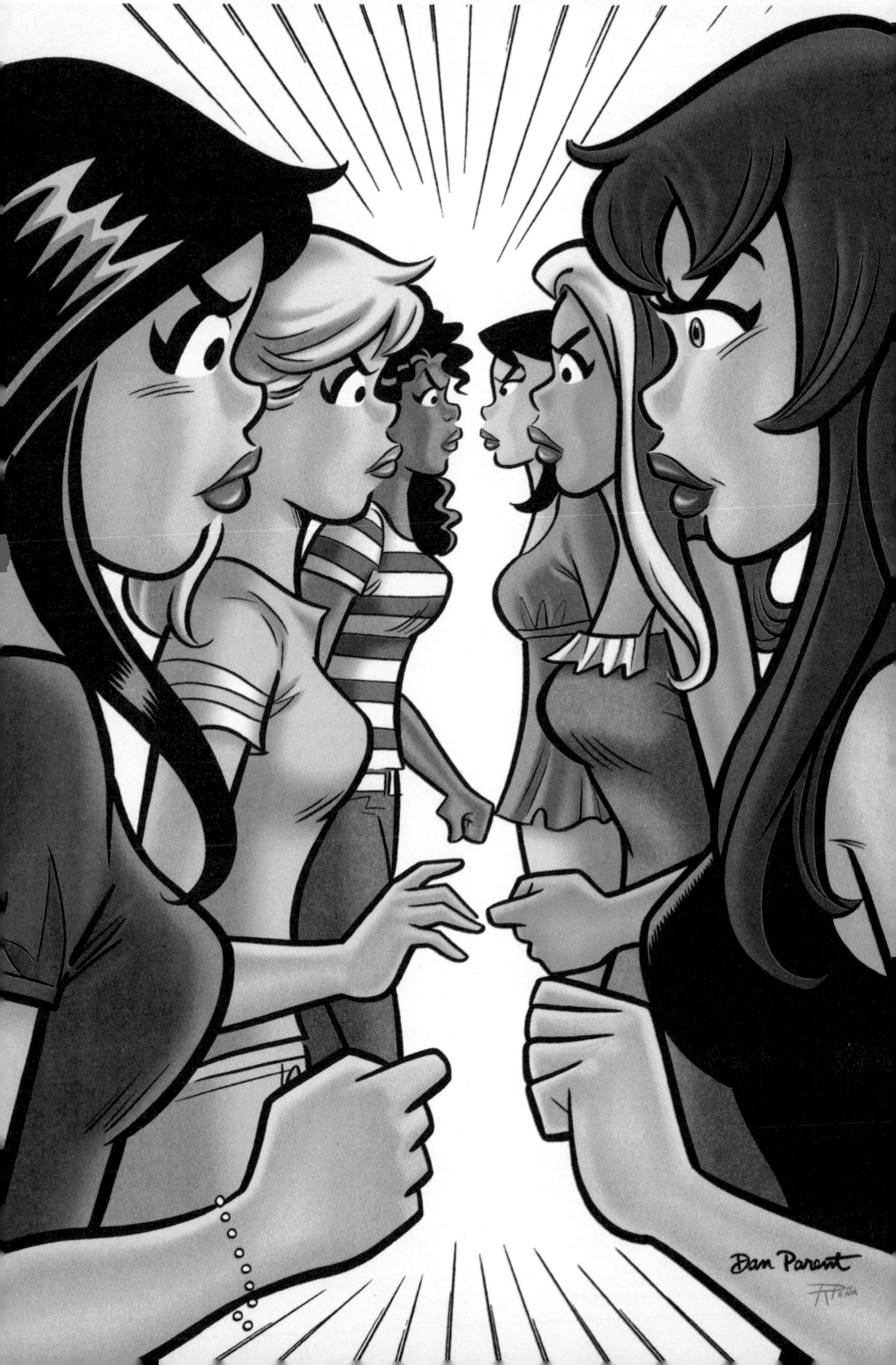
Dan Parent

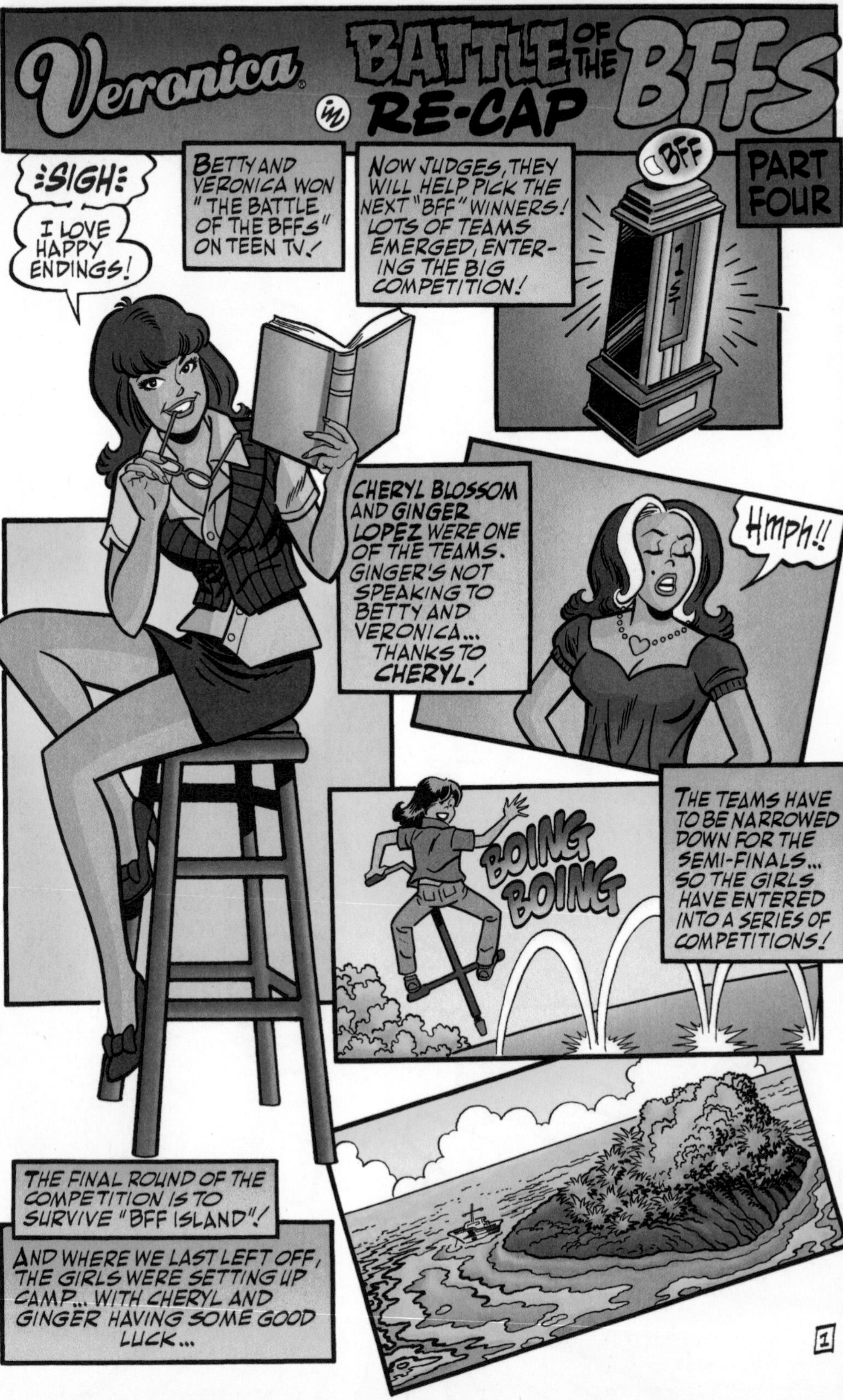

Veronica in
BATTLE OF THE BFFS RE-CAP
PART FOUR
:SIGH: I LOVE HAPPY ENDINGS!
BETTY AND VERONICA WON "THE BATTLE OF THE BFFS" ON TEEN TV!
NOW JUDGES, THEY WILL HELP PICK THE NEXT "BFF" WINNERS! LOTS OF TEAMS EMERGED, ENTERING THE BIG COMPETITION!
BFF
1ST
CHERYL BLOSSOM AND GINGER LOPEZ WERE ONE OF THE TEAMS. GINGER'S NOT SPEAKING TO BETTY AND VERONICA... THANKS TO CHERYL!
Hmph!!
THE TEAMS HAVE TO BE NARROWED DOWN FOR THE SEMI-FINALS... SO THE GIRLS HAVE ENTERED INTO A SERIES OF COMPETITIONS!
BOING BOING
THE FINAL ROUND OF THE COMPETITION IS TO SURVIVE "BFF ISLAND"!
AND WHERE WE LAST LEFT OFF, THE GIRLS WERE SETTING UP CAMP... WITH CHERYL AND GINGER HAVING SOME GOOD LUCK...
1

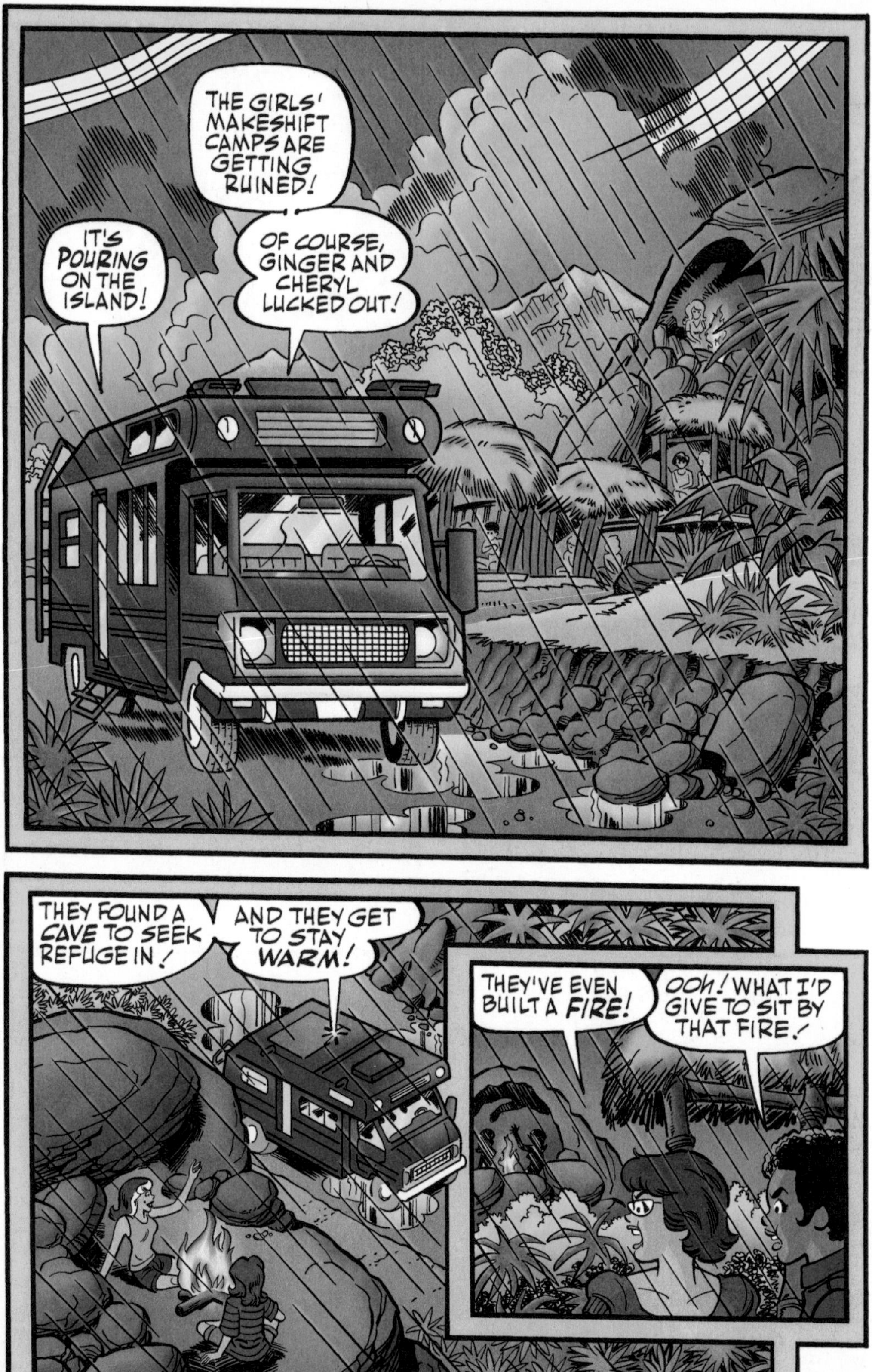

IT'S POURING ON THE ISLAND!
THE GIRLS' MAKESHIFT CAMPS ARE GETTING RUINED!
OF COURSE, GINGER AND CHERYL LUCKED OUT!
THEY FOUND A CAVE TO SEEK REFUGE IN!
AND THEY GET TO STAY WARM!
THEY'VE EVEN BUILT A FIRE!
OOH! WHAT I'D GIVE TO SIT BY THAT FIRE!

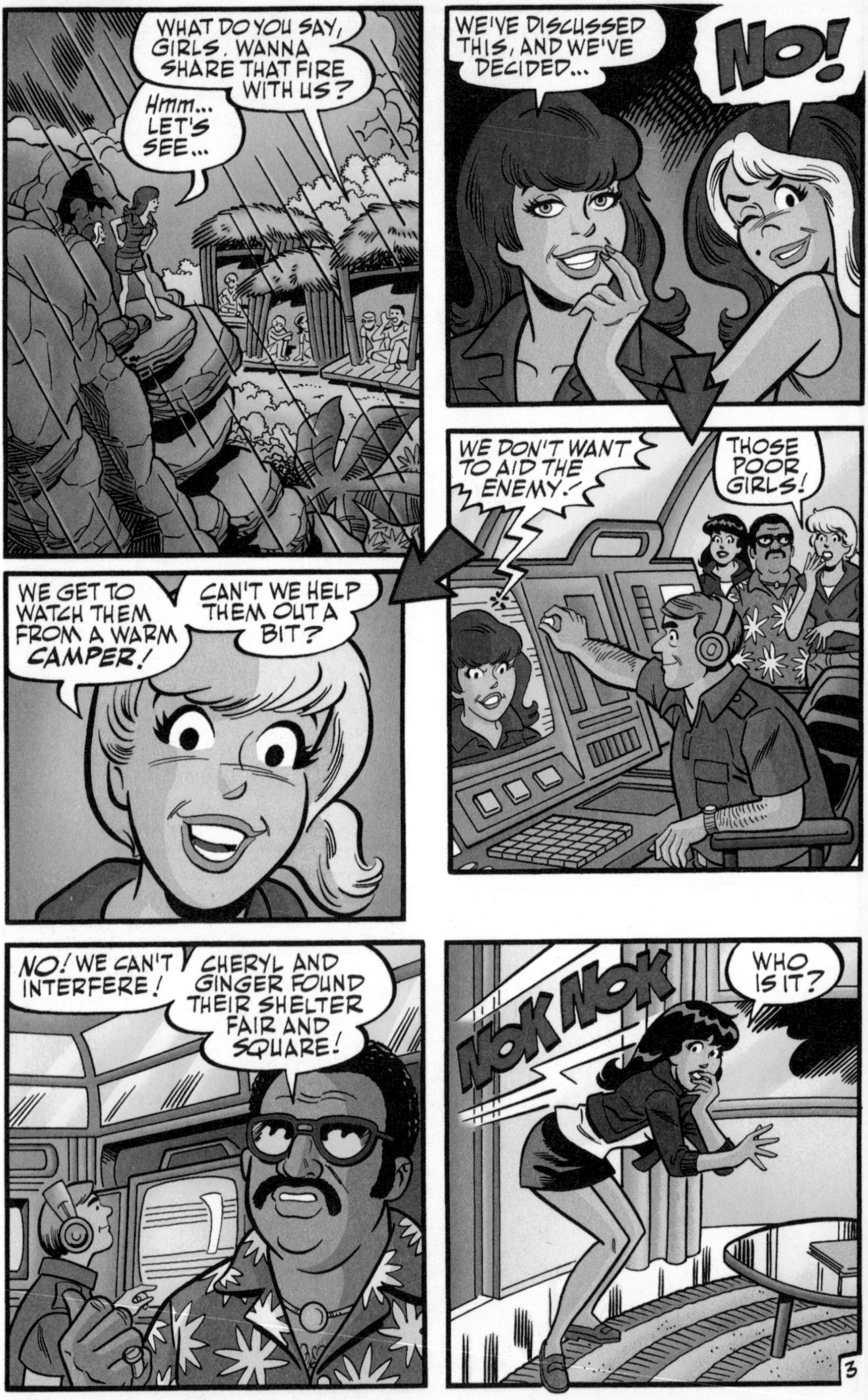

WHAT DO YOU SAY, GIRLS. WANNA SHARE THAT FIRE WITH US?
Hmm... LET'S SEE...
WE'VE DISCUSSED THIS, AND WE'VE DECIDED...
NO!
WE DON'T WANT TO AID THE ENEMY.
THOSE POOR GIRLS!
WE GET TO WATCH THEM FROM A WARM CAMPER!
CAN'T WE HELP THEM OUT A BIT?
NO! WE CAN'T INTERFERE!
CHERYL AND GINGER FOUND THEIR SHELTER FAIR AND SQUARE!
NOK NOK
WHO IS IT?

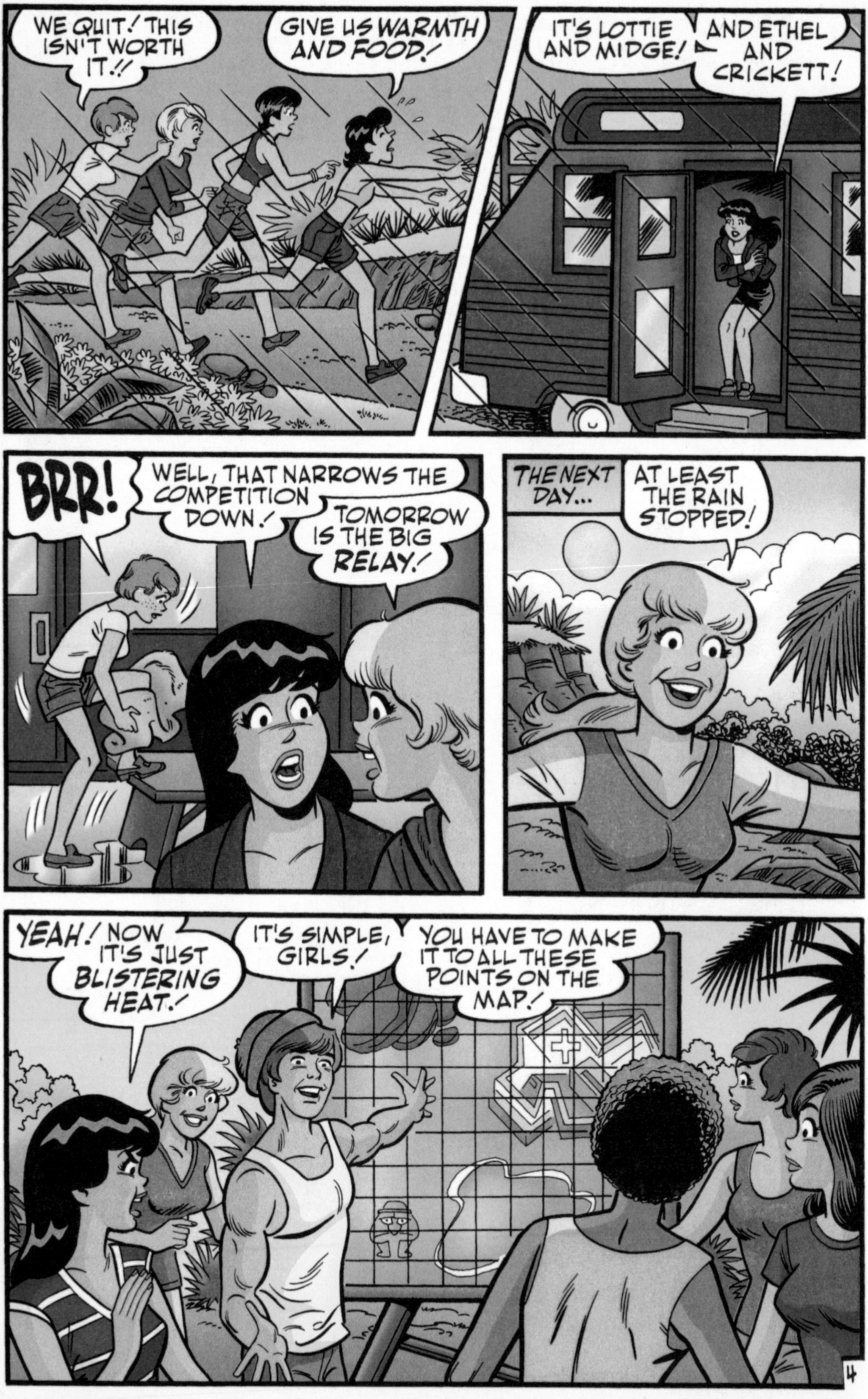
WE QUIT! THIS ISN'T WORTH IT!!
GIVE US WARMTH AND FOOD!
IT'S LOTTIE AND MIDGE!
AND ETHEL AND CRICKETT!
BRR!
WELL, THAT NARROWS THE COMPETITION DOWN!
TOMORROW IS THE BIG RELAY!
THE NEXT DAY...
AT LEAST THE RAIN STOPPED!
YEAH! NOW IT'S JUST BLISTERING HEAT!
IT'S SIMPLE, GIRLS!
YOU HAVE TO MAKE IT TO ALL THESE POINTS ON THE MAP!
4

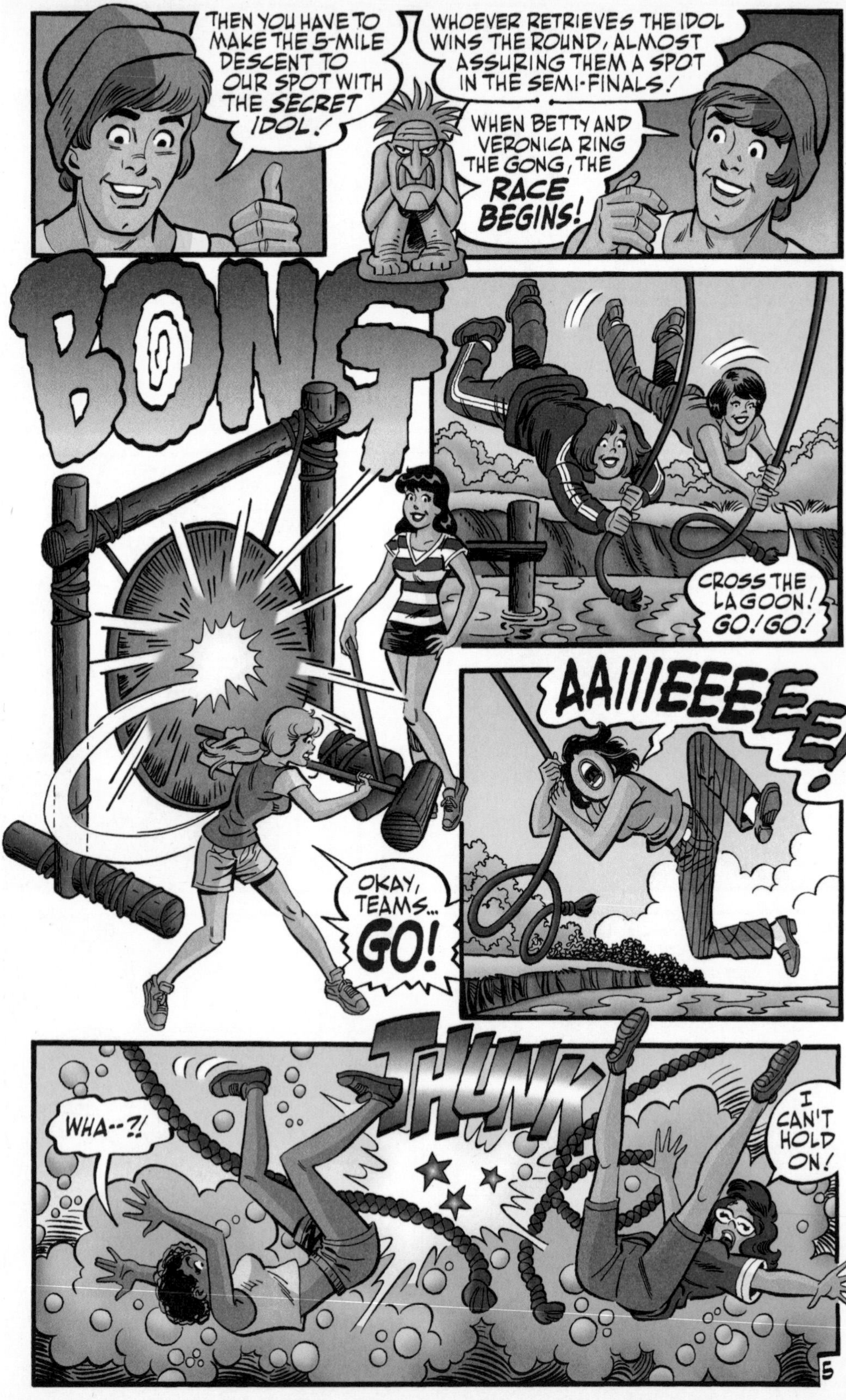
THEN YOU HAVE TO MAKE THE 5-MILE DESCENT TO OUR SPOT WITH THE SECRET IDOL!
WHOEVER RETRIEVES THE IDOL WINS THE ROUND, ALMOST ASSURING THEM A SPOT IN THE SEMI-FINALS!
WHEN BETTY AND VERONICA RING THE GONG, THE RACE BEGINS!
BONG
OKAY, TEAMS... GO!
CROSS THE LAGOON! GO! GO!
AAIIIEEEEEE!
THUNK
WHA--?!
I CAN'T HOLD ON!
5

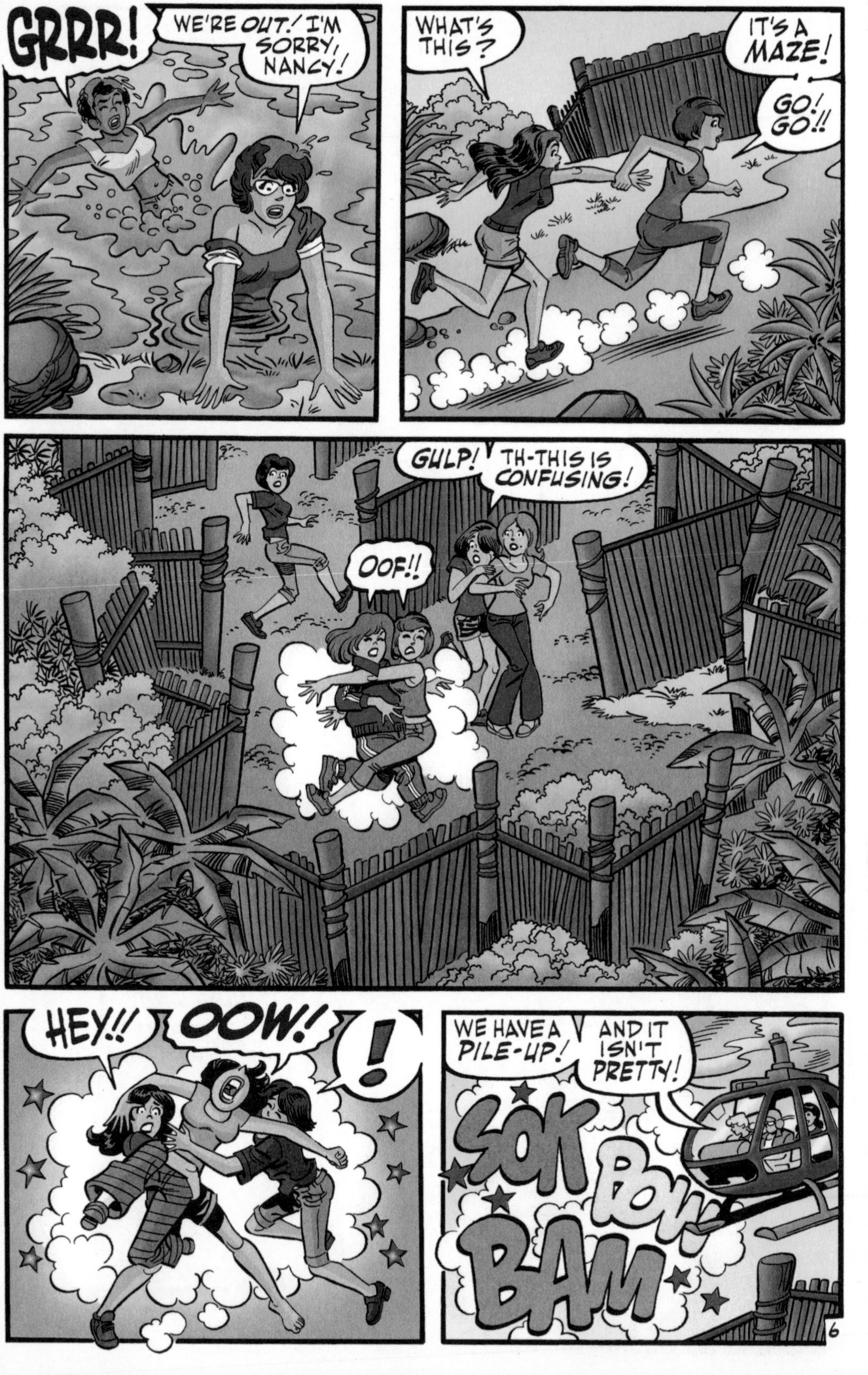
GRRR!
WE'RE OUT! I'M SORRY, NANCY!
WHAT'S THIS?
IT'S A MAZE!
GO! GO!!
GULP!
TH-THIS IS CONFUSING!
OOF!!
HEY!!
OOW!
!
WE HAVE A PILE-UP!
AND IT ISN'T PRETTY!
SOK
BOW
BAM

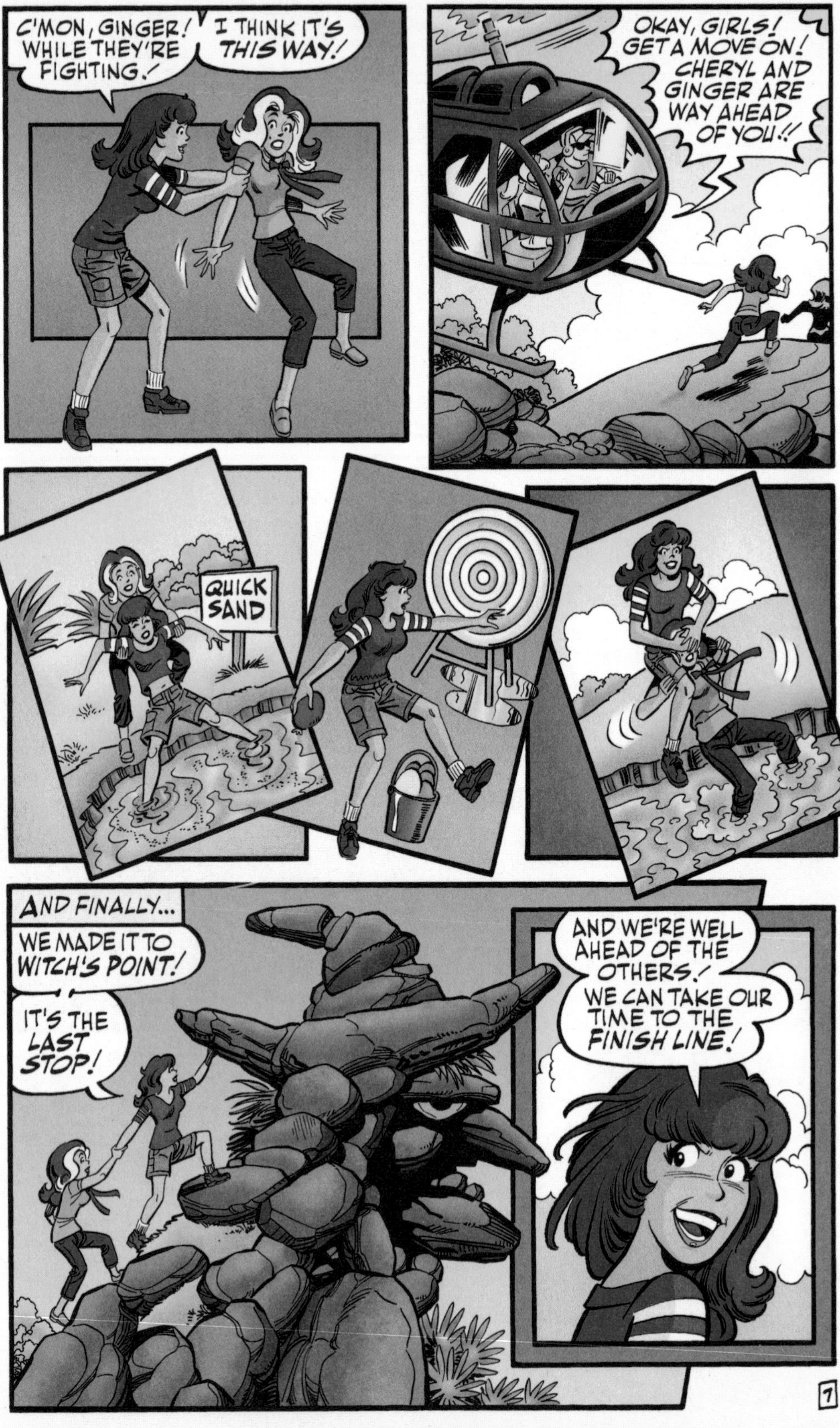
C'MON, GINGER! WHILE THEY'RE FIGHTING!
I THINK IT'S THIS WAY!
OKAY, GIRLS! GET A MOVE ON! CHERYL AND GINGER ARE WAY AHEAD OF YOU!!
QUICK SAND
AND FINALLY...
WE MADE IT TO WITCH'S POINT!
IT'S THE LAST STOP!
AND WE'RE WELL AHEAD OF THE OTHERS! WE CAN TAKE OUR TIME TO THE FINISH LINE!

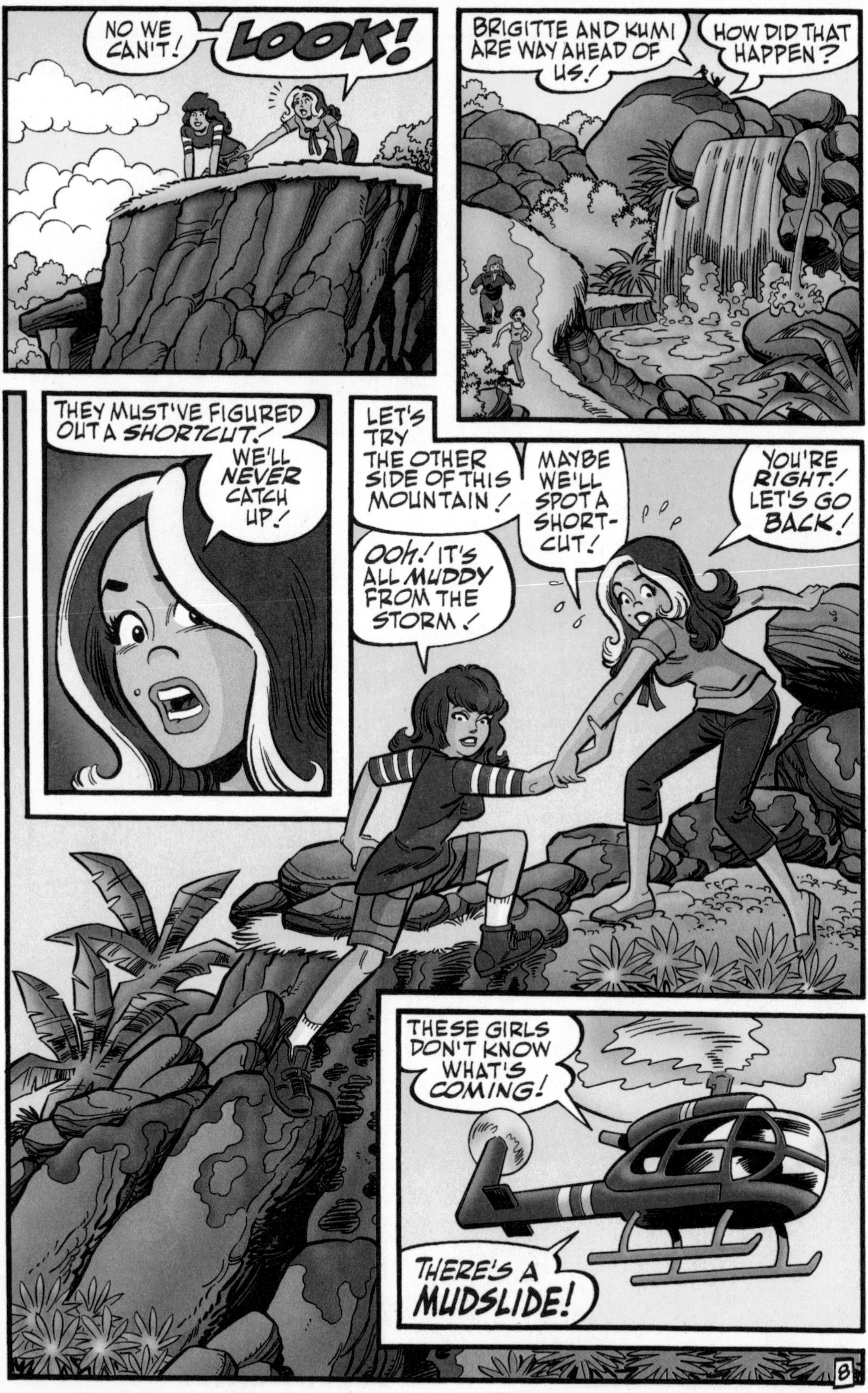
NO WE CAN'T!
LOOK!
BRIGITTE AND KUMI ARE WAY AHEAD OF US!
HOW DID THAT HAPPEN?
THEY MUST'VE FIGURED OUT A SHORTCUT!
WE'LL NEVER CATCH UP!
LET'S TRY THE OTHER SIDE OF THIS MOUNTAIN!
MAYBE WE'LL SPOT A SHORT-CUT!
YOU'RE RIGHT! LET'S GO BACK!
OOH! IT'S ALL MUDDY FROM THE STORM!
THESE GIRLS DON'T KNOW WHAT'S COMING!
THERE'S A MUDSLIDE!

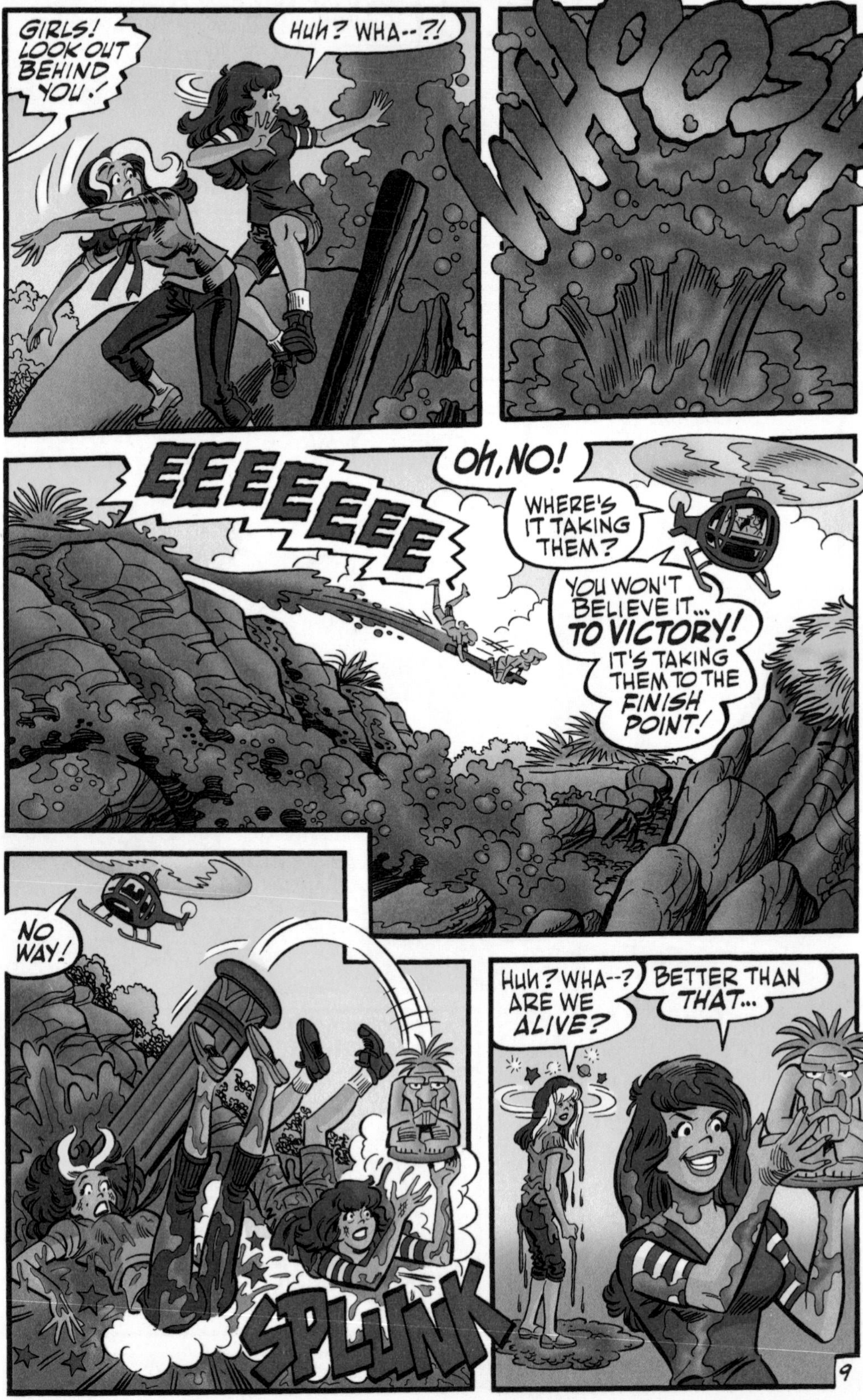
GIRLS! LOOK OUT BEHIND YOU!
HUH? WHA--?!
WHOOSH
EEEEEEEE
OH, NO!
WHERE'S IT TAKING THEM?
YOU WON'T BELIEVE IT... TO VICTORY! IT'S TAKING THEM TO THE FINISH POINT!
NO WAY!
SPLUNK
HUH? WHA--? ARE WE ALIVE?
BETTER THAN THAT...

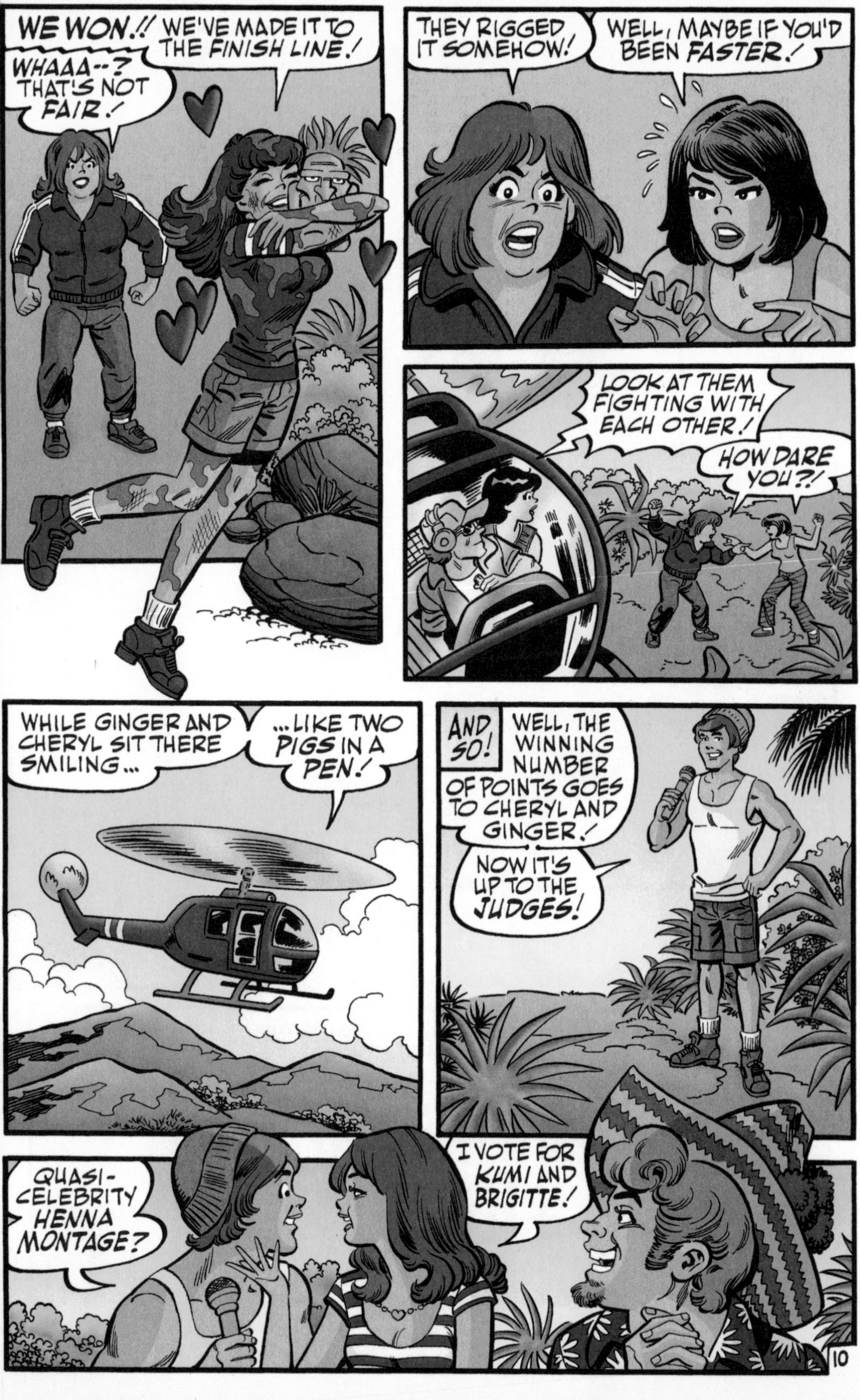

WE WON.!! WE'VE MADE IT TO THE FINISH LINE.!
WHAAA--? THAT'S NOT FAIR.!
THEY RIGGED IT SOMEHOW!
WELL, MAYBE IF YOU'D BEEN FASTER.!
LOOK AT THEM FIGHTING WITH EACH OTHER.!
HOW DARE YOU?!
WHILE GINGER AND CHERYL SIT THERE SMILING...
...LIKE TWO PIGS IN A PEN.!
AND SO!
WELL, THE WINNING NUMBER OF POINTS GOES TO CHERYL AND GINGER.!
NOW IT'S UP TO THE JUDGES!
QUASI-CELEBRITY HENNA MONTAGE?
I VOTE FOR KUMI AND BRIGITTE!

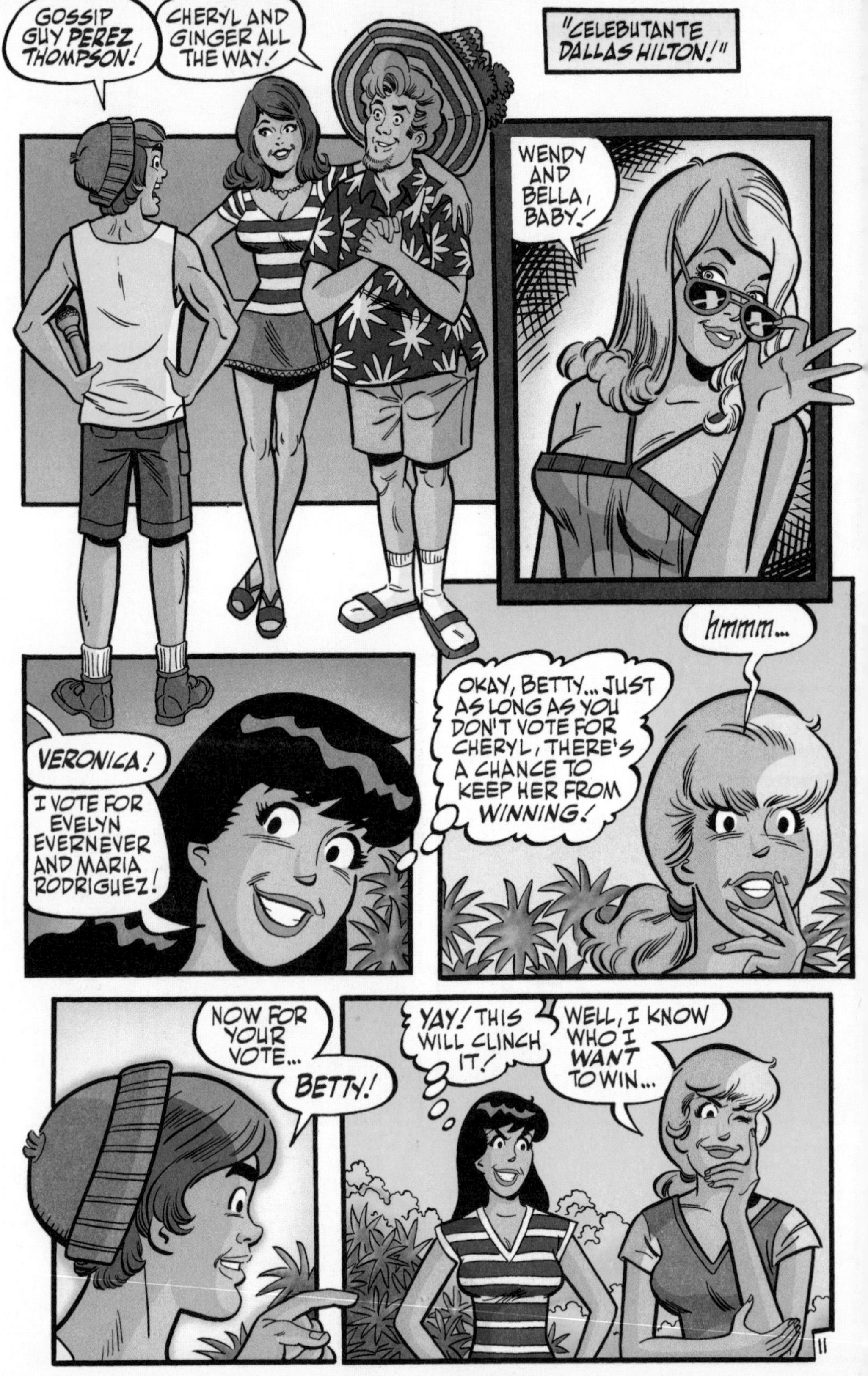
GOSSIP GUY PEREZ THOMPSON!
CHERYL AND GINGER ALL THE WAY!
"CELEBUTANTE DALLAS HILTON!"
WENDY AND BELLA, BABY!
hmmm...
VERONICA!
I VOTE FOR EVELYN EVERNEVER AND MARIA RODRIGUEZ!
OKAY, BETTY... JUST AS LONG AS YOU DON'T VOTE FOR CHERYL, THERE'S A CHANCE TO KEEP HER FROM WINNING!
NOW FOR YOUR VOTE...
BETTY!
YAY! THIS WILL CLINCH IT!
WELL, I KNOW WHO I WANT TO WIN...

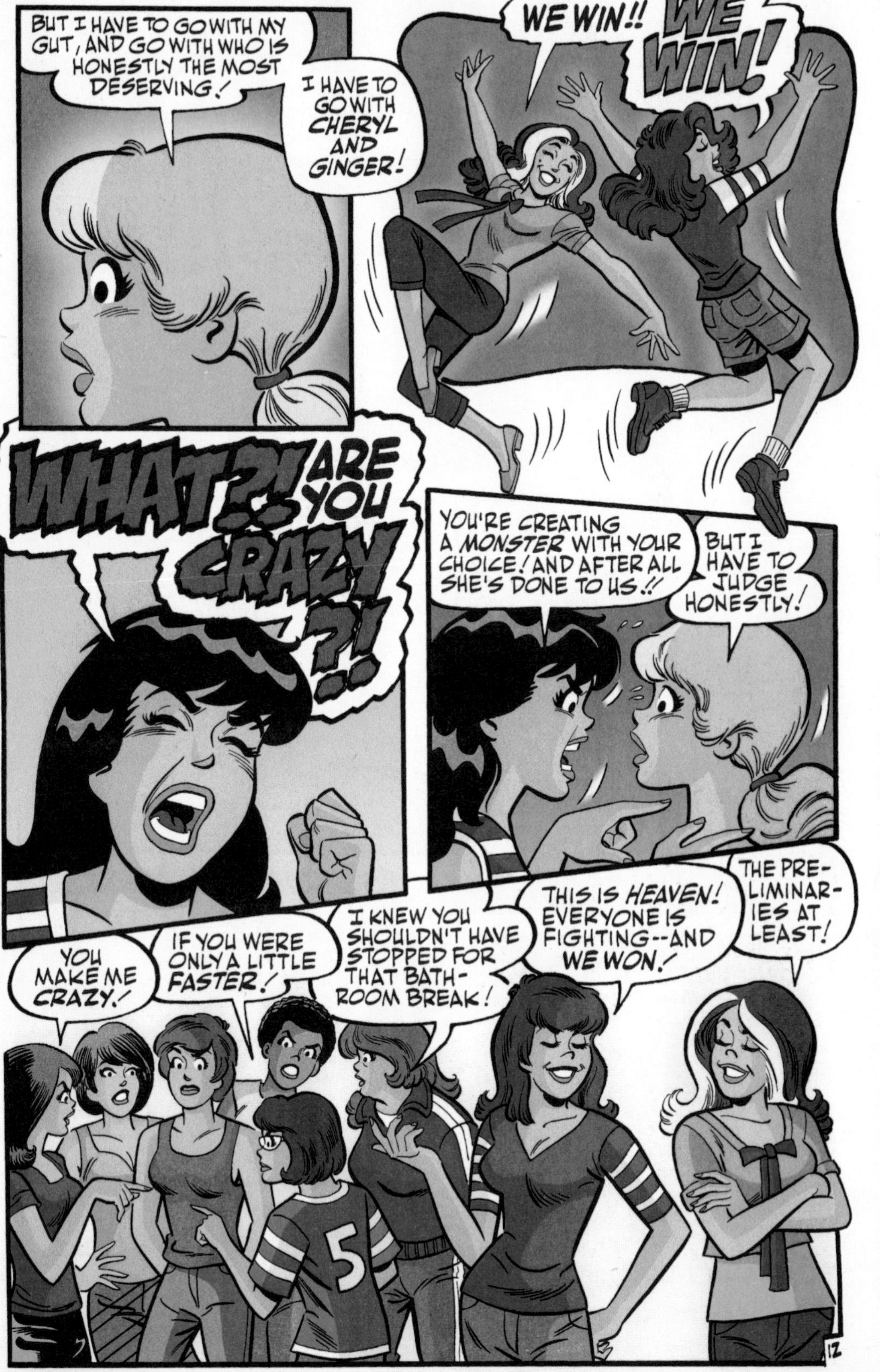
BUT I HAVE TO GO WITH MY GUT, AND GO WITH WHO IS HONESTLY THE MOST DESERVING!
I HAVE TO GO WITH CHERYL AND GINGER!
WE WIN!!
WE WIN!
WHAT?! ARE YOU CRAZY?!
YOU'RE CREATING A MONSTER WITH YOUR CHOICE! AND AFTER ALL SHE'S DONE TO US!!
BUT I HAVE TO JUDGE HONESTLY!
YOU MAKE ME CRAZY!
IF YOU WERE ONLY A LITTLE FASTER!
I KNEW YOU SHOULDN'T HAVE STOPPED FOR THAT BATH-ROOM BREAK!
THIS IS HEAVEN! EVERYONE IS FIGHTING--AND WE WON!
THE PRE-LIMINAR-IES AT LEAST!
12

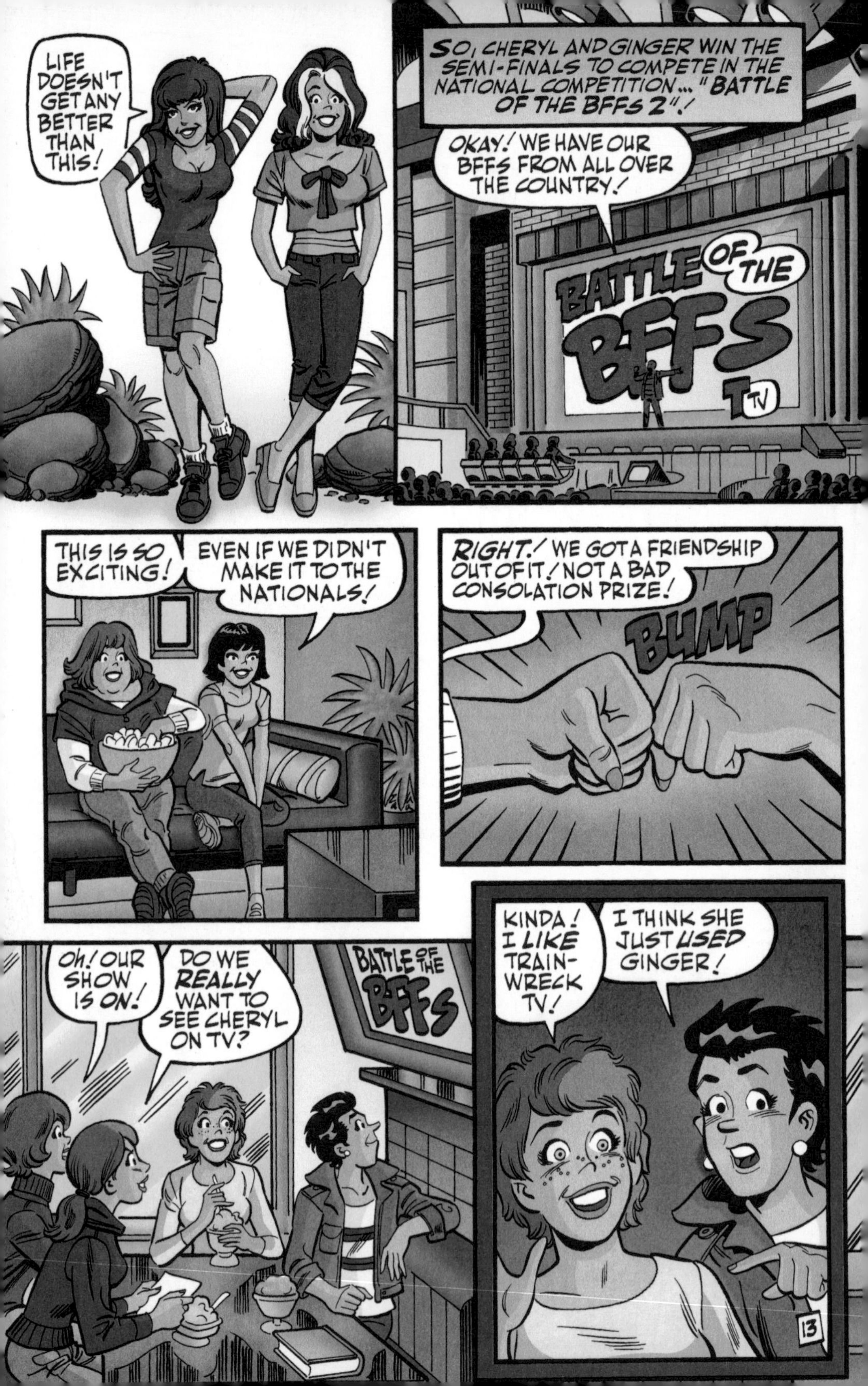
LIFE DOESN'T GET ANY BETTER THAN THIS!
SO, CHERYL AND GINGER WIN THE SEMI-FINALS TO COMPETE IN THE NATIONAL COMPETITION... "BATTLE OF THE BFFs 2"!
OKAY! WE HAVE OUR BFFs FROM ALL OVER THE COUNTRY!
BATTLE OF THE BFFS
TTV
THIS IS SO EXCITING!
EVEN IF WE DIDN'T MAKE IT TO THE NATIONALS!
RIGHT! WE GOT A FRIENDSHIP OUT OF IT! NOT A BAD CONSOLATION PRIZE!
BUMP
Oh! OUR SHOW IS ON!
DO WE REALLY WANT TO SEE CHERYL ON TV?
BATTLE OF THE BFFs
KINDA! I LIKE TRAIN-WRECK TV!
I THINK SHE JUST USED GINGER!
13

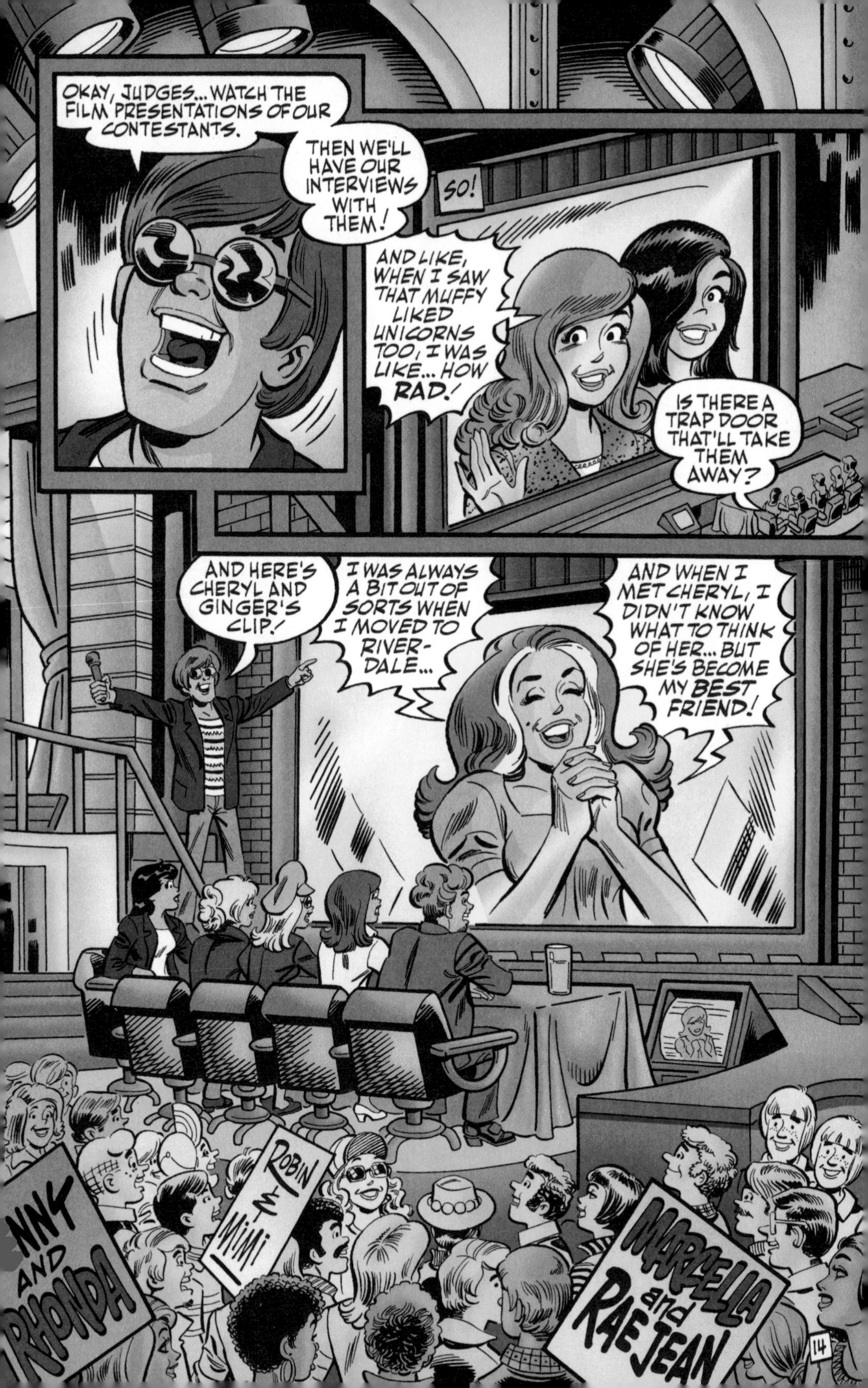

OKAY, JUDGES... WATCH THE FILM PRESENTATIONS OF OUR CONTESTANTS.
THEN WE'LL HAVE OUR INTERVIEWS WITH THEM!
SO!
AND LIKE, WHEN I SAW THAT MUFFY LIKED UNICORNS TOO, I WAS LIKE... HOW RAD!
IS THERE A TRAP DOOR THAT'LL TAKE THEM AWAY?
AND HERE'S CHERYL AND GINGER'S CLIP!
I WAS ALWAYS A BIT OUT OF SORTS WHEN I MOVED TO RIVER-DALE...
AND WHEN I MET CHERYL, I DIDN'T KNOW WHAT TO THINK OF HER... BUT SHE'S BECOME MY BEST FRIEND!
NNY AND RHONDA
ROBIN & MIMI
MARCELLA and RAE JEAN

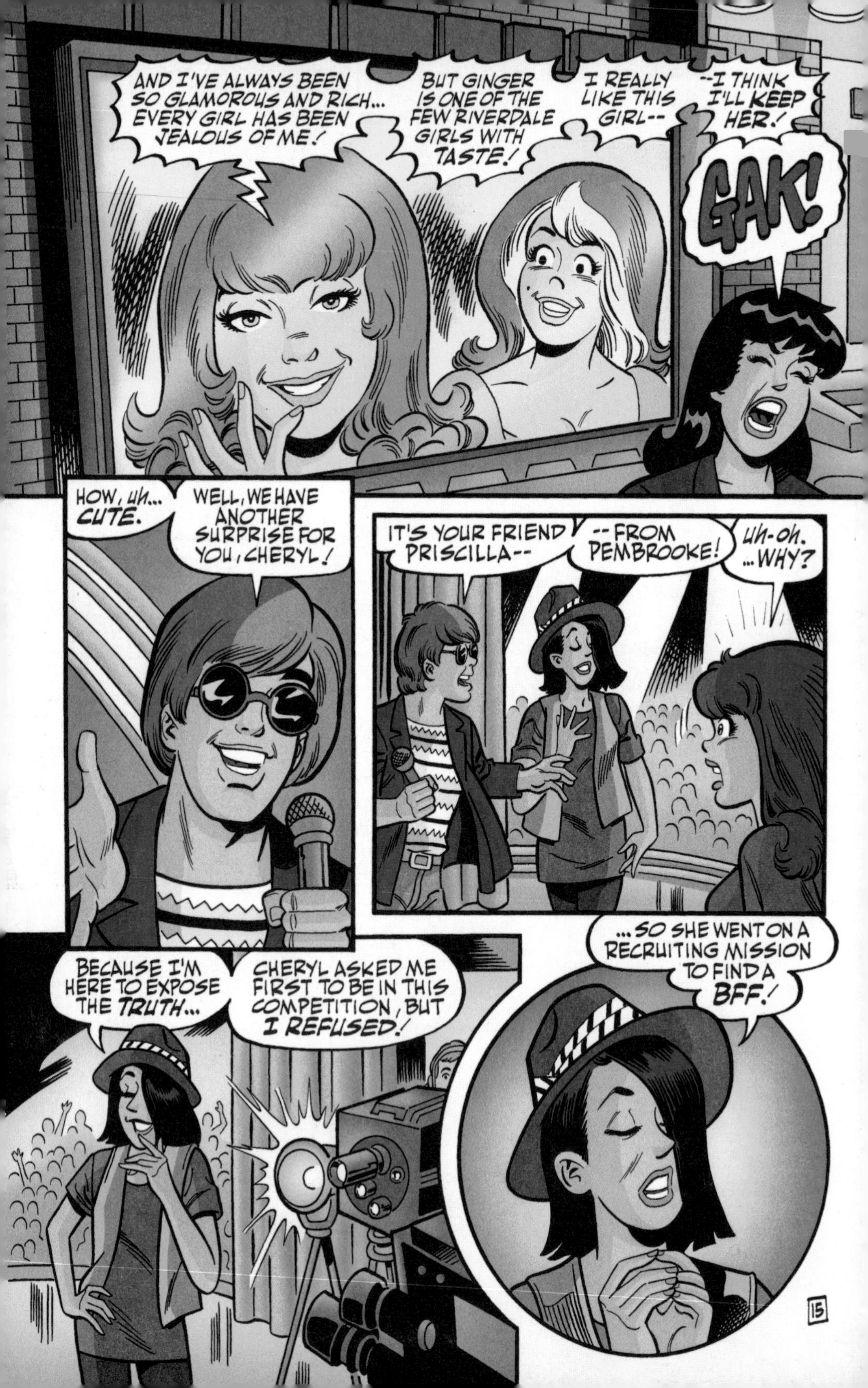
AND I'VE ALWAYS BEEN SO GLAMOROUS AND RICH... EVERY GIRL HAS BEEN JEALOUS OF ME!
BUT GINGER IS ONE OF THE FEW RIVERDALE GIRLS WITH TASTE!
I REALLY LIKE THIS GIRL--
--I THINK I'LL KEEP HER!
GAK!
HOW, uh... CUTE.
WELL, WE HAVE ANOTHER SURPRISE FOR YOU, CHERYL!
IT'S YOUR FRIEND PRISCILLA--
--FROM PEMBROOKE!
uh-oh. ...WHY?
BECAUSE I'M HERE TO EXPOSE THE TRUTH...
CHERYL ASKED ME FIRST TO BE IN THIS COMPETITION, BUT I REFUSED!
...SO SHE WENT ON A RECRUITING MISSION TO FIND A BFF!
15

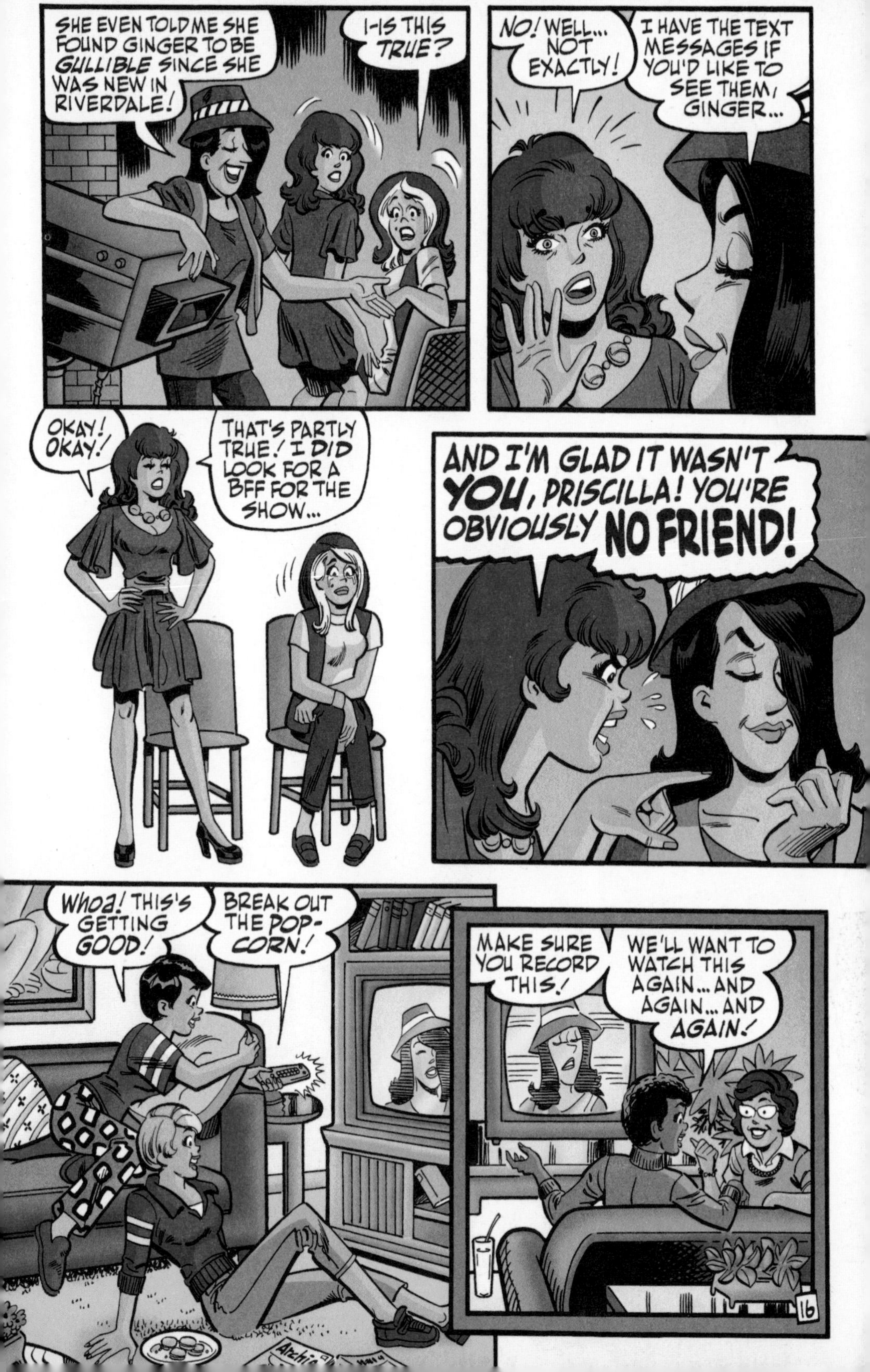
SHE EVEN TOLD ME SHE FOUND GINGER TO BE GULLIBLE SINCE SHE WAS NEW IN RIVERDALE!
I-IS THIS TRUE?
NO! WELL... NOT EXACTLY!
I HAVE THE TEXT MESSAGES IF YOU'D LIKE TO SEE THEM, GINGER...
OKAY! OKAY!
THAT'S PARTLY TRUE! I DID LOOK FOR A BFF FOR THE SHOW...
AND I'M GLAD IT WASN'T YOU, PRISCILLA! YOU'RE OBVIOUSLY NO FRIEND!
Whoa! THIS'S GETTING GOOD!
BREAK OUT THE POP-CORN!
MAKE SURE YOU RECORD THIS!
WE'LL WANT TO WATCH THIS AGAIN... AND AGAIN... AND AGAIN!
16

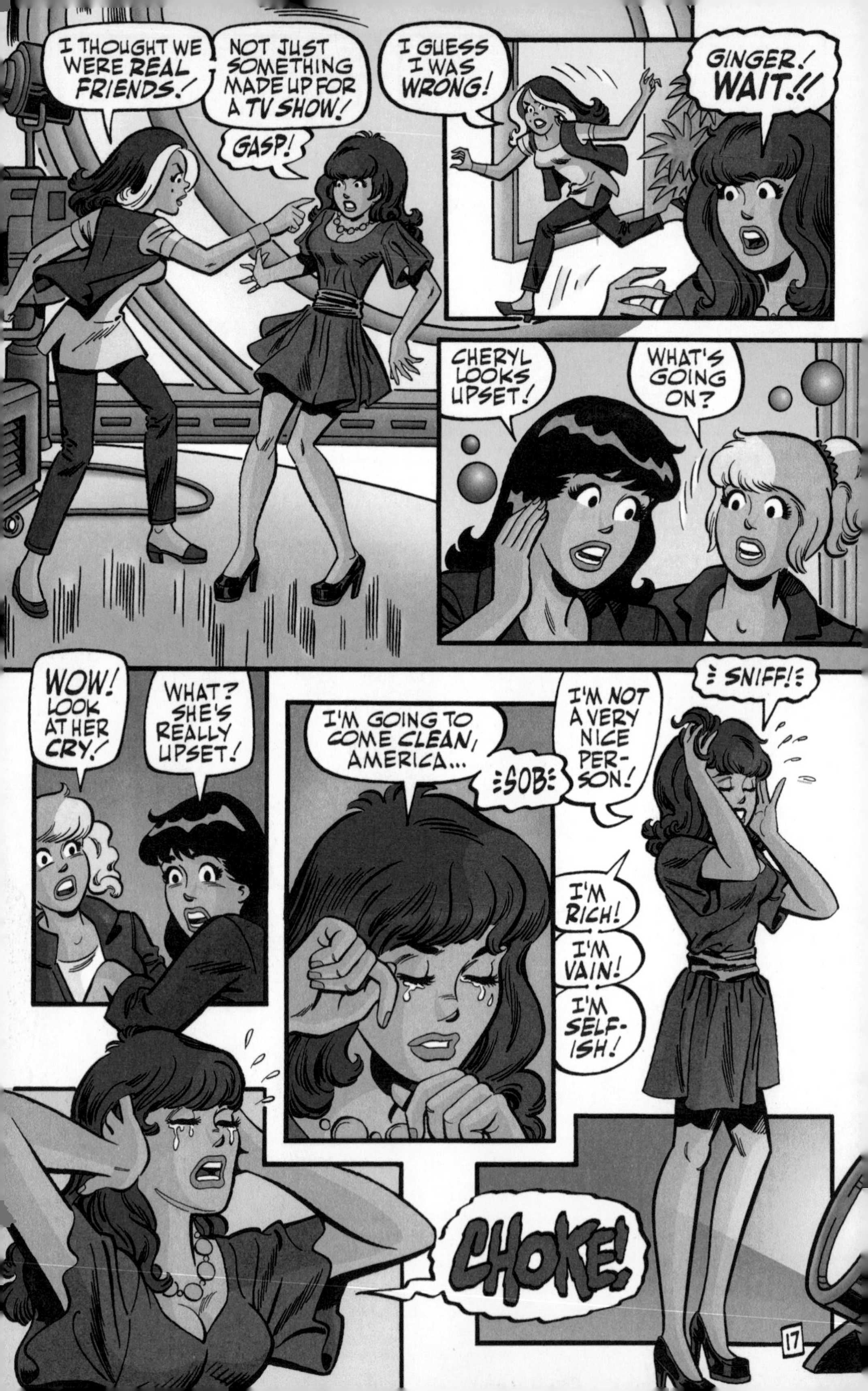

I THOUGHT WE WERE REAL FRIENDS!
NOT JUST SOMETHING MADE UP FOR A TV SHOW!
GASP!
I GUESS I WAS WRONG!
GINGER! WAIT!!
CHERYL LOOKS UPSET!
WHAT'S GOING ON?
WOW! LOOK AT HER CRY!
WHAT? SHE'S REALLY UPSET!
I'M GOING TO COME CLEAN, AMERICA...
SOB
I'M NOT A VERY NICE PER-SON!
SNIFF!
I'M RICH!
I'M VAIN!
I'M SELF-ISH!
CHOKE!

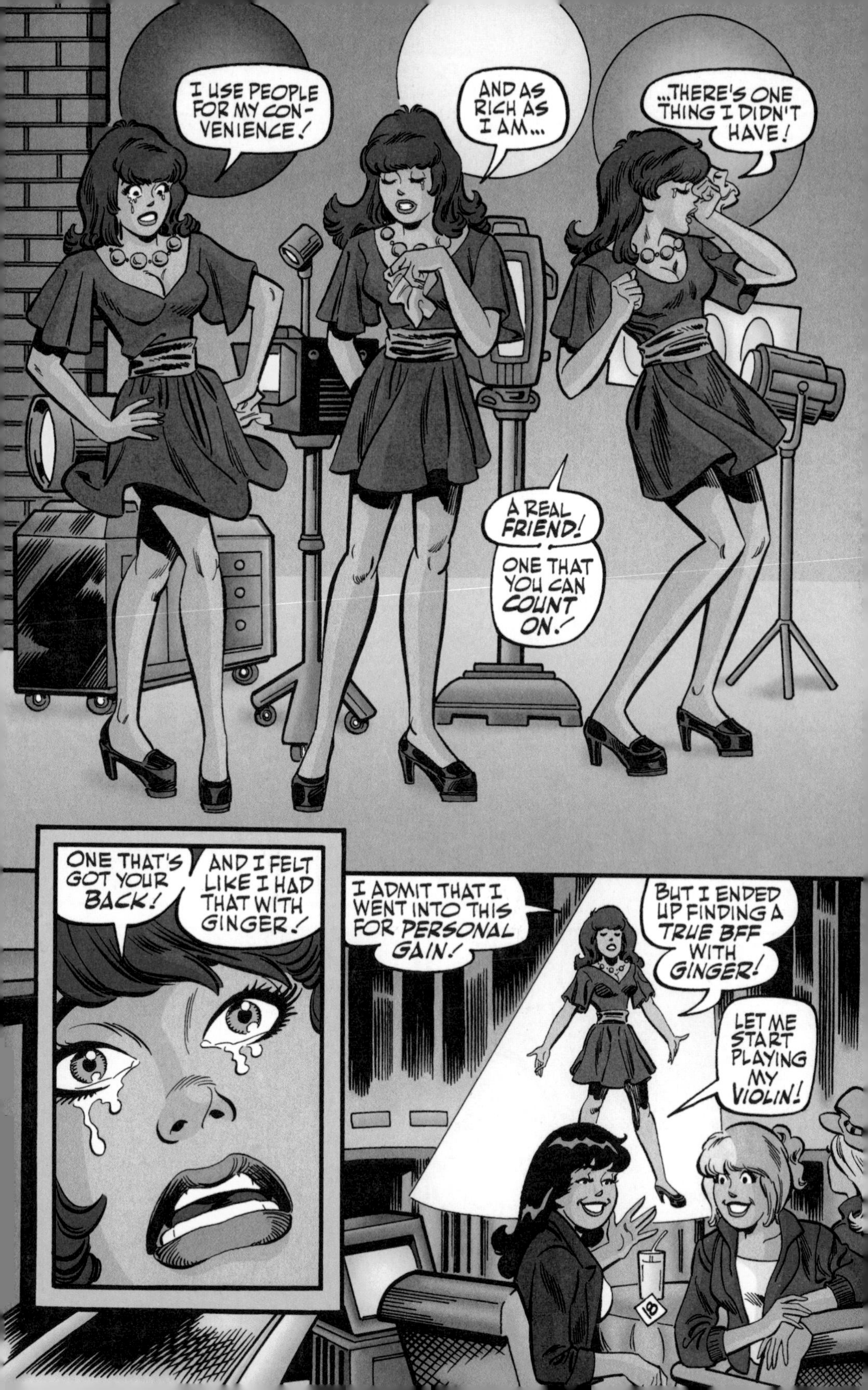
I USE PEOPLE FOR MY CON-VENIENCE!
AND AS RICH AS I AM...
...THERE'S ONE THING I DIDN'T HAVE!
A REAL FRIEND!
ONE THAT YOU CAN COUNT ON!
ONE THAT'S GOT YOUR BACK!
AND I FELT LIKE I HAD THAT WITH GINGER!
I ADMIT THAT I WENT INTO THIS FOR PERSONAL GAIN!
BUT I ENDED UP FINDING A TRUE BFF WITH GINGER!
LET ME START PLAYING MY VIOLIN!
18

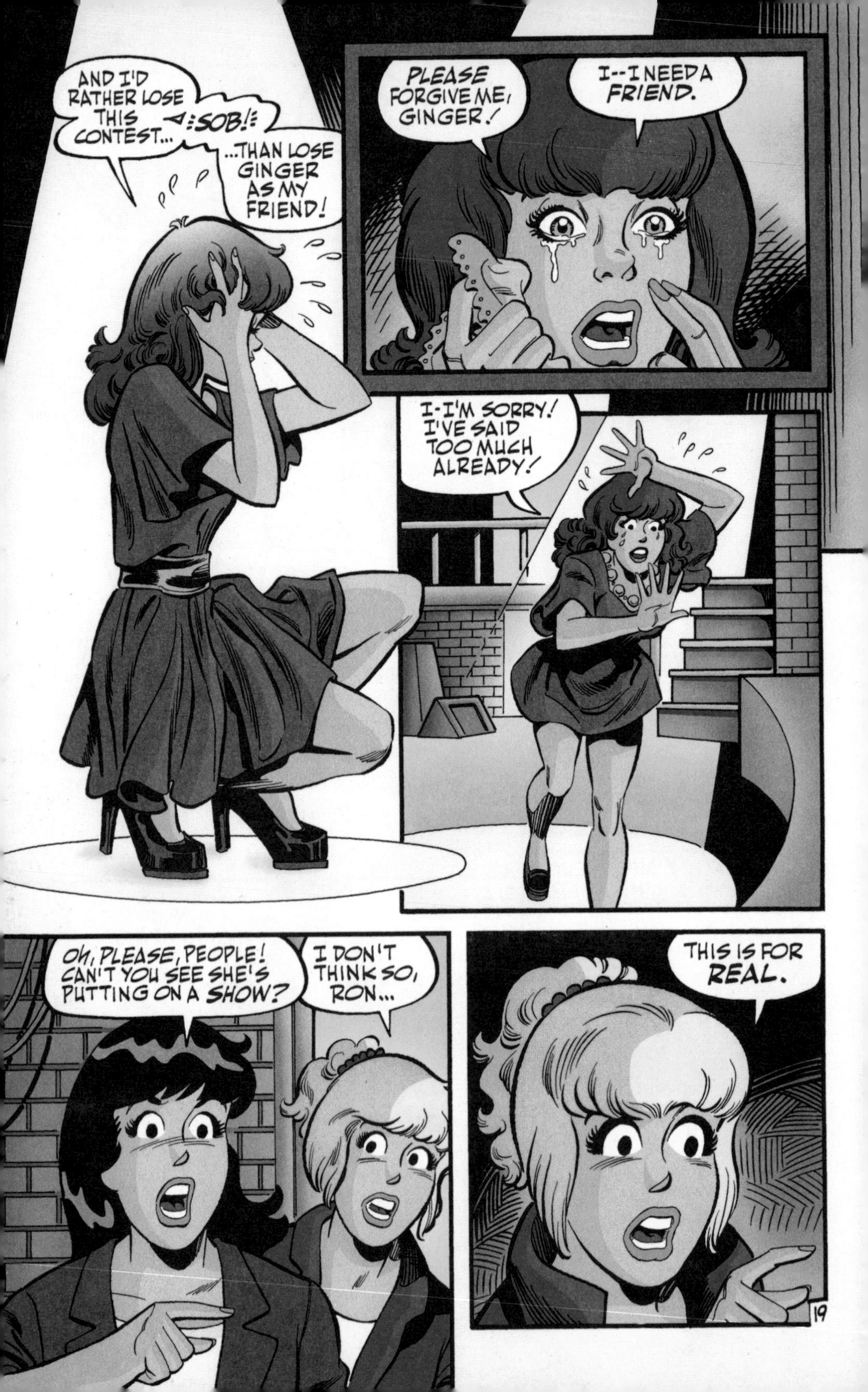
AND I'D RATHER LOSE THIS CONTEST...
SOB!
...THAN LOSE GINGER AS MY FRIEND!
PLEASE FORGIVE ME, GINGER!
I--I NEED A FRIEND.
I-I'M SORRY! I'VE SAID TOO MUCH ALREADY!
Oh, PLEASE, PEOPLE! CAN'T YOU SEE SHE'S PUTTING ON A SHOW?
I DON'T THINK SO, RON...
THIS IS FOR REAL.
19

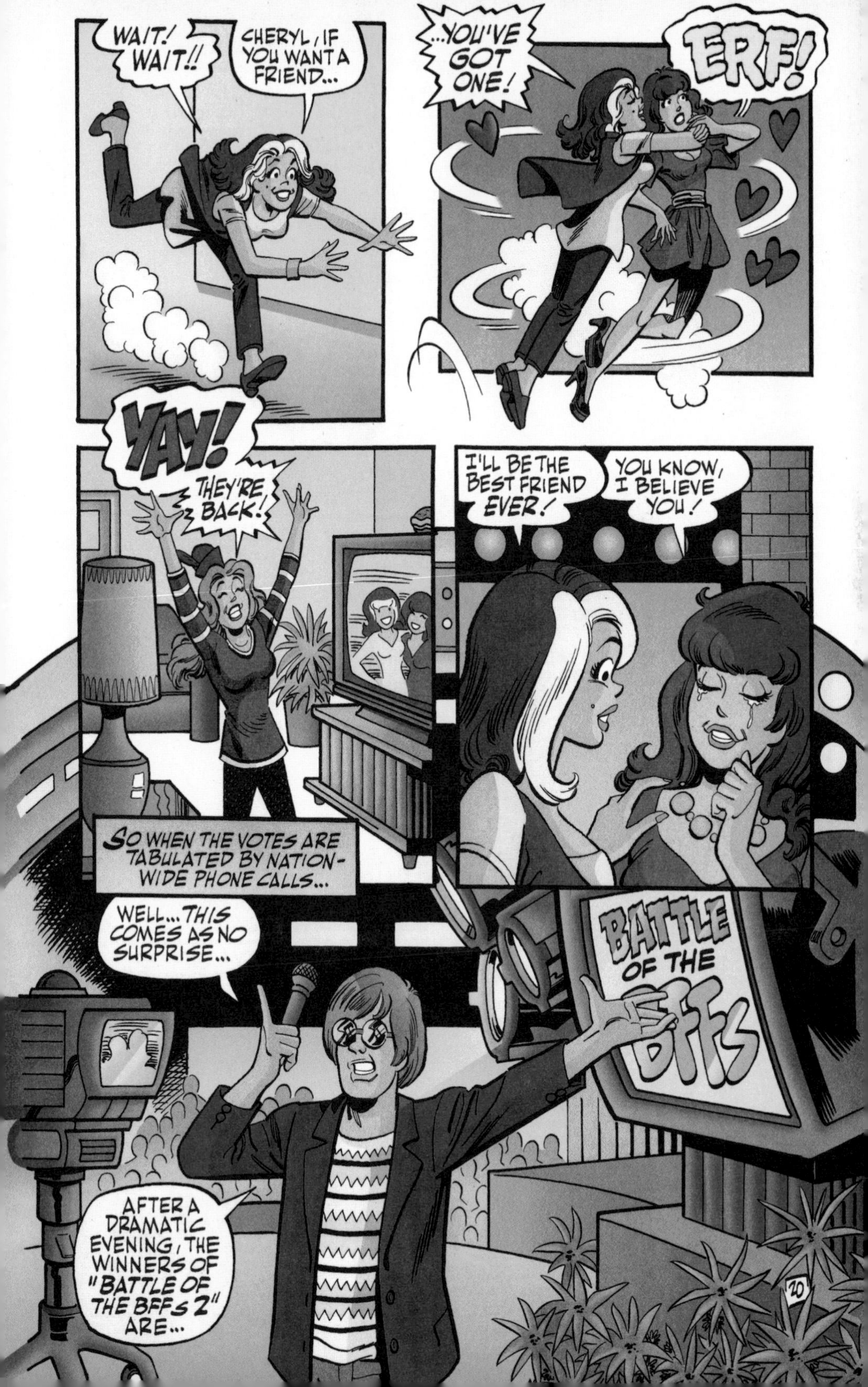
WAIT! WAIT!!
CHERYL, IF YOU WANT A FRIEND...
...YOU'VE GOT ONE!
ERF!
YAY!
THEY'RE BACK!
I'LL BE THE BEST FRIEND EVER!
YOU KNOW, I BELIEVE YOU!
SO WHEN THE VOTES ARE TABULATED BY NATION-WIDE PHONE CALLS...
WELL... THIS COMES AS NO SURPRISE...
BATTLE OF THE BFFs
AFTER A DRAMATIC EVENING, THE WINNERS OF "BATTLE OF THE BFFs 2" ARE...
20

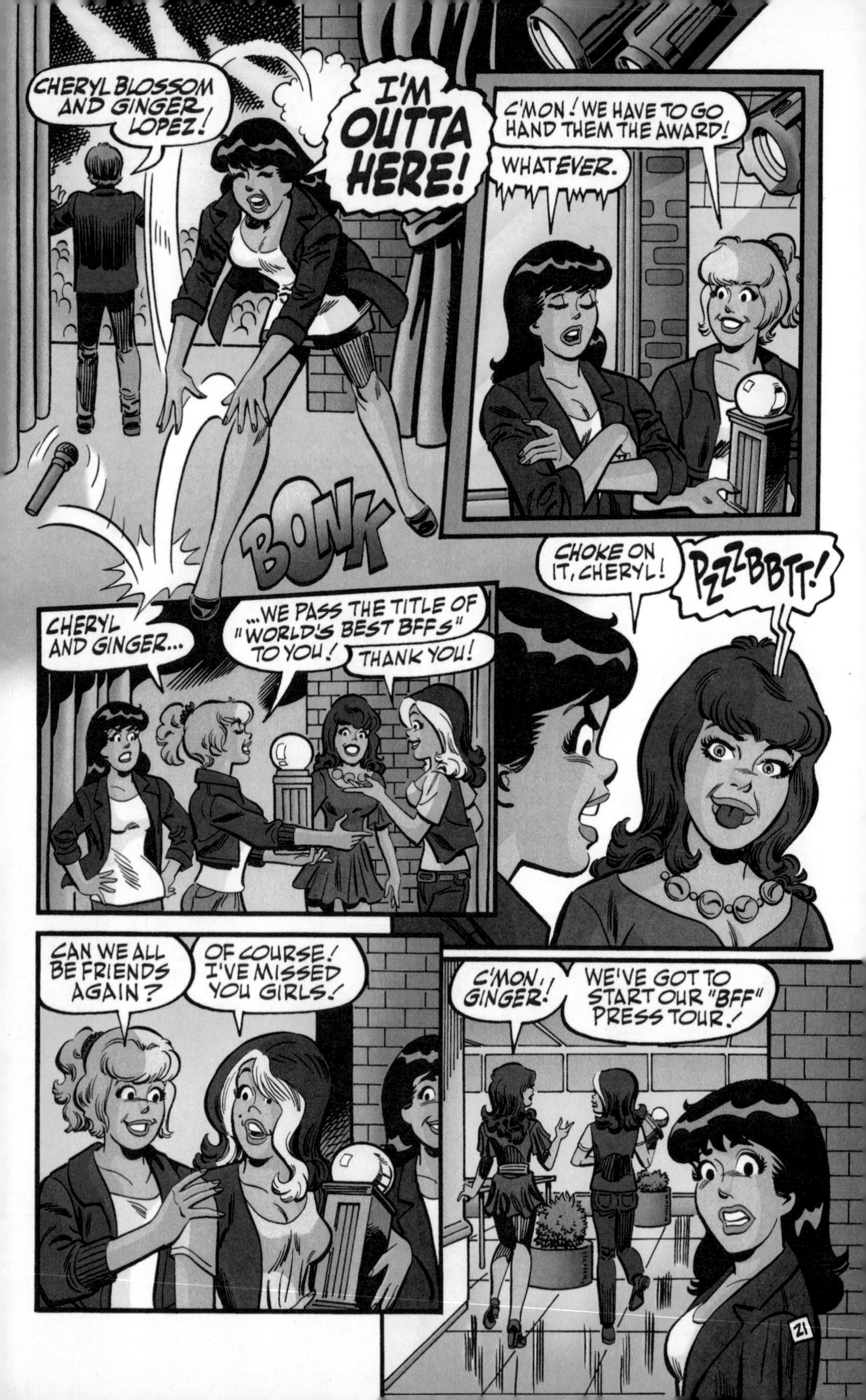
CHERYL BLOSSOM AND GINGER LOPEZ!
I'M OUTTA HERE!
BONK
C'MON! WE HAVE TO GO HAND THEM THE AWARD!
WHATEVER.
CHERYL AND GINGER...
...WE PASS THE TITLE OF "WORLD'S BEST BFFs" TO YOU!
THANK YOU!
CHOKE ON IT, CHERYL!
PZZZBBTT!
CAN WE ALL BE FRIENDS AGAIN?
OF COURSE! I'VE MISSED YOU GIRLS!
C'MON, GINGER!
WE'VE GOT TO START OUR "BFF" PRESS TOUR!
21

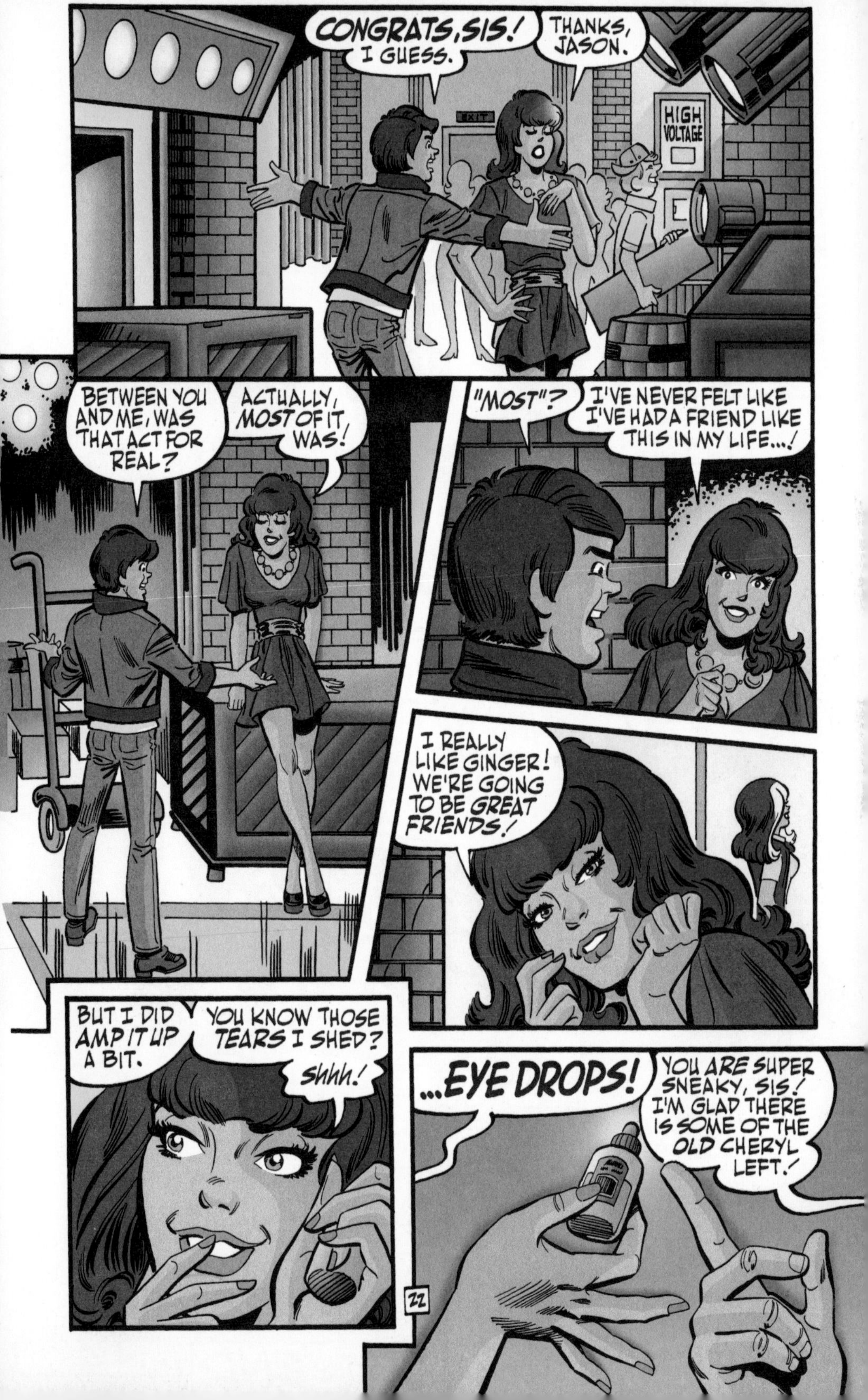
CONGRATS, SIS! I GUESS.
THANKS, JASON.
EXIT
HIGH VOLTAGE
BETWEEN YOU AND ME, WAS THAT ACT FOR REAL?
ACTUALLY, MOST OF IT WAS!
"MOST"?
I'VE NEVER FELT LIKE I'VE HAD A FRIEND LIKE THIS IN MY LIFE...!
I REALLY LIKE GINGER! WE'RE GOING TO BE GREAT FRIENDS!
BUT I DID AMP IT UP A BIT.
YOU KNOW THOSE TEARS I SHED?
shhh!
...EYE DROPS!
YOU ARE SUPER SNEAKY, SIS! I'M GLAD THERE IS SOME OF THE OLD CHERYL LEFT!

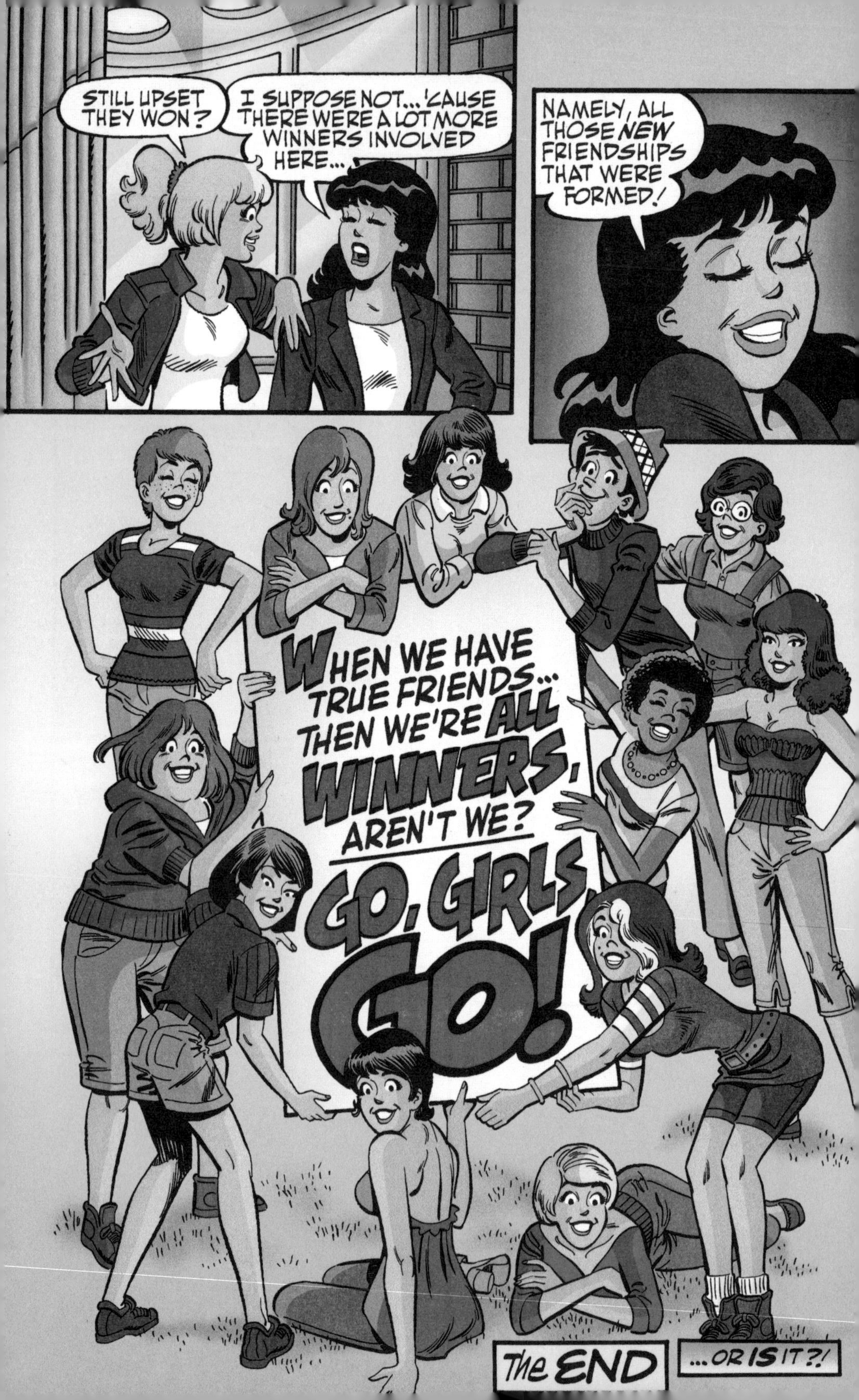
STILL UPSET THEY WON?
I SUPPOSE NOT... 'CAUSE THERE WERE A LOT MORE WINNERS INVOLVED HERE...
NAMELY, ALL THOSE NEW FRIENDSHIPS THAT WERE FORMED!
WHEN WE HAVE TRUE FRIENDS... THEN WE'RE ALL WINNERS, AREN'T WE?
GO, GIRLS, GO!
The END
...OR IS IT?!

Betty and Veronica

BFF Profiles

Few things go together as well as Betty and Veronica! Not too many girls can date the same boy and all be in a band together for years and STILL manage to be friends, but Betty and Veronica make it happen!

Betty's middle class upbringing is worlds apart from the posh lifestyle of Veronica Lodge; Veronica likes glitz and glamour and loves to shop in the ritziest stores for hours on end.

Betty, on the other hand, is the girl-next-door who loves the simple things in life, and is more of a "get-in, get-out" bargain hunter. Sometimes, it seems like the only thing these girls have in common is their mutual love for Archie! But who says opposites don't attract?

No matter their differences, and even though they constantly find themselves involved in disputes over Archie's affection, these two have remained the best of friends since childhood. They're always there to help each other out (or team up to help out others) in the end!

Did You Know:

• The Betty-Archie-Veronica love triangle started in an early Archie Comic, when Archie wrote to Veronica asking her to a dance in Riverdale. He accidentally sent the letter; he really wanted to ask Betty Cooper, and was only daydreaming. Even after he realized he had sent the letter, he did not think she would really come. Veronica accepted the invitation, thinking that a dance would be fun. At the time, she lived in a much bigger city and begged her parents to go, and Archie had to struggle to keep his dates with both girls.

• Betty is a Jack (or should we say Jacqueline) of all trades- she has worked as a writer for the Riverdale High school paper, an assistant teacher at the local elementary school, a babysitter and a mechanic, just to name a few!

• Mr. Lodge has indicated in a few stories that he moved his family to Riverdale to prevent Veronica from becoming spoiled. Admittedly, his plans were not a success.

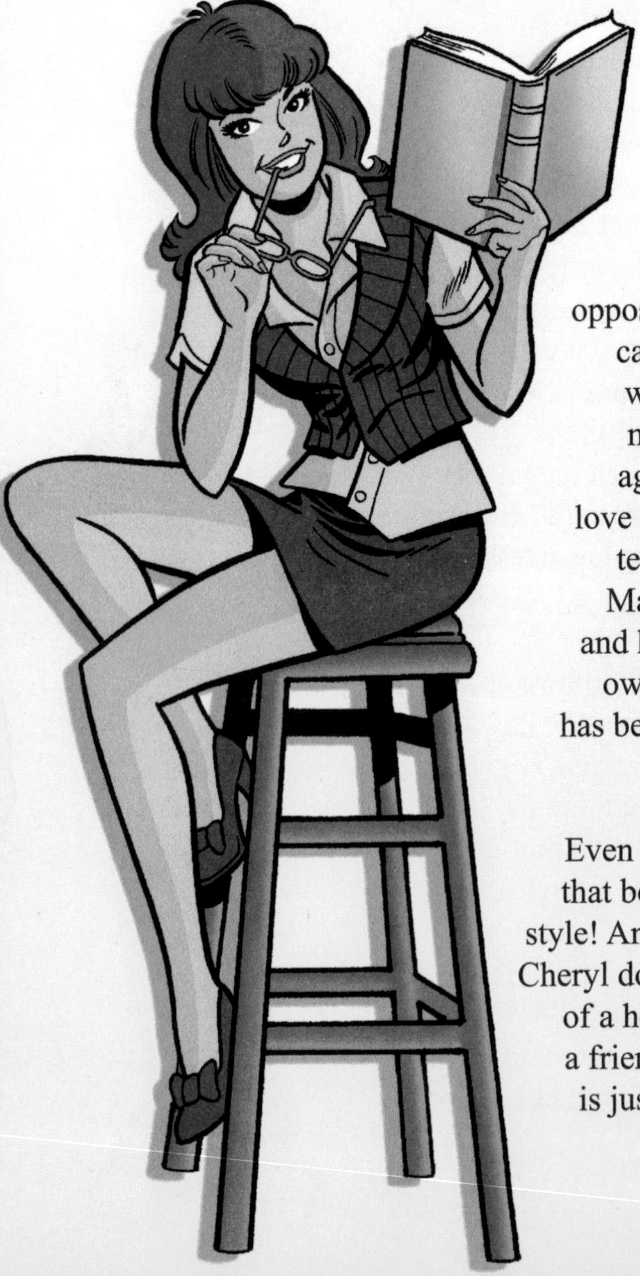

Can a "townie" and a member of Pembrooke elite actually be BFFs? Wait - can anyone actually be Cheryl's BFF?! Apparently while some girls form friendships over a mutual love, others do so over a mutual hate - in this case Betty & Veronica brought Cheryl & Ginger together - but not in a good way! While opposites do attract, in this case Cheryl and Ginger were able to bond over more than just plotting against B&V, they both love fashion! Ginger is the teen editor for "Sparkle Magazine" in New York and has even designed her own line of clothing that has been featured in several fashion shows!

Even Veronica has to admit that both of these girls have style! And maybe, deep down, Cheryl does have good enough of a heart to keep Ginger as a friend! (Or maybe Ginger is just as mean as Cheryl!)

Did You Know:

• Ginger was originally created as a replacement for Cheryl. In the early 2000s, Cheryl's hair was re-colored and the text was changed to have her be replaced by Ginger in some story reprints. Many fans were not happy with this change, however, so Cheryl was brought back once again, and Ginger was given stories of her own as a separate character.

• Initially, Ginger had Cheryl's personality, and so appeared to be a rival of Veronica. But with Cheryl's return, Ginger's mean streak was dropped and she became a much nicer character.

• Cheryl has shown her kinder, softer side. In the "Queen B" series of B&V Friends Double Digest, it was revealed that Cheryl actually has a soft spot in her heart for animals - often adopting pets from animal rescue shelters!

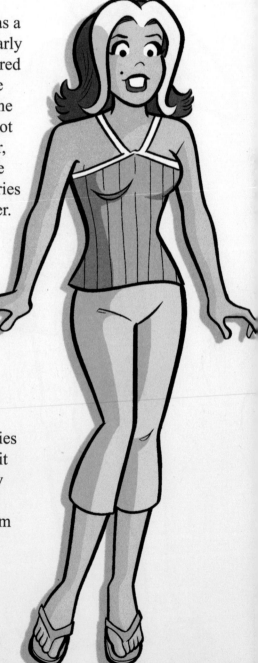

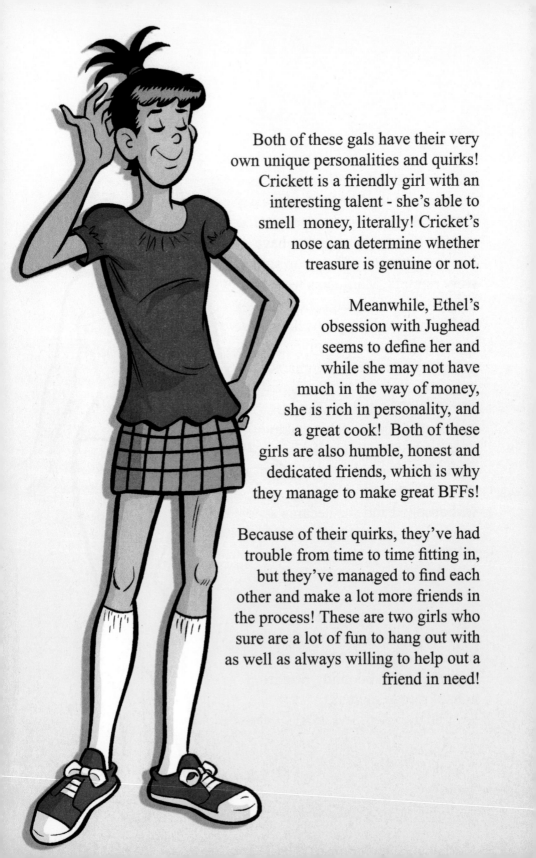

Both of these gals have their very own unique personalities and quirks! Crickett is a friendly girl with an interesting talent - she's able to smell money, literally! Cricket's nose can determine whether treasure is genuine or not.

Meanwhile, Ethel's obsession with Jughead seems to define her and while she may not have much in the way of money, she is rich in personality, and a great cook! Both of these girls are also humble, honest and dedicated friends, which is why they manage to make great BFFs!

Because of their quirks, they've had trouble from time to time fitting in, but they've managed to find each other and make a lot more friends in the process! These are two girls who sure are a lot of fun to hang out with as well as always willing to help out a friend in need!

Did You Know:

• Ethel Muggs was originally named Ophelia Gleutenschnable. Also, Jughead willingly went on dates with Ophelia. In one gag, Archie asks Jughead why he asked Ophelia to the dance, and Jughead replies that she was different: "She's the only one who'll go with me!"

• Cricket appeared in the mainstream stories as well as the pre-Pussycats Josie series, including a story in which Alexandra Cabot tried to use Cricket's unique ability to her own selfish advantage.

• Ethel's obsession with Jughead began as a result of Dilton's Electronic Mate Selector choosing Jughead as her perfect mate!

• In addition to her unique sense of smell, Cricket also used to fall in love with any boys who had a great deal of money. She once pursued Archie, thinking he had money since he was dating Veronica.

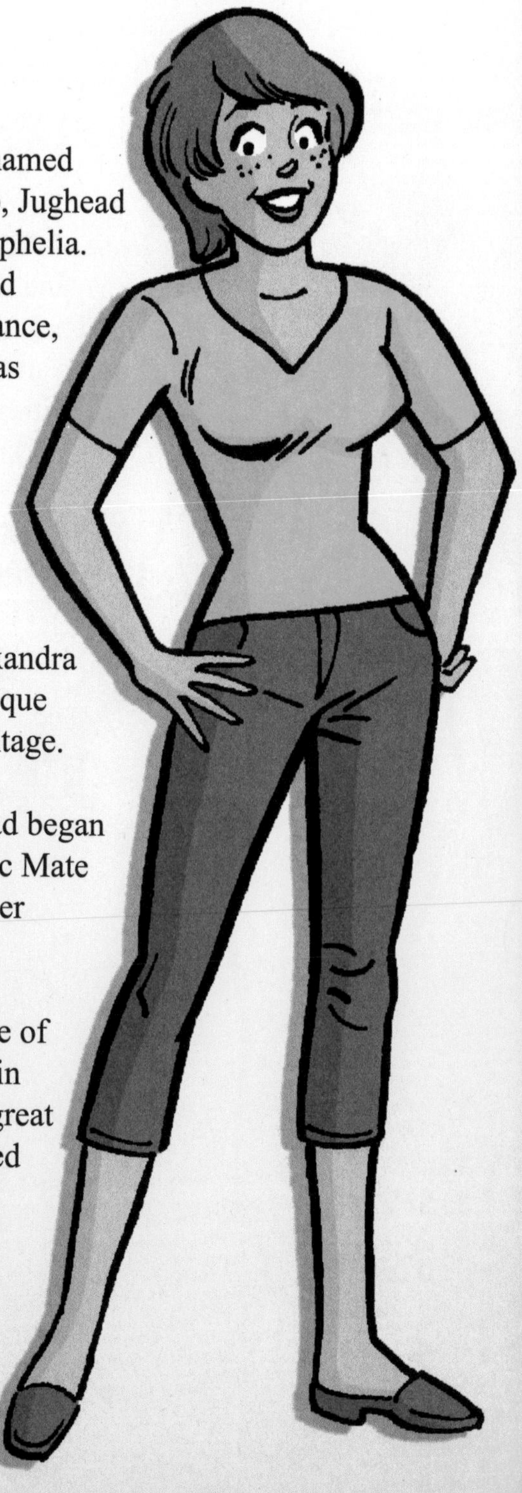

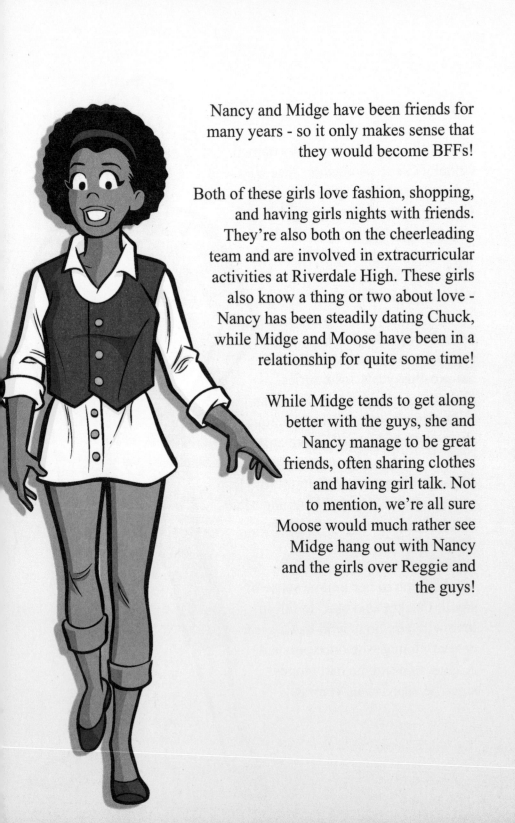

Nancy and Midge have been friends for many years - so it only makes sense that they would become BFFs!

Both of these girls love fashion, shopping, and having girls nights with friends. They're also both on the cheerleading team and are involved in extracurricular activities at Riverdale High. These girls also know a thing or two about love - Nancy has been steadily dating Chuck, while Midge and Moose have been in a relationship for quite some time!

While Midge tends to get along better with the guys, she and Nancy manage to be great friends, often sharing clothes and having girl talk. Not to mention, we're all sure Moose would much rather see Midge hang out with Nancy and the girls over Reggie and the guys!

Did You Know:

• Nancy's last name was "Harris" when she first appeared, and has occasionally been "Jackson" or "Baker," before officially becoming "Woods".

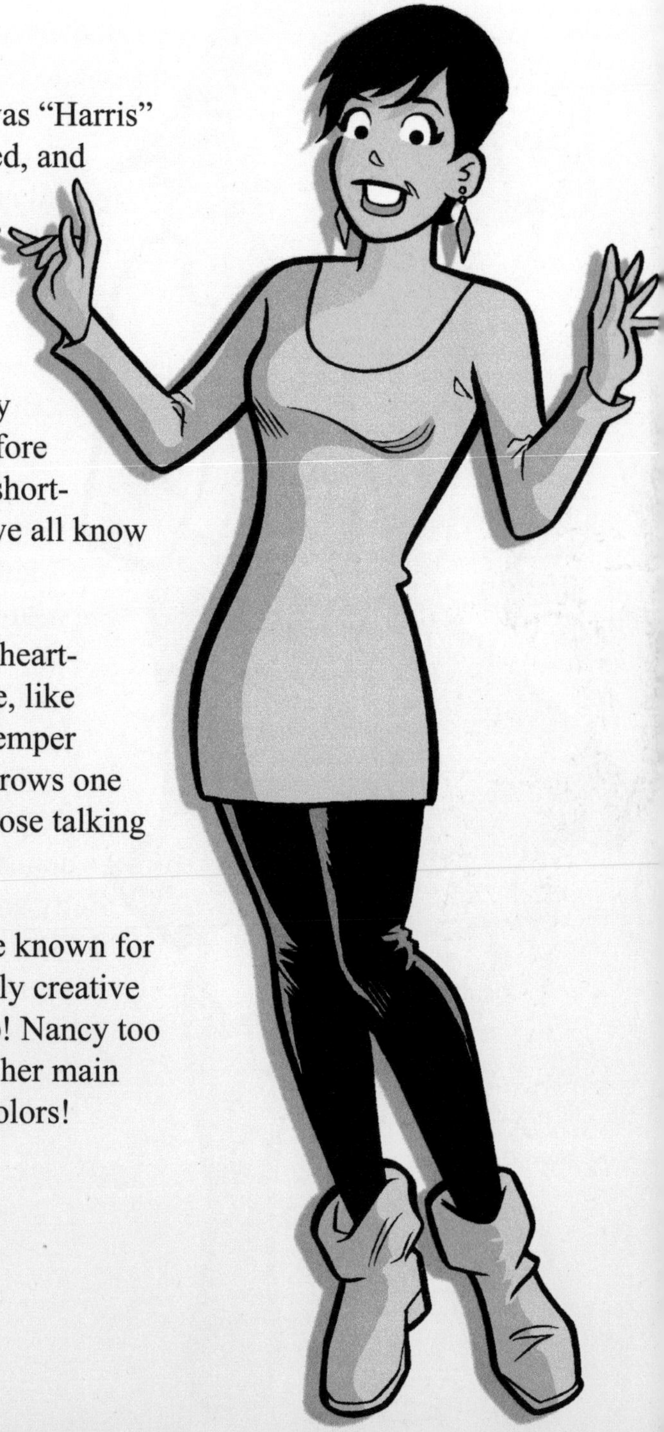

• Midge was originally called Lottie Little before being turned into the short-haired heart-breaker we all know and love!

• Speaking of being a heart-breaker herself, Midge, like Moose, is not shy to temper tantrums. She often throws one when she sees her Moose talking to other girls!

• While Chuck may be known for his art, he's not the only creative one in the relationship! Nancy too has an interest in art - her main medium being watercolors!

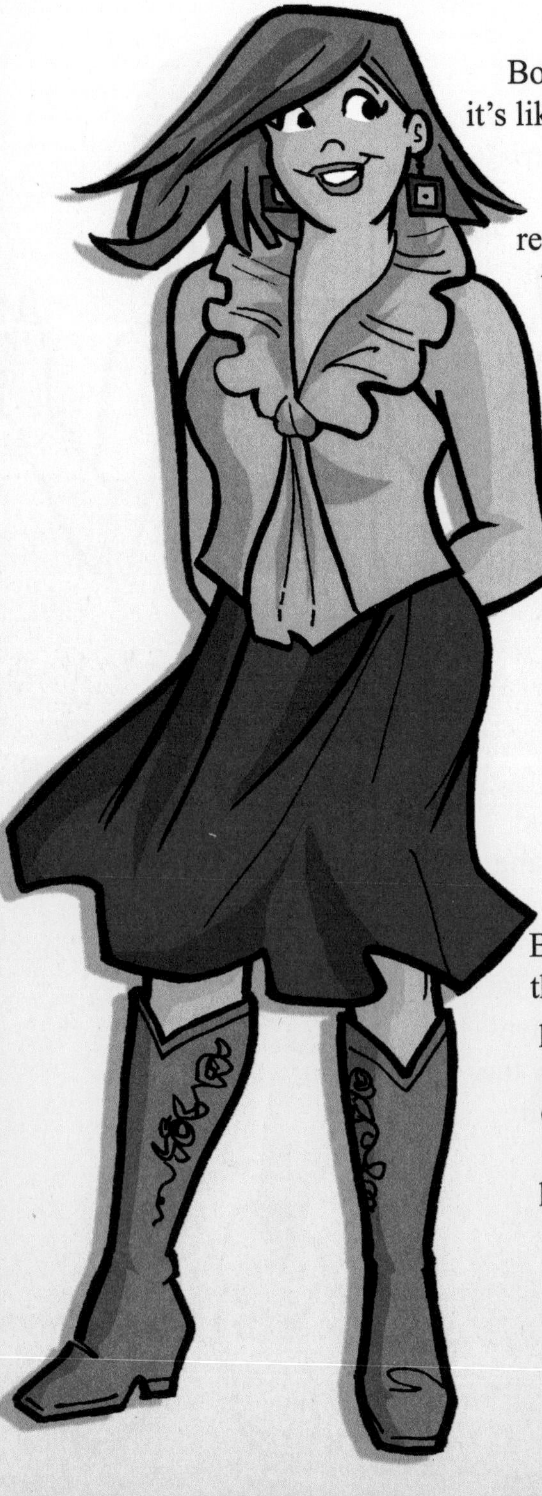

Both of these ladies know what it's like to be the new girl in town!

Kumi moved to Riverdale recently and has been adapting to life in America, while also getting better at learning the English language.

Brigitte was an exchange student from Waynesboro High, in Centerville, whose kind nature helped her to easily fit in with the Riverdale crew. In fact, Brigitte's so kind, she even offered to give singing lessons to Cheryl Blossom.

Both of these girls had help adjusting to Riverdale from Betty and Veronica, and while they come from very different places and backgrounds, now the two can learn from each other! It also helps that Kumi and Brigette both have fun-loving and kind personalities.

Did You Know:

• Brigitte is an accomplished singer who once did a music duet with Maria Rodriguez's boyfriend, Frankie Valdez, and even has her own record deal!

• Maria was jealous for some time at Frankie and Brigitte's friendship, but she soon realized that they were just good friends and everything worked out well.

• At home, Kumi's mother keeps up Japanese tradition and etiquette.

• When Kumi first came to Riverdale, she felt childish and immature compared to her Riverdale High peers, but fortunately Betty and Veronica made Kumi feel right at home in Riverdale!

• Brigitte has also been known to occasionally date Dilton.

What happens when nerds collide?? They have the potential to be BFFs, that's what! That's right, these two have more than just a little height in common!

Lottie and Marcy first met at Sci-Fi Con and realized that they both have similar tastes in entertainment. Their mutual interests in sci-fi and technology, as well as their favorite TV show - "Space Trek" - brought them closer as friends and cemented them as the quintessential "geek girl" BFFs of Riverdale.

Hopefully in their attempt to out-geek each other, they don't end up having any serious fights! Marcy can get a bit extreme when it comes to her science fiction! Not to mention, Lottie's love of conversation makes for a good match for Marcy's talkative nature!

Let's hope this "geek squad" can have an "out of this world" friendship!

Did You Know:

• Lottie Little originally debuted in the '50s, and was later redesigned into Midge!

• Marcy eventually got a step-family when her mother, Elsie, married a man named Max Wells. Max turned out to be the father of Bryan, a boy Veronica was dating at the time, thus making them cousins. I guess it was back to Archie for Veronica!

• Lottie's character originally showed a love interest in Jughead.

• For a while, Marcy acted as band manager for the Archies! She's also been a helpful accomplice to Betty and Veronica when they take on the roles of the Spy Girls!

It's about time these two girls found their BFFs! A girl needs more than a boyfriend or a doll to be her confidant!

Maria Rodriguez and Frankie Valdez may have been dating for years, but girls have to stick together! Evelyn Evernever is a pal from way back when they were kids, but over the years the gang all seemed to slowly drift apart, coming back into the picture every once and again. It's great that these two girls could reunite after all this time and become even better friends!

Maria's fiery nature provides a great contrast to Evelyn's more timid self - they can both learn how to grow in different ways from each other! Though let's hope Maria can find Evelyn a steady boyfriend like she has with Frankie! Although, now that Evelyn has returned, she might end up setting her sights on Archie. After all, he is the first boy she's ever kissed!

Did You Know:

• Much like every other couple in Riverdale, Maria Rodriguez and Frankie Valdez have had their ups and downs, but they still have managed to stay together after all these years!

• The first boy Evelyn kissed was good ol' Archie Andrews! That's right! Betty & Veronica may have a new challenger for the heart of their "Archiekins".

• When agents B&V had to rescue Archie from a villainous kidnapper, it turned out to be none other than Evelyn Evernever herself! Let's hope she's worked out whatever issues she had back then!

• Maria was originally introduced as the daughter of the vice-principal Mr. Rodriguez. While Maria continued to appear, her father did not. It looks like she had something in common with the next two...

These girls are not only creative and eccentric, but are both also relatives of some famed staff at Riverdale High!

Wendy Weatherbee is the niece of, you guessed it, Mr. Weatherbee and Bella Beazley is the daughter of none other than Riverdale High's own lunch lady, Ms. Beazley's (I know, we were shocked, too...) Wendy, or Double W as she likes to call herself, is quite the individualist. She has an odd sense of fashion and keeps some strange pets, including a tarantula named Tara and an iguana. Poor Wendy, though, can never find a steady date. All the boys avoid her for fear of permanent detention! While Bella has less of a hard time finding dates, her talent in the kitchen pales in comparison to her beauty!

These two can not only bond over their familial similarities, but also help each other in the love and food departments!

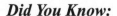

Did You Know:

• Wendy's father, Tony Weatherbee, is actually the Bee's twin brother! The Weatherbee twins grew up very different. While Waldo was studious and serious, Tony was more interested in socializing and motorcycle riding. Over time, the two brothers fell out of touch due to their strained relationship.

• After Wendy came to Riverdale, her father and uncle put aside their differences.

• Wendy tried (often unsuccessfully) to date Jughead, Dilton, and Bingo Wilkins!

• Wendy has dated both Archie and Reggie much to the shagrin of her uncle!

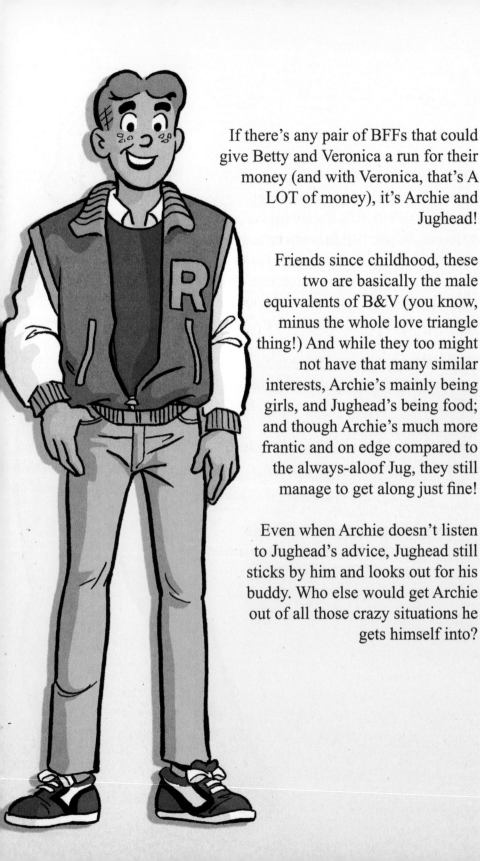

If there's any pair of BFFs that could give Betty and Veronica a run for their money (and with Veronica, that's A LOT of money), it's Archie and Jughead!

Friends since childhood, these two are basically the male equivalents of B&V (you know, minus the whole love triangle thing!) And while they too might not have that many similar interests, Archie's mainly being girls, and Jughead's being food; and though Archie's much more frantic and on edge compared to the always-aloof Jug, they still manage to get along just fine!

Even when Archie doesn't listen to Jughead's advice, Jughead still sticks by him and looks out for his buddy. Who else would get Archie out of all those crazy situations he gets himself into?

Did You Know:

• When Jughead first came to Riverdale, he was in a bad mood and tended to dismiss Archie. However, Archie tried to cheer him up, becoming his first friend in Riverdale.

• Archibald Andrews' original nickname when he was first introduced was "Chick."

• Jughead did have a steady love interest at one point in time - January McAndrews, the 29th Century descendent of Archie Andrews, as well as his co-star in *Jughead's Time Police*!

• Speaking of ancestry, the Andrews family originated in Scotland, with great-grandfather "Andy Andrews" immigrating to the United States and befriending Moose Mason's Russian ancestor, who was emigrating at the same time.

• Jughead's hat is not only a key part of his style, he also considers it a good luck charm! In fact, when his hat is taken from him, misfortune seems to come his way.

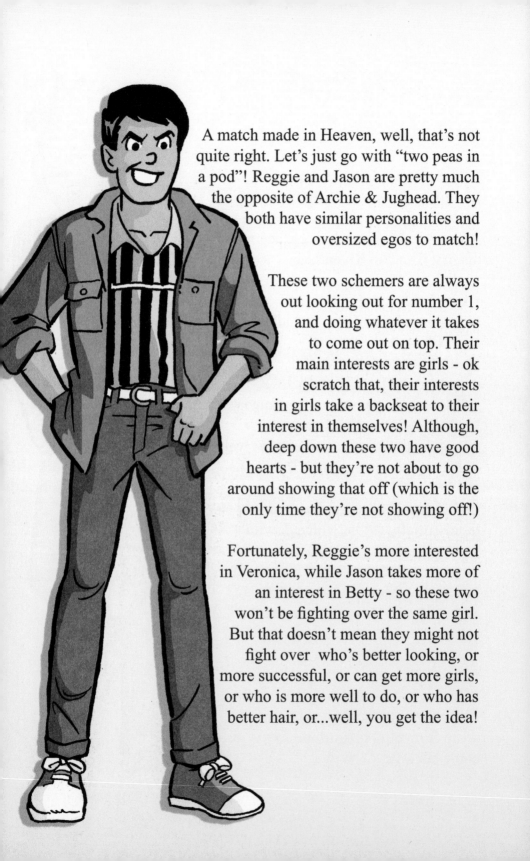

A match made in Heaven, well, that's not quite right. Let's just go with "two peas in a pod"! Reggie and Jason are pretty much the opposite of Archie & Jughead. They both have similar personalities and oversized egos to match!

These two schemers are always out looking out for number 1, and doing whatever it takes to come out on top. Their main interests are girls - ok scratch that, their interests in girls take a backseat to their interest in themselves! Although, deep down these two have good hearts - but they're not about to go around showing that off (which is the only time they're not showing off!)

Fortunately, Reggie's more interested in Veronica, while Jason takes more of an interest in Betty - so these two won't be fighting over the same girl. But that doesn't mean they might not fight over who's better looking, or more successful, or can get more girls, or who is more well to do, or who has better hair, or...well, you get the idea!

Did You Know:

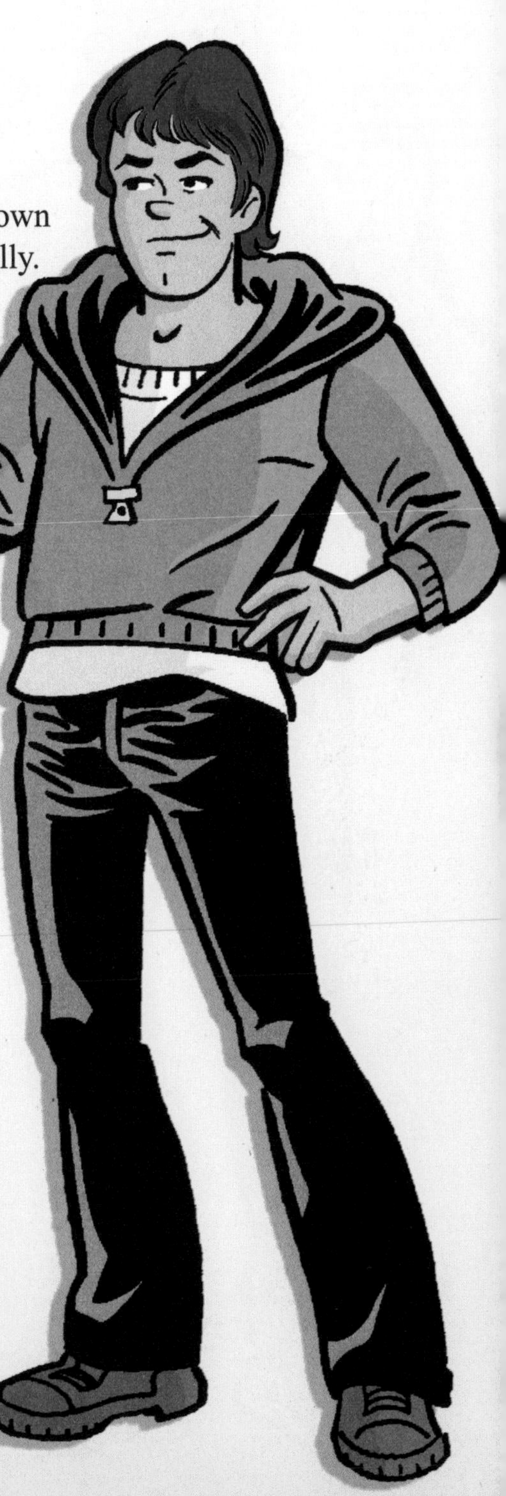

• While Reggie often vies for Veronica's attention, he is also known to date Cheryl Blossom occasionally. At one point, before she began dating a boy named George, the two tried going out together. Although Cheryl mainly uses Reggie as an alternative to Archie.

• Despite Reggie's upper-middle class status, he is often shown as being very cheap.

• Although the two are rivals, Jason is shown to have respect for Archie, and vice-versa.

• Though depicted as arrogant and self-assured, Jason can sometimes be found practicing how he'll ask Betty out while in front of a mirror!

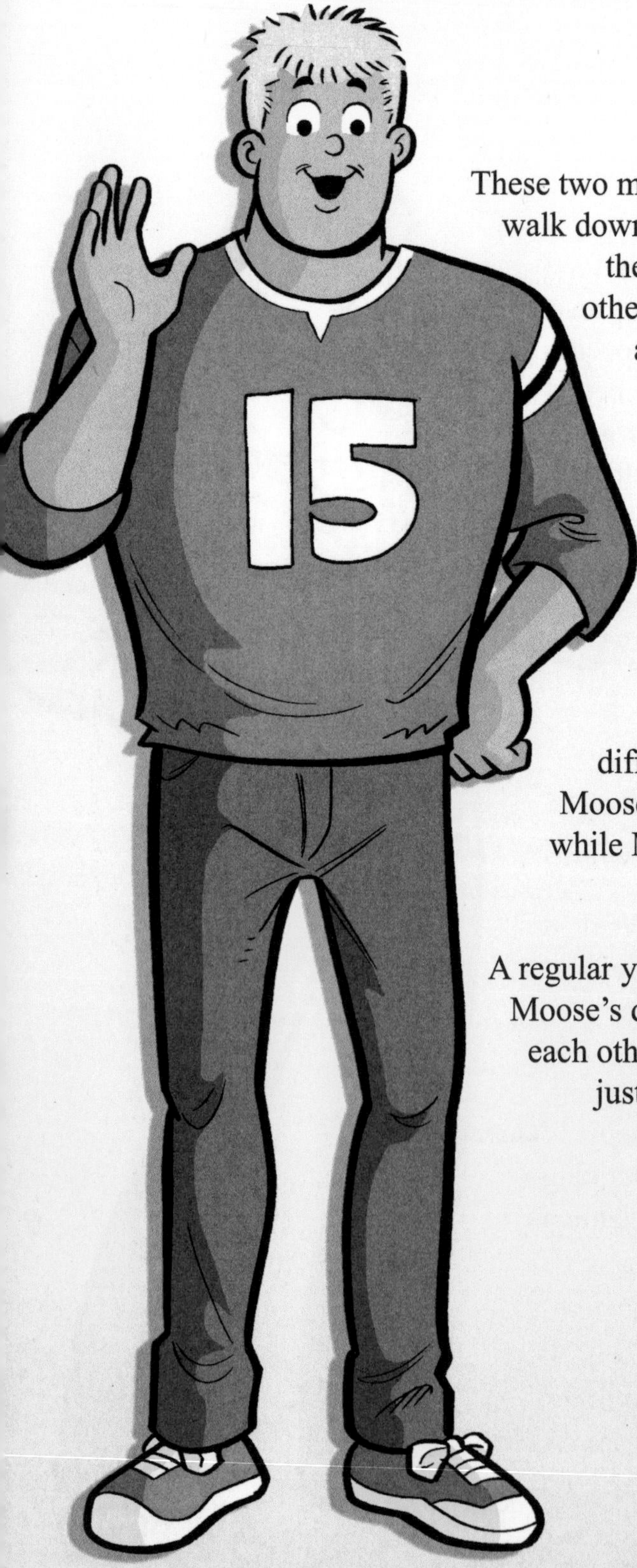

These two may look silly when they walk down the street together, but these two BFFs have each other's backs through thick and thin! Moose always takes care of his little buddy and will always go out of his way to help him! Likewise, Dilton is always the first person to stick up for his big pal!

Despite intellectual differences, Dilton can see Moose's philosophical nature while Moose admires Dilton's intelligence!

A regular yin and yang, Dilton and Moose's differences complement each other in the best of ways - just like true BFFs should!

Did You Know:

• While Moose is very protective of Midge, the only two guys he's fine with her talking to are Jughead and Dilton , whom he knows would never come between him and Midge. If he is unable to take her to a school dance, he usually insists that one of them take her instead. Though, despite Dilton's shy nature, he has dated his fair share of girls, too, including: Ethel, Cheryl and Brigitte. What a cassanova!

• Even if intimidated by him, all of Moose's friends never want to see him fail and are always willing to help him study!

• Dilton has, in the past, been the one to stand up for Moose - even going as far as pouncing on Reggie for making fun of Moose!

• Dilton has been given the opportunity on numerous occasions to start college a year early, but knowing he'd miss his friends too much, he decided against it.

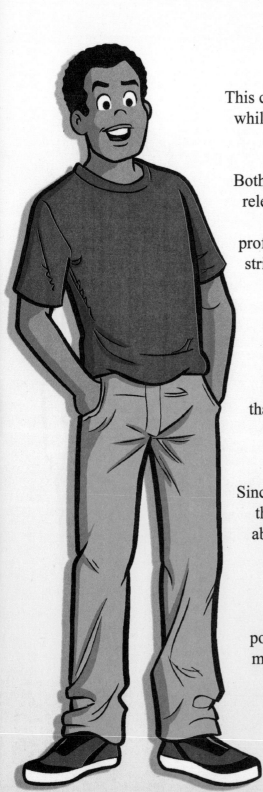

This creative duo can be great friends while helping each other out in their artistic endeavors!

Both of these goal-oriented guys are relentless in achieving their artistic dreams. Chuck wants to be a professional comic book and comic strip illustrator, while Raj wants to be a filmmaker!

Both of these guys have been guilty in the past of getting under people's skin by being so preoccupied with their hobbies that they ignore any and everyone around them, much to Chuck's girlfriend Nancy's dismay!

Since they're both so obsessed with their respective hobbies, they are able to respect each other's needs when it comes to the creative process.

With Chuck creating sets and posters for Raj's films, they could make a career out of being BFFs!

Did You Know:

• In his first few years in Riverdale, Chuck was often a sidekick to Archie as the two of them solved mysteries and was often portrayed as a shy loner, contrary to his true nature of a fun-loving, outgoing artist.

• However, by the early '90s his interest in cartooning took shape and is now one of his most notable traits, as well as being a confident, mature teenager!

• Raj has a sister, Tina, who is a year younger than him. However, due to her good grades, she was bumped up a school grade and is now in the same class as Raj, Archie and the gang!

• Dr. Ravi Patel (Raj's father) often wishes his son would take up more serious pursuits, though his attitude seemed to change when the students of Riverdale High took a trip to India.

BEST FRIENDS!
FOREVER!

Betty and Veronica
STORYBOOK
The Wizard of Oz
Cinderella, Sleeping Beauty
Alice in Wonderland

Betty & Veronica: Storybook

The ladies of Riverdale live happily ever after when they take center stage in four classic fairy tales!

ISBN: 978-1-879794-60-3

THE Archie BABIES

The Archie Babies

Before they ruled the halls of Riverdale High, Archie and his pals were kings and queens of the playground!

ISBN: 978-1-879794-72-6

The Magic of Sabrina the Teenage Witch

The magic is back with this collection of Sabrina's most spell-binding tales!

ISBN: 978-1-879794-75-7

The Magic of
Sabrina
THE TEENAGE WITCH

Archie
THE MARRIED LIFE
TWO WORLDS. TWO LOVES. TWO DESTINIES.

Archie: The Married Life Book One

Collecting the first 6 parts of the critically acclaimed Archie Marries Betty and Archie Marries Veronica storylines.

ISBN: 978-1-936975-01-3

The Best of Archie Comics

70 years of laughs in one convenient package!

ISBN: 978-1-879794-84-9

THE BEST OF
Archie
COMICS
THE BEST STORIES OF THE PAST 70 YEARS!
OVER 400 PAGES

THE ARCHIE WEDDING
Archie
WILL YOU MARRY ME?

The Archie Wedding: Will you Marry Me?

Archie has finally chosen! The winner is... BOTH OF THEM!

ISBN: 978-1-879794-51-1

The Archies & Josie and the Pussycats

Two of the hottest bands get together to make some sweet music!

ISBN: 978-1-879794-61-0

THE Archies Josie

Archie COMICS

LOOK FOR THESE AND OTHER GRAPHIC NOVELS AT COMIC SHOPS AND BOOKSTORES EVERYWHERE!

ALSO AVAILABLE ONLINE AT ARCHIECOMICS.COM

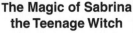